HIDDEN PIECES

HIDDEN PIECES

A MISTY PINES MYSTERY

MARY KELIIKOA

First published by Level Best Books 2022

First edition

ISBN: 978-1-68512-156-3

Cover art by Christian Storm

This book was professionally typeset on Reedsy.
Find out more at reedsy.com

To Dad—Whose heart was always at the Oregon coast. I believe Sheriff Jax Turner is a man my father would have liked.

Praise for Hidden Pieces

"Hidden Pieces is an intense novel offering hair-raising twists and turns and differing plots making it difficult for the reader to discern the culprit. Surprises arise to give the story more power and excitement. A page-turner up to the conclusion this is an exhilarating and spine-tingling read."—*New York Journal of Books*

"Mary Keliikoa has raised the bar with *Hidden Pieces.* Moody, evocative, yet propulsive. Well Done!" — Matt Coyle, bestselling author of the Rick Cahill crime series

"Mary Keliikoa delivers a tightly plotted and tense page-turner with haunted, relatable characters and an ending you won't see coming."—Heather Chavez, author of *No Bad Deed* and *Blood Will Tell*

"The disappearance of a teenage girl has dark implications for the small community of Misty Pines when the crime is linked to a decades-old murder. Keliikoa has a knack for writing nuanced investigators, and haunted-yet-relentless sheriff Jax Turner is no exception. An absorbing and expertly plotted mystery."—Tessa Wegert, author of *Dead Wind*

"Mary Keliikoa's *Hidden Pieces* is a delicious page-turning mystery full of secrets and revenge. Dogged yet emotionally vulnerable, Sheriff Jax Turner a hero for our times. Fans of twisty police procedurals are in for a treat!"—Joanna Schauffhausen, author of *Gone For Good*

"Do we really know the people in our lives? *Hidden Pieces* is a memorable, if not unnerving, reading experience that moves like mist touching everything. The story, with the loss of a child at its core, straddles the line between mystery and psychological thriller, and Mary Keliikoa deftly demonstrates how grief and loss can be insidious and unrelenting."—Gabriel Valjan, multi-award nominated author of the Company Files and Shane Cleary Mysteries series

"Wow! What a novel. It crackles with realism, a page turner that sucks you in and won't let you go till the last page. *Hidden Pieces* is a slow burn building tension as each layer is revealed. Domestic thriller and mystery fans will get their money's worth."—David Putnam, bestselling author of The Bruno Johnson series

"Dark, tense, and loaded with hairpin twists, this series launch shows Keliikoa's deft hand with plotting and character, including the highly relatable series lead, Sherriff Jax Turner. Keliikoa expertly weaves together a desperate search for a missing child with long-held secrets that threaten to upend the case. The final pages will leave you breathless."—Edwin Hill, author of *The Secrets We Share*

"Mary Keliikoa's new series debut will keep your pulse racing and your heart aching for the brave and sympathetic Sheriff Jax Turner, a tortured lawman who gets a second chance to save a young girl in danger. Fast-paced and expertly plotted, with lots of twists and turns, *Hidden Pieces* will have you turning the pages as fast as you can. I can't wait to return to the Misty Pines and I can't wait to see what Sheriff Turner gets up to next."—Sarah Stewart Taylor, author of *The Drowning Sea*

Zero Minus Four Hours

Less than a breath consumes the moment between decision and commitment. But he'd run through the scenario countless times. *He* wasn't the factor he worried about with so many variables out of his control. His throat tightened at this unfamiliar place. He coughed to release the tension.

The school bus would soon crest the hill. More farm workers would arrive. Some had already started their daily tasks. Kids would be racing to their stops.

Only one interested him.

The distance closed to where she stood; her flowing brown hair mesmerized him, along with the freckles across her nose. Her small frame swam in her oversized sweatshirt. Wide lips protruded over her braces. A backpack hung off her thin shoulder. Oblivious. He slowed, noting her red-rimmed eyes. She'd been crying. Fragile. Innocent. Weren't they all?

For a beat, he thought about driving by. But another chance to find her this isolated might be long in coming. If he stopped, there'd be no turning back.

Every muscle clenched as he eased to the edge of the road, punching the down button on the passenger window.

"Allison," he called. She wiped her eyes quick with her sleeve. But he'd seen her pain. He'd use it. "Everything okay?"

"Fine," she said with a quiet defiance.

He nodded, kept the conversation light and on point so she wouldn't fear him. Familiarity created trust. His heart thumped against his ribs and chest; the rush of blood crashed in his ears. He couldn't remember the words he'd said to get her into his vehicle, but he didn't need to. Her hand gripped the handle.

She slid in, her backpack between them, her shoulders rounded. Head down. He waited as she pulled the seatbelt across her chest, clicking it into place.

"Ready?" He checked the rearview mirror.

She nodded. Silent.

He passed the driveway to turn around.

"Where are we going?"

He recognized the lilt of the last word. That instance between realization and worry. The moment had come fast—the window slamming shut. He gripped the rag he'd readied earlier and smashed it onto her face.

Her eyes went wide. She gasped and slumped into the seat with a final bounce of her chin on her collarbone.

His hands steadied on the wheel, and he depressed the gas pedal.

No turning back.

Chapter One

Sheriff Jax Turner swerved his patrol car off Highway 101 and took a sharp right onto an unmarked dirt road leading to the beach. Tourists didn't come to Misty Pines for the summer to swim in the ocean or the lakes. Too much mist; too much murkiness. The few outdoorsmen drawn to the area for fishing off the ragged ocean jetties had long gone for the season.

His Glock 22 rested on the seat next to him, along with a miniature wooden chair. He'd finished carving it during another sleepless night for a dollhouse he'd never complete, for a tea party that would never happen.

Jax followed the smooth road as it transitioned into rock, his upper body swaying and bouncing with the uneven terrain. When it leveled, he floored it, the tires spinning before they found their footing on the sandy flat.

Aimed toward the sea, he parked on a stretch of solid pack a few yards from the surf. The foamy fingers of the ocean reached for his cruiser, coming up short. The weather report called for ninety degrees in the city located eighty miles east, which meant an inversion for everyone on the coastline. His future, or lack of one, floated in the horizon, where gray ocean met gray clouds, both soon to be indiscernible in the impending fog. Damn, he was tired of being tired.

The window down, he sucked in the brackish scent of the seaweed-littered shores. Seagulls swarmed overhead. Their plaintive cries sent a wave of grief through him.

Misty Pines should have been a fresh start, a place to heal the wounds of the past. Instead, the salty air had entrenched itself in the ten years since he'd arrived. The torture would never end on its own. An hour spent unloading his ammunition at the shooting range into a silhouette target hadn't helped this time.

Except he hadn't unloaded all of it.

He leaned over the passenger seat to retrieve two sealed envelopes from the glovebox. A dragonfly drawing done with blue-green Crayola and glitter slid out. He fumbled and then caught it before it floated to the floor. His finger trembled as he traced the wings, remembering Lulu's soft pink cheeks. He laid his daughter's gift on his lap and propped the envelopes on the dash right before picturing them splattered in his blood. They'd accuse him of many things when they discovered his body. He wouldn't let heartless be one of them. He placed the items back, securing the latch.

At least when they were found, the people who'd cared about him once would know why. One letter was for his former partner, Detective Jameson. He would understand if no one else did. The other to Abby. Ten years married, and their only child lost to cancer.

Lulu's brave smile flashed in his mind, making the lump in his throat swell. Abby said she didn't blame him, but he blamed himself enough for them both. And despite what she said, the light had dimmed in Abby's eyes the night their little girl passed. Their marriage died that day too. They just hadn't properly buried it until last year.

He balanced the gun on his lap and held the miniature chair in his hand, letting the gulls' cries and the roaring surf fill his mind one last time. The rearview mirror reflected his weary eyes and the bags that had taken up residence under them. He ran his broad hand over his graying sandy hair and back around to the stubble on his chin.

Time to get to it.

He lifted the gun, holding the barrel in his mouth. The cold, metallic weight pushed against his bottom teeth. His throat closed, and he forced a swallow. *Quit stalling.* Eyes squeezed shut, sadness flooded his chest. Regret shoved him. Don't think. He drew in the cool air through his nostrils one more time. Held it. Waited. Was this what he really wanted?

"Jax," his radio crackled to life. "Sheriff…please…."

His eyes flew open, and he withdrew the gun from his mouth. Trudy. Had he heard something in her tone? Hard to tell with her voice coming in and out. He wouldn't miss the shoddy technology in this godforsaken place. No. He was imagining it. He shook his head. Raised the gun.

"Sheriff Turner, we have a Code Ten-Fifty-Four. Urgent. Response needed."

Lost child or runaway. Could be either. He'd been equally useless in both instances in the past.

"Sherriff Turner. Answer your damn radio." Trudy's voice blared that time.

He bristled and lifted the receiver off the hook. "What're you talking about, Trudy?"

"There you are. It's Emily Krueger's kid. She didn't get on the school bus."

Allison. The little girl with the gap-toothed smile who used to wave when he walked past the bookstore. Not so little now, right? A teenager?

"Emily check with her friends?"

"No one's seen her, hon."

"Have Chapman handle it. I'm a little—"

"Gone this week," Trudy said. "Alaska fishing trip. Remember?"

Right.

He scrubbed the exhaustion from his eyes. "On my way."

He dropped the mic into its holder and secured his gun. Hopefully, this wouldn't take long, and he'd be back in an hour to contemplate finishing the job.

Chapter Two

Emily and Allison Krueger lived a mile out of town on Bay Creek Road. Jax tooled his patrol car down the pasture-lined street until their overgrown gravel driveway came into view.

A tenth of a mile up the drive, he passed a red barn and pulled in front of a white two-story farmhouse with black shutters. The towering firs surrounding the house made it invisible from the street. A lone rocker moving with the light breeze accompanied a flat bench on the covered porch.

Jax downed an energy shot, wincing as the cool liquid coated his gut, and transmitted his location to Trudy at the station before stretching out of his cruiser. He half-expected a panicked Emily to meet him before he cleared the driveway. Instead, she answered the solid front door after a couple of knocks, wearing a pink bathrobe, her auburn hair in a ponytail. Puffy-eyed, she sniffed and swiped her fingers underneath her lashes.

The image was far different than when he'd seen her in town, put together, standing behind the counter at her bookstore. She came in early and stayed late. About eight years ago, her husband left her to raise Allison on her own while he moved to Portland to marry a shrink. Being left was something he and Emily had in common.

"Come in," she said, closing the door behind him and leading the way to the small living room filled with pictures of Allison and into the dining room. "Coffee?"

"Please." He'd take all the help he could get to clear his head.

Emily disappeared into the adjoining kitchen while he pulled out a straight-back chair from the table and sat down. She returned, setting a steaming mug in front of him. The coffee sloshed over the rim and spread onto the red vinyl tablecloth. "I'm sorry."

Jax dropped a nearby napkin onto the spill. "It's fine, Emily. What's this about Allison? Trudy said you reported her as lost or runaway."

Emily withdrew her trembling hands and wrapped her arms around her body. "I only told Trudy she hadn't gotten on the bus."

He stretched his neck from side to side. "Let's start there then. What time did Allison leave the house?"

Emily slid into the chair across from him. "Around seven, like usual. I was in the shower."

"You sure she didn't walk to school?"

"Positive. Allison's best friend Kylie called an hour ago, wondering if Allison was sick or in trouble because she hadn't responded to her texts. I made a few calls to her friends and their parents right away. They haven't seen or heard from her either."

"Were there any signs last night that she might not go to school today?"

Emily lowered her head. "No. I mean, we had a fight last night."

"About?"

Her brow furrowed as her eyes rimmed with tears. "She wants to live with her dad in Portland, and I told her no."

"She ever done this before?"

Emily twisted the tie on her robe. "She's stormed off mad, of course. What kid hasn't? But not responding to Kylie is unusual."

That part had caught his attention too. "How old is she?"

"Fourteen."

Friends were everything at that age. At nearly eleven-thirty, it had been a little over four hours since Emily had been out of contact with her daughter. "I'm assuming you've reached out to your ex-husband to see if he picked her up?"

"Daniel was my first call. As I suspected, she did call him after our fight, but he told her to go to bed, and things would be better tomorrow. He's not keen on her living with him either. He divorced the whore he left me for, and now he's enjoying his life—easy when you don't have to worry about raising another human being."

She made it sound like a burden. He'd give anything to have that back.

Emily must have seen the pain in his eyes. "Sorry. I mean..."

"It's fine." It would never be fine.

"There's more to do in the big city," she continued, "and a dozen more ways to get into trouble. Don't get me wrong, Allison's a great kid, but fewer options are better. Even if she's bored as hell around here, it's my job to keep her safe. You know?"

He did. Whatever it took. He liked boring. Even if boring could cause teenagers to go off the chain. Spray paint the bridges near town. Spinout in a neighbor's yard. All tame in comparison to his previous city life where gang shootings were the norm and no night was complete without scattering the prostitutes down on North Mississippi. If Allison was headed into that cesspool, it'd be hard to get her back.

"I'll want a list of her friends and their numbers."

"I can text that to you." Emily went to the buffet drawer and withdrew a purple spiral notebook.

"Include her dad, and I'll want a current picture." He stood, trying to shed the weighted blanket of apathy. He wouldn't leave any stone untouched, not like last time. "I'll want her cell number, and a list of other places you think she could be." All scenarios were on the table. Allison was missing—of her own volition or foul play—until proven otherwise.

Emily nodded, her face drawn, her chin trembling. Overwhelmed.

He softened. "It's routine to get this up front. Nine times out of ten, kids are found wandering less than a mile away. You said she wants to live with her dad. She's likely halfway there, whether he's aware of it or not." The prospect of her hitchhiking terrified him. He wouldn't panic Emily, even though fear had already taken hold. "Don't start worrying yet."

She hugged herself tighter.

"When we're done, I'll drive along the route to see if I spot her. I take it you haven't done that?"

She didn't meet his eye. "I've been so distracted this last year. She's become difficult. She used to hang out at the store with me; read the books I was reading, and we'd discuss them." She sighed. "Now she barely comes out of her room or carries on a conversation."

Emily was drifting into guilt. Or was it more than that? Emily's reserved demeanor had felt a bit off from the start, although everyone had their own way of processing emotion. Still, most parents would be bouncing off the walls. If it had been Lulu, he'd have been up and down those streets a dozen times already. Most people didn't understand the dangers of what hid out in the open, among the ordinary. He wished he didn't know. "Mind if I check her room?"

Emily didn't look up, her focus on gathering his requested information. "Last door on the left."

Down the narrow hallway, he studied the row of hanging school pictures of Allison. Much had changed from that kindergarten photo of her with no front teeth and a pixie haircut to the more recent ones showing her brown hair long, a mouth full of metal, and a hint of mascara.

He quelled the ache the pictures lit in him and noted a man's work jacket hanging over the back of the hall chair. Allison's father might have left Emily for "that whore" but a man's jacket—casual, cast off, not hanging by the front door—meant Emily might not have let the grass grow under her feet, either.

Allison's all-pink hangout had Taylor Swift posters pinned to every flat surface. Among the obvious teen must-haves—makeup, jewelry, and brightly colored twine bracelets—a mixture of stuffed animals and dolls occupied a chair and the corners of the room. He noted a pink bear with a white tutu in the mix. Trudy had given Lulu one just like it on her second birthday. Her squeal of delight rang in his ears as if she was next to him, clinging to his pant leg. She would have been nine in July. He squeezed the feeling down deep. Four years with her hadn't been enough.

In the off-white armoire across from the door, the drawers and cabinet revealed a young girl who loved mysteries and collected sand dollars—a stark contrast to another fourteen-year-old girl's bedroom he'd gone through many years ago when working a case in Portland. Her entire life had been stuffed into a duffel bag.

Allison was clearly loved and cared for. Nothing he'd found so far indicated she'd left with going to the big city on her mind. "Emily," he hollered.

Emily appeared in the doorway. "Yes."

"Have you checked her clothes to see if she took any with her?"

She nodded. "Everything's here, except her big coat. It's not cold enough for her to need it yet. It could be at a friend's house, I guess."

"Coat here yesterday?"

She closed her eyes. "I can't remember."

"How about her phone?"

"I'd have to pry it from her hands to get it away from her."

"You try tracking it?"

"Yes, but didn't come up with anything."

An internet connection wasn't a required element for the *find my phone* app to work, but it was easily turned off or inaccessible if cell service didn't reach, like through the coast range. "Check her social media?"

"She posted a selfie a week ago on Facebook. Nothing since. Not even likes."

"Any other accounts?"

"Not that I know of." Flush crept up her neck. "Guess I wasn't always paying attention."

"Don't beat yourself up. It's hard to stay ahead of what's available to teenagers." Trudy might have a better idea about the different platforms they could check out since she had a slew of grandkids. "How about computer use?"

"Only for homework projects. Some time on the internet, but mostly she uses her phone for that."

He grimaced. "I'll be another minute, but I'll want to check that computer myself before I leave." There could be online friends Emily wasn't aware of.

Emily nodded and left Jax to continue. He'd been trained to look for signs of possible foul play or violence. His cursory search revealed none. Allison had woken that morning, dressed, and made her bed. Not many teenagers he'd known did that. Certainly not him.

On his way back out, he ducked into the bathroom. Tinted and flavored lip balms, concealers, acne medicine, and fruity body sprays littered the counter. Allison's domain. Nothing appeared out of place. He passed by Emily, hunched at the dining table again, and slipped out the front door.

Flashlight in hand, he walked around the house, aiming the beam underneath before heading for the outbuilding. The barn door creaked as he opened it. A horse whinnied and kicked at the stall; the smell of dirt mixed with urine and manure hit his nose. He eased in, leaving the door ajar. Listening. Watching. Cobwebs hung off the rafters. Bird droppings splattered the concrete floor. Four horse stalls lined the right side. A bay paced impatiently in the first one, closed in behind a barred door. Something had him riled.

A swish-swish sound came from the farthest stall. Wood cracked. The horse neighed again.

"Allison?" he said.

Another creak echoed in the small space.

"You need to come out here. This is Sheriff Turner. Whatever the problem, it can be worked out."

A loud click. A gun being engaged?

Adrenaline flooded his veins. He stepped behind a wide beam and drew his weapon, his back pressed against the wood.

The barn doors swung open, pinioning him in a slice of sunlight. Heart slamming, he whipped around and leveled his gun.

Emily jumped back, eyes wide.

Shit. "Get out of here," he commanded.

A rake crashed to the ground, rattling on the hard-packed floor behind him. He turned. A raccoon and her babies scurried into the aisle from the last stall, eyeing him and Emily before loping out the back.

Jax shoved his gun into his holster, off his game by a mile. The energy shot had only put him more on edge. "You okay?" he asked.

Emily raised a hand to her chest. "I'm fine. You?"

"Thought I heard something." If he intended to find Allison, and not look like a fool in the process, he'd better pull it together fast. He could have pressed that trigger on the beach and been done, but he hadn't. He couldn't half-ass it now. If for nothing else, Emily's sake.

At the stall, Emily swung open the top half of the door. The bay hung his head out, and she scratched his nose. "You did. Riley's a good watch horse. Unfortunately, he's not a fan of raccoons."

"Good to know."

"I was out here a couple of hours ago to feed him, though. Didn't see any signs Allison had been here."

Emily hadn't received the call that Allison hadn't shown up at school at that point. He strode to the stall where he'd heard the noise. Straw and dirt had been raked into a pile against the back wall. A white piece of ceramic poked through, catching his attention.

He knelt, gathering the shards. A piggy bank.

When he turned, Emily's face matched the color of the pottery. She clapped her hand over her mouth.

"How much was in there?" he asked.

"Most of her allowance for the past two years, and every birthday gift from her grandparents since birth." Her voice trembled.

Jax stared at her for a better answer.

"Five hundred. At least." Her body let loose a shudder, and she folded her arms over her chest, gripping her robe in her fists.

Five hundred was enough to get far away from Misty Pines.

Jax jogged back to the house with Emily on his heels. At the computer, he hammered at the keyboard, opening file after file as Emily alternated between pacing and hovering over his shoulder. Allison had done a report on the Civil War and a few searches for a US history timeline. She could have cleared her search field, but what remained was the usual ninth-grade stuff.

Emily gnawed on her thumbnail. "She's run away, hasn't she?"

"Possibly, but that doesn't change how we'll approach this. I'll get an APB and her name into the national database right away."

Emily tensed. "National?"

"It's standard, Emily. It's accessible by all law enforcement with the pertinent data. That way, when she's found, the agency will know who to contact."

Her eyes widened with concern.

"It won't come to that. I'll find her," he said, shoving aside the hollow feeling that he hadn't always come through.

Emily sent him a list of Allison's friends, along with a description of what she'd been wearing: blue jeans and a gray sweatshirt, red sneakers, and carrying a black and white paisley backpack. At least she was dressed well enough to keep her warm in the fifty-degree fog.

"I'll be back to you soon." Jax placed his hand on Emily's arm. "If you hear from her, you call me direct."

"Please find her and bring her home, Jax."

He attempted his most reassuring smile, leaving her in the doorway, tears streaking her face.

In his car, he grabbed the radio from his dash and put out an APB to all surrounding jurisdictions. At the end of Emily's driveway, he got out and scanned the area where Allison might have waited for the school bus. He focused on the roadside and the grassy verge, his stomach acid churning. Was there a torn button or dropped lip gloss or glittery hair clip—anything—that shouldn't be there? Or had she walked off attempting to get to Portland on her own?

Birds chirped while the wind rustled through the pines and firs off to the north. A slice of cobalt sky fought its way through the mist.

Nothing out of place. The ground yielded no clues.

His driving the route out of town produced nothing, either.

Allison Krueger had a good head start and might very well be headed to Portland. But twenty-five years ago, when he was a young detective, two girls had run from a bad situation on a similar rural road. Their trek had started out innocently until they encountered a person with a different plan.

In any situation, there's a window of forty-eight to seventy-two hours in which to find the missing before the trail cooled. Or worse. The last time his failure had cost a fourteen-year-old girl her life. If he was to have one last case before returning to the beach, finding another missing teenager seemed fitting.

Maybe this time, he'd make a difference.

Chapter Three

Steven was spiraling. Again. Elena Massey could hear it in her brother's endless torrent of nonsense that filled the message he'd left on her cell. She'd heard it before, many times.

After ten years in private practice, she'd become fluent in the idiosyncrasies of desperation. She brought Steven's number up on her phone and stared at the only picture she had of him on her desk. He'd made no eye contact, and his baseball hat hid most of his face. Camera-shy and elusive. The picture summed him up perfectly.

"Elena." Her receptionist's voice interrupted from the intercom.

Elena jumped, hitting the red button. "Yes, Stacey?"

"Your one o'clock is here. I'm heading to lunch."

She held back a sigh. "I'll be right out." Elena hit the SEND button on her cell anyway. If she could connect with him, she'd set up a time to talk. Five rings later, he didn't answer.

She hung up. He wouldn't get off that easy.

Got your message. She texted. *I'm available in an hour. Call me.*

The ringer silenced, she aimed for her purse and tossed her cell. It landed on the floor. Another one of those days.

Swooping up the phone, she dropped it in her bag, catching a glimpse of her reflection in the compact mirror that had popped open. She ran her fingers over her freckled nose and cheeks. She'd been told she was cute. Cute was hardly what a thirty-five-year-old clinical and forensic psychologist banked on. Her natural brown waves had come from her mom, her five-nine-frame from her dad. Her sister, Madeline, had been an older version of her right down to their fine features. Cute sometimes came at a deadly cost. Or had for Madeline, who'd been murdered twenty-five years ago today.

Elena's heart squeezed. No going there now. She had a client waiting.

She smoothed her silk blouse, tucking it into her straight black skirt, before rubbing the back of her neck. Her earlier nap hadn't cleared her impending headache, and she pushed off her edginess.

Grace Manheim was skimming a magazine when Elena entered the waiting area. "Come in, Grace."

The mousy blonde passed Elena, eyes locked on the carpet, and made her way to the overstuffed chenille couch. She dropped onto the cushions and started picking at her fingernails.

Elena settled in the chair across from her, crossing her legs, a notepad on her lap. She flipped to Grace's page from their last visit. "How're you doing since our last visit? You been journaling like we talked about?"

Grace nodded without looking up.

Elena assessed her client's mood. Pensive. Off. "Have you accepted any of his calls?"

Grace shook her head.

"When's his release date again?"

"Next week."

She browsed her notes. "I have it down for early next year."

"Good behavior," Grace said.

She'd ask Loran about that when she saw him tomorrow at her own weekly session. Like her, Dr. Kavorian worked with the inmates at the federal prison, as well as at a couple of the smaller ones where Grace's ex was incarcerated, recommending parole.

It was a heavy gig, peering deep into their hearts and souls, deciding which ones had the best chance at rehabilitation. She enjoyed the responsibility of making a difference in society. She didn't mind the control, either.

Deep down, she wanted her sister's killer to pass through the system someday. She'd hoped that she'd recognize him if he did—she'd never admit that to anyone. Grace's eyes were on her.

"The important thing is a game plan," Elena said. "Would you consider changing your phone number? It would send a clear message to your ex-husband that you don't want anything to do with him."

Grace nibbled at a hangnail on her right index finger without answering.

Her client harbored the illusion it was better to know what her ex had on his mind than to shut him out. While Elena didn't agree, she hadn't blocked Steven's number. Of course, he was her ex, but he was difficult. Did your brother rise to the same level of needing to be iced out of your life?

"I was thinking," Grace started and then looked away again.

Elena clutched her pen tighter, sensing what would follow those three little words. "Yes?" She kept her tone professional.

"I should give him another chance."

Grace wasn't mentally ill, but low self-esteem caused by a cold and detached father was proving just as debilitating as any psychological disorder. Elena didn't want to lose Grace to this asshole who'd been in prison for nearly running her over with his car. "I see. You've been communicating with him then?"

"He's been writing me." A shy grin crossed her face. "Poetry. Short notes. Long thoughtful letters. He's changed."

Elena fought the urge to scoot to the edge of her chair for emphasis. "People tell you many things when they're in the apologetic part of their cycle. If you go back, he'd start in slowly with comments that you were to blame for his incarceration and the argument that got him there. That would be the preface to him lashing out again. Only you might not escape his wrath next time."

Grace's bottom lip quivered. "I miss him."

"He's been in prison five years. It's not him you miss." She checked her tone. Being hard on Grace wouldn't help. She leaned forward and put a comforting hand on her leg. "Have you been doing the mirror exercises we spoke about?"

Grace's hangnail oozed blood. Elena snatched a tissue from a nearby Kleenex box and handed it to her, nodding at her hand.

"Sort of." Grace pressed the tissue against the rip. Blood seeped through. "I have a hard time looking at my reflection."

"I understand, but it's a good way to start changing the inner dialogue. To start believing all the good things about yourself."

"I'll try again."

That's all she could ask. A half-hour later, Elena walked Grace to the door. "Promise me you won't accept his calls in the meantime?"

Grace agreed, but the likelihood of her following through was slim to none. Family of any kind was often a weakness. Hopefully not a fatal one for Grace.

Since Stacey hadn't returned from lunch, Elena rounded her receptionist's desk and pulled up the computer calendar she maintained, moving the chocolate red foiled hearts stacked near the mouse. Sugar addict or secret admirer? With Stacey's long red hair and tiny figure, it wouldn't surprise Elena if she'd caught someone's eye. Today's appointments appeared on the screen.

Nothing for the next hour, but Gervais would be in around five. Elena had recommended him fit for rehabilitation. A gang member accused of being a runner, he was young at the time. With the right incentives and education, she believed he had a chance. She'd been right—so far.

They didn't all go as well, and the Board didn't always respect her recommendations. Perhaps she was kidding herself that she had any control.

Back in her office, she pulled out her phone—nothing from Steven.

I'm calling you, she texted. *Answer.*

Her brother's phone rang and rang before finally picking up. "Leave a message."

"Hey, sorry I missed you earlier, but I'm here for you. Whatever it is, I can help."

The phone buzzed in her hands. Her ex-husband Daniel. She switched to him. "Hey, Danny. Can we talk later? I've got a lot going on and…."

"Elena, it's Allison." His voice trembled. "She didn't get on the bus today. She's missing."

The phone slipped out of Elena's grip. Not Allison. The past crashed in like a riptide, jerking her under. She scrambled to get the phone back to her ear. "I'm on my way."

Chapter Four

Jax rushed into the sheriff's station along with a burst of wind that swirled the paperwork on Trudy's desk.

Headset wrapped around her head like an air traffic controller, she shot him a scowl while anchoring the papers. "I understand, Mrs. Jansen." She didn't miss a beat. "However, there's not much we can do about your laundry missing off the clothesline." She tucked a pure white strand of her bobbed hair behind her ear. "No other reports have come in about a clothing thief on the loose. It could be a crow. My grandmother used to tell stories of one with a penchant for colored socks. Wouldn't touch the white, but Lord if he wouldn't grab the red ones."

Small town problems. Jax would take a dozen bird capers to one minute of a missing child case. He hovered at Trudy's desk to speed her up.

"I'll let Sheriff Turner know. In the meantime, how about you take a look-see around your yard? If a varmint did get to the shirts, they might be under a bush somewhere."

Jax's mouth opened to interrupt. Trudy held an index finger in the air. At twenty years her junior, he was a fool to think he was the one in charge.

"Oh, you do? Wonderful. I'll tell the sheriff he needs to give those squirrels a talking to." She tapped the button on her headset. "Well, don't you look like hell. You not sleeping, hon? Because you sure don't look like you are."

Jax grimaced. "I'm fine."

"You've been many things this past year. Fine isn't one of them. You're working on that dollhouse all hours of the night again, aren't you?"

He shifted his weight at her ability to see through him. It had been more like five years that he hadn't felt connected to his body, let alone anyone or anything else. "You on Facebook?"

She straightened. "I am, along with Twitter and Instagram. My granddaughter says Tik Tok and Snapchat are all the rage, but I don't get the appeal." Her lips pressed together. "You haven't found Allison?"

"Not yet." He handed her his notes. "Need you to monitor her accounts and let me know if there's activity. I've already blasted the APB, but NCIC needs uploading and Allison's photo released to the outlets listing her as a possible runaway. You might as well get started on the subpoena for call data records, too."

"Will do. Have you called Abby?"

Jax pushed himself off the desk. "Why would I do that?"

"Because the FBI has resources we don't."

"Right. They're also scavengers who try to take over."

"Is that the real reason?"

Damn it, Trudy. "Get that file going for me, please," he said.

"You know, Abby living two towns away doesn't mean she's gone forever. She could have transferred out of state. Seems she would have if she intended to get away from you. What are you waiting for?"

"Divorce is final." Jax needed mothering like he needed a hole in the head. He frowned at the thought. "Just do what I ask, okay?"

"I'm serious about Abby—"

The front door opened, saving him from further commentary on his personal life.

His three young deputies, Garrett, Matt, and Brody, had arrived wearing their county-issued khaki military pants, boots, black T-shirts, and vests. Mirror images of him, without the official badges. He wished his full-timer, Deputy Chris Chapman, was among them, but he'd have to make do with this clutch of inexperienced boys. Not fair. They'd trained; everyone started somewhere. Might as well be with a missing persons drill.

"What's up, Chief?" Brody said. With his dirt-brown wispy hair and pale face, he barely looked old enough to drive.

Jax perched on the desk next to Trudy. "Allison Krueger's missing."

"The bookstore lady's daughter?" Brody asked.

"Emily, yes." His deputies leaned in as he brought them up to speed. He hadn't expected to see their faces again. Or had he? Trudy had interrupted him on the beach, but he'd hesitated. Uncertain of what he wanted—other than to be rid of the pain. How much more would he have caused by going through with his plan?

He silenced the internal debate. They had a girl to find. "Someone needs to interview the school bus driver on that route. Maybe they saw something. Same with the ticketing agent at the Greyhound station. Can't be too many teenage girls purchasing tickets out of town the past few days. If Allison did, someone should remember."

"I can do that," the oldest reservist, Matt, said. When he wasn't called up for duty, he was stocking shelves at the IGA off Main and courting the coffee baristas at the Dutch Brothers in West Shore.

"That'll work," Jax said. "Brody, I'll have you with me to canvass the neighborhood."

"What about me?" Garrett asked. Another one Jax had known since he was a teenager. He had a baby face with a crew cut and the body of an NFL lineman. He was biding his time until the Portland police department had an opening.

"You'll be driving the 101 south up to Highway 26. If Allison's on foot, she won't have gotten far. If she's hitched a ride with a friend, they could've made some stops." The same might hold true if she'd accepted a ride from a stranger.

Garrett's face drooped with disappointment. With a police future on the horizon, Jax understood Garrett's desire to be in the thick of the action. But first, he had dues to pay; sweeping Hwy 101 with an eye for a missing girl was a start to paying them.

Jax returned his attention to Matt and Brody. "Any questions?"

Matt shrugged. "Sounds like it won't amount to much. Allison probably got mad and stormed off for the day."

The straight-faced deputies turned to Jax for a response. He could tell them about the things he'd seen. Women beaten and strangled. Children molested, murdered, or left like garbage in the forest. The scars and nightmares that haunted those who worked on behalf of those victims. These boys had no idea.

Instead, he strode to the copy machine, punched in five copies, and placed Allison's picture on the glass. While the color photos churned out, he scanned her innocent face. Best case scenario, teenage angst and hormones had sent her packing, and determined to get to Portland. But he couldn't take that chance.

"Look," he said, "even if we're ninety-nine percent sure it's that simple, that one percent could mean the difference between life and death. We slack off, and she ends up in the trunk of a car, or a ditch, or…." He grabbed a roll of Tums from his pocket and popped one in his mouth as images of a dead girl, bound and gagged, rose from the past. He wouldn't go there. "These first hours are crucial, so we hunt like bloodhounds. If she shows up at a friend's house and turns out she forgot to tell her mom, then you boys get to sleep easy, knowing she's safe. Until we have eyes on her, we keep our noses to the ground."

* * *

"Got nothing," Brody said an hour later, sliding his lanky body into the passenger seat. Jax had him question the neighbors on the north side of Emily's street while he took the south. "Either they weren't home, had already left for work, or weren't paying attention."

Jax frowned. "About what I heard. Or they didn't have any view of the main road and hadn't left their house today. Did you check at the Commissioner's place?" Better Brody than him.

"Rang the call button at the gate. No answer," he said. "If you think she's run off, Chief, why aren't we all driving the roads out of town searching for her?"

Jax turned up the scenic driveway lined with maples that led to Glenn Hill Farm & Orchards. "We're too small to waste resources until we're sure. We check close first, get statements, eliminate possibilities, then go from there."

Eliminating possibilities included a visit to the farm that was next door to Allison's bus stop.

He'd last been here when Lulu was three to pick strawberries in the U-pick field. He could still see Abby with the summer sun reflecting on her black hair, hands on her slim hips, chiding him for letting Lulu eat more than she was putting into the bucket. He'd just winked at his daughter, who'd giggled, and threw his hands up in surrender to his wife.

"You're as thick as thieves, aren't you?" Abby had said, joining their laughter.

Guilty as charged. Not much appeared to have changed on the farm since.

The leaves were a mixture of green and vibrant reds and oranges. Past the maples, the cherry and pear orchards began. Besides endless rows of fruit trees and seasonal berries, one part of the hundred-plus-acre farm was filled with wandering alpacas, horses, and sheep. The property contained dozens of buildings designated for livestock, agriculture, and a riding arena at the center. The place was expansive, with too many places for a young girl to disappear into.

Jax pulled his cruiser in by the open-air arena, and he and Brody got out. They scuffed through shavings and dirt on their way to the small office. The smell of saddle leather, grime, and manure filled Jax's nose like it had at Emily's place. Cattle roping was set up in the arena.

The lead man, Vince Wallace, met them before they made it to the building. He was shorter than Jax's six one by a few inches, but lean and fit from hours spent working the farm.

"Morning, Sheriff. What can I do you for?" A trickle of sweat ran down from Vince's brown hair that slicked back and revealed a streak of gray. He wiped his weathered hands on a rag as he approached. "Hope you aren't here looking for papers. We run an upstanding business."

"I'm not INS." Jax reached out a hand that Wallace shook. A red substance discolored the man's fingertips. "How's business?"

"Not bad." He pulled his hand back, following Jax's gaze. "Sorry about that. Just had to perform surgery on one of our alpacas that tangled with a barbed wire fence."

"Animal going to make it?" Jax asked.

"Sure. I'm an old pro at repairing livestock around here. Could be a vet I do it so often. As for the farm, not a bumper year on pears, but cherries paid the bills." He scanned the sheriff and then Brody. "If you'd like, I can wrangle up half-a-flat for you and the missus. If I remember correct, she makes a mean pie."

Jax's eye twitched while forcing a smile. Wallace remembered a life that Jax hadn't lived for quite some time. "Appreciate that, but not today."

Wallace nodded. "What brings you by then?"

"Neighbor girl, Allison Krueger, didn't get on the bus this morning. Was hoping you, or someone here, saw her out at the bus stop."

"Or making her way down the road with her backpack," Brody added.

Jax nodded.

One side of Wallace's mouth curved in a half smile. "That little thing with long hair? Cutie always has her headphones on." He chuckled. "Kid's going to go deaf. I can make out every word when her music's blasting."

"That would be the one." Brody looked him up and down. "So, you did see her?"

Jax noted the shift in Brody's attitude. Wallace had given a more detailed description of a young girl standing on the road than he'd expected. But they were neighbors.

He shrugged. "I've seen her before. Not this morning, though. Been busy." He lifted his hands.

"What time did everyone arrive today?" Jax asked.

"Six-thirty, a bit before sunrise, like most days."

"Mind if I chat with some of your crew?"

"No, but the only ones near enough to take notice would be José and Francisco. They were on the picker closer to the main road earlier. They're out there now, matter of fact. If you got a sec, I'll take you to 'em."

Wallace hopped behind the wheel of a four-seater Kawasaki Mule. He grabbed a tin of Copenhagen off the dash, pinched the chew before tucking it in his cheek, and slipped the container into his front pocket. Jax rode shotgun, and Brody climbed in the back. Wallace revved it and had them bouncing down into the orchards before either of them could strap in.

The thinning leaves and large trunks of the old cherries lined a near-perfect pathway through the property. Francisco and José scaled down from the bucket of a story-high John Deere picker at their arrival. They kicked through fallen leaves over their direction.

Jax pulled Allison's picture out of his shirt pocket after Wallace had made an introduction. "Afternoon, gentlemen. Looking for a young girl who lives in the area. Hoping you might've seen her."

Francisco glanced at Allison, then at his watch. "Not me. I been busy running the beast. You, José?"

"Not today. Can't see that part of the road anyway from here. But I've seen her before. She do something?"

Jax pulled the picture back. "She's missing."

"No can help, Sheriff," José said.

He shifted on his feet. "How about any vehicles in the area between seven and seven-thirty?"

Both men shook their heads.

"Not much goes by here," Francisco said. "When the machine's running, can't hear anyway."

"Sí," José said. "Saw the Millers just a bit ago. You know, boss man, the ones that give us a hard time when we spread lime."

"He's talking about the people behind us," Wallace said.

Brody jumped in. "You didn't see the school bus or whether it stopped in front?"

José adjusted his face scarf. "Nope."

Francisco looked at his watch again. "No idea. Like I said, we were running the picker."

His body language felt off. "You need to be somewhere, Francisco? You seem preoccupied," Jax said.

He shifted. "Don't want to be late for my kid."

"Picking one up?"

"No. Wife's having our baby this afternoon. She's three weeks overdue, and her doc is only at the hospital today. But I had to work, you know. Got bills to pay. New mouth soon to feed." Francisco's tan face blanched.

Inducing would have him antsy. "Congrats. You're in for a ride." Jax didn't add how sometimes rides came to abrupt halts and nearly killed you on impact. Even if they didn't, you'd wish they had.

"Thanks, Sheriff. Appreciate that," Francisco said.

Jax turned to Wallace. "If you don't mind, I'd like to go back up and take a look around the rest of the farm."

"Got a warrant?"

Odd reaction. "Didn't think I'd need one."

"Got something to hide?" Brody interjected.

The farm boss bristled.

Jax cleared his throat. Brody hadn't learned tact yet or cultivated the skill of knowing when to push, when to hold back, how to get people talking. "It would be appreciated, Vince. You know kids. She could be hiding out here to teach her mom a lesson for upsetting her." Although that didn't explain why she hadn't answered Kylie's texts. "She might have even gotten herself hurt and can't respond."

Wallace shrugged. "I'll keep an eye out. Best I can do."

Jax met the older man's eye. There was a missing kid—nothing should be more important than finding her.

Wallace didn't blink. The steeliness of his eyes signaled he wasn't easily moved. He spat again. "Ain't my place, Sheriff. Owners don't want people poking around their private property, and I've got to respect their wishes and enforce them." He reached in his shirt pocket for a refresh of the chew.

Jax gritted his teeth. Without a search warrant, and no present legal authority to obtain one, he couldn't do much else.

Jax's radio beeped. "Matt here, Sheriff. You there?" his reserve deputy said in his ear.

Jax walked away, leaving Brody with the three men, and responded. "Whatcha got?"

"School bus driver, Mrs. Elderman, might have a lead."

"She's seen Allison?"

"Kind of. You should hear it in person."

He didn't like the sound of that. "On our way." He returned to the group. "If you see her, or find her hiding in one of your buildings, I'm your first call."

"*Vale*," Francisco and José said.

Wallace lifted his chin in the air.

Back in the patrol car, Brody said, "You seem intense. Everything okay?"

Jax didn't answer. Driving over to assist in the interview had his sixth sense jumping. As did the feeling that Vince Wallace was hiding something.

Chapter Five

"Calm down, Mrs. Elderman," Jax said for the third time since he'd walked into the school bus garage office. "No one's in trouble."

The seventy-two-year-old woman sat in a soft chair while Jax took the wooden one across from her. Matt and Brody fell back to give them room.

"I should have known when Allison was at her stop and then wasn't." She wrung her hands. "I'm always in Emily's store, seeing what she has on sale. She knows me. It would've been easy enough to call and ask her if Allison had changed her mind and was riding with her today."

"Let me be the judge of that," Jax said. "How far were you from Allison's stop when you saw her to begin with?"

"At the top of the ridge by the water tower."

That had to be at least a mile away. Bifocals framed Louise Elderman's almond-shaped and alert eyes. Aside from carrying a few extra pounds, she appeared healthy and capable. "That's quite a distance. You're sure it was her?"

She nodded, her hands now clasping and unclasping in her lap. "Pretty sure. I have eight stops between the tower and my last stop, which is Allison's. I go as far as the park, turn around, and head back to the high school."

"I understand, but—"

"I always look ahead to see who's waiting. I hadn't quite crested the hill, but I saw that except for the three stops right before Allison's, someone was at each one. It took me about ten or so minutes to get to the end. When I did, she was gone."

"You're certain you could see that distance?"

"It was overcast, but the sun had peeked out. I'm fairly certain."

The sun could have also caused a glare, which could be deceiving. "Were you paying attention to whether she was there the whole time as you moved through your route?"

The woman frowned, shaking her head. "I got focused on picking up the other kids and waiting for a few that were running behind. I didn't pay attention again until I was at the one right before hers, and she was gone."

"You said that no one was at the stops before hers."

"That was true at the point I glanced from the ridge, but Dylan Marks came racing down the driveway when I approached. He nearly missed me."

"He normally run late?"

"Always. I'd figure this being his senior year, he'd start improving. He hasn't."

Jax rubbed his chin with a bit too much vigor. Dylan was Commissioner Marks' son. Avoiding Marks might not be as easy as he'd hoped. He addressed Matt. "Get to the office and have the principal pull Dylan out of class." He should also take the opportunity to speak with Allison's friend, who notified Emily in the first place. "Have him get Kylie Reynolds too. I'll be there shortly."

"You got it." Matt rushed out of the bus barn to the adjacent high school. Brody remained at the door.

Jax returned his focus to the older woman. "Anything else you can think of that might be relevant?"

She looked past him at the wall. "I did notice at some point a car pulling out from the farm that's close to Allison's stop."

"Did you catch the make and model?"

"It could have been a station wagon, but I'm not one hundred percent on that."

Jax hadn't seen a vehicle matching that description at the farm. "Did Allison get in that car?"

"No idea. One of the kids who'd gotten on the bus tripped. I had to pull over and make sure he was okay. I got distracted and, like I said, stopped paying attention."

Tension crept into Jax's neck. It could be worth exploring—or might be nothing at all. He pulled a card from his pocket and started to stand. "If you think of anything else, please call me or Trudy at the station."

She clutched his card. "I hope Allison's okay. She seemed different this year."

"How so?" Jax asked, dropping back into the chair.

"Nothing drastic, I guess, but more withdrawn. I've seen it before with the incoming freshmen."

"Does she interact with kids much on the bus?"

"Not really. She sits at the back listening to music."

The image of Allison was taking shape, but nothing that equaled someone who'd run. "Thank you. You've been helpful."

Mrs. Elderman didn't move, holding her hands, palms together, at chest level. "There is one other thing." Jax waited. "I'm sure it's nothing. Kids and parents fight all of the time."

True. The way she said it, though, had him on alert. "What kind of fighting?"

"I mean, being a single mom and all. I don't envy Emily one bit. It must be hard."

The tension in Jax's neck tightened. He didn't have time for hemming-and-hawing. "What is it, Louise?"

"This past week, Emily's been chasing Allison down the driveway. Screaming. Calling her names. By the time I get there, Allison's red-faced and near tears, and Emily's halfway back up the driveway. She doesn't even wave goodbye to her daughter. The other day, I caught Emily at the stop shaking her by the arm. Allison hid her face, but she'd been crying. She raced to the rear of the bus while Emily ignored me and walked away."

Emily had made it sound like their fight was only last night. It could have been a continuation that reached a boiling point. "Only this past week?"

Mrs. Elderman nodded. "I don't want to get Emily in trouble. She's a good lady."

He agreed. She handled the book drive for the children's hospital and was part of the PTA. But every parent could be pushed to the limit. Or they could push their kids to theirs.

Either way, Emily hadn't painted a complete picture of her and Allison's relationship, and he'd need to revisit that. Jax covered the woman's fidgeting hands with his own and squeezed. "Thank you."

Brody followed him out. "She could be playing hooky," he said.

Jax turned to his deputy. "Kids don't usually skip out by themselves. If she was with friends, we'd know about it." He directed Brody to assist Matt in gathering Dylan and Kylie while he touched base with Trudy to update the NCIC with the vehicle information. Chapman's experience would come in handy about now because Brody was missing a vital clue, one that told them clear as day Allison wasn't taking a day off from life. She'd smashed her piggy bank and taken $500. For what purpose? Not to just goof off on a school day. She had bigger plans, and it was their job to find out what they were.

* * *

Dylan's daddy was a big-shot local politician, and Dylan did okay with the football. Those two things had him believing the world stepped aside and cheered when he entered a room. People kissing the ground one walked on, and the coaches and teachers giving free passes had that effect. Hell, Jax had experienced that himself. He'd been a decent lineman and could have ridden to college on his talent. He'd joined the Navy instead, bent on being a sailor like his father. Not that doing so, or anything subsequent, had gained him his old man's approval.

Jax had also seen how fast those accolades could disappear. One bad pass, one knee injury, and kiss those dreams goodbye. The fact Dylan could be in for a rude awakening when he ventured into the real world wasn't his problem.

"You didn't see a thing?" Matt asked.

Dylan slunk halfway out of his chair, arms over his chest. Air Jordan tennis shoes and brand-name jeans hung off his butt. If it wasn't for his belt with interlocking Gs as a buckle, they might be piled at his ankles.

"I told you, man. I was late."

"That normal?" Jax asked.

"It's seven-thirty, man. They should start school at noon or something."

Jax lifted an eyebrow. With Daddy being the County Commissioner, he was surprised Dylan hadn't figured out a way to make that happen. Especially since Daddy jumped to do lots of things on his behalf. Or at least tried. After Dylan got his DUI, even the Commissioner couldn't stop the judge two counties over from pulling Dylan's license out of his entitled little hands. "Let's pick another day then," Jax said. "Did you normally see Allison standing at the bus stop?"

"I guess. She's in her own world, though. I swear, I didn't see her this morning. I barely caught the bus."

"You spend any time with Allison on campus?" Jax said.

Dylan's upper lip curled. "She's a freshman."

"Wouldn't want to mess with your reputation?" Matt said.

Dylan rolled his eyes.

"Do you know any of her friends? Or have you heard rumors about her wanting to take off?" Sometimes kids talked. Heard things in the halls, during assemblies, P.E.

The door burst open, and Commissioner Troy Marks strode in like he owned the room and everyone in it. He only had a few inches on Jax, but he walked with a constant upward tilt of his chin to look like he was towering over everyone.

With smooth hands that hadn't seen a day of physical labor, he straightened his blazer over his white button-down. His Levi's ended at his ankles, giving him a nerdy vibe. He must have something official happening since he often wore running attire, logging miles around town for some upcoming race. Dylan's jock attitude had been inherited. "Afternoon, Jax. What brings you to the school, calling my boy out of class?"

"Morning, Troy." Jax ignored Dylan's smug look. "Simply asking if your son has seen one of his classmates, who happens to be your neighbor. She didn't get on the bus this morning."

Commissioner Marks smiled. "Ah, Sheriff, my boy doesn't see much of anything."

Dylan's smugness faded to annoyance. "Thanks, Dad."

The Commissioner waved him off. "You know what I mean, son. We don't get involved."

"In finding a young girl that's gone missing? Seems odd to draw a line in the sand on that," Jax said.

"In anything."

This had nothing to do with Allison or interviewing Dylan. He and Troy had a history of disagreements, including the one time he'd made noises about Jax not being fit to serve after Lulu's death. For the most part, they managed to function in the same town if they each stayed on their respective sides of the street. When their paths did cross, however, Troy never missed an opportunity to let people know who ran the show.

But right now, this was Jax's interview. "Seems like the good people around here would be interested in an opinion like that. Especially if something bad has happened to Emily's daughter."

"Emily's kid?" Commissioner Marks glanced at his son.

Jax caught the slight exchange. "Yes. Emily, who owns the bookstore. Her daughter, Allison."

"I know who she is." Marks tugged on his coat collar. "Hope she finds her soon. Let's go, Dylan. You're done here."

Jax stepped in front of the Commissioner. "Whoa, Troy. Am I missing something? Your son's a potential witness. He can answer questions if he likes."

"Except my boy doesn't feel like it, correct?" The father and son locked eyes.

Dylan stood. "Whatever."

"Then what about you?" Jax said. "Were you out running this morning? Did you see Allison or anything unusual in the neighborhood?"

"I was enjoying a cup of coffee with the fire chief, like I do many weekday mornings."

The Commissioner stepped around Jax before he could say another word, and Dylan followed.

Matt looked at Jax. "What the heck was that about?"

Dylan was holding back something. Whether that was Allison's whereabouts was unclear. What was clear was Commissioner Marks didn't want his son opening his mouth. "Good question."

Brody ran in, huffing and trying to catch his breath. "I missed Kylie. She had early release. I tried to catch her, but she was on her bike and hit the road toward town. I wasn't sure if you wanted me to follow."

"Let's not scare the girl to death." It wasn't Brody's fault he was green. If Jax didn't take the time to school him, he'd never learn. "I'll find her myself." He turned back to Matt. "What do we know on the Greyhound station?"

"On my way there next," Matt said.

"Allison's been missing for six hours, and we have almost nothing to go on. You should have gone there first," Jax said.

"Sorry, sir."

His whole team was inexperienced. Why the hell did Chapman have to be away right now? He clenched his hands to dispel his mounting blood pressure. "Brody, go with him and get it done. I'll catch up with you back at the station."

Outside, Jax pulled an energy drink from his pocket and downed it as his deputies sped off. No wonder his gut hurt—but he had to push through. He'd hoped to have Allison home by now. Expected to be back on the beach. Instead, he didn't even have a solid lead.

He ran his hand over the top of his head. Allison was at the bus stop, and then she wasn't. She'd been fighting with her mom regularly, but her mom had failed to mention that when questioned. Allison had been withdrawn and moody, not like herself, for a few months. She'd smashed her piggy bank open in the barn where she hoped no one would hear her or see the evidence. She was a girl running from something or to someone, but not a kid playing hooky or going to the mall, or hiding out in a friend's house.

What he didn't understand was why no one but him seemed overly concerned. Wallace put up a roadblock, Troy Marks and Dylan were stonewalling, and even Emily hadn't been forthright.

Only he was taking Allison's...Allison's what? Departure? Abduction? Murder? His brain ran to the darkest places a man's thoughts could go before he pulled himself from that edge. She was missing. That was reason enough to take her seriously.

Chapter Six

Daniel and Roper, a darling yorkie-poo that she and Allison had brought home from the Humane Society five years ago, met Elena at the door. *Hello* hadn't even left her mouth before Daniel enveloped her in his arms while Roper pawed at her pant leg for attention. "Thank you for coming. I certainly didn't expect you to make the drive."

"Of course, I'd come." They stood joined for a long moment in the entry as she scanned the home they'd once shared. Or more like the home where she'd spent the weekends. The long narrow hall leading to the living room and the kitchen to the right looked the same as when she'd taken the last of her things a year ago. Only Roper remained of their life together.

Elena leaned into the smell of Daniel's citrusy cologne, grounding her—reminding her of the good times. Saturday morning cartoons with Allison. Sunday morning breakfasts in bed. Long chats by phone during the week when she worked from her house in West Shore. Images of Roper bounding alongside Allison, demanding pets and playtime and puppy kisses were just as fresh today. Living on the coast meant she was close to her work and private practice, but it required her to navigate a long-distance relationship with Daniel. Or not navigate....

Still, she remembered feeling safe here. There were so few places that felt true.

Once Daniel released her, she cleared her throat and bent to gather Roper in her arms. She kissed the top of his bony head. The little furball relaxed into her arms, hungry for her attention. He missed her every bit as much as she missed him.

"Coffee?" Daniel asked, leading her to the kitchen.

"Please. What've you found out?" she asked.

"Nothing yet." He fiddled with his fancy Keurig and hit brew. "Allison's not responding to my calls or texts, and Emily hasn't heard an update from the police. She's waiting at home in case Allison comes back. Guess I am too."

"The museum's okay with that?"

"I told them I had to work from home today. Since Allison's done this before, I didn't want to concern anyone yet."

She nodded, remembering. "It was just after her ninth birthday, wasn't it when she was found at the ice cream parlor in town?"

"Yes. Because her mother had promised her, and then reneged." He shook his head.

Elena chuckled. It was easy to laugh now, but at that time, she'd had them worried. "Stubborn girl."

His mouth held a smile, but she knew better. His moves were rigid as he tapped the counter, waiting for the cup to fill with coffee, and promptly started the next one.

"Black?"

"Sugar today, if you have some." She sat down with Roper on her lap, caressing his silky fur. She'd spotted his sad snaggle-toothed face first that day at the shelter, but once Allison saw him, there was no question he'd come home with them. He'd needed massive amounts of dental work, which he got right away. Allison's smile every time she held Roper was enough to make it worth every penny.

Daniel was scanning her face. "A lot on your mind?"

"Sorry, yes, I was lost in thought and fighting a headache." She frowned. "It's that time of the year."

His eyes widened before he closed them. "I'm sorry. With Allison missing, I..."

"Don't apologize. I wouldn't expect you to remember." She almost said *anymore*, but even during their marriage, she'd had to remind him of the anniversary of Madeline—Maddy's murder.

"I have some biscotti around here." He opened cupboards until he found the container and grabbed two. "We could both use a little comfort food."

It would take more than that, but she took it, grateful. She balanced Roper, who had now curled into a ball on her lap, and ripped off the wrapper, dipping the cookie into her mug. "When was the last time you spoke with Allison?"

"Last night. She wants to live with me."

Allison had begged to move in with them over the course of their eight-year marriage too. Usually when her mom was clamping down the parental controls. "What did you tell her?"

"That I can't let her. The modern art exhibition is going live next month at the museum, and I'm running around the state half the time acquiring pieces. It doesn't make sense."

It didn't, but she felt for the little guy on her lap who must spend too much time alone or with a sitter. Alone could wreak havoc on the mind. At least Allison would give him the love he deserved every minute she could. Their unbreakable bond was why Elena had let him stay when she could have used the company herself. But Roper would have missed Allison. When she was in the room, everyone else became invisible. "Was Allison upset?"

He took a drink. "Of course. Told me that I didn't love her."

"Laying on the guilt."

He shrugged. "Pretty much."

She'd caught something else in his expression "You know her running away isn't your fault?"

Daniel closed his eyes. "She hasn't been happy lately. I could have let her think she could move here after the school year, if nothing else."

Elena's eyebrow arched.

He sighed. "I know. Lying betrays trust and is never a good idea."

"And you do have her trust." She sipped the coffee. "Teenage girls wanting to leave the moms who they identify with is often just a phase—a natural progression as a teenager searches for autonomy." True for many, but she'd have never wanted to be away from her own mother. If she'd known the day that her parents had gotten into their car would be their last, she'd have strapped herself to the grill to stop them. That one moment had changed everything for her, Madeline, and Steven.

"Earth to Elena." Daniel interrupted her thoughts. "I was just saying you're right, before I lost you." He lifted the coffee to his lips. "I've seen that look before. Something else is bothering you."

A chill ran up her arms, and she wrapped her hands around the cup, letting it warm her. "I'm sorry. Steven called earlier today."

Daniel lowered his mug without drinking. "Impeccable timing, like usual. What trauma is he experiencing now?"

His tone took on that familiar irritation Elena had grown to expect when Steven's name entered the conversation. Not that she blamed Daniel. "He can't help that his condition has left him terrified of people."

"Terrified, or hates them in general?"

She rubbed the back of her neck to ease the tightness that had crept from her shoulders into the base of her skull. Her taking care of Steven had caused too many fights, and neither of them needed that right now. "Anthropophobia is a real illness. His need for isolation and not wanting to meet you were never personal."

"That's not what I took personally. It's the demand he puts on your attention. You and Madeline were the ones in that foster care...." He stumbled, searching for the right word, but there were no right words. The white rock and plastic flowers sunk in around the perimeter of their foster home had fooled everyone into believing that the Simpsons were a happy, wholesome couple. Daniel glanced out the window, then cleared his throat. "It wasn't your fault you were put in that situation or for what sent you out that night. You were the ones who were put in harm's way, not him."

"I know."

Daniel drained the rest of his coffee and muttered. "Not to mention what happened after."

She closed her eyes. She didn't want to talk about what had happened to her and Maddy. Her life wasn't at issue. It was her brother who was in trouble and needed her help. Daniel had never fully understood that.

"Steven was homeless, scared, alone. Everyone handles trauma differently. But his illness makes everything he endured amplified."

Daniel's voice softened. "You're right. Forgive me. Allison missing has me on edge."

"There's nothing to forgive." Despite everything, he was a fine man. He'd tried. "Steven's frustrating; I get it." Daniel had never been good at sharing his emotions, but the strain in his eyes said what he couldn't. "Enough about my brother."

He reached his hand out to her. "I care what's happening in your life too."

She took his hand and squeezed. It had been like this once—talking and sharing. Her therapist, Dr. Kavorian, had encouraged her to trust more... talk more... be more emotionally available. Now she had so few people she lowered her walls for. She wished Allison's disappearance hadn't been what drew her and Daniel together.

Their marriage could have been something wonderful had she let Daniel in all the way. Her home in West Shore and the distance worked well in the beginning. Then she'd gotten comfortable with that distance, her own life, and the space for Daniel and Allison vanished. She rubbed her forehead.

"Are you taking the medicine that Dr. Kevorkian prescribed?"

She laughed at the slaughtering of her doctor's name. "It's Kavorian. Lord, Daniel."

"There's my girl."

"And yes. I see him tomorrow."

Their conversation turned back to Allison and his exhibit at the museum for the next hour until the coffee was gone and a stack of biscotti wrappers littered the table.

Daniel placed his hand on her arm, the warmth grounding her. "Thanks for coming. It felt good to talk, to keep my mind occupied. It won't be long now. The phone will ring any second, and Emily will be on the other end telling me Allison's back home, safe. There's no need for you to stay. I know you need to get back."

She did, but she hated to leave. "Are *you* going to be okay?"

"I'll be better when she's home. But I'm fine."

Elena lifted Roper off her lap before standing and kissed him again on his head—one, two, three, four times in quick succession—before setting him on the floor. She already missed that toothless bundle of fluff.

Daniel's phone rang, startling them. Daniel jumped out of his chair and grabbed his cell that he'd left next to the coffee machine. "This is he. Certainly. Can you hold one moment?" He placed his hand over the speaker returning to the table where he sat back down, his shoulders slumping forward. Not the news he was hoping for, then. "It's the police. They want to ask me a few questions."

"I can hang out."

He shook his head. "I'll fill you in later."

She met his eyes. "You're sure?"

"I am."

She did have her client coming in. Admittedly, she'd also feel better when she got a hold of Steven and knew what his deal was. Elena searched Daniels' face. "They will find Allison."

He hung his head and nodded. Perhaps he had tears he'd rather she not see, too.

After a long hug, she left him in the kitchen, talking, and climbed into her car, feeling the weight of the day in her upper back. She tried Steven again—and left another message.

It wasn't like him not to respond. Daniel had been right that her brother didn't just call to chat. He came barreling into her life when something was wrong, which she'd already determined by his voice. But was he not answering because something had physically happened to him this time?

She'd get to her office and see her five o'clock appointment. Then she'd drive out to his place and pray he wasn't lying dead on the floor.

Chapter Seven

Jax waited on the phone while Daniel finished a conversation. He intended to circle back to Emily, but it would be good to hear the issue from the other side before he did.

"Thank you for taking my call," he said when Daniel came on the line. "I understand you spoke with your daughter last night?"

"Yes. She called. Any idea where she's gone yet?"

"Working on that and looking for some insight. Emily mentioned she and Allison had a fight before she called you."

He hesitated. "I, well, yes."

"Is their fighting a common occurrence?"

"I wouldn't say common, but mothers and daughters notoriously have issues, don't they?"

"I imagine that can be true." Although Daniel seemed to be downplaying it. "Did they have more than what you'd consider normal?"

"Not that I've been privy to."

"You must know what prompted last night's disagreement, though."

"Yes and no. Allison was unhappy about something Emily had done. She didn't elaborate—only said that her mother was a hypocrite and didn't respect her privacy."

Jax had reasoned that Allison's attitude, as described by Emily, was typical teenage behavior. He hadn't pushed Emily on why Allison wanted to move away. In the future, he'd heed his own advice and not make assumptions. He hadn't done a proper interview with Emily to explore the undercurrent in that household—an error he would remedy. "Has she complained of that in the past?"

Daniel paused. "Not really, but Allison hasn't had an interest in boys until this last summer. That might have something to do with her wanting more privacy. Granted, that's only a guess."

"As in 'don't go through my stuff and read my love letters?'"

Daniel hesitated again. "Like 'I don't want you to know I'm seeing someone.'"

"Emily doesn't know?" Jax said, although he couldn't see her holding that back if she did.

"Correct."

"Why would she tell you and not Emily?"

"Because Emily overreacts."

Maybe, but he also sensed Daniel Krueger liked having one up on his ex-wife. "Was this boy she liked older?"

"Don't know."

"What's his name?"

"She didn't say."

Jax shifted in his seat at the lack of answers. He didn't want to judge a father that didn't press for them, but had Lulu taken an interest in a boy, or girl for that matter, he'd make sure the very least he knew about them was the name and grade. Their address. What their parents did for a living. "Were they casual or serious?"

Daniel sighed. "I hate to break her confidence like this, but…."

Jax gripped his phone. "Mr. Krueger, we believe she walked off of her own volition, but we don't know why, or for that matter, with who, if anyone. Looking like the bad guy in her eyes should be the least of your worries right now."

"Absolutely," Daniel stammered. "I suppose I'm hoping she just needed time to cool down, and she'll be walking up Emily's driveway any minute."

"We all want that," Jax said, aware that wanting and having were two different things.

"Of course. In answer to your question, serious enough. Or was. Only reason I was privy to the information was Allison wanted birth control, and she's on my insurance. With Misty Pines' gossip mill, going to a local doctor wasn't an option. I arranged for her to visit a clinic here in Portland."

"Recently?" Jax asked.

"August."

"You said it *was* serious?"

"Teenagers run hot and cold. As for the birth control, they're going to have sex with or without parental consent. I figured either help get her protected or be culpable if she got pregnant. I chose option *A* and hoped we'd raised her to be smart enough to use it."

Emily's frustrations were justified if being walled out by Allison and Daniel was common practice. "Seems like a mother should be involved in those kinds of choices."

"Except Emily's way of protecting Allison would include not letting her out of her sight, and that's not practical."

Practical or not, he would've sided with Emily on that one. "Are Allison and this boy still together?"

"Not to my knowledge," Daniel said. "A few weeks ago, she said it was a summer thing that didn't end well. I'm assuming that's still the case."

"And you're sure Allison didn't say who she'd been seeing?"

"She didn't."

"Why didn't you press her?" A relationship that had progressed to sex would have guaranteed Jax running fingerprints and a full-blown background check. Oh hell, who was he kidding. He'd lock Lulu in her room.

"It's our agreement. Allison can come to me for anything, and I won't interrogate her. Besides, she can be elusive. Even if I'd asked her twenty times, she might not have told me."

Not even near a good excuse. That's what parents did. Badger until they got the information they needed to keep their children safe. "How about overhearing a conversation?"

"I don't generally...wait, she did talk about him with her friend, Kylie, once. She was whispering, but I thought she'd said he had great hands and...."

"And?"

"And they weren't just good for football." Daniel's voice had a tinge of regret. Finally.

Jax's grip was once again tight on the phone. "Ever hear the name Dylan Marks?"

Daniel was quiet for a moment. "I can't be sure."

Jax knew someone who might—and she was next on his list.

* * *

If Kylie was on her bike, she'd either be headed for home off Pacific Avenue, where she lived with her aunt, or what passed for a shopping mall in town, a strip of half-dozen boutiques along the west part of Chautauqua Street.

He drove by both and found her at neither. Only when he was halfway down Main Street did he recognize the blonde behind the counter of *A Book Above*. His eyes on Kylie, he skimmed his rims, parking too near the curb.

Inside, a couple of shoppers had their noses in books near the back of the store. He didn't recognize either of them. He'd served this community for a decade. Before burying Lulu five years ago, he could've told you the names of most everyone who called this place home. Where they lived. What they did for a living. Now he barely slept, was obsessed with completing a dollhouse that would benefit no one, and lived on energy shots and antacids. He hadn't cared who came or went from this hole of a town, relying on his deputy, Chapman, to pick up the slack. Was that disconnection going to cost Allison?

"You work here?" he said to Kylie once the jingle of the front doorbell subsided.

"Sheriff Turner." Her eyes widened. "Yes. I mean, sometimes, if Emily's busy. She texted earlier, wanting to stay close to home. I told her I'd open, for a few hours anyway. Have you found Allison?"

"Not yet. Have you seen any activity on her social media, or talk to anyone at school who might have a clue about where she's gone?"

She shook her head, frowning.

"What can you tell me about Allison and Dylan's relationship?"

Kylie's eyes darted to the back of the store, and her voice was low. "Hold on." She approached the customers and hurried them to the register.

They nodded at him while they checked out, sadness in their eyes. They knew his story, whether he recognized them or not. The sheriff who'd lost his kid and whose wife had abandoned him, leaving behind a shell of a man to run this town. He'd long ago tired of their pity. Hell, he'd tired of his own.

He picked up a novel and thumbed through the pages, trading their glances and well-meaning sighs for a man with a wooden leg and a lackluster exchange of cannon fire between pirate ships on the high seas. But his focus drifted to the children's book table.

Lulu's favorite, *Llama Llama Red Pajama*, was on display. She'd made Abby read that silly book to her two or three times every night. He'd stand at the bedroom door, watching Abby, her dark hair resting on her shoulders, reading to their little girl snuggled deep under the covers, only her eyes showing. He almost found a smile.

Kylie locked the door and flipped the open sign over. "Sorry. I don't want anything getting back to Dylan."

He shook the memory and returned the pirate book to the table. "He have a bad reputation in school?"

Kylie nodded. "He's an ass."

Dylan had been cocky, and quick to let his father fix things. Being an ass wouldn't be far behind. "Tell me about the relationship."

"It started over the summer when a few of us signed up for berry picking at Glenn Hill Orchards."

"Glenn Hill?"

"Yeah, you know the farm—"

"I was there earlier. The farm boss didn't mention anything about that." Between the station wagon that the bus driver saw leaving their drive and Allison having worked in the berry fields, Glenn Hill warranted another visit.

She shrugged. "A ton of school kids signed up for it. Me included. Our boss was Angelique, who's cool. Anyway, the pay's decent, and it's morning work. Allison couldn't beat the location. I mean, right next door."

With Dylan's DUI, it worked well for him, too, even though it was surprising Daddy Marks would let his son do *menial* labor. "Did you know Allison was on birth control?"

She turned red. "Who told you that?"

"Her father. He also mentioned she might no longer be together with the boy she got it for."

"First off, she only got it to make Dylan happy. He never stopped bugging her, so she caved. Only the more she thought about it, she didn't like being pressured and told him no. He wasn't happy about that."

Good girl. "Did Dylan end it with her?"

Her eyebrows pulled together. "She broke up with him. That hasn't stopped him from harassing her about getting back together, though. The guy doesn't take rejection well."

"Give me an example."

"Mostly threatening to blast her online if she doesn't change her mind. That was his earlier approach. Since school started, he's gone between sitting next to her on the bus and getting in her face, to ignoring her. She hates catching that bus in the mornings, that's for sure."

Except Dylan almost didn't make the bus this morning. "Is it possible they had a run-in earlier, and she took off to avoid him?" He held back his next question of whether she thought Dylan would do something to make sure she wouldn't. It was a leap. Timing would have been tight to incapacitate Allison and then hop on a school bus. He'd seen no signs of a struggle when he scanned the bus stop. Other than Dylan's pompous attitude and adolescent libido, Jax had no proof of an interaction gone sour.

"It could have happened that way. Only thing is, Homecoming's this Friday. If she didn't want to catch the bus, she would've texted, or like, gotten in touch since. She wouldn't go all silent. We're going to the dance together, and we were stoked about shopping this afternoon. She planned to sneak money out of her savings for a dress we'd picked out at Vintage Violet."

He raised his eyebrows. "Pricy."

"She said she had enough." Kylie looked down at the ground. "Anyway,

I'm worried. She wouldn't miss shopping voluntarily."

If the money was being used for a Homecoming outfit and not an escape to Portland, then Allison woke up with every intention of going to school. "Does Allison talk much about fights with her mom?"

Kylie rounded the counter to the register, where she popped open the till. "Sometimes." Her voice got quiet.

"Go on."

She wouldn't look at Jax. "Mostly normal stuff, I guess."

"Like?"

"Clean your room. Take out the garbage. Quit talking on the phone."

"Was she on the phone to you last night when things erupted?"

Kylie shook her head.

"She'd told her mom she wanted to live with her dad. Did she want away from Dylan that badly?"

She closed her eyes and shrugged. "She misses her little dog, Roper. Says he's the only one that gets her." Her chin trembled.

There was something in the way she held her head. Her shoulders rounded. "Does it bother you she was willing to leave you behind?"

She ripped the money out of the drawer. "Misty Pines is for old people. I get why she'd want to leave."

He frowned, trying not to be offended.

"You know what I mean. Stuffed shirts. Small town people puffing out their chests, thinking they're special. If I had a dad an hour away, I'd try to get there, too."

Kylie's father had died years ago in a boating accident. Her mother had gone off the rails with drug addiction. If her aunt hadn't stepped in, Kylie would be a foster kid. He knew how that could end sometimes. Kylie had been one of the lucky ones, even if she didn't think so. "Is it possible she wanted to get out of here bad enough she'd start walking?"

Her face crumpled. "Allison doesn't even like P.E., and we talk constantly. If she isn't calling me, then…." Tears rimmed her eyes. "Then she can't. Which means something bad has gone down. I think Allison's mom isn't telling you everything."

Jax's shoulders tensed with the idea that he'd missed something crucial. "Like what?"

"Don't know. I tried to call Allison last night, but she didn't answer. Twenty minutes later, I got a text that she hated both her parents, and she'd tell me everything tomorrow. Today."

"I have a witness that said Allison and Emily had been fighting all week. Did she tell you what those arguments were about?"

She looked away. "Allison was tired of being questioned. It gets old."

"Questioned about what?"

"You'll need to ask her mom." Her body grew rigid.

"I'm asking you." Who was Kylie protecting—Allison or Emily? His gaze bore into her. "Did those fights ever get physical?"

A knock on the glass made Jax turn. An older couple stood, noses to the window, waving at them.

"You can let them in," Kylie said. "I don't want Emily to lose a sale."

Jax held up his index finger to the couple, indicating *just a second*. "Then answer the question."

Kylie's chin dropped to her chest. She didn't answer. She didn't have to.

Chapter Eight

"He thinks he's so superior." Emily's red face nearly matched the color of her hair, still up in a ponytail. She'd changed into hunter-green sweatpants and a matching sweatshirt, but wore no makeup. The lines had deepened on her forehead and around her mouth since his earlier visit. "He acts like he's better than me because she confides in him. He thrives on that, you know. He even kept that small dog that he and that woman he was married to adopted just to make sure his house is *more fun*." She used finger quotes on the last words.

"I understand it can feel that way." Jax had opened with a brief description of his conversation with Daniel after getting her settled into the living room. It had been eight hours since anyone had last seen Allison. After hearing what the bus driver and Kylie had to say, Emily was a suspect until she wasn't. Abuse happened far too often.

"You don't know the half of it," Emily said. "Allison worships Daniel because he plays the hero. It's not easy doing this alone, being the disciplinarian and the breadwinner."

Jax noted the twitch around her mouth and looked for other signs of a quick temper. "Juggling those roles can be hard." He said. "How upset were you that she idolized Daniel?"

She shrugged. "Does it matter? There's nothing I can do about it. Allison doesn't realize her father is only into himself. She wouldn't be happy there, but you can't tell kids anything."

He hadn't expected there'd be much warmth toward her ex, but would that have pushed her and Allison's argument into something physical? "Let's put Daniel on the side for the moment. What do you know about Allison's relationship with the neighbor boy Dylan?"

"Nothing. That's what I'm telling you." She jumped up and paced the room.

"Let's take it back a few steps. Summer starts. She decides to make extra money."

"Right. She'd started to ask for things I can't afford, and Glenn Hill was hiring. I wasn't that excited about it. I mean, it's a big place with lots of people coming and going. But I checked it out and decided it was fine. Besides, she begged for some independence, and I didn't want to argue." She looked away. "Since she became a teenager, it feels like that's all we ever do."

"So, you told her yes?"

"Exactly. You have to pick your battles. I got her up at six, packed her lunch, and she'd head out for the morning. I didn't see her again until I closed the store."

"Did her not helping at the bookstore upset you?"

"No. Because of the hours, she'd sleep in the afternoon."

"Any personality change during this time?"

"Just what I'd told you before." She sat down and clasped her hands together. "But since school, she's been withdrawn and spending more time in her room. I did the same thing at her age. Freshman year is hard. New school. New faces. I wanted her to hang out with me, but I'm tired myself, you know?" She looked at him, her face pained. Hoping for sympathy?

"Did you know Allison had called Daniel about getting on birth control?"

Her face flushed again as she shot off the couch. "What the hell is Daniel thinking? Oh my god, is that what you think has happened? That Allison's run off with some guy. With Dylan?"

"Not Dylan. We've already interviewed him." Jax moved both of his hands in a lowering position.

She took the cue and dropped back onto the cushion. "Our communication sucks, but he should've told me. I have a right to know these things. She's too young." The dam broke, tears filling her eyes. "Jax, she's too young. Where is she?"

He swallowed the lump in his throat at her emotion, but he wouldn't let it cloud his judgment. "That's what we're trying to find out. Did she do her chores without much hassle?"

"Like most kids. Hit and miss."

He held back a grimace at her choice of words. "Did that upset you when she wasn't pulling her weight?"

She threw up her hands. "Again, I was the same way. Worse. Why all these questions? We're wasting time. Why aren't you out searching for her?"

He rested his elbows on his knees and scrubbed the sides of his face with his palms. Attempts to lead her into admitting she may have crossed the line had failed. When did he lose his edge? Like he didn't know. But Abby accused him of being a jerk—more than once—and right now, he had to ask the tough questions for Allison's sake. "Why were you two arguing?"

"I already told you about that."

"You told me you two quarreled last night, and that's why you believe she took off. You didn't say why you argued, and I'm hearing stories of you chasing her down the driveway to the bus and Allison in tears. What caused things to get so heated?" Closer, but he was still holding off, giving her the chance to come clean.

Her posture stiffened. "The usual stuff."

"The usual stuff doesn't generate screaming unless it's a touchy subject. Or you're having major coping issues."

Her mouth trembled, but she stayed silent.

Jax's back muscles grew taut. She had one last chance to step up and be a real mom, none of this wishy-washy almost-telling-but-not-quite-going-there. Surely she'd admit to her part in driving her kid away if that helped find her. "Is there anything you want to tell me, Emily?"

Her eyes squeezed tight; she shook her head.

He leaned in. "Did you do something to Allison?"

Her head jerked up. "What?"

Jax's gaze never left her face. "Things happen when people fight. Hands get raised. People lash out. Is that what happened? Did she push you over the edge?"

"No. Never. Why would you say that?"

He reached for compassion, but no part of him could fathom hurting a child. "You admitted to fighting. Words can lead to fists being thrown. Accidents can happen."

"Not here, they don't."

A lie. She'd put her hands on Allison in the driveway. If she was willing to do that in public, what was she doing in private? The fog that had clouded his mind was lifting; anger did that. As did desperation. A kid—barely out of bubble-gum lip gloss and unicorn scrunchies—was out there somewhere on her own. Tough love was all he had.

"Did you hit Allison?"

Tears poured down Emily's face.

"I'm going to ask you again," he said, her tears putting him on edge. "Did you hit your daughter? Did she leave because of you?" Or did she not leave at all?

"How dare you." Emily gulped back tears. "She's my kid. My only kid. You wouldn't understand. Teenagers make you crazy." She dropped her face into her hands, weeping. "They say the most terrible things. But you're wrong. I didn't...I wouldn't...I haven't driven her away. I would never hurt my daughter."

He wouldn't let her anger at his accusation stop him until he was certain. "If that's what occurred, Emily, I can only help if you tell me everything."

"I have told you." Her raised voice had tipped over into hysteria. Her face was puce, the veins in her neck bulging.

"What are you holding back?" Jax pushed again.

Her breaths came long and measured now. He'd seen inner battles at play in abuse cases. A child had been shaken too hard, and the result of unchecked rage had decimated a family. Even with the evidence glaring, the parent made up alibis and justifications for such a horrible act.

Emily could have overheard Allison speaking with Daniel and came unhinged after she got off the phone. Jax searched her face for signs of guilt. He scrutinized her hands for cuts, bruises, trauma.

She glared at him, then jumped up from the sofa and marched out of the room.

"Emily," he said.

She didn't respond.

Jax followed her to Emily's bedroom, where she approached her bed, her back to him. "What're you doing?" he said as she lifted her mattress. His hand rested on the stock of his gun secured in its holster. Waiting could cost him, but he wanted to believe she wasn't reaching for a weapon.

She turned slowly, a glass pipe, tin foil, and a small paper-wrapped packet in her palm. Tears streamed down her sunken face. She held it out to him.

"What's this?" Although he knew heroin when he saw it.

"I found it in her bedroom yesterday."

"Set it down on the bed." In an instant, the tone and tenor of the case had changed completely. Allison wasn't just a missing teenager who'd had a fight with her mom. She was a missing teenager with a dangerous habit.

Emily put the pipe down.

Black tar hung off the tip. Heroin would explain the change in Allison's mood and the fights with her mother. Did it add up to running away—or did this go deeper? A drug habit could lead to associating with shady characters. This wasn't the odd bong with friends on a Saturday night. This was hard shit that took down grown men. And it was in his town. "Have you seen signs of drug use before this?" he asked.

"Nothing. I don't believe it's hers."

He'd heard *it's not mine* so many times in his career, he'd lost count. "If that's true, then why not tell me earlier?"

"Because I confronted her about it last night, and she was furious I'd been in her room. When I heard she hadn't gone to school, I figured she was still angry with me, and you'd find her out walking and haul her butt home. Scare her straight. I didn't want you to immediately jump to her being a junkie or for her to be in trouble for drugs. I didn't want you to write her off... You know...junkies go missing. If you thought she was *like that,* you might not, you know...Anyway...She swears they're not hers."

"Whose then? Kylie's?"

She shook her head.

"How about your boyfriend? Who is he? I want to talk to him."

She stiffened. "What boyfriend?"

"The man's work jacket on the chair in the hallway."

"That's mine," she said quickly.

Jax kept his eyes trained on her. It was impossible to know if she was jumpy because her daughter was missing or for some other reason.

"The barn gets cold, and it's dirty out there," she added. "But to answer your question, I don't know who these belong to, and she's been missing assignments at school, which is why we've been arguing for the last week. As for the pipe, I didn't come right out and accuse her of drug use. Instead, I tried to get her to talk about any stress she's been feeling. Anything I could think of as to why she had these in her room." She drew in a shaky breath. "It never dawned on me she might be getting pressure from a boy. That could be the reason she's been struggling. This could be his. I've been so oblivious." Her eyes started to tear again.

He couldn't lose her to self-pity now. "Did Allison say anything else when you pressed her?"

"What she always says. Leave me alone." Emily's shoulders drooped. "I should've told you about them right away. I only wanted to protect her."

Her voice had grown weary. Her whole body slumped. Her face slacked with relief for unloading the burden of the pipe. She could be telling the truth. But he should have asked her about potential drug use from the start, and he hadn't. He'd have to do better for Allison. "That doesn't explain the chasing her down to the bus stop."

"Never said I was perfect at questioning her." She swiped the tears off her face. "As for last night, she freaked when she realized I wasn't giving the drugs back. Said she'd be in trouble and that I had no right to go through her stuff. That's when she called Daniel."

Jax recalled something else Daniel had said. "Why would she call you a hypocrite?"

Emily plopped down on the bed, her eyes on the pipe. "Maybe the fact I drink and came unglued about the drugs. I admit, I haven't been easy. I work all day. Drink too much wine at night. Daniel must seem like a dream.

Museum curator. Fancy sports car." Her nose wrinkled. "Before his divorce, Allison talked about her stepmother being cool."

"The shrink?"

She nodded. "Everyone else gets the glory. Me, I'm shit because I'm the one that has to keep it together and make the hard decisions every day."

"Would she have contacted her stepmom?" Jax asked.

"No. They only ever saw each other on the weekend, and she's been out of the picture for over a year now."

Jax nodded, even though it appeared there was much that Emily didn't know about. "Any other theories where Allison may have gotten those drugs?"

"None. But Sheriff, I would never hurt my little girl. You must believe me. Please bring her home."

The memory of Lulu's tiny body in her casket gripped him. She'd laid on the white satin in a pink chiffon dress, all of the joy and energy that had left her unable to sit at the dinner table for more than ten minutes, gone. He and Abby would argue on whether it was better to make her sit or let her run. Like they had a choice. That little girl owned them. Soon they'd be laughing, and Jax would be chasing her to her bedroom and nuzzling her neck with his stubbly cheek. He could still smell her berry shampoo. She'd squeal, and Abby would chide them for roughhousing.

He'd have given his life to bring her home and relive those simple moments in a never-ending loop. He'd contemplated doing just that to get the ache to stop.

He put his hand on Emily's shoulder and pointed to the pipe. "Those are going with me."

Outside, he retrieved rubber gloves and an evidence bag from his trunk. On his way back in, he ticked off the list of people that the drugs could have belonged to. Truth was, anyone. Kids at school. A co-worker at the farm. Kylie. Dylan. Allison could be lying, and they were hers.

Except Allison told Emily that she'd be in trouble if they were gone, which implied she might be holding them for someone. If it was for Dylan and he wanted them back, that could explain why he'd been in her face like Kylie said. The same held true if they belonged to someone else.

Did the drugs or Dylan have anything to do with where she'd gone off to? Jax had to hold that possibility open. He'd have his men start asking questions of Allison's inner circle of friends and move outwards. But if Allison wasn't back by morning, he might have to make a call to Chapman and cut his fishing trip short.

In Emily's bedroom, Jax placed the wrapped packet and drug paraphernalia into the bag.

Emily tracked his every move. "Is Allison going to be in trouble for this?"

Jax sealed the top. "Her having it is the least of my concerns. More relevant is if it ties to her disappearance."

She nodded. "Okay." She was calmer, less guarded. Jax believed she'd come clean—several hours later than ideal, but at least he had something to go on now. A lead. Kind of.

Jax's cell rang. It was his deputy, Garrett. "What's up?"

"Yeah, Sheriff, I found that car you sent the APB out for."

He straightened. "Where?"

"Osbourn Park."

"Driver?"

"Not with the car. But there's, well—"

"Spit it out," Jax said.

"There's a swirly patterned pack in the backseat. Like the one you described Allison left with this morning."

Not just a potential lead. Actual evidence. He couldn't get out of that bedroom fast enough.

Chapter Nine

The ache at the base of Elena's skull had blossomed into a full-blown migraine behind her eyes by the time she pulled into the driveway of her one-story bungalow. After leaving Daniel, she'd taken the winding route back to her office, finding it hard to focus.

She'd managed to get through the forty-minute session with her client, but she was only ticking the boxes and letting him ramble instead of steering him to success.

Inside, she kicked off her shoes, taking in the quiet and slightly obstructed view of the Columbia River she had from the back windows. She pulled the cord that lowered the blinds. Even the partial view brought in too much light for her eyes to handle.

She'd bought this secluded home at the far end of the West Shore's waterfront at an auction before she'd met Daniel. It had been a godsend. She loved it there and the town with every tourist amenity that included the Lewis & Clark trail and a fisherman's wharf. Even an elaborate maritime museum. A museum she'd hoped Daniel would apply to after they'd married, since it would have kept him close to Allison in Misty Pines just twenty miles west. Instead, he'd gotten a job in Portland right away, unable to pass up the prestige of big city museums.

She'd stayed behind, maintaining her private practice and part-time job at the prison. What did it say about her that she hadn't been willing to give up her life here to follow Daniel—and Allison? She rubbed her temples and rolled her neck. The pain didn't ease.

She flipped on the living room's overhead light and lowered the dimmer switch, giving her just enough light to pick her way across the room without bumping into the ottoman or coffee table. She beelined it for the bathroom and the medicine cabinet for her migraine pills. The pressure had built like a freight train crashing through her brain and banging at the back of her optic nerves.

Steven not answering had her concerned; Allison missing had her on edge. She rubbed her eyes. It was more than the fact she was missing—Allison was too much like Madeline. Not only in appearance, or their attitude that they could slay the world, but their impulsiveness. And that likeness to her sister, more than anything, had played into Elena's decision to keep her connection with her stepdaughter limited after the divorce. She hoped Allison had simply taken off in a tantrum, and she'd be back home for dinner. But often, life didn't go according to plan.

Elena checked her phone. No recent calls or texts. She tossed two pills and ran the water, cupping it into her mouth before swallowing. Her options to help Allison were limited until she heard from Daniel, so she'd focus on what she could do—find out what happened to her brother.

Once the medicine knocked the pain in her head to a five, Elena changed into jeans and a sweater and slid on her darkest shades.

She made the fifteen-minute drive to Steven's place in the sleepy coastal town of Megler located across the bridge in Washington. Its sole diner opened for breakfast and lunch, and it boasted one gas station at the far end that housed a convenience store. The signage along the roadway indicated that bait, tackle, and coolers were big sellers at the store. Fishermen of all sorts ran through there every morning on their way across the span that connected the two states to catch a charter out of the basin.

Steven rented the upstairs room above the only laundromat. Well, they both did. His disability left her brother unable to hold a job, so Elena had co-signed the month-to-month contract and paid the $500 deposit.

When she pulled in front of the glass-walled building, she expected to find Steven's black Nissan Pathfinder parked in the farthest stall. Instead, only an oil stain caused by the leaking motor remained. He might not be home. Or he'd finally taken the clunker in for repairs.

She glanced inside the laundromat to find it empty and rounded the building to the side entrance. She'd just opened the stairwell door leading to Steven's apartment when a man's voice came from behind.

"Ms. Massey, is that you?"

She turned and smiled at the older gentleman, who was Steven's landlord, as he approached. "Mr. Tannenbaum. How've you been?"

He pulled his pants up, snug under the belly that flopped over his beltline. "Good. Haven't seen you here in quite some time."

"Work has kept me busy, but I thought I'd stop by and check on my brother. Everything been okay with him?"

She detected a grimace under his full gray beard. "Suspect so. Although he does keep to himself."

Elena nodded. "He's quite reclusive, as I've mentioned." Would she ever stop explaining for him? "But I haven't been able to reach him by phone. His Pathfinder's gone. Did you see him leave?"

"Sure did. When I opened this morning sometime around six, I saw the tail-end of his truck going down the road."

Awfully early. "How about last night?"

"That too. When I was closing, his light was on, and he was moving around up there."

"Signs of life are good," Elena said more to herself than the landlord. Relief filled her chest. "What time was that?"

"After ten. I'd worked in my yard earlier and fell asleep watching the news. Before I knew it, it's nine o'clock, and I hustled over here to lock the place. Normally do that around seven. Used to be more of a night owl until I hit eighty." He grimaced. "Now it seems every time my butt hits the chair...."

She smiled. "You don't look a day over sixty."

"Liar. But thanks." He chuckled, and then gave her a sympathetic smile. "It must be hard. I had an aunt like him. The garbage piled around her place to the point it took two dumpsters to clear her out. Fact, I didn't even know she'd died until weeks later, and the neighbors complained of the smell. Finding her in that mess, well, it took...." He must have seen the panic in Elena's eyes. "I'm sorry. Didn't mean that's the case with your brother."

She waved him off. "I know you didn't. How horrible that was for you and your family."

He nodded. "Makes you wonder what drives people to draw inward like that, but I'll give Steven at least this much. He's clean and quiet."

The need to control when things had once felt so out of control. Inward was safe. Walls were protective. How she hadn't become a recluse herself was a miracle. "The perfect tenant."

He chuckled. "Guess you could say he is. Well, won't keep you. Only here to refill the vending machine. If you need anything, give me a shout."

She nodded and stepped into the narrow stairwell. Dark and dank, the smell of dryer sheets seeping through the walls at least made the space tolerable. Steven had been out driving one night and saw the sign in the upstairs window of this place and left her a message to check it out. Most residents of Megler lived on the outskirts—that's what Mr. Tannenbaum had said when he'd given her the grand tour. It was then she understood the appeal. With so few people around, Steven would be left alone—essential for his mental health.

She knocked first. When he didn't answer, she used her key and poked her head into his place. "Steven," she hollered.

With no response, she went inside. The first time she'd stood in the middle of his apartment, the hum and gurgles of the washing machines and the thumping of the driers below unsettled her. Steven never complained. There were no sounds now.

In the kitchen, she inspected his cupboards. Crackers. Cheese Whiz. Top Ramen. She'd bought him a case at the warehouse store last year. He'd made a small dent. The coffee pot was empty and cold, but water droplets in the carafe suggested recent use. The refrigerator contained bottled water, condiments, a loaf of bread, and cheese void of mold. A good sign that he had food in the house, but she would've felt better with fruits and vegetables in the mix.

In his bedroom, the bed had been made. In the bathroom, a dripping faucet had left a yellow ring in the sink. A dirty puddle circled the drain in his shower. The towel was damp—not wet. He'd likely showered last night when Mr. Tannenbaum had seen the light. Had he decided to get a job she didn't know about? She often sensed he held back on her when he left messages, which as she'd told Daniel, had been a few months now.

Until this morning.

Anything was possible.

In the living room, she inspected the gaming system she'd bought him for Christmas a few years ago, along with a dozen games. The Getaway game had been inserted. She never understood the desire to play out roles of war, bank heists, and cat and mouse scenarios which spoke to the need for control.

Steven did have his demons. Being separated from her and Maddy when they were whisked into foster care had been difficult. Maddy's murder, devastating. By the time they were reunited years later, he'd withdrawn and never reemerged from his protective shell.

She'd been living with the guilt of that outcome. Not that she'd had the ability to do anything as a child, but he must blame her for not finding him sooner when she was able—to reunite what was left of their family. She blamed herself.

"Where are you?" she said aloud, scanning the room. At the small dinette table, a carved wooden cross rested on yesterday's newspaper, acting like a paperweight. She touched the cross and turned back to the living room. The coffee table had nothing on it. Tabloids were stacked on the end table. A glimmer of something shiny caught her eye between the pages of *Us*.

She plopped down on the sofa, grabbing the magazine. A bracelet slid onto her lap. The letter "A" dangled from a silver-linked chain. Holding the delicate jewelry in her hand, her throat tightened. She'd given a similar piece to Allison for her twelfth birthday.

Turning the fine metal in between her fingers, she felt a hollow indent. Her stomach fluttered. An indent that could have held an opal—Allison's birthstone.

How would Steven have Allison's bracelet? Allison hadn't gotten on the school bus over ten hours ago—about the same time Steven had left his message. Her heart pounded. It had to be a coincidence. When would they have ever had an interaction? They'd never even met.

Hopping off the couch, she paced the room. She had to be mistaken. Steven could have found the bracelet, and it just happened to look like Allison's. There must be a thousand of them circulating in the world. She clutched the bracelet in her hand.

She should call Daniel and let him know what she'd found. Although if there was a logical explanation, the trust she'd worked years to establish with her brother would be in ruins. She owed him the opportunity to explain.

There had to be a reason he had a similar bracelet. She'd hunt him down and find out what it could be.

Chapter Ten

Jax pushed the speedometer well past the legal limit to Osbourn Park. He'd directed Garrett to stay put until he got there, then he promised Emily he'd be in touch soon.

The memory of another time when he'd raced to a forest park because the body of a young girl had been found clouded his mind. But Garrett had only seen a backpack in a car. Not Allison. No signs yet that he'd failed. Again.

En route, he'd called Brody and Matt. They trailed him all the way. Their initial inquiries at the Greyhound station had produced no leads. He hadn't updated them on Allison's potential drug use, but questioning the kids at school and digging into that rancid hotbed of who-knows-what would wait until they knew what they had waiting for them.

Twenty minutes later, they pulled in next to a light blue station wagon and Garrett pacing the parking lot.

Jax catapulted out of his patrol car. "Any signs of Allison or the driver?"

"Nothing. I finished a perimeter search, and Trudy just relayed the owner information on the car," Garrett said.

"Spill it," Jax said.

"It's registered to a Vince Wallace."

"That jerk lied to us, Chief," Brody said.

Jax eyed his deputy. "Let's not make assumptions until we find the driver."

Garrett pointed at a backpack tucked behind the driver's seat. "You want me to break the window?"

Jax studied the paisley bag that resembled the one Emily had described. He tugged on gloves and grabbed the baton from his belt. It was against a few laws, but Allison might not have time for search warrants. If anyone had to answer for it, it'd be him.

The glass cracked and crumbled with one solid hit. Jax punched the stubborn glass around the edges with his nightstick and reached in, pulling out the backpack.

He swung the bag onto the hood. Pieces of gravel and dirt stuck to the underside. He unzipped the top and dug into it, finding a non-descript hairbrush. Next, he pulled out a Social Studies textbook and flipped over the cover. *ALLISON* had been written in block letters. Confirmation. What he didn't find was her phone. She could have that on her. Perhaps a good sign. The only one.

He'd wanted to find clothes. The coat that Emily had mentioned. A phone charger. Her wallet with the money from her piggy bank. Indicators she'd run away. Instead, he found earbuds at the bottom—the ones that Dylan and the bus driver had consistently seen her wearing. For a girl that always listened to music, he'd expect them to be with her.

The other items consisted of lip gloss, gum, and a sketchpad full of butterfly drawings. He remembered the morning Lulu brought him the dragonfly picture she'd drawn, so proud. Dressed in her flowery nightgown, she'd jumped between him and Abby, waking them from a sound sleep. They'd smothered Lulu's face and curly hair in kisses before they rolled out of bed together for pancakes. The diagnosis of cancer came a month later, and everything about their normal life changed forever.

Like Emily's would if he failed to bring Allison home.

Jax flipped the pack over to find two zipped pockets. He ripped open the largest and withdrew a tin of chew. He clutched the container. Drugs in her bedroom or not, he couldn't picture Allison shoving a wad of snuff into her cheek.

Jax scoured the parking lot, his gaze directed at the bathroom facility erected between two hiking trails.

Garrett followed his focus. "Already searched there."

Jax nodded, assessing the two paths. "Whoever's driving this car likely has Allison with him or her."

"You think she's here with a girlfriend?" Brody said.

He glanced at the tin and then at the young men surrounding him. "No, I don't. Matt, you're with me. Garrett and Brody, take the other trail." He pointed to the marked 3.4-mile hiking loop. The inversion caused by the sweltering heat on the other side of the coastal range had light mist rising from the ground. "Stay in radio contact if possible. If you find the driver, approach with caution. Heads up and eyes open. We have no idea what we're walking into."

All four hit their respective trails. With each step, he and Matt went deeper into the woods. Jax felt the clock ticking down. He wanted to jog, but he couldn't take the chance that he'd step on a branch and alert the kidnapper to their presence. Or that he'd miss something.

He took lead as they single-filed over a wooden suspension bridge. Matt was talking about statistics and how kids were often taken by people they knew. Matt was right, but Jax tuned him out. If drugs were involved, Allison might have unknowingly drawn in dangerous people—people who'd stop at nothing to get their fix. She was just a kid; she knew nothing of society's rancid underbelly.

Sweat permeated Jax's shirt at the thought.

He maintained his focus on the waterway below, at the thatch of water hyacinths crowding the embankments, and the moss-covered rocks, looking for signs of disturbance. Of violence. Of blood.

His mind clicked between the present and the memories that nightmares were made of etched in his mind. Twenty-five years ago, the emergency operations center in Portland received the call that two foster girls had gone missing during the night. He and his partner, Jameson, had answered that call.

Like Allison, they initially believed the girls had run away. Walking the route they'd taken revealed another terrifying theory. Tire marks from a large sedan marred the roadside gravel. Blood droplets splattered across a portion of pavement and rocks. Fifty yards away, more blood in the field. DNA would later reveal it was familial. The blood on the road from Madeline; the other, her sister. Whoever they'd encountered that night had incapacitated them both, loaded them in his car, and disappeared.

The hours had ticked away before they'd received a call from the girls' abductor. He'd taunted the police. Told them *catch me if you can* before he finished off the girls. The call had been made from a remote phone booth near the coast. Unlike today where street cameras caught someone picking their teeth, they didn't exist then. Still didn't in small towns. There were no witnesses.

For seventy-two hours, he and Jameson had worked every angle and came up short. At hour seventy-three, the call came from a hiker with the grim news that she and her dogs had discovered the body of a young girl south of Misty Pines.

That girl was Madeline Massey. Like his daughter Lulu, whose leukemia he could not cure, he'd failed her.

A day later, they'd found Madeline's sister wandering miles in the opposite direction. She'd escaped, but with no memory of what had occurred. Jax often wondered what happened to her.

He'd tracked her for a while.

Then he didn't.

He'd stayed on the case for years. Jameson still might since he worked for the City. The location of the actual murder had eluded them. He and Jameson held different opinions on the perp, but Jax had always felt the killer lived close to the dump site. That he knew the coastal area where he'd left the body. That belief may have played a larger part than he'd like to admit in his moving to Misty Pines after marrying Abby. Watching for the killer to resurface somewhere among the coastal communities. Waiting for him to make a mistake. Listening to see if he bragged about it in a smoky bar.

Until Lulu died. Then nothing seemed important after that.

Until this morning.

Until Allison.

Jax emerged from the forest into a clearing with Matt right behind him. A trickling stream led to a large inlet. Jax's eyes narrowed. On the water's edge, a scraggily man wearing a grimy white T-shirt was gutting a fish.

When he saw them, he tossed the knife aside and ran.

Chapter Eleven

The man was wiry and fast. Jax ran faster. He had the scrawny guy on the ground, secured, and on his feet within minutes.

"Call in the rest of the team," Jax ordered Matt, while he patted the man down and worked to get his pulse in check. The last time he'd run like that was in the academy. Hadn't cared much for it then either.

Jax turned the man away from him and pulled the wallet from his rear pocket before sitting him down on a nearby boulder. "Where's the girl?"

"What are you talking about?" he asked, smirking.

Jax flipped open the man's wallet. More like kid. Twenty-nine. "Innocent people don't run." He was within a hair's breadth of finding Allison, he could almost taste it.

Brody and Garrett piled into the clearing, eyes ablaze. They would have given anything to make the collar. They were enthusiastic; he'd give them that.

"What are you doing out here, Richard Johnson?" Jax asked.

"It's Rick. What's it look like? I've been fishing. And you'd better let me get that trout on ice. Took me all day to get a bite, and I'm not losing my dinner."

Jax tossed the wallet to Garrett. "Run him."

Garrett trotted over to the river where he'd call Trudy to check for priors.

The kid's face reddened, and his eyes darted from Garrett to Jax. "L-l-look," he stuttered. "I forgot to buy a fishing license, that's why I ran. This is police brutality."

"You forgot to spend thirty bucks at the risk of a fine ten times that?" Jax said.

"I—"

"Don't *I* me. You ran because you're guilty." Jax addressed his men. "Brody, Matt, search the area. Find her."

They nodded.

"Who's *her*?' Rick said.

Jax turned his attention back to the kid. "Is that your station wagon in the parking lot?"

"I borrowed it."

"From?"

"I don't have to answer you." Rick lifted his chin. Defiant.

"Then we can do this at the station." Jax reached for Rick's arm to bring him to his feet.

"Wait." The young man grimaced. "Can you do that? I've done nothing wrong."

"You bet I can." Allison's backpack in a car he admitted to driving there was reason enough to take him in. But the quicker he had answers, the quicker Allison came home. "But if you start talking…."

Rick shook his head. "Fuck," he muttered. "My uncle will go ballistic if I don't bring back his car."

"Who's your uncle?"

"Vince Wallace. He works at—"

Jax's gut tightened. "I know where he works."

Wallace hadn't mentioned Allison working on the farm all summer, or that his nephew borrowed his car. What else had he failed to mention?

"Then you can call him if there's a problem. I work the night shift there."

"Oh, there's a problem. That missing girl's backpack is in your car."

A bead of sweat formed on Rick's upper lip. "What backpack?"

"Don't give me that. If you're not the one who put it there, you would've seen it when you got your fishing gear out."

He frowned. "I didn't. I swear. I wanted to fish. That's all I was doing. The trout are running. I know all the places to go, and this spot is prime. Uncle Vince, he rarely lets anyone mess with his stuff, let alone borrow it.

Today, he got up on the right side of the bed, and I jumped at the chance."

"And the backpack didn't catch your attention?"

"My gear was in the backend. That's all that was there. Uncle Vince drives the car to and from work. You should be asking him these questions. Not me." He shifted on the rock, perhaps realizing he'd implicated his uncle.

Jax's jaw tightened. "Next, you'll tell me that's not your chew in the bag."

Rick didn't have time to answer before Garrett appeared at Jax's side. "Bad reception. Trudy's calling me back."

Jax nodded and scanned Rick's face. "What time did you leave the farm?"

Rick blinked. "I was off around seven thirty and got out of there the minute I had the keys."

"So, you picked the girl up from her bus stop and brought her out here?"

"No."

"Did you see anything suspicious when you left? Any vehicles cruising the area?"

He shook his head.

"How about anyone out walking when you were headed this direction?"

"Nothing."

"Do you know Allison Krueger?"

His eyes flashed. "That's who's missing?"

"You do know her?"

Rick shifted again on the boulder, trying and failing to find a comfortable angle. Jax had him where he wanted him, off balance and squirming. "I mean, I know of her," he said. "Lives next door, I think. Worked in the fields this summer."

"What made you notice a young girl like that?"

"Yeah," Garrett piped in. "You a pervert?"

Rick glared at Garrett.

Jax needed to get the conversation back on course. "You do drugs, Rick?"

"What are you talking about?"

"Heroin? You dealing to the kids that work the farm?"

"Hell no." The guy's voice ticked up a notch.

"Sure about that? Allison was holding a stash for someone she was concerned about. Was she concerned about you, Rick?"

"I don't touch that shit. Did you check with her boyfriend? Dylan something. That's usually the place to start."

"Quit trying to shift the blame," Jax said, although interrogating Dylan—"my Daddy's the commissioner Marks"—was high on his list.

Rick's eyes narrowed. "I'm just saying they had their issues."

"What kind?" He'd heard a few variations at this point.

Rick shrugged. "He was a little handsy, okay? I mean, I get wanting to kiss up on your girl, but it seemed more than that."

"How would you know?"

"I helped Angelique get the summer workers organized in the morning by assigning them to their fields. I noticed then."

"Thought you left after seven-thirty?" Jax said.

"Usually, but because my shift crosses with them arriving, sometimes I'd assist Angelique, who's pretty cool."

Her name had come up twice now. How *cool* was she? Or how cool was Rick? He could be lying about how well he knew Allison and throwing Dylan out as a diversion. "Why did Dylan's behavior cross a line?"

"Because Allison didn't appreciate it. Her friend, a little blonde she hung out with, was always stepping in to defend her and trying to get Dylan to back off."

"Did it get physical?" Jax asked.

"Angelique wouldn't have allowed that. Anyway, you asked me how I knew of her. That's it."

Matt and Brody had returned. They stood in a semi-circle around Rick. Matt shook his head at Jax. They'd found nothing.

Jax folded his arms over his chest. "So you'd like us to believe you came here for a day of fishing, but you didn't see Allison, no one out near the bus stop, no cars on the road, and the backpack just appeared like magic in your vehicle."

"Well, I may have seen a rig way ahead before I even turned onto the main road."

"What kind?"

He thought about it. "SUV."

Matt rolled his eyes. "That's helpful."

"What color?" Jax asked.

"Black, maybe. Not sure. I was focused on getting here."

"You have no idea when it entered the road you were on, or where it turned off?"

"No."

"Get a look at the driver?"

Rick shook his head. "Never caught up to it."

Jax wasn't sure he bought it, but he wouldn't ignore any possible lead.

Garrett's cell rang, and he walked back toward the river.

Jax waited while Garrett finished his conversation and motioned Jax to meet him halfway, where he relayed in a whisper what Trudy had found out.

Jax strode back to the boulder. "Brody, call in the tow, and let's get some men and women from the volunteer fire department up here to do a more thorough sweep. There's five more hours of daylight. Let's not waste them. We're short on manpower, and Allison could be anywhere in this forest. Can you coordinate that for me?"

"Yes, sir."

Rick shot up off the rock.

Jax had his hand on Rick's shoulder before he made it to his feet, forcing him back down.

"Matt, I want that car dusted and checked for signs of Allison and foul play. Bag the backpack and get it to forensics in West Shore for a full workup, including prints on everything in it. Garrett, transport Rick here to the station and get him in holding."

"I answered your questions. You promised—"

"I promised nothing. It's interesting that you noticed Dylan being handsy with Allison and yet failed to mention you recently got out of prison for raping a young woman."

Rick's face flushed. "I didn't do that. She was my ex-girlfriend, and she thought she was pregnant. Her dad was a minister, and she was afraid of him. That's all it was."

"A jury felt different."

"They were wrong. I didn't do anything to Allison, or anyone else. You have no reason to take me in."

He had every reason.

Rick continued to protest as Garrett secured him, and Jax ignored the kid's proclamations of innocence on the trek to the parking lot. He was more absorbed in his own anger, building with each step. The kid was lying. His whole *the jury got it wrong* crap was bullshit.

If Rick Johnson did time for rape, odds were he did the crime. And if true, why not set his sights on a pretty girl standing on the edge of a road who was angry at her mother? Desperate to get to her father. Trusting because she would have seen him on the farm during the summer. Vulnerable.

By the time the group reached the parking lot, Jax's teeth were clenched so tight a sharp pain shot through his left molar. He wasn't near done trying to find out what Rick was hiding.

Chapter Twelve

Jax punched in the office number before he'd even left the park. "Trudy, it's Jax."

"You got Allison, hon?"

"Getting closer. I need an expedite on those call records. Tell them it's being moved up to abduction and get that ping on Allison's phone."

"Abduction?" Trudy's voice had a sharp edge. She wasn't one for hysteria, but Jax could imagine her face, creased with worry.

"If they won't ping her, call me back. I'll raise hell." Over ten hours had passed since Allison had vanished. He'd held onto the faint hope that Allison's departure had been voluntary, but Allison's backpack in the possession of a sex offender who lived next door had annihilated that, taking with it the last shred of patience he had in his arsenal. "I also need a search warrant for Glenn Hill Orchards. Call Judge Rulli's court and get that rolling."

"Judge is out of cell service until tomorrow. I'll find out if there's an alternative, except you know how he is."

He did know. Few things happened in Misty Pines that necessitated a search warrant. When things did go down, the judge wanted to be involved. It was unlikely there'd be someone else available. Even if they could find a judge, those guys were golf and drinking buddies who wouldn't dare to infringe on Judge Rulli's turf.

"Work your magic, Trudy. Do whatever it takes. Butter up his secretary and see if there's a workaround."

"You got it," Trudy said.

Before clicking off, he asked one last question, even if it galled him to do so. "How did I not know that Rick Johnson was a member of this community?" He expected her to remind him that he'd been oblivious to everything around him for the past five years.

"Because he didn't register," she said, then paused. "Jax, maybe you should call Abby. The Bureau could offer the resources you need."

Abby again. Had he been so out of it that Trudy didn't believe he could bring Allison home on his own? He'd never missed his deputy, Chapman, more than right now, but that didn't mean he wanted *their* help. "They don't know Misty Pines like we do. Appreciate the concern, but me and the boys got it handled."

He crushed the off button on his cell with his thumb. The only good news was, by not registering as a sex offender, Rick had violated his parole. His own actions ensured that Mr. Johnson wouldn't be worrying the good people of Misty Pines with his presence any longer. Although that didn't answer the question of where he had Allison.

Jax's tires spun in the gravel on the side of the road. *Focus.* He couldn't go skidding off into the bushes. Getting an admission out of Rick while his men scoured the woods and riverbanks and Trudy worked on getting his search warrant were the first order of business. Wallace might be involved as well. And he couldn't bank on Brody and his team of volunteers to find Allison before he needed that warrant. The twang in his gut said it wouldn't be that easy.

When Jax reached the station, Trudy was working the phones. He bypassed her and went straight to the interrogation room where Garrett had Rick Johnson waiting. Jax dismissed his deputy to assist Matt in getting the backpack and the car into evidence, leaving Rick to him.

The interrogation room housed a cold metal chair chained to a metal ring bolted into the cement for the accused and an unbolted, but equally uncomfortable chair for the officer on the other side of the rectangular table. Jax stood in the doorway, staring at the sex offender. Perhaps he'd served his time, but he didn't buy rehabilitation. Those people took responsibility and registered when they moved into a community, as was the law.

Rick didn't meet his gaze. He stared at the floor, his hands cuffed to the table. He smelled of stress, sweat, and fish guts even from a distance. And guilt, for sure.

Jax pulled out the chair across from him, letting the screech of metal on the hard floor fill the room. He opened the file Trudy had prepped that referenced Rick's previous conviction.

Rick paled as Jax flipped through the papers.

Jax raised his eyebrow. "You didn't tell me you liked them so young."

Rick lifted his eyes, trying to see into the file.

Jax pulled it closer. "Says here you were twenty-three, and she was...what?" He ran his index finger along the page. "Sixteen." He dropped the file. "Is that why Allison caught your eye?"

"Told you before. I saw her in the fields during the summer, and only noticed her because of her boyfriend."

"Okay, we'll go with that. Where do you have her now?"

"I don't have her anywhere."

"Right." Jax scanned Rick's face for signs of discomfort. He was scared, but Jax had been at this game long enough to know he couldn't draw conclusions. Get this wrong, and he'd waste valuable time.

"And my ex, just so you know, said she was twenty-one. She looked older. You know how it is."

"I don't know, Rick. I don't date children."

Rick sighed and cricked his neck. "She said she was twenty-one. I swear."

"Where'd you meet?"

"At a football game."

"High school?"

"Yeah."

Rick had been cruising the high school girls, expecting to find a woman in her twenties? Not likely. "Seems like you've always enjoyed hanging out with young people."

Rick stared at the floor, the right side of his mouth twitching. "If you're going to twist what I say into me liking young girls, I'm done talking."

"Making an observation. That's all. Let's talk about Allison."

"Already told you."

"When did you approach her at the berry fields?"

"I didn't."

"Did she reject you? Did that upset you?"

"No and no."

"Wouldn't be a stretch, would it? Isn't that why you raped your ex? She broke up with you. You were angry."

"No effing way."

Jax fanned the pages of the file. "That's not what her friends said."

"They lied. It wasn't like that." He swallowed hard. The guy was rattled. "We'd broken up, but she wanted to talk. I met her at the bar, and she was acting all weird and out of it. I thought I was doing the right thing by getting her out of there. Then she started coming on to me, like she wanted me back. We went to the lake and, you know. I swear it was consensual."

"Thought you said she was out of it?"

"But I didn't know why. I mean, she grabbed me. What am I supposed to do?"

"Take her home."

Rick sighed. "Yeah. Anyways, I did get her home later that night. A few weeks later, I have police at my door, arresting me for rape."

"Why would they do that if you weren't guilty?"

"I told you. Her dad. And her friends would back up anything she said."

Jax had to force his eyes not to roll back in his head. "So, you're the victim?"

"Yes. No. I'm just saying there's another side to the story. Either way, I was screwed, literally, because it turned out, she was a minor, and there you go."

"Yeah, there you go." Jax knew bullshit when he heard it. "Where's Allison?"

"Don't know."

"How did her pack get into the backseat?"

"Didn't know it was there. I was out there doing my own thing. Started out a great day, you know. Out of every place there is to fish for miles around here, that's the best."

Jax ignored Rick's rambles and stretched his neck, fatigue from his shitty sleep last night taking hold. "Here's the thing. If you're keeping Allison somewhere, now's the chance to come clean."

"But—"

Jax raised his hand to silence him. "If something happens to her because you didn't tell me her location, or you've already done something to her, and I find out you held out on me, I'll throw every charge I can find at you, son. Do you understand?"

Rick's eyes rimmed red. "But I didn't do anything. I have no idea where she's gone. I was fishing. That chew you asked me about before is what my uncle chews. I don't touch it."

It could be another attempt to take the focus off himself, but the car belonged to his uncle, and Jax had seen that brand of chew in Wallace's ATV. In his pocket. Had Wallace been covering for his nephew from the beginning? Another conversation was warranted. Now. No, an hour ago. Time was moving in the wrong direction.

He didn't want to stop working over Rick, though. Either direction he went, he needed another boost of energy to continue. Adrenaline could only take him so far.

Jax stood. "Where is she?"

"No idea."

Jax strode to the door and slammed it behind him. He'd let Rick sit there and think about the mess he was in for a minute.

He walked into his office and found a report on his desk. He reached for an energy shot in his top drawer and found half of an egg-salad sandwich wrapped with a note from Trudy. "Eat."

Closing his eyes, he unwrapped the food and downed it in two bites. He leaned back in his chair and perused the report from the cell phone company's ping on Allison's phone. Inconclusive.

Matt appeared in his doorway. "Evidence is logged, and a search is underway at Osbourn Park. Nothing so far."

Jax stood abruptly, feeling the energy-inducing effects of the food and the drink. "You're with me."

Chapter Thirteen

Jax and Matt pulled into the farm. He could have directed Matt to drag Wallace in for questioning, but he wanted to have eyes on the farm himself. He'd sensed Wallace was hiding something from the beginning. Was Rick that something?

Unlike the last visit, no one greeted them near the arena. They found Wallace in a ten-by-ten wood-paneled room off the barn at his gunmetal desk, his head down, and filling out paperwork, a framed picture of Wallace and his wife askew on the wall.

"Gentlemen," he said when they shadowed his doorway. "What brings you back to Glenn Hill?"

Jax entered. "Still looking for Allison Krueger. Got a few more questions for you about that."

Wallace tilted his head. "Okay. What's the problem?"

There were plenty. Including why hiring an unregistered, sex-offending relative posed no moral dilemma for Wallace. Even while women and young girls like Allison milled around the property every day.

"What do you really know about Allison's disappearance?" Jax said.

Wallace swallowed, the first sign he might be nervous. "As I've said before, nothing."

"Then why was her school pack in your car?"

Wallace's brow formed a V over his eyes. "In my—oh shit."

"Yeah, oh shit," Matt said.

"You have my car?" Wallace said, confused.

Jax's blood pressure rose a notch. "Answer the question."

"I wondered where that son of a bitch nephew of mine was," Wallace said.

Jax curled his hands into fists. "In custody."

"For what?"

"Answer the damn question."

Wallace's mouth pulled into a hard line. "I've no idea. I found that backpack on my way in this morning about fifty yards up in a ditch."

Jax stopped. He'd expected him to simply deny knowledge, confirming Rick was lying. "*You* found it?"

"That's what I said. Kids leave things lying around the farm or on the road all the damned time. I saw the pack and grabbed it to look through later and get it back to where it belonged."

"If that's all you did, how'd your chew tin get into the pocket?"

Wallace frowned. "It's not mine because I didn't put it there."

"Why didn't you mention that backpack this morning? And don't tell me you didn't put that pack together with the missing girl that lives right next door."

"If I had a dollar for every bag, cellphone, jacket, you name it, I find… Anyway, I no sooner got settled than Rick rushed out to borrow my car. The boy likes to fish. I said yeah. End of story."

"How about the fact Rick is a convicted rapist? Another item you failed to mention."

Wallace waved his hand dismissively. "If I thought for a second he wasn't wrongly convicted, he wouldn't have a job here."

Jax paced the small space, his nerves rapid firing, eying the papers on Wallace's desk. "Since you're so confident about him, then you shouldn't have a problem me looking around the farm."

Wallace straightened. "Already told you, not without a warrant."

He sounded concerned. "What're you hiding?"

"Nothing. Owners don't allow random searches. Period."

"They have a problem before? They involved in drugs?"

"Course not, but I do what I'm told, and they're adamant about it. Besides, my nephew has rights. You don't get to tear this place apart simply because he works here."

"What about Allison's rights? She's fourteen, and she's out there."

He met Jax's glare. "Me and Rick have nothing to do with that. And if you search the premises without permission, you can count on me to call Commissioner Marks."

"What's he got to do with anything?"

"His cousin's a civil rights attorney in L.A., and he owns this place. He doesn't take kindly to rogue cops. Don't need him flying up here coming down on my ass. He's left me in charge. I take that responsibility seriously. Wish I could be more helpful."

After Marks' response to questioning Dylan, he wouldn't give Jax access either. "What are you afraid I'll find? Proof that Rick did something to Allison? Or...?"

They locked eyes. "You accusing me of something specific?"

"You tell me."

Wallace cleared his throat. "I'm familiar with every inch of this farm, Turner. If she was here, I'd know."

"You might not be as aware as you think."

"You aren't either."

"What's the supposed to mean?"

"People talk. After you left this morning, I found out Abby divorced you a while back. Rumor is you haven't been right for some time."

The low blow hit Jax hard. He may have been disconnected. He may have been a lot of things. Unless someone else in town had lost a child to cancer, they couldn't understand. To hell with anyone who condemned him for that. But he was not about to lose another fourteen-year-old girl. "Screw you and this entire town. I will get that subpoena and I will search this farm."

"Until then, can't help you."

"Can't or won't?" Jax ground his teeth. He understood stubborn. His father had been a fucking mule. Unrelenting. Abby had accused Jax of being just like him. She wasn't wrong about that. But not wanting to help find a young girl? Jax hovered on the edge of losing it. "Wait here," he barked at Matt. "Don't move a muscle, Wallace. I'm calling the station. And don't touch a damned thing before I find out if I have my warrant."

Jax gave Matt *the look*. Chapman would have understood that it meant *don't let this slimebucket out of your sight*. But would Matt? They didn't have that kind of connection. "Keep your eyes on him, you understand me? Holler if he moves."

Matt nodded, his hand on his weapon. Overkill, but...Jax sighed. They had so much to learn and so little time to learn it in. He walked out of the office, slamming the door behind him.

He called Trudy, who confirmed that Judge Rulli would not be available until tomorrow. Her magic wasn't working, but she wouldn't give up. He took the minute to rein in his anger—to wrap his brain around what Wallace had said. Jax had been out of it. What else had he missed while absorbed in his own pain?

Rick Johnson might only be the beginning. Allison had gone missing because he hadn't been paying enough attention. He'd sworn an oath to keep the town's people safe. He'd failed, at the very least, Allison.

The night Abby left him, before the slam of that front door reverberated the entire house, she'd warned him he'd lost sight of his job, of their marriage, of himself. She'd been right. But the need to find Allison had reeled him back. He intended to find her, regardless of who owned this property.

He had a few minutes before Wallace got antsy. He walked into the arena outside Wallace's office. A thick rope hung on the roping dummy. He inspected the hard and stiff fibers. It wouldn't be the easiest thing to tie around small hands and ankles.

He kept walking. Observing. Sensing. He found himself standing at the end of the arena looking out at a green pasture and another barn. Allison could be held in there, or one of the many other buildings that dotted the property. Rick had her backpack. He was a sexual predator. But did he have time to hide Allison on the land if he left here just after seven-thirty? Was it more likely that he would have stashed her somewhere on his way to the river? Or had he circled back when his uncle wasn't looking?

Or did Jax need to take a closer look at Wallace? Did he have time to do something to Allison, and then lend out his car?

Getting a crew to search the ditch where Wallace said he'd found her backpack for any evidence was imperative. It was on the main road. Wallace couldn't do squat about him looking out there. With even one tiny sliver of evidence, they'd be able to link foul play to Rick or Wallace, giving him legal cause to come into the property for a full search.

He texted Trudy to coordinate with Garrett and work the phones to get some more volunteers out there ASAP and scour the ditch, the road, every lane leading to and from the farm. The forensics lab in West Shore should be getting back to him soon on the pack. He needed more people. The days of he and Jameson having the Portland Police force at their beck and call would be welcome about now.

Jax rubbed his forehead to ease the tension. He crossed through the sawdust and chip-filled pathway to the barn. At first glance, he counted twenty stalls.

A young man caught his attention at the far end, shoveling manure into a wheelbarrow. When he straightened and swiped the sweat from his brow, Jax trotted in his direction.

"Dylan," he hollered.

Dylan glanced his way with a quick smile. "Yo, Sheriff. What's up?" The cocky attitude he'd seen earlier had dissipated. Hard work took it down a notch, or was he an A-grade actor? Son of a politician, he'd have learned how to lie to the public when he was in diapers.

Dylan leaned his shovel against the stable door and ambled towards Jax.

Jax had planned to take him in for questioning, but he wouldn't miss this opportunity right now with the Commissioner or his civil rights attorney cousin anywhere to stop him. "I'm looking for Allison and talking to Wallace. Didn't know you still worked here?"

Dylan stiffened. The smile faded, and he cleared his throat. "Yeah. Stayed on after the summer work to clean stalls after practice."

Jax nodded. "Well, we didn't get to finish our earlier conversation. So glad to see you."

Dylan pushed his sleeves up, revealing a fancy leather watchband.

A little overdressed. "I want to know why you lied to me."

Dylan turned away, grabbed the shovel, and started shoveling again. "I didn't."

"Oh, c'mon. Sure you did. You played it off like Allison being a freshman was beneath you. Except I know about your relationship with her, and word is it didn't end well."

"Word's wrong."

"Don't think it is."

Dylan ignored him.

"When did you see her last?"

"School, I guess. In the hallway."

"When?"

"Yesterday."

"Did you talk to her? Harass her to get your drugs back?"

Dylan stopped in mid-shovel. "What?"

Jax ignored the boy's shocked reaction. "I found a pipe and heroin, and Allison was afraid whoever they belonged to would be upset if they didn't get it back. Rumor says you wanted to make her life a living hell. Were those your drugs? Did you do something to her?" While Rick and Wallace had the backpack, he wouldn't let any possible connection go unchecked.

Dylan rested the tip of the shovel on the ground and glared at Jax. "Look, man, I liked her fine. But it was a summer thing. As for drugs, I'm an athlete praying for a scholarship. You know why? Because my dad is bent on me going Ivy league, and I want to go to U of O. That's where the best football players come from, man, and I want to be one. He also doesn't want me around girls. Says all they do is screw with your head. So, the only way I get to choose my life is if I pay my own way and make my own rules. So, no, I stay away from drugs, and I sure didn't do anything to Allison." His face flushed red. "I got nothing else to say."

There were always two sides to every coin. Dylan might be flashing him the bright and shiny kid with a heart side. But it remained true that the flip side Jax already knew about regarding Allison wasn't as pretty. If anyone was screwing with someone, it was Dylan.

"If the drugs aren't yours, whose are they? Who's pushing that shit? Rick Johnson?"

"No clue. Who the hell is Johnson?"

"Wallace's nephew. Works nights."

He shrugged. "Never heard of him."

"He's heard of you."

"My dad's the Commissioner. Most people have."

That part was true. "How about stuff around the farm in the last twenty-four hours. Anything unusual?"

"Nothing. Man, I do my job and get out of here." He started shoveling again with more determination. "I need to finish and get to my homework."

"You sure—"

"I'm not answering any more questions without my dad."

Jax wanted to shake the kid. Get him to give up something that would send him to where Allison could be. But he had Rick in custody and Wallace. If Dylan lawyered up, he'd get nothing. This was one time he needed to tread softly.

"You go ahead and do that, son. I know where to find you if I need you again."

Dylan rolled his eyes, turned his back on Jax, and worked into another corner of the stall.

Jax clenched and unclenched his hands to reign in his frustration. On his way out, he glanced inside each of the stalls, inspecting them corner to corner for anything that signaled Allison's presence. He found nothing.

Ten minutes later, he stood at the door of Wallace's office, his hand on the knob. He refocused on why he'd come here in the first place. Rick Johnson had something to do with Allison's disappearance, and Wallace could be covering for him. But with the new information that Wallace had found that backpack, he couldn't discount him either.

Jax's walkabout hadn't answered any questions or given him probable cause to ignore the need for a warrant, but his gut said Wallace wasn't telling him the whole truth. Starting with the story that he'd only found her backpack on the road. He'd instruct those volunteers to go inch by inch of the ditch and Allison's bus stop to make sure nothing was missed.

In the meantime, Jax needed to buy himself time. He walked back into the office.

Wallace hadn't budged, his legs stretched in front of him, relaxed.

Matt, however, had his hand still near his gun. Jumpy. He eased it away once Jax was in the room, but sweat permeated the young deputy's shirt. They'd need to talk about that. Later.

"Find anything interesting out there?" Wallace asked.

Jax motioned him up with his head. "I'm taking you in under ORS 162.325."

Wallace's face blanched. "What are you talking about?"

"We've got your car and nephew in custody. You're refusing consent to let us look around. Hindering prosecution is a Class C felony, my friend." Although whether he'd charge him with that was yet to be seen. He'd have forty-eight hours to make that call.

Wallace didn't respond.

Jax stepped behind his desk, handcuffed him, and walked him out the door and across the arena with Matt following.

The farm was silent. A chill settled into Jax's bones. He was missing something. It gnawed at the edges of his brain but didn't show itself. What was it? Damn, he needed sleep and manpower and a search warrant—and a teenage girl no one seemed willing to talk about.

Chapter Fourteen

Elena drove through Megler, making a stop at the only gas station at the far end. The young man tending the register recalled Steven had been by just after six that morning, confirming Mr. Tannenbaum's recollection. The attendant remembered her brother because he came by on occasion to fill up, but the young man couldn't say if this morning he was alone.

She couldn't decide if that was good or bad.

With that information, she headed west. At least she had a timeline to work from. Last night about ten, the landlord had seen Steven in his apartment. At six this morning, he'd driven his Pathfinder less than a mile and filled its tank. Around seven-thirty, he'd called her and left a jumbled and nearly incoherent message about wanting to make things right. God, she wished she'd been awake when that call came in. What she couldn't reconcile though was why he hadn't returned any of her calls since and when or how he'd come upon a bracelet that resembled the one she'd given Allison.

To cross paths with Allison, Steven would have had to travel to Misty Pines, on the other side of the river in Oregon. Even if that were the case, with his illness, he'd likely return to where he was the most comfortable. It was only a theory, but a place to start.

As she drove, she resisted the idea that even if Steven had Allison's bracelet, he had her too. As a therapist, she required that she be brutally honest with herself. She loved her brother. She'd do anything she could to shield him from the world. She'd proven that over and over again. But Allison had her heart. Her sweet stepdaughter, who'd taught Roper to play dead and won first place in the Dog Tricks section of the Ocean Sands Dog Show a few years ago. Who'd taken Elena's ache away for wanting a child. The same Allison who wouldn't say boo to a goose.

But in all honesty, until she knew for certain that Steven was involved, she was also thinking about herself.

If she called Daniel, she'd have to talk to the police, answer questions, dig up all that pain and angst of the past…and for what? She hadn't confirmed that Steven had anything to do with Allison's disappearance. Or that the bracelet even belonged to Allison. One like it could be found in any mall, and Steven could have stumbled upon it at one of the many beaches in the area.

It couldn't be her stepdaughter's. Steven was a hermit, not a kidnapper. She kept pressing the bad thoughts down—one thought, one deep breath, one thought, another deep breath—until they were fully submerged.

Every car that passed going the opposite direction had her full attention. But none matched Steven's vehicle. That would have been too easy—a word that had never described their relationship. Elena massaged the back of her neck, trying to ease the mounting tension.

Entering the town of McGowan, she cruised past the long-abandoned railroad yard and St. Mary's Church with its wooden steeple and worn stairs leading to red double doors. Neither she nor Steven had ever attended church. That's why the cross on his table had stuck out. After what they'd gone through, deciding to take up praying wasn't probable. If there was a God, he'd forsaken them both long ago.

Easing down on the accelerator, she kept it around sixty, heading to the next town. With phone in hand, she hit redial and left yet another message. "Buddy. Call me."

She tossed her phone on the passenger seat with enough force that it bounced onto the floor. Communication always came on his terms. He showed up in her life when he wasn't coping. Like the time he had a severe panic attack after throwing his new jeans in with his cotton briefs, and they came out an ugly gray-blue. He'd left a frantic message saying it was the kind of ugly that made him want to hit himself until he couldn't see anymore. He hadn't answered her call then either, but he'd heard her message and a bit later let her know he'd calmed down. He was okay. As soon as he was back on track, he withdrew again.

What had caused the meltdown this time? It could be that this being a milestone year for their sister's death was especially hard for him. Tension festered into a headache now at the base of her skull.

The *Welcome to Chinook, Population 457* sign blurred as she whizzed by. Steven had mentioned once about moving here. The town was just big enough for him to be anonymous. A stop at the grocery store, and down at the fishing basin, didn't find him or his car.

As she drove, her mind drifted to early last year when Daniel had asked for a divorce—a request she hadn't seen coming. Looking back, a blind man would have seen the rift growing between them. So consumed with work, she hadn't paid enough attention.

In the year prior, she'd stopped driving to Portland on the weekends. With Daniel's job at the museum, he rarely offered to drive to the coast. A busy schedule was as good an excuse as any. Except he'd never liked the ocean, or the rain, or the incessant mist in the area.

Whatever the reason, no matter how much she told herself she'd be okay, it was for the best, and they'd be better off apart. She'd been a mess. Like some sixth sense, Steven had contacted her. At least, that's what she thought at first. Only he didn't call to console her. He had his own set of issues. Angry at the world. Battling demons. Wanting to take it out on someone, like that one man before. At least that time, she'd been able to talk him down. As usual, she'd forgotten about her own problems as it became all about him.

For the most part, that had always been fine. She cared deeply about Steven and helping him through his issues. It was unorthodox for her to treat him, but he wouldn't talk with anyone else, and she was qualified to do it. She loved him enough to try. But if this time his drama included Allison, a little girl whose life she'd been a part of, she might not be so understanding.

She entered Avalon, the last place she'd search before calling it a night. In a little over an hour, it would be dark, making it even harder to find him.

Through the main stretch of town, she rolled through the stop signs and past shops that had already flipped over their closed signs. She willed a Pathfinder to be parked on the main strip, a side road, a parking lot. Nothing. Had he found a tavern? He liked scotch, of all things. It was possible. A cruise past Todders Tavern showed an array of early drinkers—none of them Steven. She drove into the boat basin. Jessie's Fish House, a barn-like structure, was perched on the pier. *Under Construction* signs were posted all around it.

At the docks, she pulled up and scanned the area. Stacks of crab pots filled with rope and buoys sat dockside near the fishing vessels, ready to be loaded. She'd love to think he'd taken a job on one of the fishing boats since he enjoyed fishing from the shore. With his claustrophobia, there was no way. The notion was ludicrous. What was she thinking?

She headed to Baker Bay. On one of the few occasions Daniel had visited, they went there for a picnic. The mouths of the Wallacut and Chinook Rivers fed into the area. From a cove, they could make out Cape Disappointment, its sheer cliffs, and lighthouse. At the time, the dramatic landscape called them, along with the sea birds and lush grasses around the bay. They'd laid out their blankets and stayed until dark. She always felt safe in Daniel's presence. Now Cape Disappointment felt like an irony and an apt description of their time together. Despite that, she'd told Steven about the magical place. He might have gone there.

She drove into the lot and parked. A few people sat in their cars, waiting for sunset. She got out and walked to the edge, scanning the bay. Sand Island was straight ahead. She and Daniel had kayaked there once—in the beginning, when they cared about trying each other's crazy ideas of fun.

Inspecting the activity on the beach revealed nothing. Until she spotted an SUV at the farthest end. Her throat tightened. She couldn't see the model. From the distance, it only looked big and black.

She jumped in her car. Turned the key, held it too long, and the starter squealed. The wheel locked. She took a long breath, backed up, drove to the end stall, and got out, making her way down the trail. Seagrasses whipped at her legs, and she sunk into deep fine sand until she was onto flat hardpack.

She jogged toward the SUV. Smoke drifted up from in front of what she could now tell was a Pathfinder. Relief flooded through her. She'd found him.

He'd lit a bonfire. He was safe, and soon, she'd have answers.

Elena picked up speed as she drew closer, her heartbeat pounding in her ears. If she approached too fast, she'd spook him. She slowed her pace to a brisk walk. The bumper sticker on the back, *Hell Hole,* confirmed it was him.

She willed herself to find patience with him while taking the last few steps and rounded the SUV. "Steven, my God, you gave me a scare."

A young couple looked up at her with wide, startled eyes.

"I'm so sorry," Elena said, her eyes darting between the SUV and them. How could she be wrong? "This looks identical to my brother's truck. I thought you were him. I mean, I've been searching for him and—"

The twenty-something man, who looked like he could have been surfing in Hawaii with his dreads, board shorts, and Hang Loose sweatshirt, stood. "No worries, but you look frazzled."

Completely. "No, I'm fine. But is this your rig?"

Dreads looked at his girlfriend, who had the same hippy vibe, then back at Elena. "We bought it this morning from some guy named Steven. You Elena?"

He sold his SUV? "I am. You did?" Her words came out fast.

The man glanced at his girlfriend again. "Yeah. Killer deal. Said he just wanted to get rid of it."

Panic welled in her. Why would he do that? He needed transportation. How was he getting around? "How much did you pay for it?"

"Couple hundred bucks."

Enough for a bus ticket out of town. Or a train. A couple of nights in a cheap hotel. That's if he could force himself away from the area. Why would he want to?

Dreads' hand was on her arm, his brow creased. "Maybe you should sit down and chill for a bit."

Not until she found Steven, but she mustered a small smile. "Mind if I look inside?"

He shrugged. "If you need to, sure."

"Thanks." If Allison had been with him, she might find confirmation, or a clue of where they'd gone. By the same token, she might find nothing, and she could continue to believe the bracelet was a coincidence. She wanted that more than anything.

The man rounded the Pathfinder and popped open the backend. "He said it was his to sell and that you'd signed over the title. Was he screwing with us? We don't want no trouble."

Elena shook her head. "No. It's his. I did." But she hadn't. He'd likely forged her signature. Had he not wanted to bother her about it, or was he afraid that she'd ask too many questions? "Did he say anything else?"

Dreads seemed to relax a bit. "No. Kept it real short."

Par for the course. She was surprised he'd been brave enough to interact with them at all. Elena scanned the inside with no idea what she hoped to find. "Was it clean when you got it?"

He nodded. "Very."

That wasn't normal for his car. He didn't think enough to even get the oil leak fixed. Her eyes inspected every fiber; she didn't see anything. "Nothing left in it at all?"

"No."

She peered out through the front window. The setting sun created shadows. She circled to the passenger side. "May I?"

The girlfriend stared at her intently and nodded.

Elena opened the door and saw the new owners' possessions, including a duffle, with a bottle of wine sticking out and a baggie containing a couple of joints. That explained why the girlfriend kept looking at her weird. She was high as a kite.

Flip-flops were tucked under the seat. A towel on the floorboard. A glimmer of something small and sand-like caught in the rug. She picked it up between her index finger and thumb. Without inspecting it, she set it into her other palm and wrapped her hand closed.

She backed away from the passenger side, not making eye contact, wanting to get out of there. "Thank you," she said, and started to walk away.

"Sorry," Dreads said. "If you want to...."

She was already too far away, and his voice meshed with the sounds of waves hitting the shore. With each step, she gained speed until her legs were in an all-out run. The migraine medicine had worn off, and her head throbbed with each stride.

She jumped into her vehicle, started it, popped the gearshift into reverse, and drove. Closer to home, her heart pounding, she finally opened her hand and glanced at the glimmer of sand she'd taken from the floorboard.

Except the iridescent speck wasn't sand.

It was the missing opal from Allison's bracelet.

Chapter Fifteen

Jax charged into the station. Matt had already moved Rick to a holding cell and secured Wallace in the same interrogation room. It was getting late, the sun was setting, and Trudy was still at her desk.

"Garrett and a few volunteers went out to the farm," she said, looking up.

"Saw them on my way in and gave them a quick briefing. You're staying late," Jax said.

"Like to be where I'm needed." She scanned his face. "Have you eaten?"

He sensed Trudy felt a lot more than she let on. Allison's disappearance was unsettling. Events like this didn't happen in Misty Pines. Until Allison was home, none of them would sleep easy. "Yes. Thank you for the sandwich."

She clicked her tongue. "That's hardly enough."

"I'm good."

"You're running on fumes, and you're going to drop." She reached into her desk drawer and withdrew a granola bar that she tossed at him.

He didn't need mothering. He needed to find Allison. He pocketed the energy bar and grabbed an energy shot from his other pocket, and was about to twist the cap off.

Trudy was at his side, hand over his, squeezing him mid-twist. "Eat." She met his eye.

Age spots had begun to take up more real estate on her thin hands. Arthritis had crooked her right index finger, but her grip was firm and her eye steely. She wasn't wrong. The stress of pushing had started to get to him without anything in his stomach.

He dropped the shot back into his pocket and ripped open the bar. "Thank you."

She nodded matter-of-factly and let go. "You'll need your energy. You're going to want to see what's on your desk before you get too far." She walked back to her command center and lifted a pile of messages. "And you better call Emily. She's called every hour on the hour with updates of who's been calling and dropping by. Anything she thinks could be important."

It had been several hours since he raced out of her bedroom and to Osbourn Park. He clutched the messages. She must be panicked. "What's on my desk?"

"Reports are in. Took the liberty to print them out for you."

The station door flew open. It was Brody, his hair disheveled and mud on his uniform pants. "Hey, boss."

"What'd you find?" Jax took a bite of the bar.

"Nothing. If she was out there, the volunteers would've found her. But she's not. No signs of anything suspicious."

Jax frowned. They couldn't have covered all that ground in that time. Brody had jumped to conclusions, hoping for the best when he should be assuming the worst. But it was getting dark, and searching would become treacherous. They didn't need to add 'rescue of a volunteer' to Allison's disappearance case. "Get cleaned up."

"Yes, sir," Brody said, heading to the restroom.

Back in his office, Jax dropped into his chair and thumbed through Emily's messages. One caught his eye. He grabbed the energy shot from his pocket and chased the rest of the granola bar. He'd put off letting Emily know the latest long enough.

Emily answered on the first ring. "Did you find her?"

The strain in her voice tugged on his heart. "No." He hesitated, knowing it would be hard to hear. "We no longer believe Allison walked away on her own."

Emily didn't say anything at first. Didn't even breathe. He remembered that moment when the doctor had told him and Abby that Lulu had cancer. There was no air in the room then and for Emily now.

"Who took her?" she finally managed.

Jax pressed the heels of his hands against his eyes. "The investigation is ongoing."

"How do you know she didn't run away?"

"We found her backpack."

She whimpered. "And her phone?"

"No."

Emily let go of a heart-heavy sigh. "What happens next?"

"We're questioning a couple of farmhands from next door right now."

"Just farmhands?" Her tone inched up.

"Yes, but I can't say much more until I'm done."

"I see," she whispered.

"We will find her, Emily." He didn't feel that certainty. He knew failure. Missteps. Time running down…and out. Suspects that hadn't given him anything.

"I know."

She believed in him. He'd borrow some of that for the moment. "How are you holding up otherwise? Are there friends or family you can call to support you?" At least he and Abby had held tight to each other for their daughter—before their world crashed. Emily needed someone. A shoulder. He'd heard it in her voice from her first word.

"My parents live in Colorado. I haven't called them yet. They're elderly, you know. I don't want to worry them unless I have to."

He didn't want her to have to make that call either. "How about friends?"

"Mrs. Elderman came by and brought a coffeecake. Kylie's aunt came over earlier with a casserole."

"What's this about Commissioner Marks?" He glanced at the message that had caught his attention.

"Yeah. That was a surprise."

A new wave of tension crept into Jax's shoulders. "When did he stop by?"

"Right after you left."

"The second time?"

"First. That's why I'd told Trudy to make sure and tell you."

So much for the Commissioner's attitude of not getting involved. He must have come after he'd put a stop to him talking to Dylan at the high school. "What did he say?"

"Just that he'd heard about Allison running away and asked if he could do anything. It was very nice of him since he's such a busy man."

"Very," he said, suspecting it was more than a social call. He kept his voice low and even. "Did he mention anything else?"

"He was curious why Dylan had been pulled out of class to talk about Allison. I told him that it appeared he and Allison had dated during the summer. He was as surprised as I was at that."

"And the drugs?"

"What about them?"

"What did Commissioner Marks say about his son possibly doing drugs with Allison?"

The intake of breath on the other end of the phone told him that Emily genuinely didn't believe Allison had been doing heroin. One breath, with a long shudder at the end, said she was ashamed, but also shocked. She'd argued with Allison, and she was pissed her kid was talking to her ex-husband rather than her, but she fundamentally believed her kid was good at the core. That said a lot.

"Does he feel the same way as you?" Jax tried to be as gentle with the question as he could. She was already under stress. No need to make it worse.

Emily cleared her throat. "I didn't mention them. I didn't see the need. That's your job, right? I don't want to ruin his son's good name, even if he was...." She trailed off. "Even if he was dating my daughter behind my back."

"I understand." He didn't, though. Not knowing didn't make it all go away. "About Allison and Dylan dating—did he tell you anything you didn't already know?"

Emily held off a sob. "Like I said, he was just as surprised as me. He was kind about it, but I could tell he thought Dylan shouldn't be messing with Allison."

Dylan had mentioned his dad didn't want him seeing girls. Not having been part of Marks and Emily's conversation, Jax had no way of knowing if the guy was lying or not, but Emily couldn't interpret that for him after the fact. He needed to help her keep calm. "They obviously played it pretty low-key."

"Yeah, low-key except for telling Daniel and getting birth control." So much for helping her remain on an even keel. "I mean, was she doing drugs with Dylan? I don't know. I don't think so, Sheriff. She's a good girl. I never saw any signs of that." She scoffed. "I wonder if Allison confided that to Daniel. He knew about everything else."

"To be fair, Daniel only knew there was a boy, not who, and I sensed he would have told me about the drugs if he was aware of them. The Commissioner say anything else on the subject?"

"Only that he was concerned about Dylan being a focal point. He's up for an athletic scholarship. The Commissioner's worried that even being questioned could throw a shadow on his son."

Being a suspect would do that. But Jax wouldn't concern himself with treading lightly. Not with Allison missing. "Thanks for the update, Emily. Every little bit helps. I'm on it."

"I'm counting on you."

"I'll be in touch."

He clicked off. He couldn't allow his irritation at Marks to cloud his judgment. Emily was counting on him. He'd get back to Marks as soon as he had time.

Jax turned his attention to the fingerprint report analysis on his desk. The prints on the lip gloss and hairbrush were consistent with the prints on the shiny cover of the social studies book. Odds were those prints belonged to Allison.

The prints on the Copenhagen tin were smudged on the top and bottom of the container, but the lid's side had a full print, and it belonged to Vince Wallace. At some point, his prints had gotten into the system. Jax's blood pressure ticked up a notch. He'd be curious to hear Wallace's story about that.

He flipped the report over and perused the information on the backpack.

The report laid out the plain facts. The style, the measurements, the brand. It included photographs of the contents, each item set out and labeled. The debris he'd seen on the side of the pack had been brushed off onto a sheet and photographed. It consisted of dirt and gravel. A scuff mark had been noted in the next picture.

The third report contained photos that were hard to see with the print quality. He opened his email, found the original report from the lab, and clicked on it. The sharp images of the photos filled his screen, sending prickles over his scalp. On the underside in a patch, chopped pieces of blue, green, and purple feathers had caught in the nylon fabric. Some had adhered to the outside. Most had been found in a zipped outside pocket. The one he'd failed to check when he'd gotten distracted by finding the Copenhagen in the larger compartment.

He'd seen feather fragments like this one other time in his life—stuck in the bloodied wounds on Madeline Massey's body. And not just there. When she'd been found in a wooded area outside of Pacific City, pieces of the same feathers like the ones in front of him had secured themselves to the bottoms of her feet and her back as well. That evidence had factored into their belief that her body had been transported after her murder.

When Madeline's sister Elena had been found later, wandering, she had the same types of feathers in her hair. He and Jameson had speculated that Elena and Madeline had been put in a trunk together. While Elena had escaped their captor, they theorized Madeline had been taken into a building where birds were either raised, slaughtered, or even product processed. They'd never been able to narrow that down. Other than confirming the feathers they'd found were not synthetic, they couldn't verify their origin with the limited testing available at the time.

What he did know was they were uncommon. Why would Allison have these types of feathers in her backpack?

Madeline Massey had been fourteen when she had been abducted and murdered. He could still see her face. Waist-length brown hair and freckled nose. His chest tightened with a sour burn. He found a sleeve of Tums in his top desk drawer and tossed two in his mouth, chewing quickly. That same description applied to Allison. He closed his eyes. Right down to the freckles.

The similarities didn't end there. Both had been out on rural roads when they were last seen. Both upset with their living situations. Both disappeared into nowhere. In Madeline and Elena's case, blood had been found at the scene of their forced abduction. That wasn't the case with Allison—that they'd found. But the similarities were too close to be ignored. Was it possible the same man from twenty-five years ago was back?

Jax enlarged the picture again. The bigger it got, the more dread washed over him. He didn't believe in coincidences.

He hadn't realized until right now, but today marked the anniversary of Madeline's murder. He had always felt Madeline's killer had lived in or had at least been very familiar with the Coastal range. Other than Jameson and a few forensic techs, no one knew about those feathers—except the killer.

Was he trying to get Jax's attention? Was he taunting him? You couldn't catch me then, and you can't catch me now. I won't let you forget.

Jax could never forget. His guilt over failing Madeline then would never go away. But if the killer was back—was he sitting in his interrogation room right now?

Wallace was old enough to have committed the crimes. Jax set the report down. But he couldn't jump to conclusions. Not without confirmation. There was one way to get that. His ex-partner's number was in his phone. He pulled it up and hit SEND. Three rings later, it flipped to voicemail.

Instead of leaving a message, he'd circle back. In the meantime, time to squeeze the lemon he had waiting and see if it produced some juice.

Chapter Sixteen

Jax glanced through the one-way glass into the holding room with Wallace. The suspect looked at his watch five times in four minutes. Jax'd had Trudy punch in Wallace's information a few minutes earlier. His prints were on file from a domestic spat with his wife when he was in his thirties.

He'd been living at various Oregon addresses over the past few decades before landing in Misty Pines. Which meant he was not only old enough to have committed the original crimes against Madeline and Elena twenty-five years ago, but he'd resided in the state and in close enough proximity to do so. That was the extent of what Jax knew about him, and while he may have the killer from old in custody—a fact which set his blood on fire—he couldn't collapse into the old case.

Finding Allison was the priority.

It was close to ten, however, and he didn't feel any closer to accomplishing that. Something had to give. With Wallace's prints on the tin found in the backpack, he had enough to press him and hard. But he'd already tried in your face/bad cop back at the farm to no avail.

He had his hand on the door when Garrett rushed down the hall, grinning.

"Sherriff," he said, catching up to Jax and thrusting a brown evidence bag at him. "We found something."

"From the ditch?"

"No. We scoured the area Mr. Wallace claims he found the backpack, but with the weather having been dry the past week, there were no footprints or signs of whether that's true or not. This, though, was found by one of the volunteers in the grass halfway up Allison's driveway." Garrett's desire to be a cop was obvious in his attention to detail.

Jax nodded and peeked inside. His grip tightened. "We'll need it tested."

"I can run it to the lab."

Jax nodded, thinking. "No. Wait." He closed the bag. "Good work."

What he'd been given, coupled with the print on the tin, had the potential to secure an admission, but it centered on the approach. The longer they could keep their chat friendly without the confines of a lawyer shutting down every question that might implicate Wallace, the better.

Jax went to the coffee pot in the main area and grabbed two cups. He strode into the interrogation room and set one down in front of Wallace. "Hope you like it black."

Wallace glanced up, an eyebrow arched, resting back in his chair. "Thank you."

Jax nodded and took a seat, crossing one leg over the other at the knee. He set the bag on the ground. Two guys, drinking coffee. Jax milked the moment, even though he felt anything but calm.

Jax set the cup down. "Let's you and me start over. Sorry to haul you in, but time's against us. I have your nephew here, and I need some answers."

Wallace opened his mouth to protest.

"I get it. He's your nephew. You believe he's one of the good guys. Let's say I don't have an opinion one way or the other. Walk me through your day, corroborate his story, set me straight, so I don't spend hours working an angle that's not an angle."

Wallace huffed. "Didn't take you for the 'calming down' type, Sheriff. Glad you're not hopping all over the place with accusations any longer."

Jax nodded. "Talk to me about a typical day."

"Starts before sunrise, and the crew arrive. I like to get the place going. Get a pot of coffee on. Ease into the day."

Jax sipped his coffee. He used to be an early riser. Now nights bled into morning. "Same today?"

"I was running late. Got there closer to seven-thirty if I remember correct."

"You said you didn't see Allison waiting for the bus on your way in, but found her backpack just sitting there in that ditch."

"Yep, when I got out of my car to secure the gate."

"If everyone is there by sunrise, why was the gate locked?"

"It was unlocked but had swung back onto the driveway. The bag caught my eye when I got out to fix it."

Jax eyed the brown bag on the floor. "All right. So, the backpack is all alone. There're no cars around. And no Allison."

"Right. I hustled up there, grabbed it, and threw it behind the driver's seat. Didn't think anything of it. Rick caught me soon after I parked, and that was that."

Jax took another sip. "He do that often?"

Wallace shrugged. "Boy doesn't have his own car, so yeah. He's always wrangling for mine to go fishing."

"You didn't put two and two together when we came by earlier that Rick wanting to rush off with your car and Allison missing could be connected?"

Wallace's eyes narrowed. "Nope."

Jax shifted. "Even with his previous conviction?"

"That case was about a girl saving her own ass and parents on a witch hunt."

"Even you noticed how attractive Allison is. You think a twenty-nine-year-old with impulse problems might not find that tempting?"

"My sister's kid isn't perfect, but he wasn't guilty in the first place, nor does he have impulse issues."

Either Wallace believed Rick's story about the girl he'd raped, or he thought it was fine for older men to date young girls. Either way, that was a dead horse he didn't need to flog any longer. "Rick ever do drugs?"

"Not that I'm aware."

"You ever hear about drugs being dealt around here?"

Wallace shifted. "Pot is everywhere these days, even before it was legalized. Can't hold that against anybody now."

"How about heroin?"

He shook his head. "Nope."

Without evidence, he'd have to let that line of questioning rest for a while.

They'd get there eventually. His men would keep looking; he'd get his warrant. If there was heroin on the premises, they'd have both men headed for prison in no time.

"One thing is bothering me about all of this," Jax said. "You say you got the pack, and Rick ran out for the car."

Wallace took a sip. "How many times do I have to repeat myself on that?"

"Just to be clear. You pulled up, and he ran out, asked to borrow the car, and took off. Nothing else."

"You're like a broken record. Yes. That's what happened."

Jax gave him a sardonic smile. "I'm only asking because I'm trying to figure out when you tucked your Copenhagen tin into the bag."

"Told you already I don't know nothing about that."

Jax cleared his throat. "Well, it's your brand."

"It's popular. I'm not the only one who prefers that brand of snuff. Doesn't mean anything."

"Except they don't have your fingerprints, and those were on the lid."

Wallace turned several shades lighter, then the color rushed back into his cheeks. "Maybe Rick took it from me and put it in there."

Jax nodded. "So, Rick *was* involved."

"No. I'm saying Rick might have seen the pack in the back of the car and stuck it in the pocket. You know. For safe-keeping."

"He says he didn't know about the backpack."

Wallace slapped the table with his hand. "I see what you're doing trying to twist things around, and I'm telling you, I don't know how it got there."

Jax waited. Patient. Certain Wallace would make a mistake.

"Tell you what else," Wallace continued. "This is exactly what happened to Rick, back in the day."

Jax raised his eyebrows.

"You say one thing, and the cops write down another. He didn't do nothing to that girl, and I'd bet money he didn't do nothing to Allison, either."

"How can you be certain?"

"I've known the kid since the day he was born. He doesn't have it in him."

Every murderer, arsonist, rapist, and child molester started out as cuddly babies. No exceptions. "People change."

"He didn't. He was and is a good kid. He'd planned on going to trade school to be an ironworker before all that mess went down and that girl screwed with his head." Wallace had a tension in his face that hardened his eyes. He must have caught himself as he inhaled, and his face relaxed. "I'm just saying, he got made an example of."

"I've got another theory."

Wallace's turn to wait.

"Want to know what I think?"

Wallace shrugged.

"You're bleating so hard for your nephew because you know who did it." Jax leaned in closer.

Wallace shook his head violently. "You're not going to pin this on me."

"Not looking to pin anything on anyone. Just looking at the facts. I mean, you did lose your temper once with your wife."

He glared but didn't take the bait. "I don't know where that chew came from. My prints being on it only means it belonged to me. I didn't put it into Allison's pack, you hear me? What you should be doing is finding out who Allison was talking to before she disappeared. That might hold a clue."

"And who would that be?"

"No idea. I'm just saying you're climbing the wrong set of trees."

Jax lifted the paper bag onto the table. He reached inside and pulled out a clear baggie containing a rag with dark streaks on it.

Wallace cleared his throat and looked away.

"While trying to figure out who Allison might have spoken to last, we found this halfway up her driveway." He paused and let the information sink in. "This was found only a few yards from where she would've been waiting for the bus. Looks like blood on here, and you were wiping your hands on one just like it this morning. It's heading to the lab as soon as you tell me where the hell you've got Allison."

"They're ten for a buck at the hardware store. Everyone's got them. They're super-absorbent…."

Jax rocked his head from side to side. "Maybe. But with the addition of this bloody rag, I have enough to hold you."

"That's bullshit."

"Tell me what happened, Wallace. How'd the rag end up on the driveway? Is this Allison's blood? Is she hurt? If you tell me where she's at, I can bring her home."

Wallace focused on his hands.

"What happened this morning?" Jax's voice rose. "Did you attack Allison at the bus stop? Did you drag her somewhere until after the bus had gone by? Did Rick take her from there? I mean, exactly how close do you have to be to someone wearing earbuds to hear their music?"

Wallace had turned to stone as he swallowed. "I had nothing to do with Allison disappearing."

"Then how come all the signs are pointing straight at you?"

Wallace was silent for a long minute while Jax's gaze bore into him. He sighed. "I must have dropped the rag when I fell."

This guy was like the game Ker Plunk. Pull out a stick and watch a marble drop. "You fell?"

Wallace didn't answer.

"Was that before or after you hit Allison?"

"I was walking up the driveway," Wallace hissed. "I tripped. I bled. A lot. I wiped myself off, and I must have dropped it."

How fast the story was changing. "Where's Allison in all of this?"

"No clue. I did exactly what I said, except after I retrieved the pack, I thought it could belong to one of the neighbor kids, and I decided to run it up to Allison's mom to check. But I took a few steps and landed on a fucking rock." Wallace flipped his hands, revealing a scuff mark on his palm. "That's when I said to hell with it. No good deed goes unpunished. I threw it in the back of my car and came to work."

"You didn't think any of that was relevant to tell me earlier?"

"I had nothing to do with Allison's disappearance. That's the truth."

"Or a well-spun story you dole out to cover your ass." He inspected Wallace's hands. "That mark only proves you could have had an altercation."

"It proves I fell."

Jax glowered at Wallace. "You'd better hope only your blood is on that rag."

"This is why I didn't say anything in the first place. I knew you'd try to make something of it and railroad me like you're doing to Rick. Not that it's helped. I'm sitting here."

"This isn't about you, Wallace. This is about finding Allison."

"I can't help you there."

"Can anyone corroborate your story?"

"Just my word."

"Yeah, you and Rick are real upstanding citizens."

Wallace sniffed. "You pressing charges against me or what? Otherwise, let me out of here."

Jax snorted. He wanted his case to be rock solid when he threw the book at him. Which meant getting back on the farm and finding Allison or evidence of where she was. He just needed the warrant or a full admission. "You and your nephew can think about what you really know tonight. Maybe something else will come to you. Like a conscience."

Chapter Seventeen

Jax strode into his office for the second time that night, the stress of the day in his legs. He dropped into his chair. It was after eleven, and sandpaper lined the inside of his eyelids.

He could use a drink. Another energy shot at this point would only fray his last remaining nerves. A drink wasn't the answer either. He didn't want to be buzzed or addled. What he needed was a bed. Not that he'd sleep, but the lack of it had contributed to his inability to stay neutral with Wallace. Or Rick. All he'd done with both was go around in circles: accuse, deny, postulate, argue, thrust, parry. Pointless.

He'd directed Matt to secure them both with the detention officer downstairs for the night. "Once you've done that, make sure you all go home, including Trudy." Someone should rest. They'd need their energy come sunup. He'd keep reviewing what little evidence they had, thinking through his next interrogation, working all the angles. He'd rest when Allison was home and in her own bed. If she was alive. He rubbed his eyes with his knuckles. Nothing had proved she wasn't—he had to act accordingly.

Jax returned to the report on the backpack and glanced at the images of the blue and green feathers still on his computer.

Jax had been a young detective when Madeline and Elena Massey went missing. He and Jameson had barely slept then in their efforts to bring the girls home. Stopping at every business on the way out of town. Interviewing the foster parents' neighbors. The girls' teachers. When they got a lead, they raced to interview the potential witness who might have seen the slightest deviation in a routine day in that area. They'd stopped at nothing.

In the end, however, he and Jameson had succeeded in rescuing Elena—but only because she'd gotten away. Their shared focus had cemented their friendship. Despite the fact they'd failed Madeline.

He scrolled through the images and back, zooming in and out to pick out the details. Was it a clue? Was he being goaded? Not a coincidence, he knew that much. He rested his forearms on his desk.

What if Allison's disappearance was somehow tied to the old event and Wallace was involved? Had he been lying in the shadows, and Allison was just one of many over the years? He couldn't go off half-cocked without more information. It was late, but he had to know.

He punched in Jameson's number again. His former partner answered on the fifth ring. "Jameson here." His voice sounded like gravel.

"You sleeping?" Jax asked.

"What's wrong?" Jameson said.

"Why?"

"Haven't heard from you for nearly five years, and now you're calling me in the middle of the night. What is it?"

After Lulu died, he could barely function, let alone talk to his old friend. Except for the yearly Christmas card Abby sent to Jameson and his wife, Gayle, they'd lost all contact. Hearing his voice now, he knew that had been a mistake. "Eleven isn't the middle of the night. When did you get to be an old man?"

"Since I started working the four-a.m. shift. Working cold case now."

There must be plenty in Jameson's life that he didn't know. "When did that happen?"

"Couple of years now. You still playing the Lone Ranger down in Misty Pines?"

"Yeah. That's why I'm calling. Something's come up I hope you can help me with."

Jameson hadn't thought much of his choice of locations. At the time, he and Abby had wanted to get away from the depressing frequency of crime in the big city, and sleepy Misty Pines seemed like the answer. Truth was,

Jax had to go somewhere else. He'd caused himself too many problems on the force by bucking authority.

Abby had saved him from himself for a while. Until Lulu. It always came back to Lulu.

Jameson grunted, probably on his way to an upright position. "Shoot."

Just like that, they'd slipped back into old times. Jax cleared his throat. "I've got an abduction case down here, and I found something." He'd been so certain the moment he'd seen it. Hearing Jameson's voice made him pause.

"Okay. Out with it. You didn't wake me for nothing."

What the hell. "It's the Massey case."

"Okay."

"You still working it?" Jax asked.

"It's on my list of unsolved, of course, but that trail's been iced over for years."

"What if I told you it might be thawing?"

"I'm listening."

He told him about the feathers found in Allison's backpack.

"Feathers?" Jameson said.

"They match the multicolored fragments that were found on Madeline's body and on Elena's clothing." A silence hung between them. "Did you hear me?"

"You had a hard-on about those feathers years ago, but that evidence never went anywhere. Don't go down that road again."

Jax gripped the phone. They both knew not bringing Madeline Massey home had dug into him like a barb, ripping into the meat of him, making him hard to work with. He'd left very few standing bridges by the time he'd left Portland. "It's different this time."

"Is it? Or are you reaching for something that's not there."

"I'm reaching to bring home a young girl who's the same age Madeline was and who has disappeared with a lot of similarities."

"You have no suspects in the current case?"

"I do, and he's of the age to have been involved in Madeline's murder. You have access to the old case files?"

"I can get them pulled from the warehouse, if necessary."

"I know it takes a day, but I need them sooner. Like yesterday. The clock is winding down. I don't want Allison to go down with it."

Jameson sighed. "Do you have anything you could send my way so I can look at what you've got first?"

"I'll send the report and pictures right now. You'll understand when you see them. They're the same."

"You really think the killer is back?" Disbelief had crept into his tone.

"I'm saying when I saw those feathers—look. Sometimes you have to work from the gut."

"I'll give you that. You should be talking to Abby about this, though."

Jax's left eye twitched. "Why would I do that?"

"Because the FBI has a division that genetically tests feathers now."

"A feather testing division?" His turn to sound disbelieving.

"Yup. A whole wildlife evidence department. Federal money gets you a slew of perks these days. Apparently, they can tell you the species they originate from and even what they might have been used for."

"Why haven't we done that with the Massey evidence already?"

"We? There's no we."

Jameson clearly hadn't gotten over Jax leaving. "Sorry, I mean…."

"It's fine. You married Abby. You moved to the coast. I get it. You owed me nothing."

Maybe, but Jax understood his anger for leaving him high and dry. "Why haven't you sent them to the FBI for review?"

"I've been buried deep in other cases; it just hasn't happened. Send me your reports showing what you found. If it's like the evidence we've got here, I'll send Abby what I have for comparison's sake. You'll have to do the same with your stuff."

Jax clenched his hand to dissipate the tension. He'd been doing a lot of that over the last twenty-four hours. "And you'll get up and do that now. Time…"

"You don't have to say it." He heard rustling. Jameson climbing out of bed. "It's okay, honey. I'll be right back."

Jax winced at having woken Jameson's wife. "I appreciate your help. How's Gayle?"

"Better now," he whispered, and then his voice got louder after he left the bedroom. "She finished her last round of radiation a couple of weeks ago."

A lump formed in Jax's throat. "Radiation?"

"Yeah, breast cancer. Diagnosis came last year."

Jax hung his head. "I hadn't heard. I'm sorry."

"Don't be. You've had enough of your own crap to deal with. You didn't have to deal with mine."

It was no excuse. Despite what Jameson said, he heard the strain in his voice. "Those reports and pictures should be over to you any second."

"Call Abby."

Jax stretched his neck. "Give Gayle a hug."

Silence sat between them like a golden ring. Each wanting to grab onto it, wanting to say something to make it right. Asking Jameson for help might be a way toward bridging the gap.

Jameson cleared his throat. "If you don't have much going on, can we see you at Thanksgiving? Gayle would love that. And the kid…they've missed you."

Rachel. Jameson's only daughter. An adult now. He missed them too. But that morning, Jax had been in a different place mentally. Now, he wasn't sure what he planned to do when he found Allison. Or if he didn't. He closed his eyes. Thanksgiving was too far away to make promises. "I'll see if I can swing it."

"Good enough."

Jax disconnected, confirmed the email had sent, and stared at the phone. Abby was the last person he wanted to talk to. But waiting for morning and Jameson to get the material from the warehouse felt like a dead stop.

At home, he had his own files on the Massey case that he'd kept over the years. While he couldn't remember exactly what he'd retained, he was pretty sure copies of photographs were among the items. Whatever he had wouldn't be as good as original evidence, but he couldn't let the hours tick away without pushing forward.

He grabbed the case file, paperclipping the lab report on top, and scanned the document again on the way to his car. He ducked inside and secured his gun. He glanced at the report again.

A loud slap against Jax's car window launched his stomach towards his scrotum. He dropped the file and forensic report onto his passenger seat and instinctively moved to retrieve his weapon. His eyes darted upward to see a gigantic palm print. The hand pulling away from the window was attached to Commissioner Troy Marks.

"Open up." Marks slapped the window again.

Jax met Marks's scarlet face with a snarl as his stomach slid back into place. He didn't have time for this, but the quickest way to get this over with was to kiss some political ass. He punched the down window button. Did he smell beer? "Commissioner. What brings you out to the precinct this time of night?"

"Thought we had an understanding about your leaving my boy alone."

Dylan had run right home to Daddy. "That was until I learned that he and Allison had been dating."

"Dylan's dated lots of girls. Allison's no one special, I assure you."

"He mentioned you have an interest in keeping his love life non-existent."

"He's going to be someone. He doesn't need anyone messing with his head."

That sounded certain. "How upset would you have been had they tried?"

"Oh, please. I already told you I was with the Fire Chief this morning. Don't try to put me or my son into any of your scenarios."

"Only trying to find Allison Krueger." Every second messing with the likes of Marks was a second not spent doing that.

"Say whatever you like. If I see you near him again, I'll come at you like a hornet. He had nothing to do with that girl running away."

The Commissioner wasn't asking, and Jax didn't intend to update him on Allison's new status. And while he didn't know precisely what he had other than two liars sitting in jail cells, he wouldn't let anyone off the hook. Even a seventeen-year-old with a high-powered daddy behind him.

"I won't apologize to you, or anyone else for doing my job." His right hand rested on the lab report next to him.

He looked up to find Commissioner Marks staring down at the files, his face pale as the moon. He wasn't about to let Marks in on any theories he was working, or evidence that had presented itself. He needed this blowhard out of his face so he could get home. Jax slid the files into a neat pile and blocked the window as best he could.

"What's all that?" Marks said.

"Nothing for you to worry about."

"Where my boy's concerned, I have everything to worry about." Marks leaned in, huffing in Jax's face.

"Duly noted, Commissioner. Now go home."

"Don't tell me what to do."

Jax reached for the door handle again to back Marks down. "Have you been drinking?"

"Of course not," Marks stuttered, clearly remembering the DUI Jax had slapped on him at one time.

"Good. I have other things to tend to."

"Then do them," he said, but his voice had lost any ire.

Marks could have expected more of a fight. They'd certainly had a few over the past ten years. Jax had pulled him over a couple of times for speeding, and he always fought those. But that sobriety stop had been the clincher. Jax had pulled over the newly-elected City Commissioner when he'd rolled through the stop sign.

The hometown boy had been riding high on his election victory and thought himself too good for a lowly sheriff to be issuing him yet another ticket. When Jax smelled the hint of wine on Marks's breath, he made him walk the line right there downtown. He'd failed. The charge didn't stick, and Marks gloated for weeks. He'd even attempted to have him removed as sheriff, but qualified candidates weren't banging down City Hall to patrol Misty Pines. They were all stuck with each other.

Jax held the steering wheel tight as he pulled out of the parking lot. Politicians and assholes, every county had them. He didn't have time for either. He gunned it to his house and didn't look back.

Chapter Eighteen

Jax hadn't pulled out his old files in years. At one time, he'd been at the top of his game as a detective and as a sheriff. But after Lulu's diagnosis, every ounce of energy went into trying to save her. And then he couldn't. From that point, even performing his regular duties of patrolling the sleepy main strip in town took concerted effort.

His well had run dry. With Allison's disappearance, and this possible past connection, that well needed filling, and fast.

He brewed a pot of coffee and shoved a frozen single-serve lasagna into the microwave before heading to the bedroom and into the walk-in closet. He retrieved a banker's box off the top shelf on what used to be Abby's side. *Her side?* More like the whole closet had been hers, filled with her work uniform of slacks in various shades of gray or black, blouses, and smart blazers. But his favorite short black dress with sequins she'd worn on their first date had hung close to his few clothes. In the corner had been her white silk wedding dress—a dress she'd dreamed her own daughter would wear someday.

He gripped the box in his hands. Now he could have screamed, and an echo would come back at him.

He plunked himself down on the bed before opening the cardboard box. His folder and notebook on Massey were in the middle of the stack of files he'd kept from his days on the Portland force.

Jax skimmed the forensics report. Madeline had suffered from a blow to the base of her skull resulting in a deep gash. "Blunt force trauma" read the pathologist's note. Jax skimmed the expert analysis to find that a solid wood object had been used to produce such a contusion. Nothing more specific.

When they'd found her sister, Elena also had a large gash on the back of her head. Their attacker had worked quickly to incapacitate them not only with physical force but a chemical as well. There were so many unanswered questions, but with scant forensics, they were left with speculation since Elena couldn't remember anything after she'd been knocked unconscious.

Jax and Jameson had hypothesized that Madeline may have never come to after the initial attack. No defensive wounds were found on her arms, and there was no DNA from her attacker under her nails. She hadn't been sexually assaulted, which was unusual given the nature of her wounds and the manner of their abduction. Sick sexual fantasy often underscored the abduction in the first place. This suggested they'd been dealing with someone whose sole motivation was power and control.

Madeline's body had been found in a briar bush next to an open marsh. The lack of scratches implied her body had been placed, rather than killed, there. The feathers were another clue. The fragmented pieces weren't naturally occurring and could have come from a nearby manufacturing facility. Jax had never completely agreed with that theory, based more on gut than solid evidence. The truth was with so many possibilities and sources, the feathers on Madeline and Elena could have come from anywhere.

His gut also said the multicolored feathers found in Allison's backpack were the same as in the Massey case, but his notes didn't reflect an actual description of the Massey feathers. A formal report didn't seem to have been generated at the time. The science of evidence collection and analysis had changed dramatically in the last two and a half decades—Jameson's suggestion to call Abby wasn't off base.

He wasn't eager to make that call to his ex-wife, but what he wanted was beside the point with Allison still out there.

He grabbed his cell. It was after midnight. He'd apologize later.

Abby's line rang four times before going to voicemail. "Abby, Jax here. Call me when you get this message. It's urgent."

He'd done what he had to do, and now he waited. Again. Waiting for a confession. Waiting for a call from a witness who might have seen something and hadn't come forward yet. Waiting for a lead to present itself. Waiting for his men to get some rest so they could be ready to tackle tomorrow with fresh eyes and minds at daylight.

A luxury he wouldn't allow for himself.

He found a whiteboard in the closet, removed a landscape picture from the wall, and hung the whiteboard in its place. He paced and jotted the pieces of the puzzle in black ink on the board. Between seven and seven-thirty a.m., things in Misty Pines changed. He needed to brainstorm. This wasn't the time for neat rows. He wrote down everything he could think of, ranging from one side of the board and back.

Rick Johnson at Osbourn Park.

A phantom black SUV?

The backpack.

Wallace.

Feathers.

Drugs.

He stepped back and scanned the board. Did drugs play into Allison's disappearance or not?

Dylan. He circled Dylan's name, adding several question marks. How did that little fart fit into the picture?

The farm.

More question marks. Wallace was hiding something. Jax drew an arrow linking "The Farm" to "Wallace." Then he wrote Massey, another arrow. Another question mark. But he couldn't stop there.

He drew arrows from Wallace, the farm, Rick, drugs, Dylan.

How did this puzzle fit together?

He chewed the end of the pen. He hadn't found evidence of Allison at the farm, but Wallace's sketchiness only fueled his desire for that search warrant.

Jax circled different parts of his diagram in different colors and jotted more. After thirty minutes of scribbling, he remained frustrated. His mind was doing exactly what the whiteboard showed: running in circles. He needed a break.

He strode to the garage where Lulu's wood dollhouse was laid out in pieces. Lulu had giggled with delight when he showed her the plans. He'd promised her he'd finish it before.... He swallowed. He hadn't finished, and now he wasn't sure if he would—or could. Still, he felt closest to his daughter when he worked on it. And it eased his mind. He grabbed a piece of rubberwood and his knife and took it back into the house, and grabbed his food from the microwave.

In the living room, he laid open the files and stared at them as he slid the blade across the soft pulp of the block until it began to take shape into a table. With each pull against the wood, the thin sheaths floating off, he felt conflicted at letting even a moment pass of not being out there. He couldn't lose the feeling of being useless. He glanced at his cell for Abby's return call. Its silence mocked him.

He stared at the board. It yielded no secrets. It was just a whiteboard with a bunch of names and squiggly arrows going nowhere. With his gun on the coffee table next to the knife, he laid back, propped a pillow under his head, and switched his attention to the forensics report. Feathers. There were a few on the outside, but several in the pocket. Had they been planted to get his attention? Was it a coincidence? A game? Did Wallace factor in, or was he missing something?

* * *

Jax bolted upright at pounding on the front door and squinted at the sunlight streaming through a crack in the front window blinds. Shit. He'd dozed off.

He rolled off the couch wearing his uniform from last night, the report sailing to the floor along with the wood shavings. Falling asleep was the last thing he'd expected to do. He slapped his tongue against his teeth. His stomach growled. He hadn't touched his lasagna or much else in the way of food since yesterday. Along with that and the lack of sleep the previous night, it was no wonder he'd passed out.

He walked to the entry and caught the scent of his day-old sweat. He looked through the peephole and winced.

Abby Turner...no, Kanekoa now, stood on the step, a manicured hand on her hip, black hair framing her oval face, her skin the shade of almonds. A trace of blush and mascara accented her rounded cheekbones, a trait of her Polynesian father. Her sharp green eyes belonged very much to her red-haired Irish mother who'd never liked Jax much. Her light gray pantsuit fit her just right. He glanced at the wrinkles in his shirt and ironed them with his broad hands, and then opened the door.

She pushed past him. "Finally. What's wrong?"

Jax moved to avoid getting run over and smoothed his hair standing on end. "What do you mean? I asked you to call, not come over." How did she manage to look so good? So normal? How was that even possible after what they'd gone through?

"You called in the middle of the night saying it's urgent. What did you think I'd do?" Abby's eyes were glued to what littered the coffee table. Her gaze skimmed the whittling project and rested on the gun. Her eyes narrowed, then softened. "Is there something you need to tell me?"

He picked up the glass of water from the table and finished it. "It's not what you think." Since they'd both always housed their guns in a safe when they were home, and she knew of his depression, Abby must be thinking the worst. The worst was yesterday morning. "Like I said, you only needed to call."

"Obviously, that's not true. Did you ever call that counselor?"

No counselor could bring back their daughter. But he had gone for one session. Long enough to hear that his desire to finish the dollhouse didn't mean he was crazy. "Don't need anyone trying to shrink my head." He carried the glass to the kitchen. "Did you?"

She followed him. "Yes. He's helped."

"I can see that. You look amazingly well-adjusted." He almost succeeded in keeping the edge out of his voice. It hurt that she'd left. She'd wanted another child after Lulu, and he couldn't give that to her. His heart had closed. Shriveled was more like it. Seeing her again now had his stomach in knots.

Her eyes scanned him on her way to the refrigerator, where she opened the door and inspected the few contents. "I've kept moving to survive. Based on the mess out in the living room, you're still working on her dollhouse."

He didn't answer.

"When are you going to let that go?" She opened and closed the empty crispers. "You have to find a way to let go of the pain—at the very least, you have to find a way to live with it."

"Like you did so easily." He set the glass down with a sharp clank on the counter. She'd come here worried about him, and he was being unforgivable. "Look—"

She slammed the fridge door and crossed to the pantry. "That's not fair," she said before he could get an excuse out.

He crossed his arms over his chest. She couldn't be idle for two seconds. Always had to be looking. Inspecting. Keeping her hands in motion. "Yeah, that's right. It's not. I just sometimes forget how good you are at separating from your emotions. Everything in its place."

Her lip twitched. "Why did you call?'

She didn't take the bait. Abby was a far better person than he was about this whole mess. Better to just get to it. He had to think of Allison. "I need an assist on a case."

She tucked a piece of her hair behind her ear. "Okay."

He had her attention. "I understand the FBI has a division that tests feathers."

"Among other things." She wrinkled her brow. "What kind of case you working?"

"Remember Allison Krueger? Emily's kid?"

"Of course. Lulu and I would see them at the grocery store sometimes. Lulu adored Allison. She'd share her Skittles with her."

A pang hit Jax's chest. He hadn't known of Allison's kindness to his daughter. "She's been abducted."

"Shit." Abby's face fell. She caught herself and shook it off. Personal feelings would only cloud their judgment. They both knew that. They needed to act like the law enforcement pros they were.

"We found her backpack."

Abby nodded, waiting. It wasn't only that she was good at compartmentalizing; she was good at everything. Trudy and Jameson had been right to tell him to pull Abby into the matter. His brain always did better when paired with hers.

He brought her up to speed and handed her the forensics report. "I think they could be connected to the case Jameson and I worked, back in the day. The two girls." He waited.

Abby nodded. "I remember."

"These look pretty much the same to me."

Abby squinted at him. "You connected these two cases based on the feathers?"

She sounded like his old partner. "Hoping you can tell me. They look identical to the naked eye. If they are, then that killer could be back."

"That's a stretch."

"It's a similar MO." He gave her the bullet points. "It's also the anniversary of the first case. I'm telling you, the presence of those feathers is no coincidence."

She gave him a small smile. "Then I'm happy to have my department take a look."

He nodded. "Appreciate that. I've been in touch with Jameson, and he's transferring the old evidence from the warehouse. It might already be over to you."

"Perfect."

His shoulders relaxed a little. They were good at talking work. Besides being Lulu's parents, it's what they'd done best. Touching on emotions had always gotten them into trouble. "Thank you."

Abby rested her hip against the counter and opened the cupboard next to her. "So where are you on locating Allison?"

He tried not to look at her lips, with the hint of the plum lipstick she always wore. Even on the first day they met at a Blazers basketball game—standing in line for a hot dog, no less. "I've got two suspects in custody, and I'm expecting my search warrant any time for Glenn Hill Farms."

Abby closed the cupboard and pushed herself away from the counter.

"Who are the suspects?"

"The leadman, Wallace, and his nephew, Rick Johnson."

She stiffened, her expression tight. "Vince Wallace?"

His shoulders tensed. He'd seen that look before. "Yes. He's the boss at Glenn Hill, and Rick's his nephew, who is also an unregistered sex offender with a history of messing with young girls." Jax laid out the rest of what he had on Wallace, some of it conjecture. "There were also drugs found in Allison's bedroom that she told her mom she was holding for someone. Not sure if or how that relates to them, yet, but I'm working all the angles."

"You just said you think there's a connection to the old case. How could Rick or Wallace be tied to that?"

"Based on age alone, Rick couldn't be. But Wallace is plenty old enough. I forgot to mention, that backpack was found in Wallace's car."

"Was he living in the area twenty-five years ago?"

"According to records, yes. And he's been non-cooperative from the beginning, which says he's hiding something."

She shook her head.

"What?"

"You can't raid the farm, and Mr. Wallace needs to be released, immediately."

His brow wrinkled. "What are you talking about?"

"It's connected to my work."

"And?"

"And part of why I went back to the bureau was because there was drug trafficking suspected in Misty Pines."

The list of things he'd been oblivious to never stopped. "Glenn Hill Farms is involved?"

She nodded.

That explained Wallace's resistance to letting them search the premises. "Even more reason for Wallace then to be in custody."

"You don't get it. It took us a while to figure out where the drugs were coming from, but we did, and I've been working the Glenn Hills aspect for the past two months. We believe trucks are bringing the drugs in from

Mexico, and the farm is turning them around and moving those same drugs out with the produce as their cover into other areas of the state. Wallace appears to be at the core, which means he's the key to bringing the operation down. That's why he needs to go back there."

"Finding Allison takes precedence. After what you've just told me, I'm even more convinced that farm needs to be searched."

"No."

He glared. "The Abby I know wouldn't choose drugs over a child."

"I'm choosing all the children. Do you know how many kids die of overdoses a year? Thousands, Jax. And Wallace. He's one of many sons of bitches that target them. I want to nail that bastard to a wall. His entire operation has to come down to do that."

"I can't agree when Allison is the kid here and now in mortal danger."

"I don't know about that. At least as far as Wallace or the farm are concerned. I have someone on the inside. They haven't reported anything suspicious on the property."

"Who?"

"Angelique."

That's why she was so ingrained and likable. "Her name's come up, but have you physically been on that farm? It's huge with numerous buildings. One person inside might miss something. And all you're doing is confirming that it's not a stretch to think Wallace could have been involved in a girl's murder years ago, or an abduction today, the way he tends to buck the law. He'll remain in custody. I need time to get out on that farm."

"I won't allow it. Let Wallace go and let me do what I need to do."

The burning sensation had returned in his chest. "If those feathers are connected, and Wallace is the connection between Allison and my old case, then I damn well can't let him know where I'm at on the investigation until I have a clue what I'm up against. He could be the killer I've been wanting to catch all of these years."

She frowned, her eyes reflecting an all-too-familiar sadness. She didn't believe him. "We're this close to nailing him for trafficking." She held her hand up with a sliver of distance between her thumb and index finger. "I'm not going to let you screw this up over some notion."

"It's not a hunch, Abby. That backpack is physical evidence. A snuff tin in her pack has his prints on them. Not to mention, we found a bloody rag halfway up Allison's driveway—a rag that he admitted was his. None of those things are a fabrication of my imagination."

"I didn't say any of that."

"You didn't have to. You saw the gun on the coffee table, and you took my call as desperation, and now you've made assumptions about my ability as a cop."

"Jax, please. I'm also aware you don't know when to quit and how it gets you into trouble."

"If that brings Allison home, so be it. I will not let anyone go based on your say-so. If Wallace goes back to the farm and starts hiding evidence, any traces of Allison could be long gone. I can't take that risk. I'm holding him until I get my warrant and know for myself."

"Can't let you do that, Jax." She was all business. No softness. Nothing of his Abby showing. It was more than he could bear.

They locked eyes for a long minute. She didn't yield. All he wanted was a sign that she got it. This search meant everything to him. He had to get it right. Saving Allison wouldn't make up for losing Madeline, but it would do *something* for his heart. If it was related, it would give justice to Elena and Madeline for the wrongs against them. He could do that. Abby had to understand.

Instead, she pulled herself up to her full height. "I'll expect to see Wallace back at Glenn Hill by oh-nine-hundred hours."

He stood his ground. "That's right. You're a federal agent, after all. Your job has always been the most important. That's why you ran out on me the minute they wanted you back."

"I couldn't sit around here and be torn up with you anymore. Besides, you didn't need me for consolation. You had your dollhouse obsession, and there was no room for me in your world."

He swallowed the lump in his throat. "We lost our daughter."

"And I was devastated, too."

"It showed. You look really heartbroken now." He regretted the words the moment they'd left his mouth. "I didn't mean—"

Her jaw twitched. "I cry for her every day, Jax. I'm just not all tied up in my own self-pity like you."

The words stabbed him. "What are you tied up in exactly?"

She sighed, indicating she'd had enough. It wasn't like they'd ever solve it. The crevasse was far too wide for that. "Release Wallace, and don't go anywhere near that farm again."

"I'll decide that, not you."

She stopped. "I'll have Angelique keep eyes on the inside. It's the best I can do. But I will tear you to pieces if you mess with me on this."

He strode to the door and swung it open. "I'll wait to hear from you on what Jameson sent over."

"Wallace gets released, or it'll be a long wait."

He glared his refusal as she marched past him. He slammed the door behind her. Who in the hell did she think she was? She couldn't tell him what to do.

Yes, she could.

The powerlessness had him off balance. At least Abby had someone on the inside watching for him now. Would that be good enough?

He strode to the whiteboard and grabbed the eraser. Then flung it against the front door, watching it fall apart.

Chapter Nineteen

Elena woke the next morning, her eyes burning from a restless night. With the discovery of the opal, she worried now that Steven had gotten to Allison and that she'd ridden in his SUV—the one he'd sold yesterday morning. A coincidence, perhaps. But what if he was covering his tracks?

State law mandated that she report child abuse. She was also obliged to report her brother or any patient if she thought they might do harm to themselves or another. She wasn't sure either of those scenarios applied to this situation. What she did feel certain of was calling Daniel, or the authorities could do more harm than good.

While she didn't know Steven's intentions if he did, in fact, come into contact with Allison, no one knew him better than she did. And no one could track him better than she could since she'd been taking care of him for so long. She rubbed her eyes. She also knew he distrusted the authorities, who he considered "useless" for not finding Madeline in time. Any attempts by them would make him dig in deeper.

Still, she weighed the options again and again. Report him? Not report him? Report him? Not?

She could lose her license if she truly believed Steven was involved in the abduction of a child, but that wasn't the worst of it. If her lack of reporting resulted in Allison being harmed, Daniel would never forgive her. She'd never forgive herself.

The visitation weekends they'd spent together when Allison was a little girl were always in the back of her mind. How Allison's freckled face and gap-toothed smile greeted her and Daniel when they woke. She'd crawl into bed with them and snuggle in. Allison would turn and hug Elena like only a child could, breaking down the walls of protection she'd built to survive. Elena's heart squeezed.

If anything happened to her stepdaughter, she'd deserve Daniel's wrath and the ostracization from him and everyone else that came with it.

Which meant she couldn't get it wrong. She had to solve this mystery and find out if Steven was involved. If he was, she had to bring Allison home safely. She had the best chance of doing that if she did it on her own.

She threw back the covers and got up, thinking of her last visit to Steven's apartment and whether she'd missed a clue of where he'd gone. The dirt in the shower had bothered her the most. It could be from a beach. Clam digging at night, maybe. He'd never shown interest in that, but she had to entertain all possibilities. Or was she kidding herself?

She was kidding herself, and she knew it.

She'd also noticed the cross on the dining table. There was another place she'd seen a cross that looked similar. The more she thought about it, it was just as out of place in his apartment as the bracelet.

She had to see clients later, so she dressed in light tan slacks, a white silk blouse under a navy blazer, and low-slung heels. She pulled her brown hair into a short ponytail and headed out. After grabbing a triple shot vanilla latte at a drive-thru, she drove. And drove.

Finding Steven would require that she think like him. Seep into his psyche. His dislike of people stemmed from his inability to detach. He didn't know how not to care. The guilt over being unable to fix things for them corroded him like acid.

She was a perfect example of that. He was so filled with sympathy and guilt for the plight of her childhood, he obsessed about what she'd gone through. But his sympathy often felt more like pity—something she didn't want. For the most part, she'd moved past the pain of her childhood. No matter how much counseling she gave Steven, he hadn't.

Guilt could be spurring him now. It was the anniversary of Madeline's murder, and Maddy would have been forty this year. A hand wrapped around her heart. She hadn't realized that until this moment. It was also the same age their mother had been when she died in the car accident. But what did any of that mean? She kept returning to the cross on his table—out of place.

On a hunch, she found herself on Highway 26, and then on the country road that led to her old foster home. Her hands shook as she pulled in front of the place where they'd lived, and where it all went wrong.

Elena didn't hate the paint-chipped mobile home for the same reasons Maddy did. Maddy hated the rats scurrying in and out of the holes in the walls at night, rummaging through the cereal in the kitchen cupboards, driving their foster mother to distraction. Elena wasn't too bothered by the rats; it was something else that tormented her. At night, when she waited for sleep to rescue her, she listened to them building their nests. If she could have disappeared into the woodwork with them, she would have.

She and Maddy had come to the Simpsons shortly after their parents died. Steven was older, so he didn't come with them. Questions of his whereabouts were always met with blank stares. At least she and Maddy were together.

But after the first day, Maddy had looked for ways to get out of there. Skipping school. Making out with the next-door neighbor's kid, Brian, whose parents partied a lot. Elena had seen rows of motorcycles in front of their house. The loud and smoky kind. The men were covered in tattoos and smelled like weeds being burned in the yard. Maddy and Brian smoked in the shed behind his house. Maddy constantly plotted her escape.

Elena kept her head down. Mrs. Simpson was a good cook. She used real tomato sauce and not ketchup when making spaghetti, and if they were good, Elena got to have extra helpings of garlic bread.

It was Mr. Simpson, who they referred to as "the mister," who had the temper—and a belt. Sometimes he visited Elena at night, after his wife had gone to bed. He made Elena squeeze against the wall when he climbed in next to her. On top of her. The hurt lessened, after a while.

If Elena didn't move, she could almost become invisible. But Maddy didn't know how to disappear into her mind, and Elena couldn't bear to be left behind. With a bag full of clothes, they walked out of the house after vodka had knocked out the mister and the missus had gone to bed for the night.

They'd made it a mile when bright lights shone behind them. Elena's insides felt like jelly. She wanted to cry. He'd found them. He'd be drunk and angry. They would pay for their disobedience. The belt would sting the back of her legs. He would make her please him again.

Nausea swept through her when the car pulled to the side of the road, and the rocks crunched under its tires. A power window opened. She expected hollering and honking. Being ordered into the car. Berated for their insolence. Instead, she heard a whistle call.

Maddy's face had broken into a grin. "It's Brian."

Elena loved her sister's smile. She almost believed her. "You sure?"

"He's going to give us a ride."

Brian was sixteen. Even at fourteen, Maddy flirted like she was a senior in high school. The fact she'd filled out her bra since she was twelve didn't hurt either. It had drawn the attention of boys wherever they lived.

"I don't know," Elena said. Besides Brian's sketchiness, he looked at her like the mister sometimes. "Let's just keep walking."

"Don't be so scared of everything."

"I'm not." Yes, she was. Scared of Brian. Scared of having to go back to that house. She didn't want that life anymore. Mostly she didn't want to live without Maddy.

Maddy grabbed her hand and squeezed. "Then stay here, big baby." A tease said with a reassuring smile. It was their way. "I'll come back and get you. I promise."

Elena nodded and watched her sister's silhouette fade and disappear into the glaring headlights. Standing on the road's edge, she shifted from one foot to the other, the urge to pee coming over her. Bad. Brian might get them to the next town where there was a gas station. She heard whispers, then Maddy laugh, but could see nothing past the lights. Waiting.

Maddy's scream pierced the air like a blade, and the blood inside Elena's hands and legs receded to her core like tsunami waters. Her hands fisted, her nails digging into the meat of her palms. Her heart jolted in her chest.

"Maddy?" Elena screamed back.

"Run," Maddy screamed. "Run."

She couldn't. Maddy needed help. But Elena's feet wouldn't budge. The car revved its engines. Maddy's scream stopped.

Elena squelched a sob and ran. Her legs felt like heavy paint buckets were strapped on. She stumbled into the field. Her heart pounding, skipping, jerking. A pinch grabbed in the back of her throat. She didn't stop. The sobs came. The thud of her feet hitting the ground. Through the grass. Echoing in her ears. A crack like lightning. Her foot caught on briers. She stifled a scream. Tried to hide. Darkness shrouded her. Closing in.

Elena gasped, pulling herself out of the memory. She blinked back tears. Madeline's gravestone came into focus. She'd been on autopilot when she left the Simpsons' house. She didn't remember turning into the cemetery.

The stone was etched with her sister's name: Madeline Renee Massey. It wasn't much of a memorial. Just a slab of granite with swirls of black and gray. Someone had put fresh flowers on the grave. Pink and yellow gerbera daisies. Her heartbeat started to calm.

The caretakers must put flowers on the lonely graves. Or maybe someone remembered it was the anniversary of Maddy's death, like the social worker who had felt guilty about placing them with the Simpsons in the first place. Or the detectives who had tried to find Maddy. A small smile crossed her face. That would be nice if they remembered.

Then she saw it. Stuck inside the flowers was a chocolate rose wrapped in red foil. The smile disappeared. Elena's skin prickled. She scanned the area beyond the headstone. Steven had been here.

Elena darted over to the path that led further into the cemetery and looked out ahead, searching for her brother. Steven loved chocolate. Whenever they disagreed, or he knew she was angry with him, she'd find a chocolate peace offering left for her. It had become their code. No one was on the pathway.

She took long strides back toward Madeline's grave and ran to the other path, leading in the opposite direction. In the distance, someone headed toward the street. Leaving. He wore black pants and a matching shirt. He had short brown hair. Steven.

She ran, her shoes slipping off her heels, her purse falling off her shoulder. As she drew closer, the man, about her height, moved faster.

"Steven?" She hollered. "Stop."

The man turned, revealing a white priest's collar. "Pardon?"

She halted a few feet away. Up close, the man didn't look anything like her brother. "I'm so sorry."

The man smiled. "No worries, child. Are you here to grieve the loss of someone special?"

His words caught her off guard. Her chest tightened. "I, I—yes, I mean, I thought you were someone else."

"Grief can do that." His eyes wrinkled with understanding. "Would you like to sit awhile? We could talk. I'm a very good listener."

They'd stopped in front of a park bench. He was a kind priest who might be willing to listen to everyone. She longed for a sympathetic ear, but she had to keep looking. "No. Thank you."

She walked back to Madeline's grave. She'd been so taken aback by the chocolate rose, she hadn't noticed the full bouquet of them near their mother's headstone that sat one row over and up. She squared her shoulders. There was no mistaking it. She was on the right path even if she had no idea where it led.

Elena glanced at her watch, not realizing the time. She had clients to see and an appointment to keep with Dr. Kavorian. That might be for the best, anyway. After all these years, he knew them both so well. Maybe he'd be able to help her figure out where Steven had gone next without her revealing what she was afraid he'd done.

Chapter Twenty

Jax stormed into the station. He'd nodded off, then tangled with Abby, and both had his emotions stirring like that angry hornet Marks had referenced last night.

Deputy Garrett straightened in his chair at Jax's abrupt entrance. "Morning, Sheriff."

Jax waved him off. "Release Wallace."

"But...I thought—"

"Just do it."

"Yes, sir." Garrett hopped up and disappeared down the back hallway.

Jax turned to find Trudy staring at him, a deep crease between her eyes. "What?"

"You tell me?" Trudy took a long drink from her cup of tea. "You came in here like thunder rolling in with dark clouds."

"It's nothing."

She tucked her chin, peering over her bifocals. "M-hmm. Have you called Abby?"

Jax's face wrinkled with frustration. "Oh yeah. It went great. Talked about old times, right before she ordered me to let Wallace out of jail."

Trudy drew in a measured breath.

Jax took a step back when she set down her cup.

"We all know how you love to be told what to do. But you clearly aren't sleeping well again."

He bristled. He'd had more than he'd intended. "Get the forensics report over to her pronto, and have the lab transfer the feathers."

Trudy tilted her head back. "Don't you shut me down. Whether you want my opinion or not, Jax Turner, you're going to get it. Your job is to find Allison. It's not to wallow in your own sorrows. Something you are good at, by the way."

His face flushed. "You have no idea what you're talking about."

"I know you've been walking around in a fog for some time. This town hasn't needed a lot of your undivided attention, and you've had Deputy Chapman and the boys to fall back on. Thank God you've come back to us, but don't be a dog with a bone. If Abby wants him released, I'm sure she has good reason."

"Abby only cares about her next promotion."

"You know she's not like that. She loves you."

"How do you know?" he snapped.

"Because she came to me after Lulu died. I told her you'd grieve, like I grieved my Tommy, but you'd pull through. You were a tough old boy. And when she'd had enough and couldn't stand by as you withered in that small house of yours, she asked me to watch out for you."

She had? "Abby ran out."

"You shoved her out. That's what happens when you withdraw and don't pay attention. But that's beside the point right now; Allison and Emily need you."

He'd hurt Trudy's feelings, forcing her to say more than she'd ever said before. She didn't pry. Not like that. She prodded and hinted, but she'd never gone after him directly. She did know his grief. Her son Tommy had been killed in Afghanistan.

Heat crept up his neck. No matter how annoyed he was at Trudy, he couldn't do his job without her. Resentment at Abby telling him what to do had him staring at the world through the end of two Coke bottles, and all he could see was the distorted view where he'd been wronged.

He wouldn't win this or any battle with Trudy, but the words to make it right escaped him. He strode into his office and slammed the door. He shouldn't have let Abby get under his skin. But that's not what ate at him. It was that he'd let everything they had fritter away. Trudy was right. He'd retracted every part of himself to survive. He couldn't afford to do that anymore.

He reopened the door and directed his question to Matt, who'd been hunched at one of the desks clearly trying to stay out of Jax's way. "Rick admit to anything this morning?"

"No, sir," he said.

"You and Garrett drum up some more volunteers and work Osbourn Park where Brody left off. Then start hitting the park areas heading back this way." They couldn't just sit around and wait for Abby's informant to report. They had to keep looking.

"Yes, sir," Matt said.

Brody had just walked in. "Morning, Sheriff."

Jax updated him quickly on the turn of events even though letting Wallace go landed like a knife to his chest. "You're going to be following Wallace anywhere the bastard goes."

"Even into the farm?"

"Not yet." That warrant would be coming, though, and when it did, he'd decide then if he'd wait any longer or not.

Jax returned to his desk, his anger dropping a notch now that the team was in action, even if it wasn't the action he wanted. With his hands tied and his deputies hamstrung, Jax drilled into the facts: Allison had been missing twenty-six hours. She hadn't left home on her own, that much was certain. She was out there with a maniac—or if he had his maniac in a jail cell, she was in a place of his choosing. He kicked his boot against his desk. Abby had let a possible serial killer back out to do whatever to Allison.

He needed to stay busy if he intended not to dwell on that fact.

The fax machine in the corner clanked and began to purr. Jameson had brushed aside the idea that the case from twenty-five years ago and this case were connected, but Jax's gut told him differently. There was something in the case files, he just hadn't found it yet.

He watched the fax pages pile in the tray, using the rhythm of the machine to refocus. By the time Jameson's case notes had come through, he was back in his skin, leaving his irritation at Trudy and Abby in the past.

He spread the papers out on his desk.

In the old case, he and Jameson had remained in a black tunnel and chased their tails until the killer made contact. He'd wanted to play a game—a rigged game that he and Jameson had lost. The abductor had never intended to return the girls. Only taunt them and lead them in the wrong direction.

In this case, the feathers could be the taunt again. But why, if Wallace was the killer of the past, would he be as careless as to be caught with the backpack in his car? Had he forgotten about it? No way. You don't abduct a teenager, plant evidence on her belongings, then "forget." The backpack was part of his cat and mouse game, thinking he could once again outsmart the authorities.

As Jax read, he felt that familiar gnaw of not doing enough to bring Allison home. A part of him had hoped she'd find a way to give them a signal with Rick and Wallace in custody. But could she? Was Allison a fighter? Did she have the guts and gumption of an Elena Massey, who got away from her abductor and made her way to freedom? He didn't have answers to those questions.

He sat back in his chair.

That wasn't true. Allison was smart. Whether he agreed with her tactics or not, she'd gone to the parent she trusted to keep her confidences and worked out how to keep herself "safe" from being pregnant.

As for the drugs, what if Allison was telling the truth? Maybe they weren't hers, and she was trying to keep a friend from harm. A moral crusader even.

The picture forming of Allison was not that of a little girl lost, but a savvy teenager who had her head on straight.

He dug his knuckles into his eye sockets. Head on straight or not, what shape would she be in when they did get to her? Elena Massey had been a mess. She didn't remember much, but she recalled the trauma of lying next to her dying sister. Then to be the one that got away.

He'd hold onto the fact that Allison would survive because Elena had—even though he had no idea what had happened to her over the years. Another thought had begun to set in. If the feathers turned out to be the same, and Madeline's killer had returned, could Elena be in danger?

He drummed the desk with his fingers. Not likely. The perpetrator had a thing for young girls. And if Abby had done what she promised, there'd be eyes on Wallace on and off the farm.

But what if he was approaching this wrong? What if Elena's memories had resurfaced, and she could offer information that might help find Allison now?

Jax went back into the office where Trudy had her back to him. He cleared his throat.

"Yes," she said, without turning.

"I need a search done on Elena Massey right away. She may still be living in Oregon, but I'm not sure."

"Elena Massey. Why does that name ring a bell?"

Trudy had a memory like a steel trap. If she could recall the name of a victim twenty-five years ago in another jurisdiction, that was something else. "I had a case involving her before I came here."

She waved her hand in the air. "That's not it." She swiveled her chair to face him, her face dark in thought before it brightened. "She was Allison's stepmother."

Jax's shoulders tensed. "What did you say?"

"Daniel, Emily's ex. He left Emily for Elena years ago. They're divorced now."

Before he could even process the information, Trudy took a call. She hit the hold button. "It's the lab. They want to speak to you."

"I'll take it in my office." Inside his office, he reeled from the implications. Elena was already involved. What were the odds? Astronomically small. "Sheriff Turner here."

"This is Jason from forensics. We're still working on processing the evidence, but the preliminary findings show no blood found in the vehicle."

Good. "How about other signs Allison was in the car?"

"There are a lot of hair and fibers to comb through. That'll take more time."

They didn't have more time. "If you can expedite, sure would appreciate it."

"Will do. But that's not why I called. We found traces of isoflurane on the outside of the pack. It's a—"

"I know what it is." Jax's throat constricted. He flipped through his old case file for the reference of the volatile anesthetic that could knock a small person out in a heartbeat. He was sure he'd seen it earlier. "How does one get their hands on that?"

"It's often used in putting animals under, so a vet supply would carry it. Course you can get anything online anymore."

He found the page. Then the word. Traces of "Forane" had been found in the throat and nasal passages of both Madeline and Elena. Next to Forane was written "form of isoflurane." Madeline's killer had ensured their compliance by knocking them out. It was how the abductor had ensured Allison's.

And Wallace had come out of the barn area yesterday, having just done surgery on an alpaca.

Feathers. Inhalant anesthesia. Jax closed his eyes. These were not coincidences. Neither fact had ever been released to the public. With the knowledge that Allison was Elena's stepdaughter, it meant one thing.

The killer was back.

And that killer was free.

Wallace was playing a game. Jax needed to find out if Elena remembered anything about her past ordeal—Allison's life depended on it.

Chapter Twenty-One

Elena Massey's practice was housed on the top floor of a historic building off Ocean Avenue. Jax knew Daniel left Emily for a mental health professional. He hadn't expected that person to be Elena.

A quick search of her bio before he'd arrived confirmed she was both a clinical and forensic psychologist, which meant one busy lady. Most people involved in forensics didn't see clients. They were immersed in the psychology of criminals.

Elena's childhood experience must have planted a deep-seated need to figure out why evil did what it did. It also might have played a part in why she lived in West Shore. With its proximity to where Madeline had been found, maybe like him, she had hoped she'd cross paths with her sister's killer if she stayed near the coastal region.

He entered Elena's offices through a frosted glass door that led to an all-beige waiting area. A woman sitting at the reception desk looked up when he entered. In her early twenties, she was dressed in a brown cowl neck sweater, her red hair in a bun skewered with a chopstick. She gave him a smile you'd give a sad child. "How can I help you?"

Even though he wore a uniform, she must think he was a potential client. If Abby had her way, he would be. "Is Elena Massey in?"

The woman turned to her computer and punched a couple of keys which produced a calendar on the screen. "Do you have an appointment?"

He pulled out his badge. "I don't. But it's important that I speak with her."

The door to an office situated beyond reception opened. "Stacey, I'll be back in a couple of hours," a voice said before Jax saw the woman behind it.

She stepped out and did a double take when she saw him.

He was taken aback. The baby-faced ten-year-old child he'd found that night had turned into a stunning woman—tall, with an air of confidence.

Jax straightened. "Ms. Massey?"

"I'm sorry, Doctor," Stacey said. "This sheriff just arrived a moment ago."

"Doctor," Jax said with a hint of pride. She was so smart and sharp and put-together, not a hint of the shattered girl he'd seen back then. How incredible that anyone could mend themselves so well. His cracks were newer and closer to the surface, but hers had been smoothed to nothingness. "I'm impressed."

Elena blushed. "Can I help you, Officer?"

He extended his hand. "It's Sheriff Turner." He searched her face for signs she recognized him and found none. "You might remember me as Detective Turner. From Portland."

She grew rigid but reached out to shake hands. "Detective, I mean Sheriff." Her voice had a slight tremble. "What brings you here?"

He held her hand in his for a beat. "I understand you were Allison Krueger's stepmother."

Elena nodded, pulling her arm back. She glanced at her secretary. "Call Dr. Kavorian and tell him I'm running late." She turned her gaze to Jax. "Please come in."

He followed Elena into her office. The space was filled with sleek metal and bamboo furniture. A glass bookshelf held colored porcelain vases and the usual psychology books from Freud, Jung, Cognitive Treatment for Anger and Depression, Treating High-Risk Patients, and even a trilogy on self-healing. In contrast, on the top shelf, a row of ceramic cottages with lights glowed. Representations of a happy home, perhaps? A signal that all things could be healed, with time. "It's great to see how well you've done for yourself."

She shut the door. "Thank you." She crossed to her desk and offered him a seat. He opted to perch on the arm of the overstuffed sofa. "It's been a process. After Maddy died, I was placed in a much better foster home. They got me into counseling and helped me get my education. That's where I discovered I wanted to help other people struggling with trauma."

"Commendable," he said, wishing this was a social call so they could catch up. "Are you aware Allison is missing?"

Elena shuffled some files, and slipped them into the top desk drawer, along with a notebook and some pens. "Yes. Daniel called me." She straightened the stapler, the blotter, a picture frame. His hands had to stay busy during stressful times too. It was one of many reasons he kept working on that dollhouse. Her eyes misted. "Have you found any signs of her yet?"

"No, which is why I'm here. When was the last time you spoke with your stepdaughter?"

Elena came out from behind her desk and leaned against it. "Daniel and I divorced last year, but I still send care packages for her and Roper—that's her dog. Squeaker toys, treats, lip gloss, hair ties and barrettes, things like that." She smiled. "I can't be there, but hopefully, my gifts tell her I care." Elena frowned. "She lives with her mom most of the time, who's never thought much of me, so we haven't talked since I left last year."

"Sounds like you had a good relationship, though," Jax said.

Elena's eyes softened. "She's a sweet girl." She folded her arms over her chest. "So, you have no idea where she's gone?"

"I have a theory, and that's the reason for my visit." He hesitated, knowing this wouldn't be easy to hear with her history. "We believe Allison's been taken."

Elena rubbed her arms, her face pained.

A wave of the old guilt hit Jax. "But I'm working hard to find her, and I need your help to do it."

"Oh?" she said, chewing on her bottom lip.

"When you and Madeline were abducted, there were a couple of items that were found in connection with your kidnapping that were never released to the public."

She rested her palm on her chest. "Like what?"

"Feathers, for one. The other isn't important other than it was withheld, so we'd have ways of confirming the person's involvement once they were caught."

"Feathers?" she said, her voice tight.

Was she remembering? "What I'm trying to say very poorly is those items, they've been found in connection with Allison's disappearance."

Elena rubbed her arms harder this time. "What does that mean?"

"That Madeline's killer, your abductor, may have Allison."

"My abductor…As in you think he's come back?" The blood drained from her face.

He shifted on the sofa arm. "The evidence and the similarities suggest it's likely."

She dropped her arms to her sides before working her right thumb into her other palm.

Abby had used that calming technique a time or two during some of their early fights without success. "What I'm hoping is that memories from that time have resurfaced. Any indications about where you were taken or places you might have seen at any point during your abduction could prove helpful in finding where Allison is now."

She shook her head, her eyebrows pinched together.

"I'm sorry to stir this up for you, but it's possible if the same man is involved, he's using the same playbook as he did before when he took you and Madeline."

"I wish I remembered, but I don't. And how would he know to have targeted Allison?" she said. "I keep my personal information locked down, one of the reasons I never changed my last name to Daniel's when we married."

"That's a good question." If Wallace was involved in both cases, how had he crossed paths with Elena to target her stepdaughter? "Have you had any odd occurrences lately? Feel like you've been followed? Any unusual phone calls?"

She lifted her palms. "Nothing."

He stood, the sofa arm digging into his leg. "How about through your private practice? You must see a number of clients." Although Allison could have spoken about their relationship at some point and Wallace overheard when she worked on the farm.

"I do, but predominantly female and a couple of younger men."

"When you work with the potential parolees, did you ever sense you'd met or knew any of them before?" As much as he believed he had his man, he couldn't lead her to that.

"Never."

It was worth the try. "No weird interactions?"

She went back to massaging her palm. "Well, sure. But generally, when a prisoner is being released, I've green-lighted it, so they lose the attitude."

"Generally?"

"There are exceptions. I don't always approve, but the board has on occasion done what it wants anyway."

"Anyone recently?"

"No." She'd put a hole in her hand at the rate she was working her thumb into it.

Another dead end. "I see."

Her eye twitched. "Before summer, though, there was one man. Late twenties. Convicted of raping his ex-girlfriend."

Jax's chest tightened. "His name happen to be Rick Johnson?"

Her mouth set in a hard line. "How did you know?"

He shook his head. "Go on."

"Well, he wanted us to believe a friend of his had slipped a mickey into her drink, and she'd come onto him. I'm sorry, but until you can take responsibility, you haven't done enough time. But he wasn't the problem."

Unless Rick had been telling the truth. He'd been consistent anyway. "Who then?"

"His family. They gave me the creeps."

Jax's shoulders inched up. "Remember anything distinct about them?" Don't lead the witness. Let her get there herself.

"One of them was a shorter man with graying dark hair that he wore combed back. I'll never forget his eyes."

Vince Wallace. Jax flinched.

Elena looked at her watch. "I'm sorry. I really have to go." She walked to her office door. "I'm already late."

Their conversation had her on edge, but he had to make sure all his bases were covered. "I know it's been a long time, Elena, but have you remembered anything about the man who took you and your sister? Did that man from the prison, the man with the graying hair, feel familiar?"

She sighed. "No."

"Are you sure nothing's come back on where you were taken? Smells. Sounds. Anything might help?"

She lowered her head. "Only bits and pieces show up, and rarely. More just the feelings, nothing definitive. But I don't know who took me." She swallowed—hard. "And I don't know who's taken Allison."

The isoflurane would have kept Elena under. It had been a long shot that she could help him definitively, but it was enough to connect Wallace. "I appreciate your seeing me."

She opened the door. "Wish I could have been more helpful." She walked into the reception area.

He was about to follow when he scanned her desk. The picture frame she'd been straightening had an odd photo in it. He followed her out. "Who's the camera-shy guy on your desk?"

She turned quickly. "Excuse me?"

"The photo."

She waved him off. "Oh, no one. I mean..." She glanced at her secretary, who was listening. Elena smiled, "Just a client I helped years ago." She looked at her watch again. "I really must go."

Jax handed Elena his business card. "My personal cell is on there. If you think of anything else, please call me."

She took the card and hesitated. Held it in front of her like she had something else to say. He waited. She nodded and turned to her receptionist. "Stacey, I'm not feeling well. I won't be back after my appointment."

"I'll clear your calendar."

"Thank you." She addressed Jax on her way out the door. "I'm sorry."

Jax turned back to Stacey and caught a glimpse of the calendar she'd pulled up on her computer screen. Dr. Kavorian, psych appointment.

He thanked Stacey. By the time he went into the hall, Elena was gone.

He took the stairs to the parking garage. A lump formed in his throat, which it did a lot these days. He didn't relish stirring up the past for her, or for himself. If he'd found her sister in time, Elena wouldn't have been so traumatized. When her face had paled, it was clear she wasn't over what had happened. The fatherly pride he'd felt earlier melted into a wish he could have done better by her.

His only shot at redemption, of making it right with Elena, with himself, was to find Allison. Elena just about confirmed he was on the right path with Wallace. Elena might not have seen the monster who committed such horrors against her and Madeline, but Wallace would have remembered her. When their paths crossed in that hearing room, he must have decided to go after Allison to torment Elena. The question remained: why, after all these years?

In his car, he hit Highway 101 back to Misty Pines. His cellphone rang. He hit speaker.

"Jax, it's Emily. I think you need to get here."

A flash of hope surfaced in him. "Allison?"

"No. Kylie has something to show you. Come now."

Chapter Twenty-Two

Jax heard Emily's high-pitched voice and Kylie's "I'm sorry" as he trotted onto Emily's porch. He rang the bell. When no one answered, he went inside and headed straight for the commotion.

"You had this the whole time?" Emily said, thrusting a puffy winter coat at Kylie.

"I've had it since last spring. I didn't just get it."

Emily had on the same sweats she'd worn yesterday, dark circles under her eyes, her hair disheveled. She hadn't slept, and the stress of Allison's absence had chipped away at her. Jax recognized the signs of losing faith.

He stepped into the kitchen. "Let's calm down, everyone."

"Thank God you're here," Emily said. "Kylie's been holding out on us."

Kylie shrunk into the chair.

Emily chewed her thumbnail. "I called her, like you said. I've been calling everyone. I asked her about the drugs. About the coat. Begging her to tell me everything."

Jax inspected Emily's face and then Kylie, who was shaking.

Emily thrust a piece of white plastic into Jax's hands. "I found this too on the farm's perimeter. Allison's phone is white."

He hadn't brought Emily up to date on the suspected drug trafficking. Now he wished he had. "They could have had you arrested for trespassing." Or worse.

"He, I mean, they wouldn't."

Jax turned the shard of plastic over in his hand. No identifying marks. No serial numbers. It could be part of a PVC pipe. Jax hesitated to steal any hope that Emily clung to, but he wouldn't lie to her either. Even if it had been legitimate evidence, her removing it made it inadmissible. "I get you want answers, but half the workers on that farm could have had a white phone at one time or another. That's if this is even part of a phone."

"But..."

He placed a calming hand on her shoulder. "It doesn't prove anything." He wanted to find evidence of Allison as much as she did. This just wasn't it.

The lines of Emily's face deepened as she tried to gain control. But grief and worry were like sand, finding the cracks. Oozing to the floor in a pile, growing, building, until they buried you alive.

"Well, Kylie has more to tell you. Don't you, Kylie?" Emily dropped into the dining room chair across from the young girl.

Kylie held out her phone to him. Allison's Snapchat account lit up the screen. He took the phone and scanned the image before setting it in front of her, working to control his anger. "Why didn't you tell me you had access to Allison's account from the beginning?"

Kylie cupped her face in her hands. She'd been crying, but she sniffed, wiping the tears that had pooled under her eyes. "I should have. But I thought Allison was messing around because our relationship has been intense lately. When she didn't show up at school, I ratted to her mom to get her in trouble. At first."

"But you told me you two had plans, and there'd be no way she wouldn't show without calling," Jax said.

Kylie nodded. "It's not a lie. She would've called me. If things were...you know...normal...."

Jax wrestled with the urge to get in her face and tell her exactly what he thought of her messing with his investigation. "What's not normal?"

She shook her head. "I have to live in this town and go to school with these kids, you know. It's already bad enough for me...."

What wasn't she saying? Something didn't add up. Emily had her jumpy. He opened his mouth to suggest they take a walk, but Emily cut in.

"I don't understand how you have her Snapchat on your phone?" Emily said, her leg bouncing like a piston. "Someone please explain this to me."

Kylie's face twisted, and she looked away. "Spyware."

"You have spyware on Allison's phone?" Jax said.

Kylie nodded.

"Did Allison know about that?" Emily asked.

"No. It's not actually on her phone. It's in the cloud. I went in through a website."

"But why?" Emily asked.

Kylie sat silent.

Jax thought back to their conversation in the bookstore. "Because you were afraid she was leaving?"

Kylie wrapped her arms around herself. "No."

Jax didn't have time for bullshit, even from Kylie. "Start talking. Your friend is missing. Tell me what you know."

The dam broke; tears cascaded down Kylie's face. "Ever since summer, Allison changed. First, there was Dylan, then talk about leaving for Portland. Wanting to try out for cheerleading. Wanting to get asked to prom." Her chin dropped to her chest. "She was all over the place. I couldn't keep up."

Emily's posture relaxed, and she reached for her daughter's best friend. "Honey. Allison adores you. You're both growing up. Things will change, but that doesn't mean...."

"Yes, it does," Kylie snapped. "She started spending time with other people and then lied about it. Told me she was here at home or that she didn't like someone. But with the app, I could see the truth."

Jax set the phone on the table. "Obviously, she cares about you. You were going to Homecoming together."

She snorted. "Only to rub it in Dylan's face."

"Allison wanted back with him?" Jax asked, sensing something in Kylie's tone, and in her face. She was jealous of Allison having other friends.

Her lip curled. "Apparently. Which I don't get."

"Were they doing drugs together?" Despite Emily's contrary belief, the heroin found in Allison's bedroom suggested she could be doing them with someone.

Kylie didn't answer.

Emily's shoulder slumped. "Kylie, we found a pipe."

Kylie shook her head. "I already told you, Mrs. Krueger, she never did drugs. But..." Kylie swooped the phone off the table and punched a few icons before turning the screen so Jax could see it.

He'd read about screen capture being a downside on that platform. Kids thought they could get away with anything because content quickly disappeared. All well and good, until someone decided to save the shot. Lucky for them—unlucky for Dylan—Allison had done just that.

Kylie pointed to the scroll button, and Jax skimmed through a series of saved pictures. In some, Dylan posed bare-chested, laughing. Blowing Allison a kiss. Then Dylan smoking a glass pipe filled the small screen. Heat crept up Jax's neck.

Jax swiped through a few more posing images before landing on one with Dylan snarling and punching a fist into the palm of his hand. The written message was "Give it back." Allison hadn't saved her response. The next image left no doubt what it had been. "Give it back, bitch, or you'll pay big time."

Emily reached her hand out, and Jax gave her the phone. Her face dropped while she went through the same images. "You know what this means?" she said.

Kylie ran her fingers through her bangs. "Yeah, Dylan's a prick."

Emily nodded. "The drugs weren't hers, Sheriff. She was holding them for Dylan." Emily straightened in her chair.

The pictures didn't prove that the heroin hadn't been done together, but pointing that out didn't seem relevant. "Did Dylan know that Allison had saved these pictures?" Jax said.

"When someone does a screenshot, the person sending the message gets a notification. That's why I think if anyone did anything to my friend, it's Dylan. Or that stupid guy that runs the farm."

The hairs on Jax's neck stood to attention. "Vince Wallace?"

"Yeah. Where do you think Dylan gets the drugs he sells?"

"Dylan's dealing?" Dylan's fancy belt had stuck out to him at the time before he'd dismissed it. The Air Jordans. The leather watch he wore while shoveling stalls. He grimaced. He should have caught on when he said he had to pay his own way because Daddy wouldn't.

She nodded. "But don't tell him I told you that."

"Why didn't you tell me?"

"Because that guy at the farm scares me. He always looks angry. And at first, I'd thought Allison, you know—" Her face crumpled.

When Jax looked up, Emily had turned ghostly white. She was shaking and crumbling in front of him.

"It's okay, Emily. We're going to bring Allison home."

"But Vince is involved?"

"Vince Wallace, yes. That's who we had in custody—who I believe has Allison."

She shook her head. "I called him right away."

Jax frowned. "What are you talking about?"

"Before I even called the station. He's the one that said she might be kidnapped. But I didn't believe that. You know. I said Allison's just mad because she found out about us. She was being a brat, and that's part of why she wanted to leave."

The information punched his gut. "What are you saying?"

"She stole his Copenhagen. It was on the end table, and then it wasn't. I know she took it. But he said he'd look for her. That he'd do anything to help find her."

"Why the hell am I only learning about this now?" Jax spit the words out.

"Because he wouldn't do anything to my baby. And I didn't want to bring that on him. You'd said you were interviewing farmhands. I thought he was helping you." She was hyperventilating.

"When did your affair start?"

She held her breath. Let it out slow. "We met when I went to check out the farm during the summer. He asked me out. I'd been lonely. You know, and he's nice. Really nice. A good listener. We didn't mean for it to happen. He's married. I own a business. I didn't say anything because he wouldn't...."

Jax's jaw hurt from grinding his teeth. "He might very well have, Emily.

My God." Everyone had held back on him.

Before that bombshell, he'd toyed with believing that Allison might be doing drugs with her on-again ,off-again boyfriend. She might have refused to return them because she planned to turn Dylan in.

If Abby was right and Wallace was running the show, Dylan could have gone to him, concerned that Allison would blow their operation sky high, which would mean Wallace needed to take her out.

A shudder ran through Jax. What if it was far more sinister? What if it connected back to what he'd started to believe about the old case?

Wallace could have targeted Emily to get to Allison from the start. After Rick's hearing, when Elena blocked Rick's request for parole, he would have been upset. She was "the one that got away," and here she was, messing with his life again.

A few local inquiries might garner him the information about Elena and the fact Allison was her stepdaughter. There was his way to get back at the girl who'd frustrated him so much, back in the day. He would have proceeded to get close to Emily, keeping his sights on Allison until the right moment. The opportunity of a sullen young girl standing on the edge of the road must have been like honey to a bee.

Jax's cell phone rang. Trudy. He marched out of the kitchen before answering. "Need you to find Dylan Marks," he said. "Garrett and Matt are still out at Osbourn Park. Let's take Brody off surveillance. I'll take his place until—"

"Jax," she interrupted. "Judge Rulli's chambers just called. You'll have your warrant within the hour."

The information settled over him. He'd told Abby he'd stand down, but how could he now? There were too many connections to Wallace, the old case, and the farm to ignore. Now Dylan and the drugs. It was all coming together.

He didn't know how the puzzle pieces would fall, but he at least had more to work with. If it led to Allison, there was no other choice. "Rally the team and have them meet me at Emily's place. Tell Brody to join us after he's secured Dylan. We're going in."

"Will do. What about Abby?"

He hung up without answering and strode to the kitchen, where Emily had a protective arm around Kylie.

He returned to the porch and paced, waiting for his team.

He had his man.

Abby would kill him for going up against her. He'd cross that bridge later. Even if the bridge sank under his feet and drowned him. He didn't care. Finding Allison was all that mattered.

Chapter Twenty-Three

The Portway Tavern wasn't busy this time of day. The neon guitars and various beer signs behind the bar barely made a difference in the dingy darkness. The corner booth had been the right choice.

Elena had swung in after leaving Dr. Kavorian's office. She'd had every intention of continuing the search for Steven, but her shoulders ached with an intensity that set her back on fire. The migraine that she'd barely managed to keep under control, now made her head feel like an overripe cantaloupe ready to split. Their session had done the opposite of what she'd hoped.

It had started with her settling into her usual spot, a crushed velvet chaise. Elena rested her body into the curve, closing her eyes.

"You seem shaken," Dr. Kavorian had said. Her friend and colleague, her mentor, had pulled up a straight-backed chair close and sat with one leg crossed over the other, his notebook open and pen at the ready. His gray hair had begun to thin on top, revealing his shiny dome. Wired spectacles framed his pale green eyes. He'd be retiring soon. What would she do then?

"It's been a day."

"Has something happened?"

She'd resisted telling him about Allison's disappearance and Sheriff Turner coming to see her. Starting one conversation would only encourage more of the same. But her friend might also be able to help her figure out how to find Steven since he knew them both so well. "It's my brother."

He'd scribbled a few notes. "He's back?"

She nodded. "Unfortunately."

"It's been a while. Why do you think he's reached out this time?"

"I'm not sure yet." There was some relief in telling that truth.

"Last time, you'd thought you'd been clear about him not dragging you into his world. How do you feel about him contacting you again?"

She'd stared at her hands. "Is it wrong to say that life is easier when he lives his and I live mine?"

Dr. Kavorian had given her a small smile. "Under the circumstances of the illness, it's completely normal. The key is setting boundaries and holding them."

She sighed. As a trained professional, she couldn't agree more. To have that information reflected by someone she trusted eased the guilt that held her. "It is normal, and yes, I know." But guilt and obligation were strong motivators.

"Are you still having a hard time creating those boundaries with him?"

Her friend wouldn't judge, but if he suspected a crime had been committed, their conversation would change. Although had a crime been committed? Sheriff Turner had an entirely different scenario he'd presented. Was she wrong in thinking Steven was involved at all?

She'd rest easier when she found her brother and could confirm that one way or another. "It's more that I'm trying to find him at this point."

He took more notes. "How so?"

Her mind had raced for details she could share that wouldn't put her friend on guard. "Not returning my calls isn't like him. He's not at his apartment. It's like he doesn't want to be found this time. What I don't get is why call in the first place?" Except the call had led her to his apartment. The bracelet on the end table led her to search for him. The cross on his table led her to the cemetery. Had Steven sent her on a scavenger hunt, forcing her to wait for another clue?

His face tightened. "So, you've been looking for him elsewhere?" Dr. Kavorian said.

"Yes. I went to our old foster home and ended up at Madeline's grave."

"That must have been hard to do, especially alone."

"I was so focused on finding Steven, I didn't think about it." Not remembering that she made the drive wasn't important. The fact was she did make it. There'd been a time when she couldn't even drive by the cemetery.

"Had he been there?"

"Yes. He'd left chocolate roses on the graves. It's the anniversary of Maddy's murder, you know." She rubbed the back of her head.

"I remembered." He tapped his pencil on the notebook. "Your headaches have returned, haven't they?"

She nodded. "Just stress."

He set the book down and got up, crossing to his desk. "Have you been taking your medication?"

"Whenever I need to."

She glanced at his notes. He'd circled Steven's name several times, creating a dark thick line. The words schizophrenic episode? next to his name.

"You think Steven is having an episode?" she asked. He could be right. His confusion could be causing the spiral. It made sense. It had happened before.

"It's a distinct possibility." He returned with a prescription and handed it to her. "This one's stronger than what you've been taking, but it should help if you take it every day."

"Will it make Steven disappear?" She chuckled, then felt horrible for suggesting it. What she needed desperately was for him to reappear.

"Only you can get him to do that. Perhaps if you could let me speak with him directly...."

"I've tried."

He nodded with understanding.

But he was right. Her psych training had taught her she'd have to deal with Steven at some point. Whether his illness controlled him or not, his actions meant that moment was now. Because the sheriff's theory about their abductor and Madeline's killer being back might not be accurate at all.

Steven knew about the feathers. She'd shared the details of the case in conversations with him after she'd found a way to gain access to her file a few years ago. Had she thought Steven would do something with that information, she wouldn't have shared it. His planting similar evidence was disconcerting. It had to mean something—unless he was playing some sick game with all of them. Her mind had raced, covering the same thoughts, desperate to find a new interpretation.

She should have come clean with the sheriff about Allison's bracelet and her concerns when she had the chance. The longer she waited, the worst it would be if Steven did, in fact, have her stepdaughter. She'd give herself until morning to find him, and if she failed, she'd go directly to Sheriff Turner, tell him everything, and let him sort it out with her.

"Elena." Dr. Kavorian's hand touched her arm. "Are you okay?"

She'd swung her legs off the chaise, meeting her friend's concerned gaze. A sudden desire to tell him about her suspicions clutched her. But she owed Steven for being there for her when she needed him in the past. Even if Steven did have Allison, he wouldn't hurt her. There had to be something else in play.

Her stomach ached. But meaning to or not, accidents happened. The longer Allison wasn't home, the greater the chance of things screaming further out of control. She had to know whether he had Allison. If he did, she had to bring her home. "Another migraine's coming on."

He sighed. "Fill that prescription."

She'd agreed but driven past the pharmacy. Now she sat in the corner booth of the dark tavern, nursing a martini. She soaked in the mundaneness of a man in his forties playing pool by himself across from the bar, and the bartender going in and out a back door, restocking.

Eyes closed, she sipped her drink, chewing the olives slowly. The gin soothed the tension behind her eyes and in her shoulders. The migraine had begun to ease. For a few precious moments, she forgot about Steven. About Allison. About losing Madeline.

She nearly groaned out loud. What was she doing? She'd never forget about Allison, the little girl she'd held on her lap to read stories to, braided her hair when she came to spend every other weekend with her and Daniel, giving Roper a bath in the sink and blow drying him until he was nothing but a ball of fluff. Losing Allison would be losing Madeline all over again.

Her eyes flew open, and she started. The man playing pool had slid across the table from her. His crooked teeth had a yellowish tinge, and splotchy stubble accented his sharp jawline. She frowned.

"What're you drinking, good looking?" the man said, finishing the beer he'd brought over with him.

She held tight to the stem of her glass. "Do men really use lines like that anymore?"

He laughed. "They do when the lady's hot, and he wants to buy her another round."

Smooth. "I'm on my way out."

His eyes drooped like a puppy's. "Why in such a hurry? You've been savoring that drink for a while now. Why not savor one with me?"

It hadn't been that long. Had it? "I need to get back to work."

"Must be a stressful job. I could help you with that in another way." He arched an eyebrow and let the implication hang in the air.

"Is this your idea of small talk?"

"Just asking." His face cracked into a grin, and he winked.

Classic narcissism. He undoubtedly had a glass ego. Rejecting his flirts could make him recoil. Or lash out. It all depended on his tendencies, background, what he'd gotten away with, how petulant and spoiled his parents let him be growing up. Those thoughts ran through her head while she took the last olive in her mouth. "I assure you that you'd be no help with any of it." She grabbed her purse and stood.

He reached out and gripped her wrist like a vice.

Her pulse quickened. She glared into his eyes. "Excuse me."

He released her. Smiled again. "Stay a while."

She tucked her purse under her arm. "Not with you."

She walked out of the bar and headed to her car. The walkway blurred in front of her. She'd only had one drink, but her legs felt unsteady.

The man from the bar had followed and had his hands under her armpit, on top of her shoulder. "You really shouldn't be driving."

"Let me go." He did. She kept walking, but he stayed behind her, close enough she could smell the beer on his breath.

"What did you mean, not with me?" he asked.

She spun around. It was late afternoon. She'd been inside there too long and needed to get away from this idiot. "I meant I had to go. I'm married, okay?"

He tilted his head. "I am too. It'll be our little secret." He grabbed her by the arm and reached for the keys in her hand.

Her eyes darted, searching for someone to help her. No one was in the lot. She'd parked near the back, but the backdoor was now closed into the bar. Why had she chosen a hidden spot? To be out of the eye of any clients who passed by, of course.

"Stop." She gripped her keys.

He leaned into her neck, kissed her. Bit her on the ear. The smell of hops and aftershave mingled in her nose. Something else. Onions. Grease. Her stomach revolted. She gagged. He smelled like the mister.

She flailed abruptly, pushing him back, but she felt off. Unstable. She hit the unlock button on her key fob. He came at her again, both hands on her shoulders, pulling her to him. Twisting, she had the door ajar. His hand slammed it closed.

He grabbed her again, this time pushing into her with his groin. Panicked, she gained enough distance to mule kick, her heel connecting with his knee.

He yelped and released his hold.

She clutched the door, swung it open, and scrambled in, locking it behind her. Her hands shook as she hit the start button and jerked the gear into reverse. Her head swam watching the man, bent at the waist, cradling his knee.

He spit at her car. "You bitch."

She didn't meet his eyes as she swerved back and then forward out of the parking lot, accelerating until she reached the main road.

This was Steven's fault. If it wasn't for him, she wouldn't be making stupid decisions like stopping at bars. She tapped the wheel with the heel of her hand. No, she had to take responsibility. It would be the first thing she told a client. She'd also tell them to take control of the situation. In this case, Steven's ridiculousness of not answering had to stop.

She hit speaker on the phone and dialed him. When the beep finished, she gripped the phone tight. "Steven Massey, you call me back, damn it. I can't keep this up. I just left a bar. A man...." Her stomach squeezed. Her chest caved in on her heart. "Never mind. Where are you?"

She started to cry. "Please. I'm...." She needed him to respond. "I almost got raped tonight. Some greasy man at the Portway nearly got my keys, and...." She gulped down a sob. She felt woozy. Sick. "Please, Steven, call me back. I need you."

Chapter Twenty-Four

Emily and Kylie remained inside, while Jax paced the porch. Ten minutes earlier, Trudy had sent him confirmation the team was on their way, search warrant in hand. The sight of two of his deputies cruising up the road, a dust trail behind them, sent adrenaline racing through him.

He had expected his crew to be in one vehicle. Garrett driving and Matt shotgun. Brody would have been in the backseat if he wasn't sent to find Dylan, and that's exactly how they were. He hadn't expected the following vehicle, however. An official Misty Pine Sheriff's patrol car.

His Deputy, Chris Chapman, had returned from Alaska.

A wide grin covered Jax's face. He couldn't remember the last time he'd had a reason to smile. His boys had done what he'd asked despite their lack of experience, even stepped up a bit, but there was nothing like having your right arm reattached.

The three men exited their vehicles at the same time and headed in Jax's direction.

Chapman held up his hand to the young deputies, and they hung back at the car. Chapman approached Jax alone, dressed in black cargo pants, long-sleeve T-shirt, and a bulletproof vest with his badge pinned to it. "Afternoon, Sheriff. How you been?"

As happy as he was, he hesitated. "Welcome back. I think. Fishing no good?"

Chapman smiled, revealing a slight gap between his front teeth. He had brown wavy hair, with bangs swooped to the side. His leathery skin reflected hours spent on a boat every waking off-duty hour. "The opposite. Fish nearly jumped onto the deck, begging to be caught."

"Limited out, huh?"

"Yeah. Kind of defeats the purpose of the great hunt. Besides, I missed you."

Jax's lip curled. "Now I know you're full of shit."

Chapman shrugged. "What's not to love about you, Sheriff?" He chuckled. "Anyway, thought I'd get back. Didn't want to miss the excitement. Guess there's been more than usual?"

Jax studied the forty-five-year-old deputy. He was a hard worker. Gave one hundred ten percent to the job. It helped that he'd never married. He always joked that *he hadn't found that rare woman who wanted to skin a deer, gut a fish, and spend a shower-less week in a tent.*

It was good Chapman had returned, given how much pressure they were under. But he couldn't have known about the case unless someone told him. "Trudy called you, didn't she?"

Chapman stretched his neck. "What gives you that impression?"

"Haven't seen you run out on a fishing trip since I've known you, limit or no limit."

He tucked his thumbs in his belt loops. "Thought you might appreciate someone by your side."

Whether he'd not been sleeping, or eating well, or off his game, Trudy didn't have a right to mother him. Unless she really believed he couldn't handle it on his own. He had wished Chapman back more than once and to even answer the original call. But now, he wasn't turning it over to anyone.

"Glad to have you for backup."

He nodded. "What do you got?"

"Wallace's hiding something. According to intel I've received, might be drugs. But I believe we'll either find Allison Krueger or evidence of where he's taken her. To this point, I've only had enough access to see the front of the property and one of the barns." Jax went on to lay out Wallace's many lies and obstructions. He hadn't allowed a search of the farm. He hid Allison's backpack in his car, hired a pedophile, was having an affair with the missing girl's mother.

Jax scrubbed his face. There was a mountain of evidence to cover and only a hillock of time to relay everything churning around in his head. "Long story short, I also believe he's involved in a cold case: missing girls, abduction, murder. There's physical evidence tying the two cases together."

Chapman's mouth was set in a hard line. His eye twitched. He clearly didn't think much of Wallace either.

"We need to get in there and do a search of every last inch of that farm." He could expand more on his theories, but it had already taken far too long to get this warrant. If their search panned out, they'd be sharing every detail over a celebratory beer after returning Allison to her mother.

Chapman stood at ease, his legs wide, arms crossed over his chest. "Sounds solid to me. Any other agencies in on the drug angle?"

Having a colleague was a nice change. It also meant he knew proper procedures. Telling Chapman about Abby's express wishes to stay off the property would only muddy the water. Better that Jax died on that hill alone.

"FBI. But they don't need to be involved unless we find those drugs."

He nodded. "Less complicated if we don't have to coordinate."

They agreed on that. "Let's prep the boys."

Brody had joined the team and confirmed Dylan was in custody. Together Jax and Chapman brought the three deputies up to speed. They strapped into their bulletproof vests.

"I'll serve the warrant," Jax said. "We need to be prepared for escalation. The presence of drugs often means weapons. So, heads up, and guns unholstered."

The three nodded in agreement. Garrett was stone-faced and ready to go. Brody nearly vibrated with excitement, and Matt worked his hands—twitchy again. Too many firsts for his young team.

Jax looked into their focused eyes and young faces. "Let's get Allison."

* * *

Wallace rushed out of his office to meet them, his face the color of blood. "What the fuck are you doing back here?"

Jax took long strides in his direction. "Good day, Mr. Wallace." He handed him the paper. "Here's the warrant you insisted I'd need."

Brown spittle from Wallace's ever-present chew had formed in the corner of his mouth. "Are you joking?"

Jax's eyes narrowed. "Deputy Chapman, am I smiling right now?"

"No, sir. You are not."

"Then I don't believe that I am, Mr. Wallace."

Wallace spit a wad of tobacco on the ground and scanned the document. "What's the basis of the warrant?"

"Probable cause that Allison Krueger is here."

Wallace growled. "She's not. I told you that."

"Just like you told me you were having an affair with Emily to get to her daughter?"

The blood drained from his face.

Jax yanked his handcuffs out of his back pocket. "Turn around."

"You have no basis to arrest me," Wallace said, but his bravado had slipped.

"I only want to know where you're at while we're executing the warrant."

Wallace hesitated but complied. "This is crazy. I like Emily, and Allison was a pain in the ass. But I didn't do anything to her girl."

"Secure him in Chapman's cruiser," Jax ordered Matt.

When he returned, his deputies descended in pairs on the farm in a systematic sweep. Jax went it alone. With a hundred acres, twenty outbuildings, and night falling in a few hours, they had to work fast and hope for the best outcome.

If Wallace was Madeline's killer, what were the chances Allison would be found unharmed? Could he have kept her alive to avoid the death penalty? Was that realistic if his purpose was to screw with Elena?

Panic rising in his chest, Jax entered the horse barn where he'd found Dylan working yesterday.

How long had Wallace been planning Allison's abduction? And had she sensed it? Kids were like dogs in that they had instincts about who was good and who was bad. Emily said Allison was furious when she'd found out about them. He'd seen the coat hanging off the chair in Emily's house himself. They hadn't been that stealthy about their affair.

Jax drilled down on his focus and checked the back stall where he hadn't had a good look before. If Allison had been there, Dylan had cleaned out any signs.

The grain silo and the fodder barn where hay and alfalfa bales were stacked to the ceiling revealed nothing either. Another building was used for birthing the animals. Probably where Wallace had performed the surgery on the alpaca. No brown bottles of isoflurane or Allison were present.

In the chicken coop, his thoughts returned to the blue, green, and purple feather fragments found in Allison's backpack. But the feathers intermixed with the sweet smell of straw on the floor were brown and white—nothing remotely like what he'd seen in the past or present case.

His shoulders crept up under his ears with every step. No Allison. And no signs of the drugs that Abby had been so sure were here. Were they both wrong?

An hour later, Jax's radio crackled to life. "Sheriff. It's Chapman. Need you to get to our location." He was with Brody. They'd been sent out to the farthest ends of the property.

Jax got their exact whereabouts. "On my way."

When he entered the agricultural barn, three men, day laborers, sat cross-legged on the ground, hands laced on top of their heads. A small woman, black hair shrouding her shoulders, stood arguing with Chapman. His deputy's hand rested on his holstered, but unstrapped, gun. Brody stood focused on the men sitting around her, his hand also on his weapon.

"What seems to be the problem?" Jax said to Chapman.

"The building was clean. However, this lady doesn't want me to get on the back of that truck," Chapman said.

"We're not doing anything," the woman said, her eyes wide. She spoke perfect English. "We just sanitized it for produce, and you'll create more work and put us behind. We need to get a shipment out tonight."

Jax scanned the pallets of apples and cherries that were binned and ready for loading.

Chapman shook his head. "We have a warrant to search the farm, ma'am. Your time schedule is irrelevant."

Perspiration beaded her upper lip. "You already searched this building." She turned to the men sitting and said something in Spanish.

Jax cleared his throat to get her attention, wishing he knew the language better. All he could decipher was that it was going to be okay. "Excuse me, who are you?" he asked.

"Angelique. I'm a supervisor here."

Abby's informant seemed more nervous than he would have expected, especially if Abby had asked her to keep an eye out for Allison. "Well, Angelique, I'm Sheriff Turner. Like my deputy said, we have a warrant. You don't have a choice but to comply or be arrested."

"Arrested?" Her voice squeaked.

She had to have been informed that by working with the FBI, she'd be protected in the event of any raids. "Your choice," Jax said.

Angelique's hands fisted, her face on fire, but she didn't answer.

Her fear response was visceral. Something wasn't right. Jax strode to the box truck and rolled open the back door. The trailer looked to be eight by twenty-four feet.

He inspected the empty space. No produce or ag products inside. Not even an empty pallet. It was clean but didn't seem reason enough to have Angelique so nervous.

Using the handhold, he swung himself up and into the panel-lined trailer. It smelled of apples. He walked to the end, counting. Twenty steps. His brow furrowed as he turned around and faced the rollup door. He paced the space again. Turned, and did it one more time, coming to the paneled wall. Still twenty steps.

He took the baton out of its sheath and tapped the solid wall. A hollow thud came back at him. Too hollow. He had a hunch.

At the back of the truck, he hopped down, ignoring Angelique's panicked gaze.

Chapman's eyes were pinched together. "You got something?"

Jax didn't respond, instead crouching under the truck. He skimmed his flashlight beam along the undercarriage. A sliding door caught his attention. It must access the area created by the false wall above. Ingenious. If authorities stopped the truck, no one would be the wiser that the space existed. An eight-by-four could hold a lot of merchandise. His muscles became taut. It could hold more than drugs.

Jax lifted his gun from its holster. "Brody, watch them. Chapman, back me up."

Chapman came to the edge of the undercarriage, gun drawn.

Jax made his way to the other side of the trap door. He met Chapman's eyes and pointed up.

Chapman nodded.

Jax positioned himself to the side of the opening, gripping the metal handle, praying Allison was in there and alive. In one motion, he yanked the handle back in his direction. Nothing. Not even bales of heroin which he'd suspected might also drop out. The sound of feet on the floor made him jump back. A torrent of Spanish flooded out. Fear. Alarm.

He kept his gun focused on the hole. "Come out, with your hands up," he ordered. "Despacio. Slowly. Now. Ahora."

The scurrying stopped. "No dispares. No dispares. Por favor."

"I won't shoot. Salir. Come out. Ahora."

A man's shoe came into view, followed by another, and then both legs. A young man, wearing a sheepskin-lined jean jacket, dropped onto all fours.

"This way," Chapman ordered the two men to his side of the truck.

An old man with tufts of gray hair standing on end emerged next. Followed by another middle-aged man. And another. In total, six men came through and stood with their hands interlocked behind their heads. All drawn and emaciated. They needed a shower and food.

Matt and Garrett had shown up. They guarded the three men on the ground and Angelique, who looked like she might crawl out of her own skin.

Jax swept the space with light, confirming it was empty. "Habla usted inglés?" he asked when he was done.

They all shook their head no.

"I got this one, Chief," Garrett said and translated questions. Why were they there? Who brought them there? Were they being paid? Had they paid to be there?

No one said a word at first, and then, without warning, the floodgates opened. They were undocumented and being transported back and forth across the border. They had to pay half their salary to the farm for the privilege to work there and to keep coming back. Jax was surprised by their candor. The oldest guy was the most willing to talk.

Jax directed Garrett to ask more targeted questions. The answers, always more words in Spanish than in English, boiled down to two points: they did bring in heroin, but only a small amount for the boss man who kept it in his office. No one had seen a young girl matching Allison's description on the property.

As they spoke, Jax's desire to rip Wallace apart grew stronger. The makeshift room they'd crawled out of smelled like a mixture of desperation and human waste. He met Angelique's glare with one of his own and motioned to Chapman. "Get them out of here and call the Feds."

"Will do," Chapman said. The undocumented would be going home, but at least they wouldn't be stuffed like sardines in a stinking hole on the ride there. He wished he could find some satisfaction in all of this, but he hadn't found Allison.

Jax, Chapman, and the deputies led the men and Angelique out of the ag building and were met with the wail of sirens coming up the farm road. The hum of a far-off engine getting closer came from overhead. The sound of blades cut through the air.

A chopper.

He'd wondered how long it would take for Abby to hear that he'd ignored her wishes. At least their arrival saved him the call. Time to cross that unforgiving bridge.

Chapter Twenty-Five

The flare of Abby's nostrils as she approached reminded Jax of a raging bull. He crossed his arms over his chest, steeling himself for what was coming.

She stormed to within inches of his face, her small hands at her side, wearing her gray pantsuit from earlier. The color matched the shadows circling her eyes. "I should have you arrested for this."

"I had new information which left me no choice. That aside, I may have done you a favor."

"Are you serious right now?" She looked past Jax and to the line of men that his deputies had secured next to their cars. "Where's Angelique?"

"In custody. Along with Wallace."

"You're not arresting her." It wasn't a question.

"No, but you might. She played you." FBI had descended on the scene. The immigration angle made it federal all the way. They could have it. He only wanted Wallace.

Her cheeks flushed. "What are you talking about?"

"My boys and I combed this place. There are no signs of a big operation like Angelique had you believing. According to the men we found, they bring a small stash of heroin for Wallace, who I'm assuming has Dylan peddling it in the high school."

Abby's face twitched. "I've been working this case for two solid months, and you've been here for two hours and got all that?"

Abby had always been street-smart and headstrong. How had she been taken in? "I did. How'd you find her anyway?"

"A disgruntled employee gave us the initial lead. We targeted Angelique as our informant based on her time and position here at the farm."

"My guess is she fed you just enough about the drugs to keep you at bay until they could get this batch of undocumented off the property. Granted, just my opinion."

"Exactly. You don't know for sure."

"No, but did Angelique notify you they'd been moving people in and out of the country?"

Abby's jaw tensed. "No."

"Then go see for yourself." He described their conditions and gave her a description of the barn at the end of the property. "They were slave labor. Any decent human being would have told you that, let alone an informant."

She turned and directed half her team to check, and the other half to step in and take custody of the lineup.

Jax motioned his deputies to step aside.

"You're still a son of a bitch."

He strode over to his cruiser and motioned her in before climbing in himself. He wasn't going to let her berate him further in front of his men, and they had a few minutes while her team went into action.

Abby hesitated before opening the door and dropping into the seat next to him. She kept glancing at her phone, no doubt awaiting word from her team lead. "I'm sorry you didn't find Allison," she finally said.

Jax's head pounded from the adrenaline. "I am too. I thought she'd be coming out of that truck compartment and that I'd be escorting her home about now."

Abby nodded, but her fidgeting said she was rehashing her own mess. She started to pick at the leather on the arm of the door. "I should have known something was off when I wanted to move a couple of times, and Angelique kept pushing me off."

Jax shrugged. "Being duped has happened to all of us. At least now that you know, you can proceed as necessary." The walls felt less solid between them. They hadn't shown each other their vulnerable sides in so long.

God, he'd missed Abby. She and Lulu had made him whole. Then there was only Abby. Why had he ever let her believe she wasn't enough?

"Higher-ups won't be thrilled."

"Screw 'em. These people were being taken advantage of in the worst possible ways. You'll be a hero."

She gave him a faint smile. "I believed Angelique. She'd brought me a few packets of heroin, and I bought it, hook, line, and sinker, as they say. After all, the heroin habit in this county is bad enough that the drugs have to be coming from somewhere...." She scraped off dirt from the glove compartment with her fingernail. The latch popped open.

Jax reached to keep it closed a second too late. The small wooden chair for Lulu's dollhouse tumbled out, along with the notes he'd written to her and Jameson.

Abby plucked them from the floorboard.

He grabbed for the envelopes.

She pulled them away, inspecting the names on them, and set the chair on the dashboard. "Apologies, I hope?"

Jax held out his hand, palm up, his heart crashing in his chest. "Give them back."

She splayed them and fanned herself. "I want to read mine."

"No, you don't."

She frowned. "It's the least you can let me do since you've essentially burned my case to the ground."

"If you'd come in for the bust and found nothing, it would be worse. At least you have something to show for your efforts." Something he didn't have.

The thought made him shift in his seat, as did the idea of her reading her letter. She'd never look at him the same. There'd only be pity.

She softened. "I'll give you that."

Her words melted him, the old hurt lessening. "Please give me the letters, Abby."

She ripped hers open.

He swallowed but kept his voice even. "Give me the damn letters."

She appraised his face before handing them to him. "Tell me what it says."

He clutched them, his mouth dry. "They say—"

Chapman slapped the hood of the patrol car, startling them.

Jax punched the window down control, relieved at the interruption. "What's up?"

"Hey, Abby." Chapman tipped his fingers in a salute. "Good to see you. How ya doing?"

Abby gave him a half smile. "Good, Chris. Good to see you again."

Chapman nodded. "Hey, boss, I'm sending the deputies out since FBI has the scene. What are we doing with Wallace?"

"Wallace is with us. We didn't find Allison, so no one goes home. I want you all back at the station, on the phones, monitoring, and we have him and Dylan to squeeze."

"I can't let you take Wallace, Jax," Abby said, her hand on his arm.

He absorbed the warmth of her touch, steadying himself. Keeping Wallace close so he could question him without jumping through hoops would be ideal. But this had become her circus. If Wallace remained in jail, he could live with that.

"Wallace stays. The rest stands," he said to Chapman.

"Yes, sir."

Refocused, he turned to Abby. "I need to push him on Allison, though, one more time."

"Then he's mine," she said.

He nodded and reached over Abby, placing the chair back in the glove compartment and stuffing the envelopes inside his vest before getting out of the car. Next chance he got, he'd toss them in a roaring fire.

If he ever ended back on that beach again, he'd be rewriting them anyway. Some things had changed. He eyed the patrol car with Wallace. Some things hadn't.

* * *

Chapman had transferred Wallace into a federal rig. Jax opened the backdoor, resting his foot on the inside step. He set his forearm on his knee and bent down. "Now's the time to come clean about Allison."

Wallace threw Jax a sardonic look. "I told you she wasn't here."

Jax frowned. "Yeah, but you know what we did find. You and your nephew will be making the penitentiary a family affair, after all."

Wallace's face dropped. "I had no idea what Angelique was doing. You've got nothing on me."

"Nothing but the kilo of heroin under your desk. Know anything about that?"

"Not mine."

Jax shrugged. "Guess you have nothing to worry about when we dust it for prints."

Wallace turned his head away.

"I might be able to help you if you'd help me," Jax said. He eyed Wallace, who continued to ignore him. "I mean, I can't guarantee it, but I have some pull with the agent in charge. She's pretty upset about the conditions of those men you were transporting, but your willingness to exchange information could soften her—like telling me where you have Allison."

Wallace's jaw was bunched.

Frustrated, Jax clenched his teeth. "Have it your way. I'll find Allison. When I do, I'll nail you for taking her. Then I'll nail you for the murder of Madeline Massey."

Wallace's head whipped around. "What are you talking about?"

"Your games are over. I know who you are."

"You know nothing about me. I demand you tell me what you're accusing me of now."

Jax stepped out of the vehicle and straightened. "The murder and abduction of two young girls in Portland twenty-five years ago. That's what."

"I was nowhere near Portland then. And I certainly didn't murder anyone."

"I've read your file. You lived in Oregon."

"I maintained a PO Box for a few years here, but my mother was dying from cancer in Florida." He leaned forward abruptly, the seat belt restraining him. "So don't put that on me. I lived there for five years and took care of my mom. I didn't expect to stay that long, but she went into remission for a while and then relapsed. You can check all that out. I was her main caretaker and had a good relationship with her doctors. It's also where I met my wife."

Jax pressed the palm against his forehead before running it over his head. Was the file wrong, or was Wallace lying again? "I'm giving you one last chance to come clean."

Wallace spat past Jax. "I got nothing for you."

He hadn't truly expected Wallace would grow a conscience. Jax slammed the door.

Abby had stayed back and conferred with her team, but as he approached, her face was tight with rage. In her hands, she gripped two white envelopes.

His hand flew to his chest, where he patted himself to find the notes he'd put there gone. They'd slipped out. His gut dropped.

She marched over to him and thrust the envelopes at him. "You're a coward."

"I—"

"Don't *I* me. You don't get to check out, Jax. This is stupidity. What were you planning?"

"Nothing."

"Obviously. When did you write these? Yesterday? When I came to your house and saw your gun. Were you about to blow your brains out, then? Or were you planning to slice your wrists with the knife you had lying on the table?"

"No. I—"

"Then when?"

He scowled. "It doesn't matter. Things have changed."

She white-knuckled the envelopes. "Things never change, Jax. The same stuff happens every day. Just in a different way. You need to learn to cope. Get your act together and quit feeling sorry for yourself. Because this…." She thrust the envelopes toward him, "…is not the Jax I knew and fell in love with."

He couldn't answer.

"You know what keeps me going?"

He shook his head.

"Lulu."

His chest tightened. "She's gone."

"She's only gone if we forget her. It's your job to carry her memory. The day we stop talking about her, stop remembering, that's the day she's gone. And you don't get to stop. If making her doll furniture is what keeps you going, then you do that. You make that enough, and you live for her. Got it?"

His jaw trembled. "Got it." She threw the envelopes at his chest, and they floated to the ground. He gathered them slowly, his heart in a vice. She did care whether he was on the planet. Even if it was only to carry Lulu with her. He'd make that do. "When are you going to get back to me on those feathers?"

She hung her head. "That's all you have after what I just said?"

"I get it, Abby." And he did. "But I have a fourteen-year-old girl out there, and I can't stop until I find her."

Her eyes softened. "I expedited the tests. Tomorrow at the latest."

"Thank you."

Back in his car, his tires kicked up gravel, and he caught Abby in the rearview, watching him drive away. He couldn't decipher whether the look on her face was gratitude or wanting to wring his neck. Probably more of the latter.

Tonight, he'd helped a few men, and who knew how many more, that had come and gone in that truck. He'd stopped Dylan's supply of heroin to pedal to high schoolers. He'd done good work. Like Trudy had once suggested, there might even be a way back to Abby.

But when he stormed the farm, he was certain there'd be evidence of Allison's presence. Instead, he'd found nothing that said where she'd gone.

How could success feel like so much failure?

At the end of the farm's driveway, he dialed Emily.

"You got her?" Her voice shook

He winced. "I'm sorry, Emily. She wasn't there. But I will find her." He tried to add that boost of confidence in his voice that he didn't feel as she sobbed into the phone.

After sunrise, he'd be at forty-eight hours with not one sign of life. Despite Wallace's denial, until he had his timeline checked out, he was still the prime suspect. But with no admissions or direction of where to go next, he had to summon hope for them both.

Where are you, Allison?

Chapter Twenty-Six

A horn blasted with a staccato beat. It grew louder, piercing Elena's brain like a spike. The horrible noise emanated from the clock next to her bed. Lying flat on her stomach, she reached out and slammed the off button.

The radio switched on. "Nice day ahead, folks. Highs in the mid-sixties." Her head throbbed with the sudden movement, her eyes squinting at the godawful sunlight coming in through the blinds.

She didn't remember pulling into her driveway. That didn't seem possible after having only one drink—or was it two? She'd been woozy and sick after leaving the bar and the message for Steven. Had she been roofied? It would explain the memory glitch—why her head felt like it could split open.

The creep at the bar must have slipped something into her drink. With the bartender in and out the back, and her thoughts elsewhere, it wouldn't have been difficult. Tears pushed against her eyes. Her sinuses pulled. At least she'd gotten away. No telling what could have happened if she hadn't.

She pried her eyes open to find herself wearing cotton pajama bottoms and a white ribbed tank top. It was five o'clock. She sank deeper into the covers, pressing her head into the pillow.

Patting the nightstand, she found her phone next to the radio, and drew it under the covers with her. No calls. Steven had ignored her pleas—a first. He'd always reached out when she called with hurt or desperation. Yet another sign that something had drastically changed between them.

The desire to stay under the covers tugged at her, but she forced herself to ooze out of bed and place her feet on the ground. The urge to pee hit her, a moment before her stomach cramped, shooting bile into her throat.

She reached the bathroom in time to retch up acid, gin, and olives—the contents from last night. Her stomach squeezed again, and she gasped for breath, wanting to die when a new wave hit her. Finally, she rested her face on the cool seat and pulled a strand of toilet paper from the roll to blot her damp eyes and blow her nose.

Hauling herself up to the bathroom sink, she cupped water into her mouth, rinsed, and spat. She was dizzy and off-kilter, but her reflection was real enough: her hair had matted and stuck to the side of her head like she'd gone to bed with it wet. Being roofied, as she suspected, would have had her sweating all night. It would also explain the severe hang-over effect, why her heart pounded, and her limbs felt heavy.

If she hadn't stopped at the bar, she wouldn't have gotten herself into that predicament. Keeping her emotions and life together had never been an issue. Steven had her beyond stressed out, but that was no excuse.

She trudged back to the bedroom, pulled on her robe, and hunted for her slippers. Two clients were on the books for the afternoon. She needed to feel better long before then to figure out where Steven had gone and whether he had Allison. Coffee might help. The caffeine would be a start to getting rid of the headache.

She reached for the doorknob. It was locked. Odd. She twisted the latch and stepped out into her living room, her eyes struggling to focus and absorb what had happened.

The blinds hung off the windows like they'd been used to do chin-ups. Dining chairs toppled on their sides. Sofa cushions askew. Papers, DVDs, CDs, all flung from the cabinets and littering the floor.

Her stomach turned again. She sprinted to the kitchen sink, stubbing her toe against something hard. She yipped, reached down, and sliced her finger on a shattered wine glass. She clasped her bloodied hand over her mouth, stepped, and tripped on the pile of utensils, cutlery, and canned foods at her feet.

Side-stepping the pile, she made it to the sink before retching more. She gulped down as much water she could bear and let the faucet run to clear the sink while she grabbed a towel and pressed it on her hand.

Had the man from the bar followed her here, and they'd fought? Being drugged, she'd be an easy mark. Was he still here? Is that why she'd locked herself in the bedroom? The thump in her chest accelerated. She swooped up a knife from the pile.

Shaking with every step, she crept through the rest of her house, her rag-wrapped hand gripping the knife in front of her. She checked the laundry room. The spare bedroom. The guest bathroom. No other rooms had been disturbed.

She dropped her hand to her side. She was alone. Back in the living room, she set the knife on the coffee table.

If not the guy from the bar, who had done this? Steven? Possibly. Instead of calling her back, he showed up. She inspected the wreckage. Drugged or not, she would have demanded to know where he'd been. If he had Allison. He might have argued with her, like he'd done in the past.

Earlier in the year, he'd called to hound her about working too much, being alone, not being able to settle since Daniel. But when she'd suggested again that he see Dr. Kavorian, he'd gotten upset and left more scathing messages that she'd ignored. She'd sensed even then he was teetering—his accusations towards her out of character. His illness had been worsening.

Had Allison paid the price for her shutting him out the last couple of months?

She shuddered at the missed opportunity and wrapped her arms around herself. *No time for pity.* She'd get showered. Bandage her cut. Get out of here and get back to finding her brother. She'd clean the mess later.

A country song finished as she entered the bedroom and the disk jockey came on. "The Dow is expected to be up in early trading," he started. Elena dropped her robe to the ground.

She peeled off her shirt. "Morning traffic is light, but construction on the 101 is causing some delays." She stepped out of her PJ bottoms and walked into the bathroom.

"In other news, a man was brutally attacked last night at the Portway Tavern."

She stopped cold.

"The bartender says the man was a regular patron of the bar who spent hours playing pool in the afternoons and evenings. His wife reported him missing when he didn't come home or return her calls. He was later found unresponsive and remains in a coma. The police are looking for anyone who may have had contact with the victim yesterday. If you or someone you know has information, please contact...."

The reporter's voice faded. Elena swayed on her feet, her tongue thick in her cotton-dry mouth. She crumpled to the floor. It had to be the man who'd roofied her.

She wanted to believe that he'd gone back into Portway Tavern and tried to hit on someone else. That the next person had been far more capable of making their point that they didn't want to be bothered. That he'd pushed someone else too far.

But she didn't believe that. When that jogger had bothered her a few years ago, Steven had set out to teach him a lesson. Her calling Steven last night had resulted in the same thing.

She forced herself to stand. That's why she'd locked herself in her bedroom. He'd come here and admitted what he'd done. She would have berated him for it. This was all her fault. She should have never told him the details when she called. She'd hoped that it would make him come to her. To call her. Not hurt anyone.

Now he gave her no choice. She couldn't save him or do this alone anymore. Perhaps she'd been stupid to think she ever could. She swallowed down another wave of nausea, dumped her purse on the bed, and dug through the contents to find Sheriff Turner's card.

A short conversation with him, and they arranged to meet. She showered quickly, pulled her hair into a ponytail, and tugged on black yoga pants with a long sweater.

Telling the Sheriff about Steven and what she was afraid he'd done couldn't be done over the phone. Especially because the sheriff was likely wrong about the old killer returning; Steven knew everything about the old case. She'd risked everything by not coming forward sooner, but she'd deal with that as it came.

She grabbed her purse and was almost to the front door when she saw it propped on the entry table.

A message.

One that only she would understand. A Polaroid picture of an iron door on metal hinges. Rusted. Massive. Old. Next to it a barrette she'd given Allison in her last care package.

Grief gripped her. Steven did have Allison. And the Polaroid...all three of them—Madeline, Steven, Elena—had been where that picture was taken together once. Right after the funeral of their parents. Before the social workers dragged her and Maddy away. They'd run there to cry. To hide. It was where their lives had changed forever.

That's where Steven had taken Allison. She slid the picture into her purse, knowing their lives were about to change again.

Chapter Twenty-Seven

By the time Elena entered the station, Jax had downed an energy shot, chased it with a pot of coffee, and the sky had lightened a shade on the new day.

After leaving the farm last night, he'd gone straight to the station. Trudy had already made a dozen calls and obtained the information back on Wallace. He'd been telling the truth. His claim that he'd been living in Florida at the time of the Massey case had checked out. Jax's theory that he'd been involved in the original case crumbled.

Feeling like a dog who'd chased his tail for no reward, he'd marched in to question Dylan Marks.

"I don't know anything about anything," Dylan had repeated in the confines of the interrogation room. His voice grated on Jax like a squawking parrot, and Jax would have loved nothing more than to flick him from his perch. After ten minutes of flat denials—the pipe wasn't his; he didn't know where Allison had found it; no, he'd never done hard drugs, never, ever—he caved. Fingerprints. Hard, incontrovertible science, gets them every time.

"Look, man, it was the farm dude's idea for us to make a little on the side. But it was nothing. I move less than a gram a week, max. I don't use the stuff and neither does Allison."

"Could she have upset someone else around the drug dealing? Someone higher up. If you're small fry, who are the sharks?"

Dylan shook his head. "There is no one else. Like...I mean...she wasn't involved like that. The only reason she even had what she did was because she caught me talking to a sixth grader in town about it a month ago. But I didn't do nothing to Allison. I swear. I didn't see her. I haven't even talked to her for over a week."

"What about the Snapchat photos, Dylan? Your threats? Where is she?"

"I don't know! I was ticked she wasn't giving my shit back to me. She said she didn't want to see me getting hurt or hurting young kids. But I finally gave up." His chin quivered as he held back tears.

Jax wanted to press him further, but Daddy Marks had crashed in again, his lawyer right behind, and shut down the conversation. He was far from done with Dylan, but did he have Allison? Sure, he was a punk with entitlement running through his blood, but based on everything he'd found to this point, he didn't believe he did.

He released Dylan. He wasn't off the hook by a long shot, but he had to stay focused, and he'd circle back. Defeated, Jax had watched them drive away.

He was back at square one. Abby would be sending him something on the feathers soon. He hoped to God they panned out. He was losing time, which meant Allison was in more danger of losing her life (if she was still alive). For the rest of the night, Chapman had manned the phones and computer to see if any hits came in. There were none.

Jax sent the young deputies home around three a.m. when they'd all turned to drooping, nodding off zombies. Chapman followed at five, promising to return after a few hours of sleep. It had been a long night, and none of them would be any good to him if they couldn't think. He'd stayed and scanned the evidence and the files. He had to have missed something that told him where to go next.

Then Elena called, giving him no clues about why she had to see him, other than it was important. Now she stood in front of him, calm, but worn out.

His eyes went to her bandage. "You need to see a doctor for that?"

Her gaze followed his, and she lifted her hand. "I'm fine. Cut it on a glass this morning."

He nodded. "Come in. Coffee?"

"Please."

He nabbed her a cup from the breakroom, and they went into his office. She collapsed in the chair across from him, her shoulders slumping like she was tied to a yoke.

His visit yesterday may have pushed her back into the past. Unfortunate, but he'd do it again if it meant protecting her and finding Allison. That didn't lessen the guilt, and he fought the urge to put a paternal arm around her and tell her it would be okay. He didn't know if that were true. He placed his elbows on his desk.

They sat in silence. She pulled her purse onto her lap. "You probably wonder why I wanted to see you so urgently."

"Thought crossed my mind."

She slipped something out of her purse and laid it on his desk, keeping her hand over the item. "I know where Allison is." She winced and slid her hand away, revealing a Polaroid of a door.

His eyes on the picture, his pulse quickened before dread sank in. Three items had been kept out of the public domain in the Massey abduction/murder case. The feathers, the isoflurane, and the fact the killer had left Polaroids of Madeline bound and dead. The images stirred acid in Jax's gut. Wallace might not have been the one, but if he hadn't been certain before the same person was involved with Allison's abduction, now he held zero doubt. "Where'd you get this?"

"In my entry as I was leaving to come here."

He'd found Elena? "Your sister's killer was in your house?"

"No. You've been wrong about that angle."

He tapped his foot, his nerves pinging. "Everything I'm finding in relation to Allison's abduction is a repeat of your case. This photo proves it."

"You mean along with the feathers and the chemical used to knock us out?"

He grimaced. "You know about the isoflurane?"

She nodded. "I was able to see the file once."

"Then you know that Polaroids showing what the killer did to Madeline were found next to her body."

Her face scrunched in pain. She'd clearly seen the horrendous images left by a demented individual. Gaining her composure, she rested her hand over her heart. "Yes, I know all of that. But you're wrong. My brother took Allison."

He dropped back into his seat. "What brother?"

"Steven."

He'd been through the file countless times. "I don't recall seeing anything about him."

"He was much older than me and Maddy, and not in foster care."

Family connections should have been noted, though, and they weren't. A rookie had assisted at the time so he and Jameson could concentrate on finding the abductor. He'd clearly dropped the ball. "How much older?"

"Eight years. Point is, I have proof he has Allison." She removed a bracelet from her purse. "This was in his apartment. I gave it to Allison on her twelfth birthday."

Jax picked up the bracelet and fingered the "A."

Elena set an opal down on the desk. "This was in his truck that he sold a couple of days ago." Next the barrette. "This was sitting by the photo this morning."

Jax's head spun. He couldn't indulge his emotions. Rage—that she'd hidden this from him, that there'd been a solid lead and he hadn't known, that Allison had been out there all this time when he could have done something about it. All that frustration would have to wait until later. No good would come of berating her for protecting her brother. He needed her to remain on his side now that she'd found her way to doing the right thing.

But getting a grip on his emotions didn't prove easy. Someone should have known about a goddamn brother.

He'd put Trudy on tracking down the social worker when she got in. Of course, Steven could've also stayed in the shadows easily during the first investigation since they weren't focused on family during that time.

It was also possible Steven had stayed hidden on purpose. "You should've told me this yesterday."

"Agreed. But I wasn't certain he had Allison after you mentioned your theory. But that hair piece...." She cleared her throat and looked away. "I'm here now. He's not returning my calls, and—" She dropped her chin to her chest.

"And what?"

"He's falling apart."

Jax scrubbed his hand over his face, the chafing sound of his day-old beard in his ears, as he absorbed the information. "If he's abducted your stepdaughter, he's doing more than that." He got up, went down the hall, and returned with gloves and an evidence bag. He took a quick picture from his cell of the photo and placed the evidence inside. Hopefully, this brother of hers had left a print that could be used later to identify him. "Where's that door?" he asked.

"In the abandoned military batteries outside of town. I believe he left this as a bread crumb to find him and Allison. We were there, us kids, after our parents' funeral."

"You haven't been there to check?"

Elena shook her head, and her shoulders inched up. "No. I called you because I think he's capable of doing bad things right now."

Jax scanned Elena's face. "What kinds of bad things?"

She bit into her lower lip. "I think he hurt the man at the Portway Tavern last night."

His eyes narrowed. "What man?"

"It was on the radio. After my doctor's appointment, I stopped at that bar. As I was leaving, a man harassed me. He tried to take my keys. And…" She swallowed. "I called Steven and left him a message about what happened. When I got home, I passed out until this morning, and that's when I heard the report of a man beaten into a coma. It was the same man who'd been bothering me."

"You think Steven did that?"

"It's a possibility. He obviously came to my house because he left this picture for me to find." Her words were measured. "He's not well."

"Define not well?"

"There've been a dozen labels for him. Bipolar, schizophrenic, delusional. Right now, he's in a manic state. I get the feeling he's playing a game with me."

Steven having a mental condition made the entire situation more unpredictable, amplifying the danger to Allison. "Why would he want to?"

"I don't know. But he could be reaching out because he's afraid he'll harm Allison, and he wants me to come for her. Whatever his reasons, he's not stupid. He'll want to cover his trail and not get caught. I don't want *covering his trail* to include hurting my stepdaughter."

Jax listened, unsure of what to think. Every family had its dysfunction. Its dark side. With what little he'd seen of Elena's current life, she'd risen above her early trauma. But Madeline's murder had damaged all of them on some levels. The fact that Steven might be involved in Allison's disappearance indicated he hadn't coped with the loss at all. "What's his number?"

Elena took a piece of paper from her purse and jotted it down.

Jax grabbed it up.

The station door smacked against the wall.

"Morning," he heard Trudy holler from the outer office.

"I'm getting this traced and calling in my team. Give me five," he said, racing out of his office to see Trudy.

* * *

Jax and company pulled into the Corps of Engineers parking lot.

Trudy had rallied who she could of the team and done a search on Steven Massey. Elena had composed herself and stood next to him while he brought Brody and Matt up to speed.

Chapman and Garrett hadn't answered their phones or their doors when he sent Brody to rouse them. Chapman and communication was sometimes an issue, but since he was supposed to be casting a fishing line in Alaska rather than on the job, he wouldn't be too hard on him. Still, he was here, and he'd have a conversation with both him and Garrett about availability. Later. Right now, he didn't have time to wait on them.

The military batteries that Elena had spoken of were cordoned off behind them. They'd been neglected for years by the state, so there were no humans to contend with, no forced evacuations necessary. Much of the area felt like Roman ruins.

At one time, concrete buildings where maneuvers were planned and executed would have stood tall. Time and the incessant moisture of the coastal range had toppled many of the structures, leaving only cement pillars. Years ago, state officials had come in and labeled the various locations. They stood in front of the map room and officer quarters. Where a floor once supported enlisted men, gaping holes with waist-high grasses swallowing chunks of concrete remained.

On their way in from the lot, Jax hadn't seen signs of other vehicles or activity. A faint whistle wafted through the decrepit buildings. Wind, not people. Bird droppings covered much of the gray surfaces. So close to the everyday life of Misty Pines, yet a land forgotten. One hell of a place to hole up.

"Do you believe he's acted alone?" Jax directed his question to Elena.

"I'm sure of it. He's always been reclusive, but he also has anthropophobia, which is a heightened fear of people."

Jax shook his head. The man would be a psychiatrist's dream. He glanced at Elena. Or a sister/psychologist's nightmare.

Brody, a few strides behind them, took it in. "He has social disorders, and he's whacked. That about the sum of it?"

Elena's forehead creased. "He can't help that he's sick." Her eye twitched. "Which is why—"

Jax put his hand on her shoulder. She didn't have to say it. "We won't hurt him if we can avoid it." His voice trailed off. There'd be no choice if it came down to saving Steven or Allison.

She closed her eyes and nodded. "Thank you."

Matt shifted his feet. "What if he won't give Allison back voluntarily?"

Jax looked at Elena and then at Matt. "Allison is coming home. Unharmed. Period." He stared hard at Matt to convey that it was up to Steven how it ended for himself.

Matt nodded. "Got it."

This was Matt's second raid in twenty-four hours. He was amped. They all were. Sleepy Misty Pines had woken up and not in a good way.

They approached the semicircular concrete structures built into the hillside. There were five of them, still intact, strung together like half a paper chain. Inside those circles were gun emplacements. The circular building housed the artillery for the big cannon-sized ordnances. The weapons would have been stationed to take out any ships approaching from the sea. Now, trees blocked any views of the water, and the guns had long been dismantled.

Jax opened the photos on his phone. The Polaroid of the door was first up. The group stayed far back and hidden while he assessed each battery until he was sure he'd found the door that matched. He called the team over.

"I agree. It looks like the picture," Elena whispered.

Jax scanned the area. Bent grass had created a pathway to the last battery. A guard station with a narrow lookout sat off to the side. Jax made sure it was clear before he approached the large closed rusted iron doors. The battery itself was the most hidden from view. Steven had picked a good location to hide Allison. Even if she screamed, no one could hear.

Jax drew his gun and motioned them over, opening one side of the entry. Coolness eased out like ghost fingers gripping him. The smell of must and damp stung his nose. He pushed down a shudder. "Stay here."

"No," Elena whispered. "If Steven is in there, you'll need me. If he's not, then at least I'll be there to comfort Allison."

Could he trust Elena not to protect Steven at her own peril? He had to believe she'd come to terms with what could happen. "You up for this?"

She nodded. "I have to be. It's my fault he's done this in the first place."

They didn't have time to explore that statement, but she clearly felt responsible for him. Still, it was dangerous. "I don't—"

"Sheriff, I'm going with or without your permission. There's an artillery room in the farthest corner. If she's anywhere, it's there. I know the way."

Before he could respond, she walked into the corridor.

"Shit." Jax flicked on his flashlight and followed.

Chapter Twenty-Eight

Matt remained in place at the battery door in case Steven made a break for it. Brody fell back, guarding the end of the hall. Jax kept stride with Elena, their soft-soled shoes almost silent in the dank space. He listened for sounds of Allison or her abductor as they headed down the narrow corridor, disappearing into the dark maze.

As they grew closer to the artillery room, Elena's steps became smaller. Her breaths, short and shallow. Jax aimed the beam of light out ahead, the blackness swallowing it whole. Elena swayed, bumping into him. He reached out to steady her and felt her body's rigidity. She gripped his forearm and froze.

"Are you going to be alright?" he whispered.

Her teeth chattered. "Fine."

Jax had to fight off his own chills with the damp cold permeating his shirt. But her grip said more than that. He washed the beam of light over her. Skin pale. Eyes shut. Lips clamped. He should have known this would happen. "Go back with Brody," he ordered, his voice low.

"No. Steven's here. I can feel it."

"Then I'll find him and Allison on my own."

She shook her head. "I can do it. I'm just... This place has always scared me. Ghosts, you know."

He didn't know if she meant personal, or those he'd heard stories of. Or both. Everyone who lived in these parts knew of the spirit of an infantryman who wandered the Oregon coast, showing himself in disparate places, but often in the forts where he'd once served. "You'll be fine. There's no such thing."

She moaned.

He didn't have time for sympathy. Allison could be waiting. Hurt. Needing them. "Take a deep breath, Elena. Let's do this or you go back."

She steadied herself, nodded, and continued making her way down the corridor. She stayed in control with each step until they reached a T. Elena pointed to the left.

Jax's eyes followed her finger, his heart hammering. A faint light illuminated an opening—the artillery room Elena had described.

They stepped out of view. He motioned her to call Steven on her phone, and she did. Jax froze, listening for a buzz. A ring. Any sound echoing back confirming Steven's presence. Nothing. The lack of noise didn't mean much. Steven's phone could be dead or silenced.

He gave Elena the wait sign with his hand, rounded the corner and, gun drawn, slunk the fifty yards to the edge of the room. His mouth was dry; the vein in his neck pulsed. He flashed the light in. No response. He stepped into the room, his heart sinking.

Elena had ignored him, and her footfalls followed. From the entry, she gasped.

He turned to see her white-faced, working her good hand, blood soaking through her bandages.

Jax holstered his gun. There was no Allison or Steven, but someone had been there. He got on his radio. "Brody, bring gloves and evidence bags."

The source of the faint light had been a gel stick. Pallets had been stacked, creating a table. Folded blankets had been placed on top. Fast food wrappers were crumpled and piled in a corner. A box of hand and foot warmers in the center. Zip ties and bungee cords littered the cement floor near the chair. A black cloth bag rested on the seat. He winced at the thought of it over Allison's head.

Something bright mixed in with the zip ties stood out. He walked over and crouched, shining the beam of light on a pink twine bracelet. His hand clenched into a fist. He'd seen a bunch of those bracelets in Allison's bedroom.

One of the hand warmers had been tossed on the floor next to the chair. His palm hovered over the top of it. Still warm. The brand lasted ten hours, give or take. Allison had been under his nose the whole time.

His jaw tensed. Where had he been? Storming a farm and interrogating a punk, both actions resulting in nothing. He resisted the urge to kick the chair and spew a dozen profanities.

Brody appeared in the entry.

Jax swept his hand over the room. "I want this place lit up, processed, and all of the evidence out of here. Let's see if the bastard left us prints and clues."

"You got it," Brody said, his eyes wide with excitement.

"I'll send Matt in and see if I can raise Chapman again to assist." Jax left his deputy and guided Elena back through the tunnels and into the fresh air. Outside, he sent Chapman a series of texts and paced until he finally responded that he'd be there. Elena's face had gone slack.

Jax finally stopped. "Where would Steven have gone?"

"I don't know." Her hands shook. "I don't understand why he'd lead me here and then disappear. Allison was here. Right? It doesn't make sense."

"Unless he wanted you to come alone. Does he know that you contacted me?"

She shook her head.

Something in the way she held her mouth. She'd kept so much from him. No reason to believe she wasn't still holding back. "You're sure?"

"I came straight from my house. I—" She stopped. Her face drained of color. "Unless he was watching me. Following me. He's done that before when he's spiraling."

Jax let out a frustrated sigh. So much for the element of surprise.

"He could be afraid that I've turned on him." She wrapped her arms around herself and rocked back and forth.

The stress was getting to Elena, but he couldn't help that right now. His own stress was about to level him.

Brody rushed through the iron door, moving fast in their direction. "Chief, you missed this." He held out a pair of latex gloves and gave Jax an envelope.

Jax pulled out the tri-folded paper inside. Scrawled in black Sharpie ink: "Catch me if you can. Tick Tock. When the sun goes down tomorrow, time will be up."

Jax's ears rang like a sledgehammer had hit him on the side of the head. *Catch me if you can.* The same words had been used by Madeline's killer when he taunted him and Jameson. Just over seventy-two hours after abduction, they'd found Madeline's body. This note implied that in less than thirty-two hours, Allison would meet the same fate.

Elena hung over Jax's shoulder, her eyes frozen on the note.

"Does the handwriting look like your brother's?"

She nodded.

Jax grimaced. He'd been wrong all along. Madeline's killer had not only been in the area, but he was related to Madeline and Elena. He knew the statistics—over fifty percent of murder victims knew their killer. "Elena, I need you to think back to that night. Did Steven take you and Madeline?"

Her eyes went wide. "I already told you I don't know who took us. But why would he?"

"We don't have time for whys." They had to concentrate on the evidence which supported the theory he had been involved before. "You must try to remember. Allison needs you to remember. Where did he take you? How did you get away? What were the sequence of events after you left the...?"

She pressed her fist against her forehead. "I don't know."

Jax had been going the wrong direction. He had to quell his rising anxiety. "You're coming with me. I need to know everything you do about Steven."

If Elena's brother wanted to play games, then Jax would play.

Chapter Twenty-Nine

Jax set Elena up in the interrogation room with a forensic artist who lived in Misty Pines and was happy to help. He'd called Detective Bergstrom, who was handling the Portway Tavern assault, and told him of Steven's possible involvement.

"Is the man going to survive?" Jax had asked.

"Likely, but he took quite a blow to the back of the head. My guess is he didn't even see it coming since there's no defensive wounds. But I'll let you know when he regains consciousness."

He was able to push off the detective's request for an interview with Elena until later since the sketch that would be broadcast of Steven could potentially help both jurisdictions.

Elena had one snapshot of Steven that she kept on her phone. Other than brown hair poking out from under a red baseball hat, the angle hid his face. It was the same picture she had on her desk.

"I'm sorry," was all she'd offered when asked why she hadn't come clean. She also didn't have any more current pictures. Childhood photos of all of them had been lost during the transition into foster care. No images of their parents, or even one of Madeline, remained.

Jax rested his shoulder against the door, inspecting Elena's movements. She'd lost her parents to a horrible car crash. The foster care system had failed them miserably when they placed them with a child molester forcing the girls to run. The abduction. Her sister's murder. Now the impending loss of Steven. She'd endured more than most. He wouldn't judge her for not jumping to Steven's guilt immediately. She was here now.

"That girl looks bone-weary," Trudy said, approaching from behind Jax and peeking through the small glass panel in the door. "As do you." She put her hand on his shoulder. "I put a bowl of chowder from the Columbia Café on your desk."

He patted her hand. His favorite. "Thank you." She did take care of him. For all he'd put her through with his bad attitude, he was lucky she hadn't hightailed it out of there long ago. "Boys back from the battery yet?"

"Yes. Getting evidence submitted to the West Shore lab I believe."

Good. He nodded toward Elena. "It can't be easy knowing your own brother has your stepdaughter and is playing mind games." He turned to Trudy. "You got anything for me yet?"

Her lips pursed when she handed him the sheet in her other hand. "I did a state-wide search for Steven Massey, and what you see is what I found. The social worker for the Massey girls died several years ago, and those case files are archived in Salem. I've put in a request, but we're looking at three to five days if I can find someone to feel sorry for me. Otherwise, we're talking thirty."

Not good enough. "How about Steven's phone?"

"It's registered to Elena."

Elena had clearly been taking care of her brother for quite some time. "And?"

"And only one cell tower serves us and West Shore. There's been a couple of hits on it, but it doesn't tell us anything specific. He also may be keeping his phone off. The Polaroid went to the lab, but the prints on it are smudged and inconclusive."

Not surprising after being shoved into Elena's purse. He skimmed the page. Steven's name showed up along with Elena's on an electric bill tied to an apartment in Megler, co-signed by Elena. A black Pathfinder SUV bore only her name. That must be the one Elena said he'd sold. The new owners have fourteen days to put in a transfer request, and they hadn't done so yet. Rick Johnson had mentioned a black SUV out ahead of him. He'd been telling the truth.

"Put out an APB on that vehicle and send Brody my way when he's back."

"Absolutely, and I could use a social or date of birth on Steven Massey, so when I broaden the search to the U.S., I don't have thousands flagged."

"I'll see what I can do."

He started to enter the room and then stopped. "By the way. About calling Chapman back from vacation. You didn't need to...."

Trudy had started to walk away and turned back to him. "I didn't."

"I thought..."

"Wasn't me."

Maybe he'd misunderstood. More likely, Chapman didn't want to admit that he'd been paying attention to the case from afar. Called a friend. Kept tabs on the scanners. While Trudy had seen Jax pulling it together, Chapman had only known of Jax flailing on the job for a few years. It rankled Jax, but how could he blame his deputy?

He glanced back at Elena. He did appreciate Chapman's return, regardless.

The artist finished and left Elena waiting in the room. When Jax entered, Elena had her face buried in her hands. He sat across from her and leaned back in the chair, pulling the picture of Steven in front of him. Short brown hair. Light skin blemished with freckles that looked far better on his sister. They shared a familial resemblance, except for the stronger jaw and the darker eyes, making Steven look angry. "It's time you tell me about your brother."

She lifted her head. "Where do I start?"

"From the beginning."

She squared her shoulders. "I didn't know him well as a child."

"He didn't live with you and your parents?"

"No, and my parents didn't talk about him much. I vaguely recall overhearing my dad saying they'd lost Steven, but I may not be remembering that correctly being a kid and the youngest at that. I never asked my dad about that either." She frowned. "The world revolved around me at that time. It drove Maddy nuts that I had more freedom than she'd had and spent more time with my dad. I think parents do that sometimes by the time they've reached their third kid. They loosen the reins. Give up the need to get it all done."

He nodded. He would've liked to have known that firsthand. "I'm sure."

"Anyway. From my dad's comment, I guess Steven has always had problems."

"When did you see him again?"

"He showed up briefly after my parents died, but more so after Madeline's murder when he'd asked the social worker if he could take me in. But with no real job or home of his own... Despite not knowing him well, it meant the world to me though that he tried and wanted to protect me."

Jax shifted in his chair. Hopefully, Trudy could expedite those files from Salem to give him another perspective. "Was he jealous of you and Madeline?"

Her head tilted to the side. "Perhaps during the years we lived with our parents. Certainly not after we went into foster care. I lost touch with him after I moved into my new foster situation, where I finally began to heal."

Jax nodded, although he didn't need to be a shrink to recognize that the level in which she funded Steven's lifestyle suggested co-dependence. "You say you didn't see Steven during your teenage years?"

"Right, or in college. My life started cruising along, and his, too. We lost track of each other until about ten years ago when he showed up needing help to get his own place. Said he was tired of wandering. The timing sucked. I'd just broken up with a boyfriend and was a complete mess. Turned out, helping my brother was a good distraction. I met Daniel right after that."

"That's when you co-signed Steven's apartment."

Elena's eyes flashed surprise, but she nodded. "Yes. And that's when I bought him his car as well."

"You know he doesn't have a driver's license, though...."

She looked at the table. "Some things I supposed I didn't want to know."

He nodded. "Can I get his birth date and his social?"

"September third." She grimaced. "Not that we ever celebrated it together. Some sister I am. I have no idea about the social."

"Would it be on the apartment application?"

She shook her head. "Since I paid the bills, I used mine. The landlord didn't care."

Jax sighed. "Go on."

"Things went back to normal after that. He'd contact me on occasion, usually when he was having emotional problems."

"Is he on medication?"

"Yes, but I can't police whether he takes them." Her face contorted. "Anyway, Daniel always accused me of running out on him to help Steven. I really thought I could, though. I've always been able to talk him down."

"At least in the past."

She shrugged. "You're probably right about that."

Or she'd been kidding herself. If she hadn't been in touch consistently, Steven could have been out doing many things without her knowledge.

Brody appeared in the door's window panel and waved.

Jax stepped out long enough to give Brody his next assignment to find someone who might have seen that black SUV around at any point. Whether it was coming or going, its direction might give them a clue to where Steven had Allison.

Elena was cupping her head in her hands when Jax returned. He cleared his throat and sat down. "Why do you believe he attacked the man at the bar?"

"As I said, I'd called Steven on my way home and told him he'd tried to hurt me." Tears brimmed in her eyes. "He can go overboard thinking he's protecting me. I've tried to help him with that, but I failed once before."

He rested his forearms on the table. "Once before?"

"A few years ago, another man harassed me when I was jogging at Cullaby Lake. I'd told Steven, and he found the guy and beat him terribly."

"I'll want more information on that."

She nodded and worked her thumb lightly into her hand again. "I only told him about the man at the bar so he'd call me and I could find out if he did, in fact, have Allison."

Good intentions that had gone very wrong. "You'd said you'd all been to the battery before. Is there any place else he might go?"

"I've been racking my brain on that. As an adult, he's been a shut-in for so long he really hasn't gone many places. But as a kid, he and my dad would have done things together, I'm sure, before I was born, before they 'lost him' as my dad said. Of course, I wouldn't know where they would've gone."

Jax cupped the back of his neck, fighting fatigue and the feeling he was missing something. "Why Allison? Does Steven think he needs to protect you from her?"

She straightened. "Allison's never done anything to me."

"Would he be trying to get back at Daniel?"

"Our divorce was amicable. I was angry at him for wanting to give up, but that's before I could admit I wanted to do the same."

"What then? Why now? Why her?"

She massaged her temples. "My mother died at the age of forty. And it's Maddy's fortieth birthday this month, as well as the twenty-fifth anniversary of her murder. My guess is the loss has crashed back in on him. It's the only thing I can think of."

A sick way to mark an anniversary or a birthday. "He had to know that abducting your stepdaughter would turn your world and everyone else's upside down."

Her face scrunched in thought. "I haven't figured that part out either or whether he truly understands what he's done. Something has changed this time, but if he lets me, I truly believe I can make him understand, and he'll come in voluntarily."

Jax picked up the sketch. If Steven hadn't been following the old playbook of the original case, Jax might have bought into Elena's wishful thinking that Steven didn't know what he was doing. But Steven knew. "The best way to do that is to let me know of anything that will lead us to him, or if he gets into contact with you."

She nodded.

He continued asking about Steven for a few more minutes. But the guy didn't have any friends. No hobbies, no place of employment. Elena's sheltering him from the world had made him a ghost in the age of digital information overload. Either that, or he operated in the shadows very much on purpose and using her to accomplish that. Steven could be a serial killer for all Elena knew.

He stood. "I'm going to get this broadcast ASAP, along with Allison's picture. If we're lucky, the public will have seen something. We could use the help."

Elena's eyes drooped. Her shoulders slumped. "Am I free to go?"

"For now, but not far. As we get closer to pinpointing his whereabouts, we'll have more questions and will likely need your help."

Jax jotted down the information on the earlier case that Elena had referenced about the jogging incident, secured the key to Steven's apartment, and walked her out.

Elena said something had changed with Steven. He wasn't answering her calls and had been leaving clues from the beginning. Not only for Elena with the Polaroid, but the feathers, the chemicals on the backpack, and now the note.

What was the end game?

He didn't know. Except the note said sundown tomorrow—thirty hours away. He had to believe Allison was still alive based on that.

They were one step behind. He couldn't shake the thought that he had the pieces in front of him. He just needed to put them together.

* * *

Before heading out to Megler, Jax pulled up the files from the assault case three years ago out of Clatsop County that Elena had mentioned.

Chapman strode in. "Got something." He laid out five pictures on top of Jax's desk.

Jax stared at the shots of the battery's dirty concrete floor, along with the chair he believed Allison had been tied to. "What do you see that I don't?"

"Blood spots." Chapman pointed to a series of dark drops near the chair and the opening to the room. "It's an odd mix of dried and fresh blood. It could be Allison's."

"Or the abductor's?" Jax said.

Chapman shifted. "Maybe."

Jax pointed to the fresher drops at the entrance. "Those could belong to

Elena. She cut her hand this morning on a glass and was bleeding through her bandages." He'd been so focused on the chair, he hadn't tracked Elena's motions at the time, and he should have.

Chapman nodded. "Either way, I've expedited the DNA tests. They've got that rapid testing available now in West Shore. Told them we were on a high wire and needed them yesterday, but they weren't feeling confident they'd get anything back on the older blood."

He'd take whatever they could give him. "Four hours realistic?"

"Two."

"Even better. In the meantime, I have a task for you."

Before he told him where he needed him to go, he brought Chapman up to speed on the old case angle.

Chapman frowned as he listened. "You think Steven Massey would have attacked his own sisters?"

"It's possible. Elena said he was in and out of trouble as a kid, although he's flown under the radar. There's not much on him in the system. That's why I want you to start here." He hit the print button and handed him a copy of Steven's picture, and explained about Elena's earlier attack. "She got away, but a Mr. Truman was almost beaten to a pulp by Steven in retaliation. That's according to Elena, who never pressed charges for the attack. According to the report Truman filed, they never caught the attacker, and Elena is only referenced as a female jogger. Maybe showing Steven's picture will make the guy remember something else about the incident."

Chapman scanned the paper. "And confirm we have a time bomb on our hands."

"That too."

Chapman nodded. "I'll check it out."

"Take Garrett with you."

Chapman cleared his throat. "I can handle it."

Jax was sure he could. He'd handled a lot for Jax. Those days were long gone. "Always good to run with a partner, and the boy needs the training. I've got that sketch of Steven out on the wire, and the local station has already broadcast it in a special report. Tips should be rolling in shortly.

But anything Mr. Truman can offer might help us build a better picture of who we're dealing with. Steven's note says his sick game ends tomorrow evening. I don't have to tell you we need to be working fast to figure out where he has Allison before we get close to that deadline."

Chapman nodded, clutching the report in his hand. "I'll be in touch."

Jax leapt from his chair. Every minute felt like the tick-tock of that time bomb. He needed to do his part and find something, anything in Steven's apartment that might answer where he'd gone before time ran out.

Chapter Thirty

Jax pulled in front of a two-story building housing a laundromat on the bottom floor. On his way into town, he'd stopped at the gas station. The guy working handled the day shift and didn't recall seeing Steven. The evening attendant had worked a double the day before and didn't answer his phone. Jax could hunt the guy down, but he'd stop on his way back out of town rather than engaging in a wild goose chase.

He'd also passed a diner a couple of blocks up—the sign in the window indicating they closed at two. It was one-thirty. The restaurant was a direct shot from the laundromat. Steven had to eat at some point whether he liked to be around people or not. Worth checking.

Jax locked his cruiser and trotted up the block. Inside, the sweet smell of sausage and maple syrup brought back memories of Sunday morning breakfasts and animal-shaped pancakes. White and yellow curtains hung on the windows, and Formica dinettes with vinyl booths lined the walls. Square tables and chairs littered the middle. An elderly couple sipped coffee in the farthest corner booth.

A sixty-something woman wearing a red checked dress and white apron greeted him with a menu and a faint smile. The fallen curls on her forehead and her weary eyes gave the impression she'd been on duty since the early shift. "Table or booth, Officer?"

He waved her off. "Neither, thank you. I'm hoping you can help me."

She tucked the menu under her arm. "Happy to try."

He pulled up the picture on his phone that he'd taken of Steven's sketch. "Have you seen this man in here before?"

She squinted at the image and tilted the phone from side to side a couple of times. "Perhaps. Although I've never seen him without a baseball hat which is why I hesitate. But if it's who I think it is, he comes in right at open and asks for a cup of coffee and an omelet to go."

"What time do you open?"

"Three-thirty." She stifled a yawn. "Guess who's here turning on the lights?"

"Hell of a shift."

"You're telling me. Anyway, I don't see him too often." She walked behind her cash register and shoved the menu to the side. "Sure I can't interest you in some pie?"

Jax's mouth watered at the suggestion. Trudy's chowder had been a start, but his sparse food intake the last couple of days was taking its toll. A happy waitress might remember details better, too. "I'll take a slice of apple to go."

She smiled, like she'd won the lottery. "You'll love it. Fresh this morning."

He pulled a ten from his wallet and turned back toward the laundromat. "Ever see him come or go from down there?"

She slipped the slice into a Styrofoam box and pushed it closed before bending low enough below the curtain's edge to see where Jax pointed.

"Nope. Course, I don't have much time to be admiring the view." The waitress handed him his pie, rang it up, and handed him his change which he dropped into the tip jar.

"You said that he was always here at open. Any ideas what brought him out so early?"

"Fishing, I suspect. But I didn't say always."

"Oh?"

"A couple of days ago, he flitted through closer to ten. Breakfast crowd was gone, and he rushed in for his regular order. The different time is what made it stand out."

The hairs on the back of Jax's arm stood. "And a couple of days ago—is that the last time you saw him?"

She nodded.

"What makes you think he was fishing?"

"He had on waders with muddy boots."

"Waders?"

"Yeah, you know, the big green kind you step into and fish in streams with."

Was this the break he'd been praying for? "Did you ask him where he'd been fishing that morning?"

She chuckled. "No. And wouldn't matter if I did. He's not a talker, that one."

Not enough to give him clear direction, but something. "You're positive it was two days ago?"

"Yup. It was my Friday, so to speak. I was off yesterday."

"He happened to be driving a black SUV?"

"Don't pay attention to that kind of stuff."

"Anyone on staff who might?"

She hollered to the scrawny man tending the grill. He didn't even know the weather half the time, let alone who was in the parking lot.

Jax thanked her and stepped out of the restaurant, a gloom falling over him. Two days ago, Steven Massey had gone off his normal routine and come to the diner later in the morning. The timing fit with Allison's disappearance. He'd have had plenty of time to get to Misty Pines, take Allison, and get back. Somewhere in there, he'd sold his truck, which could have happened right outside in the parking lot. Without a witness, it was anyone's guess.

But where had Steven been to need waders? The battery wasn't close enough to water, and there'd been no mud in the area to speak of either. Had he been somewhere before he'd taken Allison to that location?

Or had Allison not been there at all? They'd found her twine bracelet, but that could have been planted like the Polaroid. Misdirection could be part of the game. Hopefully, the DNA and test results from the artillery room would fill in the blanks. Finding the waders could tell them even more.

Jax left his pie uneaten in his patrol car and hopped the stairs two at a time up to Steven's apartment. He didn't expect to find him there, but he undid the strap on his holster and pounded twice, announcing his intention to enter.

The door swung open. Adrenaline shot through Jax, and he stepped to the side of the entry.

A stout, gray-bearded man stood with his hand on the knob. "What's all the fuss about?"

Jax huffed, releasing the tension, and produced his badge. "Sheriff Turner, Misty Pines. And you are?"

"Jake Tannenbaum," he said, eyes wide. "Were you about to bust down the door?"

"No, sir." Jax produced the key from his pocket and held it up for him to see. "Do you live here?"

"No, I own the building. Suppose you're looking for the creep who did, though?"

"Steven Massey, correct."

"That would be the one. Saw his picture all over the news. Don't want any part of that."

A half-filled garbage bag sat behind the old man. "I'm going to ask you to cease your efforts, sir. You could be contaminating a possible crime scene."

The man's face blanched as he followed Jax's gaze to the bag. "Sorry about that. Was just trying to get a head start. You're not going to tear this place up, are you?"

Landlords didn't like when the yellow crime tape came out and prevented them from making money, but he wouldn't make promises. "I'll do my best not to. In the meantime, I need to secure the room."

"Fine. Just make sure you apprehend that Massey fellow." He shook his head in disgust.

"I'll let you know when I'm through," he said, motioning the man to the door and scanning the living room for those waders.

He nodded. "I'll be downstairs." He started to leave. "You know, I feel horrible for his sister. Sweet gal. Certainly didn't deserve a brother like the one she got stuck with."

Jax agreed with that. "What was your take on Steven?"

"Odd, reclusive, and clearly has a few screws loose. Only way I knew the place was even rented half the time was I'd see him moving about at night."

Being an insomniac himself, he didn't see that as a real concern. "Other than keeping to himself, he give you any problems?"

"Never. I told Elena he was almost the perfect tenant. Now to hear he's wanted in an abduction of a young girl and for questioning about attacking a man at that tavern. No, thank you. He's out of here."

"Appreciate the information." Jax glanced at his watch. Twenty-eight hours left. His jaw clenched. Time was slipping through his fingers. "I need to move on this, sir."

"You go right ahead. You find what you need to get that little girl back, Sheriff." He shut the door behind him.

Once alone, Jax pulled on latex gloves. Finding the waders that the waitress spoke about was priority one, but he didn't want to miss anything else along the way.

He started in the breakfast nook that looked out over the parking lot and went into the kitchen. Salt and pepper, saltines, Top Ramen... little else. No wonder Steven went to the diner for real food.

Jax sorted through the few items the landlord had thrown into the garbage bag, finding magazines and an Xbox console along with a dozen games. He'd hoped maybe a brochure of fishing locations or better, a map, would be in the mix. Cases were often solved by plain dumb luck. That wasn't the case today.

In the bedroom, he walked past jeans and a sweatshirt flung over the back of a chair on his way to the bathroom. There, a dry towel hung off the sliding shower door, but dirt collared the drain. He rubbed the silt between his fingers. After he'd left the diner, Steven appeared to have come home and taken a shower.

The medicine cabinet contained a bottle of Excedrin, hair gel, and a toothbrush and paste. No medications. He'd expected to find at least a few, unless Steven had them with him. Did that mean he didn't expect to return? His shoulders tensed.

Back in the bedroom, he opened the closet. Like-new baseball hats from professional leagues lined the top shelf. Steven had the LA Dodgers one on in Elena's photo of him.

A few button-downs and sweatshirts hung off the rod, and several pairs of jeans were folded on a shelf of the closet organizer. Jax unfolded a pair and held them to his waist. Steven was shorter by a few inches and considerably thinner. In a pullout drawer, he found boxers and T-shirts, men's size medium.

What he didn't find were the waders.

Nothing under the bed. Nothing in the closet near the front door. There was another option, which he could confirm with Mr. Tannenbaum.

Jax ran down the stairs to the laundromat and found the old man inside the wash area with a wrench, tweaking a unit pulled away from the wall.

The landlord turned to acknowledge him. "All done?"

"Do you offer storage with the apartment?"

His face wrinkled. "It's not much to speak of. More of a locker, really. Good place to put extra jackets. Car tools. Things like that."

"Did Steven have one?"

"Believe he did." Wrench in hand, he walked toward the back room.

Jax followed. The back room had an array of old coin units, and a broken vending machine. In the corner, a powder gray industrial locker had been secured against the wall.

Mr. Tannenbaum pointed to B7 at the bottom left corner. It was the only locker with a padlock run through the handle. "That's the one there."

"Wouldn't happen to have a key?"

"I don't. But..." He held up his wrench. "You might want to turn around for this."

If he had a hammer, he would've pounded it off himself. "Do it."

With two swings, the padlock sprang open. Mr. Tannenbaum stepped back, and Jax opened the locker slowly. A heavy pungent garlic odor immediately wafted out before he had a visual of the waders. Garlic?

Jax leaned in, lifted one of the boots from the locker, and inspected the tread caked in mud. His nose tingled from the scent. He inhaled deeper, certainty clicking in. He'd smelled a scent like that once before—the night his naval ship had been bombed.

The sky that night had filled with murky gasses, and they reeked of garlic.

It was a trait in the chemical component found in munitions and mustard gas. Where would Steven have been that he'd have dirt that smelled like a chemical bomb?

The coastal range had been fired on by a Japanese submarine during WWII. He'd read that not every missile had been recovered, and those that remained were out there leaking and rotting in the soil. That article also indicated the home team was no less guilty. Hundreds of munitions had been buried and forgotten along the coastline.

It was possible the state would have some maps of places they thought the munitions could be. An expert that could give him some direction would be even better.

Ignoring the landlord's gaze, Jax trotted to his patrol car and retrieved an evidence bag. When he returned, he removed a chunk of mud off the waders and sealed the contents. Each area of the coast had its unique properties. If the lab could get a hit on the mud composition, that could at least give them a general vicinity in which to search. It was worth a shot.

"I'm calling in crime techs from across the river to take the rest of this in and process upstairs," he said to Mr. Tannenbaum. "Can I count on you not to touch anything?"

"Absolutely. I caught a whiff of what you did the minute you opened that door. I know exactly what you found."

"You do?"

"Two tours in Nam, my friend. You bet your ass I do. Happy to oblige."

Jax left him with instructions to let Matt and the team have access the minute they arrived, and he ducked into his car, checking his phone. Brody hadn't called in with any luck on the SUV. And Chapman and Garrett must still be out interviewing that assault victim.

At least his men were on it. He made the calls to Matt and the techs to get the scene secured, bagged, and to the lab ASAP. Another to Trudy to find him someone from the Corp of Engineers who had expertise in the munition dump sites in the area, or at least some maps.

His next call was to Elena to find out if she knew where Steven might go fishing to need waders. She didn't answer.

He slammed his hands on the steering wheel. Waiting. Again. He didn't have time for this. If he couldn't get hold of Elena, Daniel might be the next best thing for filling in some blanks on her brother. He should know something, having been married to Elena for eight years. On his way to the lab to drop off the mud sample, he made the call to Daniel, who was closer than Jax thought.

Chapter Thirty-One

Emily's place had a few more cars in its driveway than it had the last two times Jax had been there. He'd told her to find some support, and he was glad her friends and neighbors had shown up. Including Daniel.

The bookish man walked out onto the porch, Allison's stuffed bear with the tutu tucked under his arm. "Any leads yet?" Daniel extended his other hand as Jax approached.

Jax shook it. "A few, and I've come with some questions."

"Should I get Emily? She's just updating some neighbors who brought over food. She's been a real mess. Especially after you didn't find Allison at the farm." Daniel's eye twitched. "Guess we all are." Daniel shook his head. "I'm sorry. I know you're doing the best you can. What kinds of questions?"

A wave of guilt rolled over Jax. He'd been wrong about the farm and Allison, but he was on the right track now. "What can you tell me about Elena's brother, Steven."

Daniel bristled. "He's a freak, but what's he got to do with anything?"

"We believe he's abducted Allison."

Daniel's brows drew together with confusion. "How's that possible? The man's a recluse. He's never met my daughter. I wouldn't let him near her even if he'd wanted to." Daniel's face hardened. "Why are you here then if he has my daughter? You know he's nuts, right? You should be out there getting that psycho behind bars and Allison back to us."

Jax felt the stab of Daniel's anger. "That's what I'm trying to do. I need to know everything you do about him. Where he goes? What he does? Elena must have shared things over the years, right?"

Daniel shook his head. "Not much."

"The morning he took Allison, he was seen a few hours later dressed in waders. Does he have a spot he might go fishing?"

Daniel started to pace the length of the porch, his face contorted in pain. "I have no idea. I never met the guy, let alone talk to him. All I can tell you is he only shows up when his life is falling apart, and Elena always goes to him. The man was the bane of our marriage."

Same story each time. Steven's anthropophobia and severe emotional issues had a stranglehold on his sister's attention. He called. She ran. "Give me an example?"

"That's the problem. I can't. Elena didn't share details, just that she felt responsible to help him through it. I'm sure that's why she never moved to Portland with me. Living across the river from him made it easier when he needed her to jump. Even her therapist couldn't get her to set boundaries when it came to that."

"Dr. Kavorian?"

Daniel nodded. "I'd hoped their sessions would get her away from her brother. Instead, she doubled down and became more protective." He gripped the bear.

Daniel's glimpse into Elena's life fueled Jax to get Steven out of it. But it wasn't helping him find Allison. Perhaps Steven's location linked back further. "Is there any place that Elena spoke about visiting with her own family? She'd mentioned that her father might have taken Steven places before she was born. Maybe Elena visited them, too."

He clicked his tongue a couple of times. "Again, she shared very few details of her past life during our marriage. Don't get me wrong, Elena is a wonderful woman. Kind. Compassionate. She's risen above what happened to her in many ways, but even all these years later, she has layers that come up around her childhood, and how she deals with it is to clamp it down."

If Elena was suppressing layers of her life, she might be the key to finding Steven. He just needed to find ways to get in. "She must have talked about her foster care situation?"

"Not really. I had to look up what happened to her and Madeline. Any details I've gotten I've gleaned when she talked in her sleep, and I asked her about it the next morning."

"Such as?"

"Well, not specifics. More like feelings maybe is the better way to say it. She adored her father something fierce. Always felt he was the one that would protect her, her hero, and then, of course, he and her mother died, and all hell broke loose."

Jax's heart squeezed. He'd known that love once. "Did anything come out of your conversations about those dreams? Even the mention of a location they visited as a family could help."

"No." He set the bear on the bench and rubbed his eyes. "How is this helping find Allison? You should be out there looking. Have you interrogated Elena? Insisted that she tell you everything about her brother?"

Daniel's demeanor was up and down. Stressed. His nerves as frayed as Emily's. Jax's own nerves were tenuous. He wasn't getting answers fast enough. But he had to cover every base. "Please, Mr. Krueger. Human nature often dictates that people run in circles, going to places they recognize. That's even more the case with the mentally ill. According to Elena, Steven had lived with the family before she was born. I'm trying to discern family patterns, habits, things they did so I can apply them to Steven's circle. Is that all she ever said about her parents?"

Daniel grabbed the bear again. "Elena often dreamed of gardens. Apparently, her mother had a beautiful rose garden. Elena loved them. Or I thought she did. I gave her a bouquet on our first anniversary, and she cried half the day."

"Anything about her father?"

He closed his eyes. Thinking. When he opened them, they had a spark. "He was a fisherman. One time when we were out at some bay for a picnic, she saw a man off the shore, and she'd told me then. I made a joke about giving it a try sometime—clearly, I'm not the outdoorsy type. Anyway, she said her father was a natural, and she'd gone with him a few times. That might relate to those waders you just mentioned...."

Jax perked up. It certainly might.

But before he could ask where, Daniel shook his head. "But again, no idea where they fished. She didn't offer, and I didn't ask. I mean, I wasn't serious about going myself."

Emily's front door opened, and three women emerged with somber looks, murmuring in concerned voices. Two were about Emily's age. The older woman he recognized as Commissioner Marks's wife. Dylan's mother, Deanna.

"Ladies," Jax said when the two younger women passed.

They nodded, and Deanna hung back with a scowl on her face. "Sheriff," she said before turning to Daniel. "We left Emily napping in her bedroom. Poor girl needs some sleep."

"Thank you. She's hardly shut her eyes through this."

She gave Daniel a one-armed hug. "Give Elena our love too if you see her, won't you?"

Daniel hugged her back. "If I see her, I most definitely will."

She turned to Jax. Waiting. Was she expecting him to apologize? "How's it coming with finding Allison?" she finally said. "Since you let Dylan come home last night, I can only assume he's no longer your prime suspect." Her words were short but fierce.

He hadn't *let* Dylan do anything. "It's a shame your son got caught up in this, but he put himself there by associating with the wrong people and selling drugs. Drugs that Allison had in her bedroom. I will chase down every lead to find her. You should understand that. I would do the same if Dylan was missing."

She squeezed her eyes closed. When she reopened them, the anger had dissipated. "I do. Poor Emily. And I know you're only doing your job." She sighed. "Dylan is just rebelling against Troy, who has his own demons. They're the ones I'm furious with because I'm stuck in the middle trying to keep the peace. But, Sheriff, Dylan's not a bad boy. Dumb as a box of rocks on occasion, but he's not evil."

"I'll keep that in mind," Jax said. As much as he wanted to learn more about Dylan, now wasn't the time to pump his mother for information. That would have to wait. "But I didn't realize you knew Elena."

"Her family had just moved to town a few months before her parents died in that accident. I was a grade ahead of her sister in school."

He knew Elena's parents had lived nearby prior to their deaths, but because Madeline and Elena's abduction occurred in Portland, that's where their investigation had focused. He'd never known details. Was that another error on their part? "Anywhere close?"

"Not sure. Her father worked for Troy's dad during that time. He might know."

Why hadn't Troy shared that information earlier? "I'll be sure to ask," he said as she headed to her car.

Jax's phone pinged with a text. Abby had the results on the feathers.

He handed Daniel his card. "You think of anything else, call me direct."

Daniel held it between his two palms. "Don't get me wrong, I'm glad Elena is cooperating about Steven. That's a big step for her, but you might need to press her harder. No matter what she says, she defends him."

Jax promised to stay in touch and called Abby the minute he'd started his cruiser. "Give me something good," he said when she answered after the third ring.

"The feathers are chicken, dyed, and most commonly used for fishing lures."

"Lures? Aren't they too chopped up for that?"

"They're remnants and used by fly fishermen specifically. They're tied with nylon line, and some of the feathers had minuscule strands of nylon still on them."

"How about the feathers Jameson sent over?"

"Same. Both were brittle, used for the same purpose, and came from the same source. They also share the same unique dye profile."

"Mechanically tied, or homemade?"

"Die-hard fly fishermen tie their own, but the samples you provided aren't conclusive."

It was still something. "I owe you."

Abby paused. Maybe thinking about how much of his hide he wanted to extract in exchange. "You might."

Despite what it could cost him, Jax liked the sound of that. "You think about it. In the meantime, I could use one more favor." He let go of his pride. He needed Abby's help. He'd always needed her. It was time he admitted that to himself. "Got access to a hypnotherapist?"

"Yes," she said.

He signed off a few minutes later and reversed the car. Steven's waders. The feathers. Allison could be somewhere Elena's father had taken them to fish. The question was where—and was the answer hidden in one of Elena's memories?

Chapter Thirty-Two

Elena walked back into her house, cringing at the mess Steven had left in his wake. Picking up the pieces for him had become so second nature, she didn't even feel angry. He lashed out; she took it. Despite her early trauma, she'd pulled her life together. Like she'd told Sheriff Turner, the second set of fosters had been decent to her. If not for them, there was no telling what she would have become.

She took full advantage by making something of her life. She'd fared far better than Steven, who'd been left flailing in the wind after their parents' death. That's why when he'd called her, no matter the drama happening in her world, she'd been there for him. She couldn't have imagined a time when she wouldn't be. They shared the grief of their parents. Of Madeline. Of their DNA. They were family.

She passed the living room and went into the bathroom to attend to her cut. How could she stand by him now, though? He'd left that note at the battery, leaving no doubt he'd abducted Allison. He'd likely beaten the man from the bar. She unwrapped the blood-drenched bandage from her hand. But as much as she wanted to run, how could she abandon him knowing he was ill—and the only family she had left?

But what if Sheriff Turner's theory was right that he'd abducted them and murdered Madeline? Had every interaction since been measured and calculated to make sure she never put the pieces together?

Her heart ached that her stepdaughter had gotten caught up in this mess. She must be terrified, but Elena didn't know how to help her or why she'd been chosen. She didn't know where to tell the sheriff to look.

Her hand rewrapped, she was numb and tired and craving peace back in her life. She slipped into a pair of jeans, a thigh-length sweater, and boots. Despite her fatigue, she couldn't sit and do nothing. She had to keep moving. She could make a brief appearance at her office to see the clients that were on the schedule. Her poor assistant Stacey had made enough excuses to clients the last couple of days—clients who needed her guidance. Even if it was just a few minutes of normalcy, she'd grasp it. If that were even possible with Allison missing, and her brother off the deep end. Regardless, she had to try.

Leaving the mess behind to deal with later, she left for her office. She found Stacey with her nose in a book at the front desk.

Stacey glanced up with surprise and scanned Elena. "What happened to your hand?"

Elena followed her secretary's gaze. Blood had soaked through the bandage again. "Lord," she said. "A broken wine glass, and I can't get the thing to stop bleeding." She walked into the bathroom off reception and unwrapped the gauze.

Stacey came up behind her with a roll of paper towels and the first aid kit. "You should have that looked at."

Elena assessed the long deep gash. Stacey was right, but her own welfare wasn't a factor at this point. "It'll be fine." Elena finished rinsing the wound, wincing as she rewrapped it. "Everything been good here?"

"I'm holding down the fort, as they say. I rescheduled your appointments for next week."

Elena frowned. "I was hoping to see them this afternoon."

"I'm sorry. I figured—"

Elena shook her head. "It's fine."

"You know, with everything going on."

Stacey was right. How could she help anyone when she couldn't even help Steven and was worried to death about Allison? "Thank you."

Stacey nodded. "Any word on Allison yet?"

Thankfully, Stacey hadn't tuned into the local news where Sheriff Turner had made fast work of getting Steven's sketch broadcasted. Elena didn't want to have to explain his involvement. "No, but they haven't stopped trying to find her."

Stacey frowned. "Daniel must be a complete wreck."

Elena looked away. She hadn't called to check on him like she'd promised and couldn't now. Sheriff Turner would have updated him as to Steven's involvement. She couldn't bear to hear him say he was right about her brother all along. "Everyone's doing as well as can be expected."

Stacey cleared her throat. "You've got mail," she said, her voice light and clearly picking up on Elena's mood.

Elena shook off the cloud. Normalcy. That's why she'd come to the office, desperate for it more than ever.

Mail was piled on Stacey's desk. Elena picked up the electric bill while scanning the clutter. Her eyes stopped on a chocolate rose stuck in the pencil holder along with the stack of chocolate hearts near the mouse she'd seen earlier. She clutched the envelope. "Where'd you get that rose?"

Stacey blushed. "My secret admirer. It had been popped through the mail slot this morning when I came in."

"Secret admirer?"

"Yes. Someone's been leaving me goodies for the past year. I thought you knew." Stacey grabbed the chocolates and dropped them one by one back into their stack like they were coins.

Elena's hands trembled. She had thought it could be a secret admirer when she'd seen them, but the rose...

"Are they there every day?"

Stacey shook her head. "Not always."

"Any clue who leaves them?"

"Not really. Although there's a cute guy on the janitorial team who winks at me when I leave for the night."

The back of her throat ached. "What's he look like?"

"Short, blond, and sexy." Stacey fanned herself.

Elena blinked, dispelling some tension. Not Steven. But Stacey was wrong. Not about the hearts, perhaps, but about that rose. It hadn't been left by a shy night janitor. Steven had been in her office—just like he'd been at

Madeline's and her mother's graves.

Stacey could be wrong about who'd given her the hearts, too. Over the years, Elena had mentioned her secretary to Steven. How sweet and helpful she was. How good she was at her job, and at keeping Elena organized. She'd texted him a picture about a year ago of her and Stacey having fun at a conference where Stacey had been her plus one.

It was an innocent act of wanting to include him in her life in a positive way. In retrospect, Steven could have taken a fancy to her. The timing would be right.

He could have slipped in and out while the night crew was working to avoid people. But why not communicate with Elena while he was here? How much more of Steven's life and his interactions did she know nothing about?

Elena's cell phone rang. She startled and retrieved it from her purse. Sheriff Turner "Hello," she said quickly, praying he'd found Allison.

"I have a proposition to run past you," he said and spent the next few minutes detailing a plan to get her to remember details from her childhood. She'd been so good at forgetting. Who had that served? No one.

If something from her past could connect to Steven and why he'd gone off the rails, which included leaving *forget me not* messages for Stacey, she had to try.

She dashed out of her office. For Allison's sake, she'd do it. But a new truth had started to niggle at her. What if the roses left at the graves, and shoved through her mail slot this morning, weren't tokens of remembrance or mere flirting with her secretary?

What if that final rose had been meant for her—and it was to say goodbye?

Steven might not want her help anymore. He could be tired of his small and fear-filled life. What if the reason he'd taken Allison and beaten the Portway man was because he was on a suicide mission and wanted Elena to feel the pain he did? He must know there was no easy way out.

If his goal was to die, then Allison was running out of time. Elena's whole body shook as she hopped in her car and turned it towards Misty Pines, remembering the pain of when everything changed.

Maddy had told her to run, and she did. The loud crack that had filled that night's air had been followed by complete darkness. The next thing she knew, the bounce of her chin on the hard ground had jolted her awake. Her teeth ground together. She'd moaned. Had she been shot? She'd ran her hands up and down herself. No gaping holes. Where was Maddy? Her mouth opened only to be slapped closed. No sound came out. Tight hands dug into her ankles. Dragging her. She couldn't see who it was. Grasses thrashed her face. She sensed eyes boring into her. She went limp. Tried to become invisible.

She was folded into a trunk. Eyes closed. Something thrown on her face before sleep overtook her.

When she woke, she reached out to find Maddy next to her. Elena's heart squeezed. They were together. Maddy would help her figure a way out. Tears filled her eyes as she reached for her sister and shook her.

"Maddy, wake up," she whispered with no response.

In the dark, Elena searched her sister's face with her trembling hands. Sticky blood oozed from Maddy's nose and head. Her eyes were closed. She couldn't feel Maddy's breath.... Wait. A little. Too little.

Elena curled in a ball when the engine came to life, and the car moved. Thump. Swish. Thump. Swish. The car tires against the pavement reached a hypnotic rhythm. Had to think. Keep the panic down. Figure a way out.

Trunk popped. Why had they stopped? There was no time to question. Another cloth over her face brought darkness again. The tire rhythm filled the trunk. Moving again. Had it been hours? Days? Maddy was now laying closer to the trunk's opening, while Elena had moved deeper in. She felt for her sister. The blood on Maddy had dried. Her chest barely moved, and there was little warmth to her skin.

When the car stopped for the last time, and the trunk popped, she forced her mouth open in a frozen scream. Eyes wide. Staring into the abyss. She'd seen it in a movie once. She'd practiced on the mister before. A game she played. Big hands pulled Maddy out first. The swoosh of cold air rushed into the trunk against her. Don't shake. Play dead. Footsteps. Walking away. Farther. Fading.

Run. Don't look back. Run.

Chapter Thirty-Three

Jameson's number lit up Jax's cell just as he pulled into the station.

"Hey buddy, you were on my list." Jax killed the engine. "I owe you a thank you for sending your file over to Abby."

"No problem. That's actually why I'm calling. Anything come back on those feathers yet?" his ex-partner asked.

Jax leaned back in the seat. He'd missed this—their connection. "Just got off the phone with Abby a bit ago." He launched into the rundown of that conversation.

"Fishing lures. I'll be damned," Jameson said. "I'll be interested to see how this pans out. Keep me posted, will ya?"

"You bet." He was about to click off when it dawned on him that he should have picked up the phone to Jameson earlier. "Got a question. Do you recall an older brother in the Massey case?"

"You're talking about Steven?"

Jax's face slacked. "Yeah. I don't remember his name coming up."

"The social worker mentioned him later, when placing Elena into a new foster home."

"In what way?"

"From what I recall, Elena had hoped to live with him instead of going back into the system."

"We may have erred in not following that lead further." Hopefully not a fatal one. Jax quickly brought his former partner up to speed.

Jameson cleared his throat, clearly not liking the fact they'd dropped the ball any more than Jax. "Have you reached out to the social worker for more info on him?"

"She died a few years ago."

"And getting her case files will take an act of God, no doubt."

"At least in the time frame I have, yes."

"Sorry, bud. That's all I got."

It wasn't anything he could work with to find Allison. But talking to his old partner had grounded him.

Jax got out and passed Chapman's truck. He'd kept his deputy so busy from the moment he'd landed from Alaska that he hadn't even unloaded his gear. His duffel was in the back, and the cab still had his oversized coats. Pure bachelor. Abby wouldn't have let him get away with that.

But it was nearly five, which meant they had twenty-four hours to find Allison. He didn't intend to keep Chapman, or any of his deputies, any less busy. If Steven had been involved in the Portway assault as Elena suspected, he was capable of making good on his threat to harm Allison.

Inside, Jax headed for his office when Chapman intercepted him, his face flushed. "Trudy updated me the minute I got back," Chapman said. "Garrett was able to get a map of the known munition dump sites from the Army Corps of Engineers. We're set up in the incident room."

Jax nodded, following Chapman. In the room, he scanned the wall map they'd secured with thumbtacks. The cleaned-up sites were denoted by colored push pins. It looked like an art project gone wrong. "Where to start?" Jax said. "Is this complete?"

"Yes and no. According to the Corps, it covers the spots they know about. Casey Beach, for instance, was added recently when it was cleaned last year. They insist there wouldn't be any munitions left over that would cause a leakage. According to them, they're thorough. Which leads to no, because like that beach, it was brought to their attention by hikers who stumbled upon it."

"Meaning we don't know anything about where those waders were."

"What waders?" Chapman said.

Brody popped his head in. "Hey, boss."

"Got anything?" Jax asked.

Brody stared at the wall map. "Nothing. No one saw a black SUV anywhere. Holy crap, what are all those pins for?"

"Already known and cleaned up munitions sites. But given what Chapman just said, it's not necessarily where we're looking for Allison." He went on to explain about the waders in Steven's apartment. "What is possible is that Steven crossed through one of those undiscovered locations to wherever he's holding Allison."

"Which means it won't be on any map," Chapman said.

Jax nodded, but took a picture of the wall with his phone for reference anyway since it labeled different areas of the coastline. So many possibilities. Too many. If his theory was right about Steven having Allison in a location where Elena and her father had fished at one time, then only Elena could narrow down those possibilities for him.

"I saw Truman," Chapman said, swiping his wet forehead.

"You feeling okay?" Jax asked.

"Yeah, fine." Chapman frowned. "Anyway, the guy swore he was just being friendly with the lady. Big misunderstanding." Chapman rolled his eyes. "But when I asked about his assault, suddenly he was the victim. The guy came out of nowhere and kicked the crap out of him. He lifted his shirt to show me where his ribs had been broken."

"Visual ID?" Jax asked as they left Brody in the room, inspecting the map, and walked back to his office.

Chapman shook his head. "Said he didn't remember anything but a baseball cap. Sounded to me like he didn't want to remember."

At every turn, Steven was untraceable. Wouldn't Truman want to see Steven pay if he'd been hurt that badly? Was Truman scared he'd come back if he remembered too much? "Is the hypnotherapist here yet?"

"Garrett's getting her set up. Matt's waiting for Ms. Massey to arrive."

Abby had come through for him. "Good."

"You don't think it's a little extreme?" Chapman swiped his forehead again.

"If it gets Allison home, no." Jax took a seat behind his desk while Chapman remained inside the doorway.

Chapman nodded. Whether he'd admit it or not, his deputy didn't look well, but he could rest when they found Allison.

"What I do know is Abby's team identified the feathers. They were used to make lures. I just need Elena to remember where she and her dad fished." He tapped his fingers on the desk. "You're an outdoorsman. What do you know about fishing locations around here?"

Chapman crossed his arms over his chest. "Sorry, boss, my fishing's done from a boat in the middle of an ocean."

"You must know people who fish the inlets, though?"

"My buddies are all about deep-sea fishing, and we hunt in Eastern Oregon, so not a lot of familiarity with the trails around here either. Besides, you know how many there are. It's like a needle...."

"Yeah, I know." It would take hundreds of volunteers and days to cover it all. Days Allison didn't have. "Well, some old timer or Eagle Scout group might know. Ask." He couldn't hinge everything on Elena.

"Yes, sir."

Jax's computer chimed with a new email. "Forensic report is in," he said, clicking it open. The DNA test had come through. Nothing on the soil analysis yet.

"What's it say?" Chapman asked.

"Those dried blood drops belonged to Madeline and Elena." Jax leaned back. "Twenty-five-year-old evidence has been sitting right there all this time. Unbelievable." After Steven had taken the girls from that rural street, he must have laid low at the battery. But there were no signs of feathers, or excessive blood. It wasn't where he'd killed Madeline.

Chapman cleared his throat. "Anything on the abductor?"

"Nothing, or on Allison, at least in the blood samples. That doesn't mean she wasn't there." Except he would have expected more proof than the twine bracelet under the chair. "Regardless of whether it was planted or not, Steven is recreating the original case. Clearly, that means there's another place the killer took Madeline and Elena after the battery. That could be where Madeline was murdered and where he's taken Allison now."

Chapman flushed red, turning abruptly. "How about announcing yourself in the future?"

Commissioner Marks came from behind. Chapman shot him a look like they'd had more unfavorable interactions than the one last night when Troy stormed in to get Dylan. Jax, however, had expected the Commissioner to return at some point, since he'd held back unleashing in the presence of his lawyer.

The Commissioner pounded his fist on Jax's desk before Jax could get a word out. "What the hell do you think you're doing raiding my cousin's farm? You're going to pay dearly for that stunt."

Jax flattened his hands on his desk and pushed himself upright. "If your cousin has any concerns, he should be here himself."

Troy's face contorted. "He sent me, you arrogant ass, but don't think he isn't looking at every which way to sue you and get you booted from this town permanently."

After this case, he might go willingly. "He should be more worried about how he plans to defend himself for bringing in undocumented workers and treating them like livestock. At worst, he's complicit. At best, he's a complete moron." This wasn't the best tack to get information from Marks, but the man had a way of burrowing under his skin every time.

Chapman had stepped out of the room, probably to save himself.

The Commissioner's tight expression said he might spit bullets. "He didn't know anything about what was happening there. He lives in California."

"Take it up with the FBI. They're in charge over there now."

"All brought on by you and your rush to judgment."

Jax didn't want to give Marks the satisfaction that he'd been riled. But he couldn't stay quiet. "The conditions there were deplorable. Why aren't you more outraged that this was happening under your nose, too? Instead of looking at ways to ruin me, aim that rage where it belongs. And I'll tell you this, I would go back to that farm again and again for Allison Krueger. She's fourteen. Have you forgotten she's missing? You seemed to be all up in it whenever I ask Dylan questions."

The Commissioner scoffed. "Who I never want to see in here again."

Jax shook his head. "Fancy lawyering won't save him. Have you stopped for a second to realize what you're rescuing him from? He's been dealing drugs to other kids. He'll be charged for that."

The Commissioner's face flushed again. "When my cousin gets done with you, you won't have a badge."

"Do what you need to, Troy." He had to get back on track. He didn't have time for this nonsense. "By the way, I ran into Deanna earlier."

"Now you're messing with my wife?"

Jax raised his hands. "Relax. She was at Emily's place and mentioned that you knew the Massey family?"

His eyes narrowed. "Name sounds familiar, but I don't recall knowing them."

"Deanna thinks Mr. Massey worked for your father at some point."

Troy snorted. "My dad owned the cannery. He had thousands of workers over the years. But hell, that was well over twenty-five years ago. I would have been neck deep in college and into my own things."

Jax frowned. "Any idea where they lived?"

The Commissioner shook his head. "Not a clue." He tucked his hands in his pockets. "Why does it matter?"

"Everything matters until Allison's home."

That seemed to rein him in. "You getting any closer to finding her?"

Like Jax intended to share where he was on the case with Troy Marks now, or ever. Matt appeared and motioned with his head. Elena must have arrived. Jax stood again and rounded his desk. "You bet I am."

Troy straightened his jacket. "I hope for the sake of the family you don't screw it up this time. The people of this town pay you to be effective."

Jax held back a snipe as the Commissioner whipped around and left the way he'd come.

This town did deserve the best version of Jax, and they were about to get their money's worth when he brought Allison home and closed the two cases.

He just needed to get Elena talking about the past.

Chapter Thirty-Four

Elena followed Jax into a room that had been prepared to mimic a low-lit psychiatrist's office. The therapist had her cell on the table and soft music playing. Elena had never been hypnotized, even though Dr. Kavorian had suggested it a few times. But she'd studied the technique during college on her way to a degree.

Minutes before, she'd sat across from Jax in another small room where she'd helped the artist sketch Steven. Jax had asked her a few questions about going fishing with her father while they waited for the therapist to prepare. He believed the location they fished might link to where Steven had taken Allison now. She'd vaguely remembered those times but not where they'd gone. Only that she hated worms.

"But I'd tolerate those squirmy creatures to be with my dad. That I do remember." She'd always felt safe when she was with him. Like she did with Jax.

The image of the first day they met had hit her. She'd been wandering, bleeding, dazed, when finally a Good Samaritan had stopped. She hadn't had anything to drink or eat for what felt like days. The kind woman who found her called the police. Gave her water. Food. And then Detective Turner and his partner arrived.

Jax had wrapped her in a blanket and put her in the back of his car. She'd laid on the seat, staring at the back of his head and the slope of his strong shoulders, and closed her eyes. His voice had been calm. Assuring her that she'd be all right.

He'd driven her to the hospital and asked her questions then. Questions she couldn't answer. Would she do any better now with the hypnotherapist?

She settled into the cushioned armchair and leaned back. A full storage box had been placed for a footrest.

The therapist, whose auburn hair swirled on her head, gazed at Elena with laser green eyes and reached out her hand. "I'm Heather. I'll be guiding you this afternoon." She went through the basics of her credentials and qualifications to conduct the session. "Any questions?"

Elena grimaced. "I've been missing my sunglasses for a week. If you can ask me where I put them, I'd appreciate it." She hoped levity would calm her nerves. It didn't.

Heather smiled. "I'll see what I can do." She handed her a pair of headphones. "Put these on. You'll hear music, and I'll be talking into this microphone and recording the session. We'll watch it together after for any clarifications. Sheriff Turner will accompany us during that time. Is this agreeable to you?"

Jax watched from the corner.

Elena noted the tired bags under his eyes, the stubble on his face, the slouch of his stance. All because of Steven. Because she'd failed to bring him in. This whole mess was her fault. "Yes," she said.

Heather adjusted her microphone. "Sheriff, please leave the room. I'll call you once we're done."

He looked at Elena. "I understand this approach is unorthodox, but I wouldn't be asking if time wasn't running out."

"I know."

He nodded. "You sure you don't want to call in anyone for support during this?"

Daniel had once been that person. Then she'd relied on Steven. "I'm sure."

He gave her a reassuring smile.

Heather cleared her throat. "Then, if you're ready."

Elena nodded.

Jax turned on the video camera and stepped out of the room.

"Close your eyes," Heather said. "Listen to my voice."

Elena crossed her ankles and laid her hands on her lap. Listening.

"I want you to be conscious of your breathing," Heather began. "Ten, nine…. And I want you to become aware of your hands. Feel the weight of them. Imagine that heaviness and tension flowing out of your fingertips."

Elena felt the stress leaving, her shoulders sagging.

"Become aware of the muscles in your thighs. Your calves. Your ankles. The tiniest muscles of your feet. Feel light wash over you, evaporating the tightness from them. Eight. Seven."

Elena's feet and hands prickled.

"Now, visualize an elevator in front of you. The doors are opening. Step in."

Elena did.

"The elevator is going down. Down. Six. Five."

Elena's whole body tingled with the sensation of dropping further into the Earth's crust.

"The doors are opening, and there's a meadow. The grasses are long and golden. Birds are overhead. One is landing. It's large enough to hold you. Get onto the bird."

A feeling of giddiness flooded over Elena. She crawled on top of a swan, clinging to its long neck.

"Now fly. Let the bird take you. Feel the wind. Four. Three."

The sensation of the breeze on her face made her smile. For the first time in so long, she had a sense of wonder. Lightness. Relief.

"Two, One."

Elena soared above the ground, taking control of the swan, swooping above the land. She reached out, brushed her hands through the grasses, and laughed. Images of a happy life filled her mind. Allison, asleep on the couch. Roper nuzzling Allison's neck. A candlelight dinner with Daniel at Chez Lounge. Her college diploma handed to her at a ceremony on a warm June afternoon.

She pulled on the swan. It climbed upward toward the sun. She leaned into the neck and back down again they went. Like a TV going on the blink, images of darkness tried to disrupt the show, but she held tighter to the swan's neck, not allowing them to take hold. She rode the roller coaster over and over and over.

The snap of fingers interrupted the ride, and her eyes fluttered open.

She stared into Heather's calming face. "Do you feel refreshed?"

Elena must have been flying for only a few minutes, but she nodded. "I had the most wonderful ride on a swan, of all things." She chuckled, feeling self-conscious. "But I'm so sorry. I was no help to you at all."

Heather smiled. "But you were. We've got it all on tape. You were wonderful. You remembered."

She did? Elena swallowed the lump in her throat. "I don't recall saying anything."

"It happens often in people undergoing a lot of stress. You may remember even more later tonight, and in the days to come, but that's why we record the session. You can see for yourself. I'll get the sheriff."

Chapter Thirty-Five

The hypnotherapist, Elena, and Jax huddled around the monitor. Jax studied Elena on the recording as she'd gone deeper into hypnosis while the therapist had counted down. She'd raised a finger in answer to questions that Heather posed. Smiles flickered across her face like she hadn't a care in the world.

When Elena spoke, she answered the questions he'd been waiting for. "Fishing, yes. A few times." Her face had broken out in a grimace. "I only went because it was daddy and me time. Mostly I sat on the shore and looked for cool rocks while he stood in the water, whipping his pole forward and back. Forward and back."

Heather nodded. "Do you know where you are?"

Elena shook her head.

"Do you hear anything?"

"Seagulls."

"Are they on a beach around you?'

"No."

"Flying overhead?"

"Yes."

"What do you see?"

"Daddy." Elena had sounded gleeful, like a little girl.

"What's the water like?"

"Calm."

"What do you smell?"

Jax had leaned in, eyes locked on the screen.

Elena wrinkled her nose. "Fish."

"Where are you?"

"Don't know."

"Did your dad drive there?"

"Yes."

Heather had stopped, looked at some notes. "Was it right off the road?"

"No."

"Did you walk?"

"Yes."

"From where?"

"The fish shack."

Jax's shoulders tightened. That would make sense. Some place to be holed up.

"Where is that shack, Elena?"

"Don't know."

"What's it look like?"

"Wood. Dark. Red."

"Redwood?"

"No. The roof."

The questions continued for a few more minutes. But Elena didn't have any more to offer that gave a clear location.

Heather turned off the recording. "Because Elena was so young, it's possible she never knew the exact spot her father took them to fish. It's also possible the memories are buried more deeply than one session can retrieve."

Jax masked his disappointment. Allison couldn't wait for another session. But Elena had given him something to work with, and if Chapman drummed up another local fisherman or two, he might be able to fill in some blanks. If not, he had one other potential source....

"I can try again," Elena said.

Heather smiled. "The mind only gives what it can in the moment." She turned to Jax. "Now that the memories have been stirred, more could emerge as soon as tonight. I suggest you get her some dinner. Let her unwind, and they could very well start flowing. It's like removing a rock from a dam. But if you push too much, it could have the opposite result."

Elena met Jax's eyes. "I'm sorry."

"Don't be. We now know there's a dark woodshed with a red roof."

Elena scoffed. "Probably only a hundred of those around here."

"It's more than we had an hour ago. Sounds like you only lived here a short time as a kid, but I'll have Trudy do a property search to see if your parents owned land with a fishing shack in the area. There might be a record of it."

He guided Elena out of the room and left her in his office to gather herself while he found Trudy to get her on the search. "Also, get Rick Johnson brought up from the holding cells." It might be a long shot that he'd cooperate or know anything, but it was worth a try. Rick liked to fish. Elena's dad liked to fish. Long shot or not, he had to dig for more facts while he waited to hear from Chapman on whether he'd been able to tap a source.

Trudy didn't look up from her computer. "His parole officer had him transferred to Portland earlier today."

Jax clenched his fist. "I should have been notified of that request."

"You'll have to take it up with Chapman. He authorized it because of the new suspect."

"Where is Chapman?" He'd leaned on his deputy too long, and now Chapman believed he could make decisions without consulting Jax.

"He said he was hitting up the old tavern for the local fishermen you asked for and then heading to get some sleep. He'd let you know if he had anything. As for the boys, I sent them home. They'll all be back bright and early."

A headache gnawed at the base of Jax's skull.

Trudy must have sensed his annoyance. "Hon, Chris looked terrible, and you and the boys look like rags in the wind. You should go home and eat. Change your clothes at least."

Allison didn't have that option—why should he? They were so close and so far at the same time. Jax rubbed the space between his brows before grabbing his phone. He texted Chapman: *Looking for locations with fishing shacks. Red roof. Call me the minute you have a lead.*

Chapman responded with *Got it!*

Trudy kept staring at him. "Hon, we all want to find Allison, but if you boys drop in the middle of the street from exhaustion, you'll do her no good."

His jaw tightened not only at her candor, but that she was right. They couldn't stop, though. At least he couldn't. He'd find Allison alone if he had to. He wouldn't wait for Chapman's leads or anyone else's. "Set up a Skype with Johnson. I have some questions."

"On it."

"Anything more on the social worker files or search of institutions where Steven might have been living?"

"Nothing so far."

More waiting. Jax shook his head with frustration and strode to the kitchen. Despite Trudy's words of caution, he downed an energy drink. He wanted to get in his car and start searching for fishing spots himself. But with the forest floor being so dense, so boggy, such hostile terrain even during the day, heading out near dark with no real direction could equal disaster. He'd need to cool his heels until he had some answers either from Chapman or Rick Johnson.

That hope on Rick, however, came to a halt five minutes later when Trudy came into the kitchen. "He's refusing the interview."

"Get his parole officer on the phone."

"That's who I spoke with. He said his hands are tied and Mr. Johnson has rights."

What about Allison's right to be home with her mother? What was wrong with everyone? "Then get Johnson back here. Now. Tell that parole officer I have an active investigation, and Rick should have never been transferred." If Rick thought refusing a Skype interview would save him, he didn't know who he was dealing with.

"I'm sure he'll agree. He felt bad he couldn't compel him. But transfer papers take a minute."

Jax marched back to his office, where Elena was resting her eyes. "I appreciate your doing this. Hopefully, Trudy's search will give us more to go on."

"Anything to help. I just wish I could remember more."

"Are any details of the shack coming to you? Or landmarks on the drive out to the area?" The therapist said it was like freeing a dam and not to push. He didn't want to push. He wanted to kick the hell out of the rock holding in the information and let it flood out.

She shook her head. "Not yet." She stood, the color draining from her face. She listed to the right, nearly falling into him.

He reached to steady her. "What happened?"

She put her hand on her stomach and dropped back into the chair. "Hungry, I guess. It's been a long day. I don't remember the last time I ate."

He had the same issue. The therapist had said get her dinner. Let her unwind. He didn't have time to eat or relax, but he was in a waiting game anyway. And if she remembered…. "How about we grab a bite?"

She pressed her hand to her face. "That would be fine."

His gaze intensified. She wasn't in shape for eating out. "You like lasagna?"

"Sure."

He nodded and grabbed his keys from his desk. "Follow me."

Chapter Thirty-Six

Jax popped two frozen Stouffers in the microwave and left Elena in the kitchen before heading to the living room to secure his whittling knife in a drawer. He checked his phone. No Chapman, or Trudy with word she'd performed a miracle and had Rick on his way back yet. In the bedroom, he changed into a clean uniform, and washed his face, running his electric razor over the rough patches of stubble on his chin.

By the time he'd returned to the kitchen, Elena had set out the two cardboard containers of steaming pasta on the table, along with two tumblers filled with caramel liquid. His bottle of Jim Beam sat near the sink. A drink would ease his ever-present tension since Allison went missing, but getting her home would be the only relief.

He retrieved the glass and poured the contents back into the whiskey bottle.

Elena stared at him. "I'm sorry. I should've asked first."

"No worries. Just want to stay on my game." He set the glass in the sink.

She cupped her glass between both hands. "Would you prefer if I don't?"

They were just outside the eighteen-hour mark. Anything to help her relax—to remember. "After today, you've earned it."

"Thanks. And thank you for dinner. It almost feels like life is normal."

Sitting here felt the exact opposite. Besides Allison, he hadn't had guests of any kind since Abby moved out. Things were not all right. Not normal. His nerves pinged. Food was the last thing on his mind.

"You really don't recall anything from the session today?" he said.

"Nothing. One moment I'm soaring through the air. Next, my eyes are open. It felt like only a minute had passed." She took a sip of her drink. "A wonderful, stress-free minute." She swirled her fork in the middle of the lasagna but didn't take a bite. "It hasn't been easy with Steven."

That had to be an understatement.

She lowered her gaze to the table, set down her fork, and grabbed the whiskey again. "Of course, he might say the same of me."

"How so?" Jax started eating.

"Up until our parents died, Maddy and I didn't want for much. She was popular with the boys, I was carefree. A kid. Steven wasn't around, and that's telling. Then after the accident, everything fell apart for all of us. We were swept away. Steven was on his own. Then the incident."

"Your abduction?"

She nodded and brought the glass back to her lips, taking another long drink. "He's all I have left, but he's got his own issues. Suddenly I'm falling apart and needing him desperately. He probably thought I was a weak hot mess."

He shook his head. "You were a child. What you're doing now, turning your brother in, assisting in finding him, that takes courage."

She shrugged. "I guess. And I have tried to help him. To be honest, he's been such a burden, I don't know how I feel about him anymore." She finished the glass.

He knew how sadness could move into the cracks and take hold. And how whiskey had a way of filling those cracks. "Eat," he said.

She nodded and took a few bites. "I do appreciate everything, Sheriff. You know, I do remember you."

"You do?"

"Of course. You came to my rescue."

He shifted. He hadn't thought of it that way; he'd only felt failure for not finding Madeline in time. That feeling threatened him again now. "I was glad to be there for you, and to hear your life turned out so well. When I saw you in your office a couple of days ago, I was impressed."

"The day I needed to rush off to see my therapist." She tightened her grip on her empty glass.

"Has he helped?"

She shrugged. "To some degree. I guess it all depends on how much you let people in, right?" Something they both struggled with for certain. "Who's the dollhouse for?"

His stomach tightened. "You went into my garage?"

"I was looking for the pantry." She met his eye. "It's beautiful. I didn't realize you had a daughter. Did your wife get her in the divorce like Emily did Allison?" There was a slight edge to her voice.

He would have taken that if given a choice. "Cancer."

Her eyes widened. "I'm so sorry." She got up and filled her glass with more whiskey. "When?"

"Five years." His tone sounded pathetic. "Before we lost her, I promised I'd finish it. I intend to keep that promise."

Her eyes narrowed in compassion. "I get it, believe me. I'm not judging."

Of course, she'd understand. He'd sounded too curt. "Appreciate that." He needed to get the conversation back on track before he was a mess.

But it was too late for Elena. Tears rolled down her face. She tilted the fresh glass of whiskey and finished it in one swallow. Her face contorted. "That's really nice that your daughter had you."

The stress of the last few days flowed out.

The hypnotherapist had warned him about pushing too hard. He'd been careful. He couldn't know that just being a father to Lulu would have been a trigger. Elena wilted into the chair. Exhausted. The whiskey had gone straight into her system.

"You're going to stay here tonight," he said.

"I couldn't."

"I can't let you drive. Besides, if you remember any more details, I'll be right here."

She eventually dried her eyes and conceded, if she was allowed to sleep on the couch. They finished eating without another word. She rose slowly and went to the counter, and poured another shot.

"That's not the answer. It's a tricky friend. You only think it's doing you a favor."

She sniffed. "Tonight, I could use this friend."

It was his turn not to judge. He set their forks in the sink and tossed the containers before leaving her to change the sheets on his bed and tidy his room. Elena had insisted she sleep on the couch, but he'd been raised better than that.

He retrieved Elena and steered her to his room. "There're clean towels in the bathroom, and you should be good for the night."

She gave him a small smile. "Thank you."

He shut the door behind her and made his way to the living room. He secured his gun under a pillow and plopped down on the couch. His phone chirped with a text. Trudy. "Nothing on the Masseys owning property in town or out. Sorry. Rick's on his way back." Good. But that meant at least a few hours before he could get in his face for answers. Hours he didn't have when Allison was with a man who had a history of violence. Chapman hadn't texted anything on his end either.

Jax tossed the phone on the coffee table and stared at the whiteboard still hanging on the wall. He pressed the heels of his hands into his eyes, then stood and erased his previous ramblings. He began again, this time by listing out some of the popular fishing locales he knew about. He didn't include those off Osbourn Park as that area had been thoroughly searched at this point. He pulled up the picture of the map on his phone from the incident room.

To his list, he added Dead Man's Creek, Bounty Basin, and a dozen others he realized he had no idea about and quickly saw there were simply too many options. Misty Pines was surrounded by water in some form or another. He needed someone who'd been out there, fishing all their lives, who knew the inlets. If Chapman had found someone, seems he would have let him know by now.

At least Rick was on his way back. He'd boasted from their initial meeting about having fished the local spots. Said he knew where all the fat trout could be caught. Even Wallace had said his nephew knew his stuff. Jax would test that theory soon enough.

Elena could also hold the key as well, but what if the memories didn't come like the hypnotherapist suggested? Or they might come too late. He dropped back onto the couch, staring at the whiteboard until the black ink blurred.

He heard her breath before he felt the warmth of it on his neck, and then her thigh against his hip.

"Save me," she whispered in his ear. Abby?

Save her. He could do that. He wanted to. They'd endured so much together.

A tug on his pants. Save her? Abby would never ask that.

Jax bolted upright, his momentary haze lifting, and nearly knocked Elena off the couch. "What are you doing?"

Elena started and hopped away from him, dressed in a pair of lacy underwear and his Navy T-shirt that barely touched her thighs. She'd pulled her hair up into a messy bun. "I thought you wanted me."

She'd misread his understanding for something more. He caught sight of another filled tumbler of whiskey on the coffee table next to his phone. Or was it the same glass she'd poured earlier? The glassiness in her eyes said it wasn't the same. "Elena. You've had a stressful week."

"I need you."

"You need sleep." It was three in the morning. He jumped off the couch, angry that he'd nodded off, and picked up the whiskey. He took it into the kitchen and dumped it in the sink, and started a pot of coffee.

When he returned to the living room, Elena was in a chair, cradling her face in her hands. "I'm so sorry. I don't know what came over me. I guess I thought…."

He hadn't meant to cause her pain, but he wouldn't comfort her and be misread again. Abby owned his heart, whether she wanted it or not. "If I gave you that impression, I—"

The living room window shattered, followed by an ear-piercing pop. Jax dove for Elena, jerking her out of the chair and down onto the ground. He shielded her with his arms as another shot sailed into the room and slammed into a lamp that had once lit up his father's den.

He scrambled to the couch and retrieved his gun from under his pillow.

He rolled back to Elena and covered her head, peeking up to see who was assaulting them with bullets.

Instead, another shot blasted its way into the house.

Chapter Thirty-Seven

The shooter had to be Steven. If he'd only meant to issue a warning, one shot would have been enough. His intention was clear—he wanted Jax dead.

His eyes glued to the window, scanning for any movement outside, Jax reached for his phone and called Chapman. His deputy panted into the phone, like he'd been startled out of a deep sleep. "I'm under fire. Get here now," Jax said.

Chapman lived a few miles away. Hunkering on the floor until he arrived wasn't an option.

"It's Steven," Elena said.

Jax hadn't let her move since he'd pulled her to the ground. "That's my guess." Either Steven realized Jax was getting close and had to be stopped, or he believed the sheriff stood between him and his sister. He might even think Jax was forcing Elena to turn on him.

The only bright spot with Steven outside—he wasn't with Allison. Jax had to apprehend him alive so he could tell them where he had her.

He removed his protective arm from Elena and nodded to the hallway. "Get to that bathroom, lock the door, and lay in the bathtub."

On the verge of hyperventilating, Elena managed a nod. "Don't let him kill you."

A few days ago, he might have welcomed the bullet. Not now. He wasn't going anywhere, by Steven's hands or his own. "Move."

She hesitated, then army-crawled to the hallway.

Jax didn't budge until her feet disappeared into the bathroom, and he heard the click of the lock. On all fours, he clambered over the broken lamp on his way to the kitchen and into the garage. Inside the windowless space, he found a flashlight, and opened the door to the back yard. Outside, he flashed the light around, confirming the shooter hadn't made his way to the rear of the house. He locked the door behind him.

Adrenaline pumping at a record pace, he crept to the side gate. The latch was secured. He opened the gate, conscious of every creak, and made his way to the front of the house where the shots had come from. His truck sat at the curb.

From his vantage point, he had a partial visual of the outline of the trees across the street. He stared into black. Clouds shrouded the moon off to the west, offering no help. Once his eyes adjusted, he focused on the tree line. The thump of his own heartbeat in his ears made it difficult to hear anything else, but he scanned the area inch by inch. No movement. A motor sounded in the distance. Not quite close enough to be related, but hard to tell.

The last bullet had gone into the house over five minutes ago. The attack could be over. Or the shooter could be waiting for Jax to move into the open. He scooped up a stone and threw it into the yard to see if it stirred a response. It didn't.

Hunched close to the ground, he made his way to the front of the garage, keeping to the shadows. A moving target was hard to track, but if Steven took a shot, at least Jax would know where the bastard was hiding.

Staying low, Jack darted to his truck, squatting near the tire for cover. When no shots rang out, Jax exhaled. He swept the flashlight's beam underneath the chassis. All clear.

He moved to the other side of the house, using his overgrown rhododendron bushes for cover. Side yard was empty. No footprints. No broken limbs. For safe measure, he aimed his flashlight toward the road hoping to draw him out. The moment passed in silence.

Confident they weren't in immediate danger, Jax assessed the damage to the front window. The way the glass had shattered, he suspected a rifle had been used. An inspection of the bullets would tell them for sure. Whatever the gauge, the shooter had meant business.

He wouldn't be able to leave it in its present state all night unless he wanted a few raccoons for housemates. Jax walked to the garage and punched the code for the opener. Elena must be going out of her mind. Gunshots were enough to rattle anyone's nerves. He'd get her out of that bathroom and assure her she was safe before doing anything else.

Before the garage door rolled up all the way, reflections of red and white lights bounced off his house and trees. Chapman had arrived, followed by another SUV that belonged to Brody.

Chapman reversed into the driveway and aimed the spotlights on the tree line before climbing out of his car. "Shit, Turner. You okay?"

The forest illuminated, Jax scanned the property across the street. "Fine. Front window has seen better days. See you called in the cavalry." Two out of Jax's three deputies fell out of their car and hurried up on him and Chapman.

"You okay, Sheriff?" Brody said, with Garrett nodding next to him.

"He missed, that's what's important. No Matt?"

Chapman looked out into the trees. "He got called in on night crew at the store right after he left the station. The shots come from over there?"

Jax nodded. "All three of them."

Chapman's face flushed as he swiped his drenched forehead.

"Still not feeling good?" Jax asked.

"Don't worry about me. You go back inside and get dressed. Me and the boys will do a sweep."

"I am dressed."

Chapman nodded to Jax's middle.

Jax's belt was unbuckled, and his top button undone. He frowned while he fixed them and addressed his men. "Fan out and see what you can find. I'll get this window shuttered."

Chapman turned to Brody and Garrett. "We'll each sweep a quadrant, but eyes open. He could be out there."

They nodded and split up.

Jax went inside and straight to the bathroom. The shower was running.

Elena must have drunk more than he thought. She had to be completely out of it to jump in a shower with Steven outside, trying to kill them, but, with any luck, the hot water would help get her sober.

He tapped lightly. "When you're done, it's safe to come out." He disappeared into the garage to grab plywood for the window.

Half-hour later, his window covered, the team had returned and were briefing him inside his dining room.

"We didn't find anything," Brody and Garrett reported. "Scared off a couple of deer, and someone is using that back field for a dumping ground because we found old mattresses and rusted car parts."

Chapman agreed. "I also suspect the shooter came and went from that back access point. Saw some tire tracks, but nothing else. There's a couple of roads that lead out to the main one."

"No weapon?"

"Not even shell casings," Chapman said. "But it's a big area. We could've missed them."

Jax nodded. "Daylight will give us a better picture." He glanced at his watch. Four thirty. "But I have a pretty good idea who did it."

"Massey?" Chapman asked.

"You got it. He knows we're closing in. And he might have taken issue that Elena was here."

Chapman cleared his throat, his hand on his abdomen. "Elena's here?"

Jax shot him a look. He must be piecing the fact his pants had been undone to the new information, but he didn't owe his deputy an explanation. "You look like shit."

"It's not been a good night." Chapman placed his hand on his stomach again.

"Did you find me anyone at the bar who has some knowledge on the local fishing spots?"

"No. After a few beers, all I could get was fishing tales of the big ones they caught, or more often the ones that got away. No real insight on where to go. Most of the old codgers haven't been out on any trails for years." He cleared his throat. "Why'd you bring Elena here?"

"The hypnotherapist said the session might stir Elena's memories. I wanted her close in case they did." He hadn't checked on her in a while. His hot water tank would be empty by now. "I'll be right back."

The bathroom door was closed, and the water still running. He knocked. "Elena, you about done?" This time he listened for a response. Nothing. Something wasn't right. He knocked again. "Everything alright in there?"

Chapman came up from behind. "She took a shower during a shooting?"

Jax's shoulders tightened. "Weird, I agree. She might be sick from the liquor." Jax ignored the judgment on Chapman's face and returned his attention to the door, trying the handle. It turned. He pushed the door open. "Elena?" The bathroom was empty with the shower going full force. The two-by-two window above the towel rack had been slid open. "Damn it."

Jax rushed past Chapman, who stayed on his heels all the way to the front door. Jax looked out to an empty street. Had Steven doubled back and gotten to her?

Jax ran to his bedroom. Elena had been wearing her underwear and his T-shirt when she'd come onto him. If Steven had taken her, that's what she'd be wearing, or less if she'd been showering.

He checked the bed and the corner chair and found nothing. He popped his head into the master bath, believing he'd find her clothes and purse there. They were gone. She'd left the safety of the guest bathroom and gotten dressed. He frowned. She'd run.

"Jax," Brody yelled from the kitchen. "Got something."

Jax and Chapman hurried into the kitchen to find Brody holding a note.

Jax grabbed it from his hands and read it out loud. "I can't put you at risk. It's between me and Steven. I remember. It's what he wanted from me all along. I'll find Allison and bring her home."

Jax crumpled the paper in his hands. He grabbed his cell and called her number. It went straight to voicemail.

"What now?" Chapman asked.

Jax ran his hand through his hair. "Chapman—if you're up to it, run with Garrett—I want you canvassing every inch of this area. She couldn't have gotten far without her car."

"You got it."

"Brody, you're with me. Rick Johnson had better be back. I need to know everything he knows about local fishing holes and right now."

Chapter Thirty-Eight

Brody had secured Rick in the situation room with the maps by the time Jax walked in with a pack of cigarettes he found in a cabinet left behind by a former detainee. Dressed in a blue jumpsuit, the scruffy beard on Rick's chin had started to fill in. His hair stood on end, and dark circles shadowed his eyes.

"Hauling me back here was a waste of time. I'm not interested in talking to you."

"Right. Except I still have an active case, and you're mine until I say so."

"I'm not part of your case." Rick nodded to the cigarette. "Can I have one or what?"

Jax tapped out a cigarette and handed it to him, lighting the tip. There were rules about smoking in public buildings, but Rick had already proven he had a stubborn streak. Elena was MIA. He'd break every rule to get the information he needed to find Allison.

"When we first met, you told me you knew just about every fishing hole there was around here. That true?" Jax said.

Rick drew in a long drag and closed his eyes. "You brought me back for suggestions on fishing?"

"Answer the question."

He blew out the smoke. "Yeah, so what?"

"I need your help."

Rick barked a laugh. "That's rich. Why would I help you after you dragged me in here and accused me of stuff I had nothing to do with. And when that wasn't good enough, you targeted my uncle."

Jax forced himself to keep his cool. "It's not my fault you didn't register as a sex offender. And I was only looking for Allison at the farm. Can't help what I found when I got there, but the FBI has it now."

Rick shrugged. "Sounds like you haven't found your girl yet, huh? Some cop you are."

Jax's eye twitched. "That's why we're chatting."

Rick stiffened. "I told you already I had nothing to do with her disappearing. If you're going to keep harassing me about it, I want my lawyer."

Jax inhaled deep through his nose. "I don't think you did."

Rick lifted his chin. "Damn straight. And?

"And what?"

"You know what."

Jax folded his arms across his chest. "I'm not apologizing for arresting your ass, Rick."

Rick stared at the ceiling before taking another drag of his cigarette.

"Tell me what you know about the local fishing spots around here," Jax said, nodding to the maps. "In particular, I'm interested in places with fishing shacks."

Rick flicked the tip of his cigarette onto the table, leaving a pile of ash. "What's in it for me?"

Jax's blood pressure inched upward. "What do you want?"

"Gee, I don't know."

Jax had no time for the pissing contest that Rick clearly wanted. "Fine, Mr. Johnson. I apologize if I was hard on you."

"That's a start. But after what you put me through, I'm not feeling very motivated to help. In fact, I am exhausted." He faked a yawn. "Maybe we'll talk later."

There was no later. "Okay, Rick. But just so you know, that mess your uncle is in is about to include you. You had to know the undocumented were on the premises. So, when I leave this room, I'm calling the lead investigator with the FBI on that, who I know personally. You'll be facing federal charges in addition to your parole violation. And I tell you, those federal sentences can be long. Like years. Might never see you again, Rick. Hope I don't."

"What the fuck," Rick said, the cigarette dangling from his mouth. "I didn't know anything about that."

Jax stood. "Tell it to the feds."

"Fine. Jesus. If I help, you'll leave me out of that?"

Better. "Sure." Jax sat down. "You fish around the coastline all the time?"

"I already told you I did."

"I'm looking for a place that may have been bombed out during the war. See these maps?" He nodded at the wall. "The pins represent munitions dump sites that were cleaned up. These are not it. I'm looking for a place that's still out there."

"Bombed? Munitions? How the hell would I know anything about that?"

Jax grimaced. "You'd know it from a smell of garlic in the mud caused by the chemicals that leaked into the soil."

Rick scoffed. "Garlic? Like at a farm? Because there ain't much fishing going on at a farm."

How to put this in terms he could understand. "I think there's a fishing hole that may have some old artillery and munitions nearby. Have you been to any place like that?"

Rick took another drag. "Wouldn't make for good fishing, if there were."

"Perhaps. It might not be someplace that's currently used."

Rick shook his head. "Can't think of one."

"When I arrested you, you seemed pretty savvy about when the fish were running. Where to go. You're telling me you haven't heard any stories about places to fish that are sketchy? Places to stay away from? Are you telling me you're not as smart or the expert your uncle claims you are in this area?"

He took a drag. "He said that?"

Sort of. "He did."

Rick shrugged. "If you put it that way, there's tons of places where the fish don't bite. That's why I fish up at Osbourn. That's where all the fat trout are. But you said something about a fishing shack. And there aren't any up there."

"Tell me what I don't know, Rick. Where are they?"

He flicked the ashes on top of the existing pile. "You're thinking North

Jetty. There're some old unused shacks in that area."

North Jetty was a few miles north of town past the cannery. "Thought that was for crabbing only."

"Sure, but the inlets made for nice fishing, too, at one time. Trout. Steelhead. Even sturgeon. It's spread out and remote, but a few cabins were built around it. As a little kid, I spent time there." His eyes narrowed. Thinking. "Wait. That's right. I did until some World War II relics were found in the vicinity."

"Shells?"

"Wouldn't surprise me. That place has been abandoned for years, though. Especially after Pacific Fisheries threw up those No Trespass signs."

"The cannery?"

"Yeah. I heard they owned most of the land there. Or did. Not sure which."

The cannery had been owned by Troy Marks' family. Was his story of not knowing the Masseys true? Seems he would have known if his father was letting employees out on the property to fish. Though he also said he was off at college. "Please tell me that one of those fishing shacks had a red roof."

Rick frowned. "I stopped playing around there when I was six or seven. Can't even remember the color of my toys back then, let alone the roof of some old cabin."

A tap on the door's window got Jax's attention. Chapman waved him out, his face splotchy.

"You look like hell," Jax said after he'd secured the door behind him.

"Comes in waves, but I'm hanging in."

He needed him to. They were almost there. "Anything on Elena?"

"Garrett and I split up, and he found her. He's on his way back now."

Good. One issue resolved. Maybe things would start breaking their way. "Have him bring her to my office when she gets here."

"Will do." He directed Chapman to put Rick back in his cell. "When you're done, get me a printout of North Jetty Park and gather everyone in fifteen. Steven has Allison in one of those shacks out there. We move at daybreak."

Chapter Thirty-Nine

Brody knocked on the door jamb several minutes later with Elena next to him. Her drawn face emphasized the dark circles under her eyes. Jax motioned her in to sit.

Brody backed out of the room. "We're ready for you, Sheriff. Got the maps printed, and everyone's here except Deputy Chapman. He went ahead to set up surveillance at the entrances to North Jetty in case there was any activity before we got out there."

After this case, Jax would make time for that conversation with Chapman about him making decisions without approval. The days of Jax being disengaged and disconnected were over. Chapman would have to get used to being only a deputy again.

But he wouldn't want to do this job without him. Flu or not, Chapman was out ahead of it. Would have been nice if they could have stayed together, but Chapman could handle himself if something came up. Unlike Elena, slumped in the chair in front of him.

Jax waited for Brody to close the door and drilled his gaze into Elena. "What were you thinking to run out of the house like that? You could have been shot."

Her clasped hands hung in front of her, her head down, her back rigid against the wooden chair. "I left you a note that I remembered. What I didn't say is Steven called. He's scared. He knows he's screwed up and wanted me to come to him."

"He called you? When exactly? In between gunshots or after?" Her demeanor had changed from the woman he'd shared a meal with. Or the woman who had wanted to take him on the couch. The after-effects of too much whiskey had taken a toll.

She grimaced. "He's sick."

"What did he say? Why did he shoot at us?"

"He said it wasn't him."

"You believe him?"

She wrung her hands together. "I do."

Jax shook his head. "Well, that makes one of us. He hasn't bothered to return any of your calls, but while bullets are flying into the house, he makes contact. Did you think it might have been a ploy to get you into view so he could kill you?"

"I'm here, aren't I?"

He pinched his lips together. "It was stupid." He didn't want Elena as an adversary. It had been a rough night for them both, and they were down to just over twelve hours. That's if Steven was keeping to his word, and after last night, he couldn't count on that. Jax should be on the move, not sitting here lecturing a grown woman about her safety.

"Let's start over. You're okay, and that's what matters. Where did he tell you to go?"

Elena stared at her feet. Frowning. She could be recalling the way he recoiled when she'd come onto him.

He sighed. "Look, you had me worried."

She nodded, giving a little. "North Jetty."

A second confirmation he was heading in the right direction. "Did he say if Allison is there and alive?"

"He confirmed he hasn't harmed her, but he didn't actually tell me to go there. What he said is it was time to remember. That the only way to get past my trauma was to remember where the man who abducted me and Maddy took us." She squeezed her eyes closed, her face contorting.

Jax leaned his forearms on the desk. "Did you?"

"Not at first. Then he told me to think about some of the best days I ever had with our dad. Like I'd touched on during the session, watching him fish and tying flies up there was one of my favorite memories. But one time, we spent a couple of days in the little shack there. I also remember he'd sometimes take a neighbor kid. I recall Steven saying now he'd been there, too, before I was born."

"Who was the neighbor?"

She shrugged.

"Do you remember where the shed's at?"

"It's a trek in from the main entrance, but yes." She closed her eyes, a smile brushing her lips before she paled. "That's the cabin where Madeline died." Her voice broke.

As Jax suspected, Steven was repeating the original crime. Twenty-five years ago, he would have taken Madeline to a place he knew. That's where he'd taken Allison. Except Jax wasn't about to let it end the same way.

He jumped out of his chair. "Trudy will be here shortly. You'll stay with her until this is over and assist from a distance."

Her eyes narrowed in protest. "There are hundreds if not thousands of acres and trails up there. You'll need me, so you don't take the wrong ones."

"It's too dangerous."

"I'll recognize the cabin when I see it."

Jax shook his head. "No way."

She stood, her eyes dark, tension set in her jaw. "I know now this has been Steven's motivation the whole time. He's leading me to her and recreating the original case so that this time I can save Allison. He knows how not saving Maddy has affected every aspect of my life."

"Leaving those clues is easy to do when you were the perpetrator of the original crime. You're naive if you think he doesn't intend to kill her and perhaps you."

She stared at him. "You're wrong about that."

"Am I wrong that he hurt that man at the tavern? Or the jogger before that?"

She shook her head slowly. "He knows that was bad, but they tried to hurt me first. But getting Allison back safely now is all that matters."

"Agreed," Jax said.

"Then I'm going. Once I've done what he wants, he'll hand her over to us.

Even if I'm wrong, we have to try." She softened, putting her hand on his arm. "Please, Sheriff, I want to bring Allison home as much as you do."

Putting Elena in more harm's way tore at him. But Steven was only communicating with her, and she might be able to talk him into releasing Allison once he believed Elena would be okay. If Steven caught sight of them coming in without her, he could go deeper into the forest, or worse, harm Allison. He couldn't take that risk.

He might regret his decision. Somehow, he'd have to keep Elena safe and save Allison. A few days ago, he questioned his ability to do it. That was no longer a question.

"Fine." He crossed to Elena, who stood in the doorway, her brown hair around her shoulders, her face taut. Her posture stubborn as a mule. "But you do anything to jeopardize yourself or my team, I'll arrest you to keep you out of my way."

"Understood."

When they came out of the room, Trudy was at her desk. "According to Rick, the cannery owns the land we're heading to," Jax said. "Get Commissioner Marks on the phone. Ask him if he knows anything about a goddamn fishing shack. And find out who Masseys' neighbors were twenty-five years ago."

Chapter Forty

At sunrise, Jax pulled into the gravel drive of North Jetty with Elena in the seat next to him. The most direct way in was off the 101 to the park entrance. They'd made the drive through the morning mist in silence with Elena stoic, staring out the window. Knowing Steven would be gone forever, however things ended today, had to be heartbreaking. Jax didn't have a blood brother, but Jameson came close, and he'd be devastated if anything happened to his old friend.

They got out, his young deputies rolling in behind him. He'd expected to find Chapman waiting, but his patrol car was nowhere in sight. He must have parked farther up the road so as not to spook Steven.

What he didn't expect to see was Troy Marks' vehicle. The son of a bitch must have come straightaway after Trudy's call—and driven a hundred miles an hour to get here before them.

But there were no signs of Troy, either.

Jax got on the radio to Chapman to let him know they'd arrived and to rejoin the team. Choppy static came back in response. Jax inspected the thick forest surrounding the park. Chapman must have gone in ahead. Even though he couldn't understand the reply, hopefully, his deputy had gotten the message. Although it was clear that the dense trees would make it difficult to communicate further. Regardless, he couldn't wait.

Jax rounded his car and retrieved two bulletproof vests from the trunk. His men did the same. He tightened the Velcro straps on his own and held out the other to Elena.

She stepped back. "What for?"

"We don't know what we're walking into. We've already been shot at once today. Let's prevent anyone from finishing the job, shall we?"

Their eyes met for a moment before she relented. She grabbed the vest and slid her arms through.

"Do the trails look familiar?" he asked, cinching the vest straps at her waist.

"Yes. The middle one."

Matt approached with a map and laid it out, his hands shaking. "There're three ways in, and they appear to lead in different directions. But there's a clearing back about two miles off this middle path."

Elena shook her head. "That's wrong." She stared at the map, then out at the trails. "The memory is vague, but I'm positive the trails circle back and connect. There's a camping area where the shacks are. They sit less than fifty yards from the cliffs that run for miles behind them."

Jax cast his eye over his men. A few days of investigating a serial killer—tracking down leads, pounding the trails, interviewing and re-interviewing witnesses—and their collective skill set was vastly improved. They were fit for the job at hand and ready to be put to the test.

He briefed them on being ready, but not trigger-happy.

Chapman was out there. As was Marks. He didn't want his men shooting them on sight.

Which way had Chapman gone? For all Jax knew, he'd already neutralized Steven and saved Allison. And Marks? Where the hell was he? He didn't want to have to save that fool's sorry ass, but he also didn't want him gunned down.

This wasn't what he'd had in mind. He'd imagined himself and Chapman splitting into two teams and taking Brody, Garrett, and Matt along to bring up the rear. Now the forest was littered with friendlies as well as the enemy. Worse yet, too many players multiplied the danger to Allison.

Too much thinking, not enough action.

Jax folded the map and tucked it in his front pocket. "Brody, stay here in case Steven escapes and gets this far. Garrett, take the right trail, Matt, left." He turned to Elena. "You'll go out ahead of me down the middle. I'll be right behind."

She nodded, then wrapped her hair up into a bun and secured it with a tie she had on her wrist.

He checked her vest one last time, ignoring her eyes searching his face. A few hours ago, she'd come to him and whispered, "Save me." That momentary lapse when he thought it was Abby ate at him. Had his subconscious known it was Elena? Had he believed he could save her from her past? Because he couldn't. The only way to save Elena was to put Steven, her sister's killer, in prison for life, and get Allison back home into the arms of Emily and Daniel. Even if that meant that Elena would lose her only brother.

Jax cleared his throat. "Ready?"

They all nodded.

Jax and Elena took lead to the middle pathway overgrown with ferns, grasses, and briars. He turned to watch his men diverge onto their own routes before stepping onto the trail, gun drawn but barrel down. Fog had coated everything making the trek wet and slick. He moved deliberately behind Elena as the tall grasses swished with their strides.

They made their way for at least ten minutes, burrowing deeper into the woods. Fir trees towered to the sky around them. The earthy scent of moss and mildew filled the air. Morning birdsong broke the silence. His heartbeat double-timed as he tried to anticipate what shape Allison would be in when they found her. He pushed those thoughts aside. Ending Steven's sick game had to remain his focus.

The briars and grass thinned when they approached a fork in the road. The sound of a gunshot echoed off the trees. Had Matt been trigger-happy, or had they run into Steven? Jax whipped around, his back to Elena, listening. Searching. Where had the shot come from?

The piercing edge of a boulder connected with his skull before he saw it. The force of the blow buckled his knees.

"Elena, run," he managed before the second hit landed above his left ear.

He dropped onto his heels. A leg bumped his shoulder as his attacker rounded him. He expected to see Steven when he blinked to clear his blurred vision. Instead, it was Elena, wild-eyed, a large boulder poised above her head to finish him.

"Elena, stop," he yelled.

"I'm sorry, but Elena has to be the one," she said.

The one for what? Confused as to why she'd turned on him, he didn't intend to lie there and die either. Before she could release the boulder, he flung himself forward and got hold of her foot. Holding fast with his hands, Elena crashed to her knees, sending the boulder to the ground and rolling off to the side.

But just as quickly, she whipped around on him, beating his shoulder with clenched fists. A burning sensation raced through his arm. He lost his grip and scrambled to get upright.

Elena sprung up too.

Warm blood trickled into Jax's eyes, stinging them. Before he could get his bearings, Elena charged him. He didn't have the wherewithal to lessen the impact.

Her bony shoulder connected, digging deep into his ribs. The impact knocked the wind out of him, and he tumbled backwards, landing flat onto the ground. Elena leapt on top of him, punching his head and chest.

He crossed his arms in front of his throat to fend her off. His gun. It had flown from his hands. He turned his head side to side. Searching.

Elena saw it first. She clambered over him. He rolled onto his stomach and reached out, catching her by the ankle this time. With all his strength, he jerked her back.

She kicked with her boot.

The heel smashed into his forehead, splitting the skin. He held on as the next kick connected with his nose. What happened to the woman he'd been protecting? Most of him didn't care. Only surviving mattered.

Elena clawed the ground for leverage. Wanting the gun. But not more than him. He clamped onto her harder, wrenching her backwards. With a thud, he was on her and putting every ounce of his two hundred pounds against her.

She thrashed beneath him. Pummeled his back. Twisting his uniform in her hands, trying to grab skin with it. He lifted his body off her enough to flip her over and reach for his cuffs. Teeth grinding, heart about to explode, he stood, yanking her up by her cuffed wrists.

"What the hell was that?" He blinked to clear the sweat and blood from his vision. His nose throbbed, the pain causing his eyes to water. Damn thing was probably broken.

Elena's spooked gaze darted about, reminding him of Emily's horse that first day in the barn. A cornered animal, frantic for a way out.

Jax spat blood, panting like he'd run a marathon. "We need to find Allison. We're here to stop Steven. Together. Remember."

"I am Steven." Elena's voice had deepened.

He shook his head, incredulous. "There's no time for this."

Deep lines marred her stony face. Her eyes hardened. She'd transformed before his eyes into something else. Someone else. Her stare seared through him. The rigidity of her body carried through every pore. "I am serious."

Her hair pulled up, her jawline rigid, her eyes dark, she looked every bit that sketch of Steven. Her squared shoulders showed a determination he'd not witnessed in Elena. The once scared and guilt-ridden psychologist had disappeared. He'd seen a glimpse of this defiant person in his office an hour ago and dismissed it. The ache in his shoulder and blood streaming from his temple had him believing it now.

Jax grabbed his radio. "Brody, come in," he said into the mic.

No response. Jax might be in a clearing, but as he'd feared, the surrounding trees were working against him and his team. He'd need to get Elena back to the car. "Let's move," he ordered.

"You should have let me go. I didn't want to hurt you." The words came out of Elena's mouth, but they weren't hers. "You must let her finish, or you'll have stolen the only chance she has at redemption."

Redemption? What was Elena or Steven—whoever the hell this was—talking about? "Okay then, Steven. Where's Elena?"

"In hiding. Like always."

Jax had dealt with mental illness almost daily on the streets of Portland, especially among the homeless community. But split personality, or dissociative personality disorder as he'd heard it referenced—that he'd only read about. And he certainly didn't know what to do with it except maybe humor the one who appeared to have control. He grimaced as much from the pain in his face as the time that was ticking away.

He held Elena by the upper arm and directed her back toward the parking area. "When did you show up?" he asked.

She shrugged. "I've always been here. Waiting for Elena to need me. The first time was after her parents died. Although I was more in the background then. But I came back when she laid in the trunk with Madeline bleeding out." She smirked. "At the battery. At the shack. I've been everywhere. Watching. Knowing. Directing. When that trunk opened the last time, I told Elena to run. She was upset at me for that." Elena's voice tightened. "Like a ten-year-old child could have saved Maddy. Our sister was going to die no matter what Elena did. So, I forced Elena to save herself."

If that was true—if Elena truly was Steven—then someone else had abducted the girls and murdered Maddy. Did Steven know the details of the original case that well to have recreated it in the way he did? Elena had admitted to reading her case file. What Elena knew Steven must know. Clearly, it didn't work the other way unless the memories were suppressed so deep that the Steven personality guarded them to protect Elena.

Jax would have to reconcile it later. He returned his focus to the present danger. "Where's the shack? Where's Allison?"

Elena's face flushed. "Elena must save her. It's the only way for her to move on."

Like hell, he'd remove the cuffs after her stunt. He'd get it another way. "Have you always known who killed Madeline?"

"The night Elena escaped from him, she'd wandered for two days in the forest. I had comforted her, told her the best thing she could do was forget. By the time she found her way out, you had already recovered Maddy's body. There was no point in Elena remembering."

Elena hadn't answered his question. "But you knew." Bile rose in his throat. "We could have put the killer away years ago had she told us. You should have let her."

"She was too afraid he'd come back for her like he'd come for Madeline. I told her if she played dumb, she'd be okay. I'd make sure of it. She asked me to protect her. That's what I did. I've always protected her."

Jax half-listened, fixing in on Steven's words: come for Madeline. Had they known their abductor as kids? Was it someone they'd grown up with? A teacher. A family friend. "It's safe to tell me now. Who did it?" They cleared the path and were in the parking lot. Where the hell was Brody?

"It's not safe yet."

Jax's eyes narrowed, a horrific realization niggling at his edges. "What do you mean?"

"He knows. That's why he tried to kill you tonight. He wants to kill Elena too. Had he known she was with you, he wouldn't have stopped trying."

Dread poured into his limbs. There was someone else out there. Someone with Allison. "What does he know, Steven?"

"Everything had to be the same. Elena has to save Allison in the same scenario Maddy had been in, or she'll never be free."

What had Elena done? "You called Madeline's killer and told him where Allison was, didn't you?"

"He already knew. He just didn't realize it."

"What do you mean he knew? You'd contacted him before all of this?"

She nodded, slowly.

Troy's car was still sitting in the parking lot. Why was he really here?

Jax's mouth went dry. His deputies could already be at the clearing. Unless Elena had lied to send them off course, so only Elena made it there. The gunshot. Had one of them been killed? "Which way do I go at that fork?"

"Elena must save her."

"It's not going to happen that way." He led Elena to the patrol car, resisting the urge to tighten his grip. To force answers. "Tell me where Allison's at. It may already be too late. Do you understand? If Allison's already dead, Elena will have even more trauma to overcome. She'll know you not only called in her sister's killer for some sick do-over, but you didn't help save her stepdaughter from him. She'll blame you forever."

"I—"

"There is no I. She's the one who will go to jail for your crimes."

"Elena doesn't know anything unless I tell her. She believes I'm the brother who saved her. She'll forgive me anything. She always has."

Sick or not, anger surged through Jax at Elena's refusal to help. He was running out of time. Allison could pay the price for his not seeing the deception sooner. He had to try again. "Not if she learns the protection you supposedly provided meant the real killer went on to abduct and kill a dozen more fourteen-year-olds, just like Maddy."

Steven flinched.

"Redeem yourself. Let Elena go and tell me where Allison is."

Steven looked away.

Jax could have gone around and around, but he had a sinking feeling he'd already taken too much time. He yanked open the car. "Steven, Elena is saving Allison if she is helping me. Don't you get that? It's the only way."

Steven hesitated, seeming to calculate that information. It was the longest minute Jax could remember. "Go right."

Thank God. "Who will I find, Elena? Troy Marks?"

She didn't respond, instead slinking into the back of the cruiser.

It didn't matter. He'd find out soon enough. After securing her, Jax ran to his trunk and retrieved his rifle.

The bushes rustled, and Brody appeared, zipping up his pants. His forehead creased with worry at Jax's appearance. "What the hell happened out there, Chief? Do you need an ambulance?"

He must look like hell, but he swiped the blood from his forehead and wiped it on his pant leg. "I'm fine. Matt and Garrett are out of range. Keep trying them and Chapman to let them know where I'm headed. And keep an eye on Elena. She's not well. I'm going for Allison."

Brody nodded.

Jax grabbed his phone and texted Trudy. He needed confirmation. "I need that info on Massey's neighbors ASAP."

Elena's father had fished with some of the neighborhood kids. They'd spent time at the shack. Elena and Madeline had known their abductor. He swallowed. Since the property was owned by Troy's father, and Troy's car was in the parking lot, Jax had an idea of who that neighbor had been. The reason he'd made himself an obstacle in this investigation from the start finally made sense.

With rifle in hand, Jax re-entered the trail.

Chapter Forty-One

A red-roofed shack nestled into the trees came into view. The warped cedar siding had long since faded to gray, and crumbling, rusted nails held the boards in place. Twenty-five years ago, Madeline Massey's body had been found far south of the shack, but she hadn't been murdered where she'd been found. They'd never located the scene of the murder, until now.

Elena had been fractured into two pieces from her childhood traumas, one sick enough to believe that bringing another fourteen-year-old girl whom she loved to the same location and riling up her sister's killer would fix anything. While finding Allison was the priority, capturing the person who'd perpetrated such crimes on innocents—who not only sent Elena, but himself and Jameson, into a world of self-doubt and guilt—would be a sweet bonus.

He scanned the decrepit shack for signs of life. The stairway leading to the front door, riddled with large holes, hung askew. The wood-paned windows had long been shattered, leaving jagged pieces behind. The place hadn't been inhabited for quite some time.

There were no signs of his men. He crept around the back and looked inside. No furniture. No ropes. No food wrappers.

No Allison.

Jax reached for the back door. It dropped out of the frame with a clunk as it hit the floor. He propped it against the beaten doorjamb and stepped inside. His flashlight beam bounced around the small room, revealing cobwebs hanging from every corner. A mixture of mold and excrement burned his nose. A rat scurried across the floor and disappeared through cracks in the floorboards.

He held back a frustrated growl. His gut said he was in the right area. Where was Allison?

Outside, he checked for Trudy's response to his text. Nothing, and only one bar on his cell. He moved further away from the structure, and three bars appeared. With no time to wait, he dialed her.

"Just getting ready to text you, hon," she answered. "Got that info for you on the neighbor."

"Let me guess. Troy Marks and family."

"You'd be right."

He'd be happier if he'd figured it out sooner. "What did he tell you this morning when you called?"

"He didn't. Deanna answered and said he'd left early for a run, but when she'd looked to see if he was back, the car was gone. She hasn't been able to get hold of him."

Too busy getting here. They'd had their differences, but was a man he'd worked with for the past ten years capable of a horrible act so long ago? He couldn't believe it was true, but he couldn't deny the possibility.

"Pull up Google Earth. I'm missing something. The shack I've found isn't the right one." He took a picture of the cabin and pulled up the details. From that, he gave her the longitude and latitude of his location. He could hear the tap of her fingers on her keyboard.

"I see it clear as day, hon. But there's another one about a quarter mile north of where you're at." She gave him the coordinates.

"Got it."

A few minutes later, the shack came into view. A faint light emanated from the side window. Jax's heart picked up speed. Whether he wanted to believe it or not, he had to accept the truth now. Troy had already arrived.

Jax ducked low in front of the hedges and snuck around the building to get a better view of the situation. The tail end of an ATV caught his eye. He inched over to the four-wheeler. Mud caked the tires, emitting the same pungent odor that had been present in Steven's locker. A bog with leaking munitions must be nearby. But when did Troy get to an ATV? And where? Had it been hidden on one of the trails near the park entrance?

Jax touched the motor's hood. Warm. He clicked open the storage compartment hoping to find confirmation of the owner. Three shell casings rolled into his hand. Bet they'd match the bullets in his drywall at home. The memory of being shot at in the middle of the night rankled him.

"What'd you find?"

Jax dropped the casings to the ground and leveled his shotgun before registering it was Troy who'd popped up from the front of the ATV.

"Hands up," he ordered.

Marks hesitated but must have thought better than to argue and complied. "What the hell's wrong with you?" he whispered.

"Where've you got Allison?" Jax said.

Marks grimaced. "I don't have her at all. I'm assuming she's in the shack, but I just got here myself."

"You've come to finish her off?"

"Finish her off?" Marks' face contorted. "Is that what you think?"

"You tell me. Why are you even here, Troy?"

"I'll tell you if I can lower my hands."

Jax was close enough to end Troy if he made any move toward him. Still… "Slowly. If I see you go for a weapon…."

"Jesus, Jax. When have you ever known me to have a gun," Troy said, lowering his arms to his sides. "Look, I run towards the cannery every morning and circle back. As you know, the area has been closed and off limits for years, and there's never been any activity, until today when I heard an ATV. I decided to investigate, and some guy was cutting across the back portion of the property and heading into the forest. With the drugs found at the farm and my boy's possible involvement…." He cleared his throat. "Anyway, I wanted to see what the guy was up to."

Jax's eyes narrowed. "And you followed him by parking out at the entrance?"

"The cannery land connects here to this opening. It's a couple of miles in, and there's really no place to stop in between. When I didn't see the guy come out of the trees, I had a feeling I knew where he was going. I'd have needed an ATV to get through the mud out on those trails, though, so I took the easiest route."

Jax scanned Troy for signs of lying.

"It's the truth," Troy said.

"Right. Like telling me you didn't know the Masseys lived across the street from you. Didn't you think for one second that county records would give you away?"

Marks shook his head. "My mother might have lived across from them for a short time, but once the divorce was final from my dad, she moved out of state. And the Masseys weren't in town too long before their accident. I lived with my dad on the other end of town until I left for Berkeley that same year."

Maybe...but Elena's dad had fly fished with a neighbor kid. "I suppose next you're going to tell me you never fished with Mr. Massey?"

"What?"

"The feathers in Allison's backpack and on Madeline's body were used for fly fishing, and their father took a neighbor kid with him. You telling me you weren't that neighbor?"

He frowned, his face turning red. "I wasn't. I hate fishing." He hesitated, and then swallowed hard. "And, you have to *really* love fishing to spend that kind of time. Shit."

Jax stiffened, Troy's words settling in, his body language suggesting something Jax didn't want to consider. He'd only known one avid fisherman who lived and breathed it. Only one that had left out ahead of him this morning to get here and he hadn't been able to communicate with since.

An uneasiness swept over Jax. Only one who lived close enough to shoot a bullet through his house in the middle of the night and have enough time to get home and then back, acting as if he was riding in to save the day. Jax swallowed down nausea. He'd trusted that man with his life since he'd come aboard five years ago.

The back door burst open, followed by footfalls on the back porch. Jax caught Marks's eyes and held his index finger up to his pursed lips.

Marks nodded and followed Jax as he crept around the ATV to the rear of the house, where the expansive cliffs ran as a backdrop—exactly as Elena had described them.

Chris Chapman, dressed in uniform, clutched Allison's arm and dragged her down the steps. A red gasoline can dangled from his other hand as he swung it back and forth, liquid sloshing out and dousing the wood. Allison was blindfolded, but tears and dirt streaked her terrified face. Otherwise, she appeared unharmed.

Jax's chest tightened at the sight of his deputy. He'd wanted to be wrong. But the how and why would have to come later. Jax couldn't let him take Allison anywhere near those cliffs. He circled his finger in the air at Marks, praying he understood it meant to come around behind Chapman.

Jax stepped away from the house. "Hold it right there, Chris." He leveled his gun.

Chapman spun around and threw the gas can at Jax, who sidestepped it, before shoving Allison in front of him like a shield. "Screw you, Turner." He pulled a switchblade from his shirt pocket and flicked it open, pressing it against Allison's throat.

"Let her go," Jax commanded, relieved Chris hadn't gone for his gun. If he could avoid a shootout, Allison's odds of surviving this exchange increased.

"Get back, or she's dead." Chapman's teeth clenched. He took a step toward the cliffs.

"I can't do that," Jax said.

Allison wiggled to get away, the knife pushing into her skin.

"Allison, sweetie, this is Sheriff Turner. I need you to be patient. Everything's going to be okay." Jax found a calming tone despite his growing panic.

"I want to go home." Her chin trembled.

Her quivering voice tore into his heart. "We all do. Right, Chris?"

Chapman didn't answer.

Jax held the gun steady. "But the only way we get to do that, Chris, is if you put that knife down and step away from Allison. She's done nothing to you."

Chapman locked eyes with Jax but grasped Allison tighter. He took another step back.

Jax looked for the shot. "You don't have to do this."

"I didn't plan for it to work out this way, believe me. But Steven was bent on making Allison's disappearance look like the old case where his sister was murdered. As I'm sure you've guessed by now, I'm the last piece."

If Chapman only knew the truth. "Steven called you?"

He nodded. "He's the reason I came back early. And last night, he told me where Allison was being kept. Told me I'd pay for what happened to Madeline and go down for Allison too. He said my prints would be all over the scene. Obviously, I couldn't let that happen."

"So you thought killing me was the answer?"

"I had to wait until daylight and couldn't take the risk you might figure things out."

"If I was dead, you could get here at your leisure." Rage at being deceived by his deputy burned in Jax's gut.

"It wasn't personal. I'd hoped to avoid what we're doing now."

Jax held his deputy's eyes but focused on his peripheral vision. Troy had made progress, but he wasn't close enough. He had to buy Troy time to get in position. "Why'd you kill Madeline?" Jax said.

"It was an accident."

A sour tang filled Jax's mouth. "There was far too much blood on the road where you picked them up for me to believe that."

"Well, I didn't go there to kill anyone. But after all I'd done to find her, she laughed at me. Said she didn't want me to come for her. That she'd fallen in love with some kid named Brian." He gripped the knife tighter. "We argued, and I hit her."

Jax had interrogated that poor boy until he'd been in tears that first night the girls had gone missing. And Jax remembered Madeline's autopsy. The injuries were inflicted by a wood object. "You used a fishing club, didn't you?"

Chapman shrugged, with not a shred of remorse. His eyes flicked upwards. "Anyway, she screamed for Elena to run. I couldn't let there be a witness. I drove them to a hideout first, hoping to convince Madeline to change her mind." He scoffed. "Did no good. She could barely talk, but she hated me at that point."

Chapman took another step towards the cliff. Troy was almost close enough.

"And then you brought her out to the edge of the world to finish her off. Why move Madeline again and leave a note taunting my department to find you? You left Polaroids, for God's sake." This guy had been begging to be caught at the time, and Jax had missed it. They'd all missed it.

"Wanted you to believe it was a serial killer." Chapman had a far off look in his eyes. Another step back.

The misdirection had sent them in circles. The heat of rage crept up Jax's neck, still looking for a clean shot. "You know, your *it was all an accident* story would be convincing, except you left out the isoflurane that you used to take the girls down and keep them there."

"You stole that from my dad's stables?" Troy. He'd placed himself to the far left of Chapman.

Chapman swung his head. "Get out of here, Troy." He took another step. Too close to the edge.

If Troy would have kept his mouth shut until he was closer.... Now Jax wouldn't be able to get to Allison in time. If he took a shot, and Chapman moved an inch...

"I'm not going anywhere until you let her go, Chris. It's over," Jax said.

Chapman let out a bitter laugh. "I didn't want any of this. You and Boy Scout over there changed everything. I'd actually believed by rushing out here before you, I could get Allison back up to the main road and be the town hero."

The man was delusional. "I'll take it easy on you. It's an old case. I know you had nothing to do with Allison's kidnapping."

Chapman's face dripped with sweat. He twitched. "I'm already screwed. There's no way out."

Jax took a step closer to Chapman. "Don't do this. Ending your life, no matter the circumstances, is a bad idea. But don't take Allison with you."

Chapman shook his head. Defeated. "Oh, c'mon. You know what happens to cops in prison. I'm dead anyway."

Troy reached out for Allison. So close. "We were friends once. I won't let that happen to you. I'll pull in some favors. I can do that for you. Give me a chance. C'mon, buddy."

Chapman hesitated.

An opening for Jax.

But Elena appeared out of nowhere, coming at Chapman full throttle.

Terror filled Chris's eyes with what must have been the realization that there was nowhere to escape the force barreling in his direction.

Troy froze.

"No," Jax yelled. Dropping his rifle, he dove toward Chapman.

Time slowed as Elena crashed into Chapman's shoulder. The knife flew from his hands, and his hold on Allison loosened. Elena grasped Allison's shirt. Jax slid in and wrapped his arms around Elena's legs, anchoring her and Allison, praying it was enough.

The sound of Chris's scream echoed as he lost footing and plummeted over the cliff.

Elena drew Allison in and clutched the girl to her chest as Jax pulled them both from the cliff, his weight toppling them both to the ground.

He encircled them with his arms. "I've got you." He peered over the edge and slapped his hands over Allison's ears as a final scream and sickening thud signaled Chapman hitting the rocks below.

Troy ran to the rim and peered over.

"Any chance he's alive?" Jax asked, knowing that the ragged rock, combined with the fifty-foot drop, would make survival near impossible.

Troy shook his head.

Jax untangled himself from Elena and Allison and stood, taking them up with him.

Elena's body trembled. "You're safe now, hon. You're safe."

"Elena?" Allison said, stepping away from her voice. Afraid.

Jax took hold of Allison's arm to stabilize her and removed the blindfold. Her eyes were wide as she stared at him, and then the woman she'd once trusted. She shifted behind Jax, holding tight to his arm.

Elena's face crumpled, and she began to sob.

Whether she knew what had happened or why, he didn't know. He focused on Allison. "Are you hurt?"

Allison shook her head. "I just want to go home."

Elena's face was twisted in confusion. "Honey, let me...."

"No." Allison buried her head in Jax's shirt.

Matt and Garrett raced around the shack frowning, clearly disappointed they'd missed the action. Jax directed them to get a recovery unit to assist in retrieving Chapman's body. "And get Elena back and secured in the cruiser," he directed.

Jax turned and looked into Allison's tear-brimmed eyes, relief flooding through him that she'd been found alive. He intended to take her back to the car himself, but Troy Marks came from behind.

"If it's all right, I'll escort her out. It's the least I can do," he said.

Jax nodded. "I didn't realize you knew Chapman from the past or that Chapman had ever known Madeline and Elena. His resume said he was from Oklahoma."

He served in the Coast Guard there, but he graduated from high school here. We hung out some before he left for the Midwest." He shook his head. "At the time, he'd told me about some hot young girl he was desperate for back then. I just had no idea who he'd been talking about."

"But why did Chapman come back here?" Had he been keeping tabs on Jax all these years? Only concerned when Jax had returned to the area of the originating crime?

Troy looked away. "Unfortunately, I played a part in that. Chapman had indicated interest in being the sheriff, but he didn't have the experience, and the previous commissioner had blown him off. But when things went south with you after your daughter, well, I invited him to apply." He didn't meet Jax's eyes. "Guess I thought eventually he'd take your place, but.... Look. I'm sorry about that. And again, I had no idea...."

"Right." There's no way Troy would have been able to put the two together. How Chapman had hid in plain sight before returning to Misty Pines wasn't hard to imagine. There'd been no DNA to link him. And he might have become a cop to have an inside view of cold and active cases. Only Chris would have been able to answer that question.

Troy put a protective arm around Allison's shoulders. Jax tracked him, and his deputies, as they made their way through the clearing and back to the trails.

He found an opening and texted Brody to expect the team. He got a response back apologizing that Elena had gotten away from him.

He'd talk to Brody about that later. He had a call to make.

"Emily, it's Turner. We got her." Emotion clutched his throat. "Allison's coming home."

Epilogue

It was late afternoon, and Jax paced the waiting room of the third floor of Mercy Hospital in West Shore, where Allison had been admitted. Before he'd arrived, he'd made sure Elena was secured and had planned to ask more questions. But Elena's one call was to Dr. Kavorian, and his call was to an attorney. With the information he possessed about Elena's condition, Judge Rulli had her on a transport to Oregon State Hospital and out of his hands within short order.

Not ideal. He would have liked to understand more about how Steven could take over Elena's life in the manner he did. But at least she had her psychiatrist advocating for her, and there'd be time down the road to hear her version.

In the meantime, Dr. Kavorian had shared some insight. He'd long known about Steven. Apparently, Elena's "brother" appeared during times of stress, acting to protect Elena, but he could be reined in with medication. Or so the doctor thought. Dr. Kavorian had no idea about the apartment in Megler or that when Steven was in control, he'd created a separate life from Elena. That even when Elena was in control, he lurked. Always waiting.

Steven had managed to dupe the doctor completely. Until their last session, he'd believed Steven might be gone for good.

Crime techs from the Oregon State Police had already begun processing the cabin. They tore apart every plank in the old shack. The feathers used for fly fishing were in a workbench, and the remnants had been strewn on the floor. They appeared identical to those in the backpack and from the old case, but Abby's FBI team would verify that.

The most damning evidence found was blood that had dripped down into the floorboards. It would confirm it was the site of Madeline's murder. He hoped it would link Chapman to the crime directly, but no matter, Chapman had admitted as much. His deputy, a man he'd trusted with his life, had paid the ultimate price for his crime.

As for knowing about the shack, as a youth, Chapman had tagged along with Elena's father on a few fishing trips. According to Troy, his dad, not much of a fisherman himself, had been happy to let other people use the shack whenever they wanted.

When Troy eventually inherited the property from his dad, he never came out to survey it, believing that it couldn't be developed and that the shed had been torn down after some munitions had been found five miles south of there. That's what he'd told Chapman. Which was lucky, or Chapman might have figured out where Allison was sooner. He might have pulled off being the town hero as he'd planned. But there also were no guarantees that he wouldn't have killed Allison and burned the place down.

Chapman thought he had it all under control by staying close to track the cases that lit up their switchboard. Except this time, Chapman had been in Alaska when Emily called, and Steven/Elena's quest to alter the outcome of the past was something he'd never counted on.

Maybe Jax should have noticed the change in his deputy once he'd been brought into the loop on Jax's suspicions. Thinking back, Chapman had made sure to be other places any time Elena was nearby. He might have been afraid she would recognize him. Had even become physically ill as it began to unravel. But Jax had trusted him. If not for Elena's call setting the end into motion, Jax would still be trusting him.

After another round of pacing through the waiting room, Emily emerged through the double doors and strode toward Jax, holding her arms out for a hug. Her hair hadn't been washed. Her clothes were wrinkled. But her eyes brimmed with relief. "Thank you," she whispered in his ear.

"How is she?"

"Seriously dehydrated. Tired. Hungry. But will make a full recovery."

Jax's shoulders relaxed for the first time since this whole ordeal. "I'm just glad we got to her in time. Will Daniel stay around a while to help?"

"Yes. He's agreed to go to counseling with us, but he wants to be there for Elena too, which is commendable. Even though we've had our differences, she was sick. I never really understood what she went through as a child." Emily hung her head. "But I made a terrible mistake letting Wallace into my life. It was hard on Allison. She only ever wanted me and Daniel back together. Had we not argued the night before...."

Jax squeezed her hand. "Don't blame yourself. Steven had a plan, and he might have just tried another day. But right now, Allison needs both of you." He thought of Elena and how her inability to handle the traumas of her life had created Steven. "Don't let her feel alone. Don't let her think she needs someone else to protect her."

"We won't."

Jax smiled, knowing she was in good hands. "Think she's up for some questions?"

"She's ready."

Jax walked into the room. Daniel sat in the corner, his face slack with relief. Allison was so tiny that the hospital bed nearly swallowed her. An IV tree hung nearby with tubes connected to her hands. He resisted the urge to gather her up in his arms.

A lap dog rested on Allison's chest, his bony head tucked under her chin. Jax pulled a chair to the edge of her bed. "This must be Roper."

Allison smiled, her eyes drooping. "It is." She stroked his head.

"Can you tell me what happened?"

She sunk deeper into her pillow. "I was waiting for the bus when a black SUV pulled up. I didn't know who it was at first. Then Elena rolled down the window. She said my dad wanted to make sure I was okay and could she take me to school. Said she had a new toy for Roper." She squeezed her eyes closed. "She was so rushed, and I was so annoyed at my mom... I didn't want to get on the bus."

She poured out her heart about the drugs she'd kept from Dylan to save him from messing with kids, just as he'd said. How she loved Kylie and felt bad that she'd made her feel any different. That she'd loved Elena and even now couldn't understand why she'd turned on her.

"She didn't turn on you by choice," Jax said, not sure how much Allison could understand of the illness. "But she is sick and will get the help she needs. Perhaps someday you can forgive her."

Allison only nodded.

A half-hour later, Jax left the exhausted fourteen-year-old sleeping under the watchful eyes of her parents and drove to the station.

Brody, Garrett, and Matt were poring over paperwork when he walked in. Better to get them learning the tedious ropes now. He'd be needing them more than ever. Trudy gave him a thumbs up while she fielded a call about someone tagging old man Snodgrass's garbage can. Small town problems. The way he liked them.

Jax strode into the kitchen and poured a cup of coffee.

"Got a sec?" Trudy had followed him.

Jax took a long drink before turning to her. "Of course."

"Have you heard anything more on Elena?"

He told her about Dr. Kavorian and Daniel wanting to be there for her. "She won't be deemed able to stand trial, I'm sure. The Portway man did regain consciousness, but didn't see the attack coming, so they'll be depending on DNA. The important thing is that Elena's in a place perhaps she can heal. And I'll check in with her from time to time."

"You're a good man, Jax."

He didn't know about that. But despite the outcome, a part of him had felt a sense of closure on that cliff. He had saved both Elena and Allison. While it didn't bring back Madeline, or Lulu, some of the responsibility for that let go. Just a little.

"There is one other thing," Trudy said. "Turns out, Steven Massey really did exist."

Jax folded his arms over his chest. "You're kidding?"

"Nope. He was born eight years before Elena, but he died at birth."

That's what Elena's father must have meant when she overheard him say they'd lost him. "She could've believed had he lived, he would have protected her like most big brothers." It seemed natural that her dissociated personality would be someone who would take care of her.

Trudy shook her head. "I guess we're all wanting to be cared for on some level." Her eyes met Jax. Message received. "How's Allison?" she asked.

"Emily and Daniel are united. With what Daniel experienced with Elena, they'll make sure Allison is supported to get through the trauma. She's going to be all right."

"Good. I'm making a pot of stew for the family tonight. Did she say what happened?"

"She did." Jax gave her the bullet points.

Trudy frowned. "Poor child. What about that backpack you found with the feathers?"

Jax shook his head. "Allison was unconscious by then. My theory is the Steven part of Elena planted the feathers and then tossed the pack expecting Elena would find it at some point, and that would trigger the past. What we do know is that Wallace got to it first and set everything screwy after that."

Trudy leaned onto the doorframe. "Wallace did you a favor."

"Hate to admit it, but you're right. Even if I'm sure he rues the morning, he took it."

Trudy nodded. "You going to be okay?"

Jax picked up the coffee mug and warmed his hands. "I hired Chapman. Let a killer in our midst. Trusted him. If I'd been paying more attention, I might have caught it."

Trudy came up behind him and placed a soft hand on his arm. "Oh, hon. I pride myself on having a pretty good sense about people." She shook her head. "He fooled us all."

Trudy disappeared, and Jax dumped his coffee before returning to his office. Every part of him was spent. He looked around and then strode past Trudy and his deputies.

"I'm out," he said to no one in particular.

Once in his car, he found himself cruising the streets of Misty Pines before hitting the highway to West Shore with his thoughts on Elena and Steven.

Steven, damaged and angry at the world, had been residing in her since childhood. He'd shown up when tragedy or trauma occurred in her life. He was the sick one with all the dysfunction so that Elena could live a normal life, but he ran the show. At some point, Steven must have grown weary of carrying the burden for her and created the plan to get Elena over not saving Madeline once and for all.

Maybe on some level, everyone strived to find healing, no matter how fractured.

An hour later, Jax pulled into his own driveway and went inside. He stood in his kitchen alone, eating another microwave dinner, his mind numb and craving sleep. He crawled into bed, grabbed his phone, and texted Jameson.

"Allison is safe. We got Maddy's killer."

A minute later, he got a response. "Tell me all about it at Thanksgiving?"

"I'll be there."

He closed his eyes and didn't open them until morning.

* * *

Jax leaned against his car outside the funeral home at the edge of town. Chris Chapman was buried on a foggy Tuesday morning. The few people that filtered out of the building were a far cry from the crowd, pomp, or circumstance befitting an honored member of law enforcement. Not one person in Misty Pines didn't feel let down by what had transpired.

Troy, followed by Deanna and Dylan, were among the last of the guests to leave.

Jax nodded a greeting.

Troy approached, motioning his wife and son to go ahead to their car.

"I'm having a little get-together at the house if you'd like to stop by," Troy said. "Won't be much."

"Awfully nice of you, Commissioner, considering the man once committed murder on your property."

He grimaced. "I'm not sure nice is an apt description. I knew Chris. Went to school with him. I feel a bit responsible because I should have seen it coming."

"You and me both," Jax said, not sure they'd ever agreed on anything. Hell of a thing to agree on.

"Anyway, the invitation stands."

Jax pushed off from his car. "I'd love to, but I've been disconnected of late, and I'd like to spend the day patrolling. Town needs me to pay attention. I plan to do just that."

He nodded. "All right then."

Dylan stood next to his mother by the family car, waiting for Troy. Jax lifted his chin in Dylan's direction. "You know I have to charge your son," he said.

Troy scanned Jax's face. Maybe he hoped he could sway him. He couldn't. "I understand."

Jax nodded. "Mind if I talk to him a minute?"

Troy sighed. "Dylan. Sheriff Turner wants a word."

Dylan strode over, dressed in black pants, white-short-sleeved shirt, and black tie. His arms crossed over his chest. "Yeah?" Dylan's voice was tight.

"Thought we should catch up and come to an understanding. The dealing of any drugs at the school stops."

Dylan shifted. "It wasn't that big of a—"

Jax held up his hand. "Hasn't there been enough lying?"

Dylan lifted his chin and looked away. "Fine," he whispered.

"Good. I told your dad you'll have to be charged for your part in the dealing, but I'm willing to put in a recommendation for probation. If you take that serious, and get your act together, I'll advocate for you."

Jax could come down harder. The kid had been arrogant and condescending. He was also a teenager. Jax knew how it felt to live for the approval of a father who might never give it to him. He suspected that was the root of much of Dylan's attitude and choices. Jax had sworn to protect Misty Pines, and that meant every one of its citizens. Even the wayward, confused, and petulant.

Dylan's nostrils flared. "What's that supposed to mean?"

"It means I know you were on your way to a scholarship. You're a minor—this won't stay on your record forever. If I can help you make something good happen, let me know. I'd like to help."

Dylan's chin quivered. He only nodded and ran to catch up with his mom and dad.

* * *

The next morning, Jax woke on his back and opened his eyes. Another day. But he was grateful that he had it before him. Morning light filtered through the closed blinds. He flipped back the covers and rolled out of bed. He shuffled down the hall, stopping in front of Lulu's room. He put his hand on the door, turned the knob, and pushed the door wide.

Little girl pink surrounded him when he stepped in. Ignoring the ache in his chest, he went to the blinds and pulled them up. There hadn't been light in this room since the day they'd laid her to rest. Abby had begged him to grieve with her. He'd refused. Instead, he'd become a shell of the man he'd been, shoving everyone that reminded him of Lulu far away.

To deal with the trauma Elena had experienced, she escaped and created an alter ego that had done her far more harm than good. The sullen man he'd become was no different. If Elena had taught him anything, it was that he couldn't run from himself.

He went to the garage and returned with several boxes. He spent the next half hour boxing up Lulu's toys and clothes. When he was through, he stacked the containers in the closet. He couldn't tear down her bed. Just yet. Baby steps. But when he walked out the door, he left it open. The days of trying to forget were over. Not that he'd ever succeeded in that. But he'd focused on only the loss. Now he intended to remember it all. Every tear. Every footstep. Every tickle. Every bedtime story.

His next stop was the garage, where he focused on assembling the dollhouse. When he finished, he placed the pieces he'd carved in the rooms. Elena had once told him that people let things go when they were ready. He was ready to let this go. It was past time for someone else's child to get the joy that he'd wished for his Lulu. After the last piece was set, he carefully put it in the back of his truck and secured it.

In the kitchen, he made himself scrambled eggs. At one time, he'd had the laughter of his daughter and the love of Abby. At one time, he wondered if he'd ever have those things again. Then it hurt to want them anymore. Now he wanted them both. Only one was an option—and that wasn't even certain.

In the living room, he grabbed his phone and scrolled down to Abby's number. He hesitated. Calmed his beating heart. She might say no, but he found his courage and pressed send.

Abby picked up on the first ring. "You're calling early."

Her husky voice felt good to his ears. He cleared his throat. "You told me I was going to owe you. I figured now might be a good time to pay up."

She laughed. God, he'd missed that laugh. "What did you have in mind?"

He closed his eyes. He'd pushed her away once. She'd been angry. They'd lost Lulu. But he was different now. "I have an errand to run to the Children's Hospital if you'd like to join me. Then I was hoping we could talk."

Her breath caught. "I'll be right there."

Acknowledgements

I wrote this book back in 2018 and to say it's been a rollercoaster ever since, wouldn't quite define it. But despite the setbacks, I never stopped believing in this story. It's set at the Oregon coast, which is where I spent a part of my youth, and the atmosphere and events there have embedded firmly in my mind, I set out to tell a story that intertwined things that made me. Because of the long journey, the list is long for those who have helped get this book to this place. But I'll start with the woman who brought it to life.

Thank you to my editor, Harriette Sackler, for believing in Sheriff Jax Turner, and wanting him to be in the world. Thank you to Michelle Richter whose early notes and direction helped shape this novel and define what was important to me. Kate Pickford, love to you always and for championing Jax right from the start. To my critique partners Dianne Freeman and Jaime Lynn Hendricks whose insight and love of the story kept me believing. To earlier read throughs from Vanessa Lillie, Elise Bungo, Gwynne L. Jackson and Heather Chavez who again helped me find Jax's voice in a relatable way. And to Dawn Ius for loving Jax as much as I do and providing feedback on that final polish.

To my beta readers Jessica Jett, Bonnie Matheny, and Karenza Corder, who always make me feel like a legitimate author. To Detective James Lawrence (retired) and current Clark County Sheriff Deputy, who is always ready with the answers I need to make my stories believable. If I've missed the mark on the procedural side, it's on me for not asking the right questions.

To you my readers. Thank you for buying, reviewing, and sharing my novels. While this is a new series, I hope you will embrace Jax Turner and enjoy his journey to redemption as he unravels this twisting story.

To my husband, Robb. Up, down or sideways, he's always there for the crazy ride. You've made it fun, talking story for hours, and have grounded me in all good ways. I wouldn't want to do this without you. Aloha nui loa.

And lastly, I lost my mother this year and this is the one book I've written that she didn't get to read or hold in her hands. Although I know she's checking it out from above. So, thank you Mom for not only being my biggest fan, but always listening to this little gawky kid read endlessly to you while you cooked dinner. I have no doubt that my love of books stemmed from that time, and things will never be quite the same without you. All my love.

About the Author

Mary Keliikoa is the author of the Shamus finalist and multi-award nominated PI Kelly Pruett mystery series, and the Misty Pines mystery series featuring former Portland homicide detective turned small-town sheriff. Her short stories have appeared in *Woman's World* and in the anthology *Peace, Love and Crime*.

A Pacific NW native, she spent years working around lawyers and admits to being *that person* who gets excited when called for jury duty. When not in Washington, you can find Mary on the beach in Hawaii. But even under the palm trees and blazing sun, she's plotting her next murder—novel, that is.

SOCIAL MEDIA HANDLES:

Facebook: https://www.facebook.com/Mary.Keliikoa.Author
Twitter: https://twitter.com/mary_keliikoa
Instagram: https://www.instagram.com/mary.keliikoa.author/
Bookbub: https://www.bookbub.com/authors/mary-keliikoa

Goodreads: https://www.goodreads.com/author/show/20038534.Mary_Keliikoa

AUTHOR WEBSITE: https://marykeliikoa.com/

Also by Mary Keliikoa

Derailed, A Kelly Pruett Mystery

Denied, A Kelly Pruett Mystery

Deceived, A Kelly Pruett Mystery

Peace, Love and Crime (an anthology)

CPSIA information can be obtained
at www.ICGtesting.com
Printed in the USA
LVHW112202311022
732054LV00016B/72